W9-BKV-117

TOXIC PREY

ALSO BY JOHN SANDFORD

Rules of Prey
Shadow Prey
Eyes of Prey
Silent Prey
Winter Prey
Night Prey
Mind Prey
Sudden Prey
The Night Crew
Secret Prey
Certain Prey
Easy Prey
Chosen Prey
Mortal Prey
Naked Prey
Hidden Prey
Broken Prey
Invisible Prey
Phantom Prey
Wicked Prey
Storm Prey
Buried Prey
Stolen Prey
Silken Prey
Field of Prey
Gathering Prey
Extreme Prey
Golden Prey
Twisted Prey
Neon Prey
Masked Prey
Ocean Prey
Righteous Prey
Judgment Prey

KIDD NOVELS

The Fool's Run
The Empress File
The Devil's Code
The Hanged Man's Song

VIRGIL FLOWERS NOVELS

Dark of the Moon
Heat Lightning
Rough Country
Bad Blood
Shock Wave
Mad River
Storm Front
Deadline
Escape Clause
Deep Freeze
Holy Ghost
Bloody Genius

LETTY DAVENPORT NOVELS

The Investigator
Dark Angel

STAND-ALONE NOVELS

The Night Crew
Dead Watch
Saturn Run (with Ctein)

BY JOHN SANDFORD AND MICHELE COOK

Uncaged
Outrage
Rampage

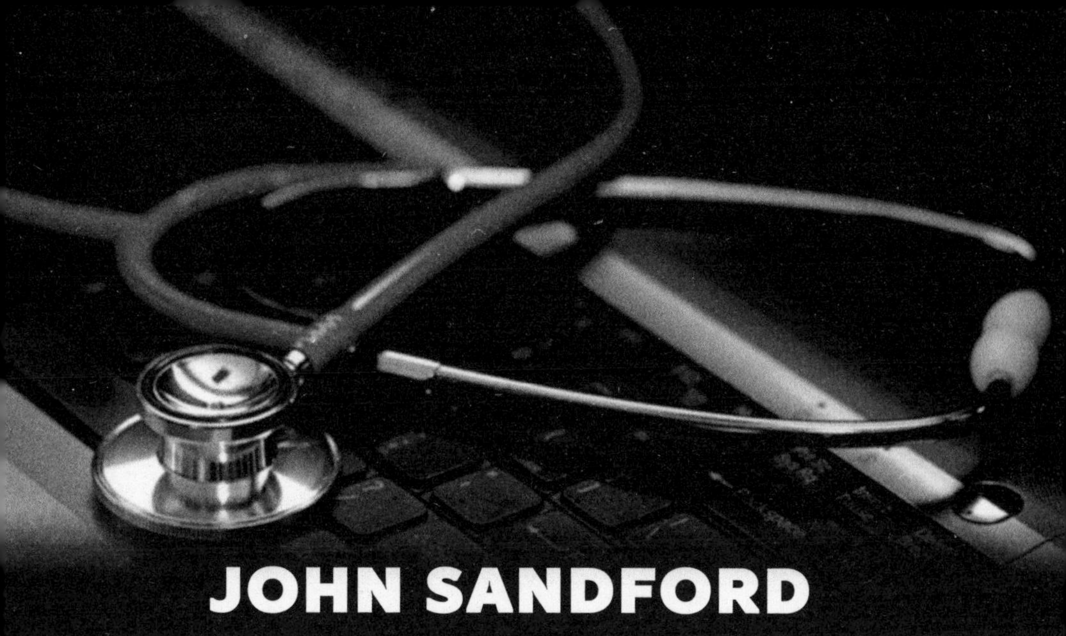

JOHN SANDFORD

TOXIC PREY

G. P. PUTNAM'S SONS
NEW YORK

PUTNAM
— EST. 1838 —
G. P. Putnam's Sons
Publishers Since 1838
An imprint of Penguin Random House LLC
penguinrandomhouse.com

Library of Congress Cataloging-in-Publication Data
Names: Sandford, John, 1944 February 23– author.
Title: Toxic prey / John Sandford.
Description: New York : G. P. Putnam's Sons, 2024.
Identifiers: LCCN 2023053882 (print) | LCCN 2023053883 (ebook) |
ISBN 9780593714492 (hardcover) | ISBN 9780593714508 (e-book)
Subjects: LCGFT: Detective and mystery fiction. | Novels.
Classification: LCC PS3569.A516 T69 2024 (print) |
LCC PS3569.A516 (ebook) | DDC 813/.54—dc23/eng/20231120
LC record available at https://lccn.loc.gov/2023053882
LC ebook record available at https://lccn.loc.gov/2023053883

Printed in the United States of America
10 9 8 7 6 5 4 3 2 1

TOXIC PREY

ELEVEN MONTHS EARLIER . . .

A dinged-up, dust-covered ten-year-old Subaru Outback bumped along a fire road that ran downhill from the Sangre de Cristo Mountains, through an old patch of controlled burn that had renewed itself with shoulder-high aspen saplings, and then back into dense stands of dark green piñon.

Lionel Scott was lost in northern New Mexico, as he had intended, but after four nights of meditation and his personal version of prayer, he could use a shower and a salad.

Now, he focused on missing the larger stones. He didn't always succeed, both hands tight on the steering wheel, glasses bouncing on his sunburned nose; every once in a while, he had to stop, get out, and move a fallen log or clump of brush. The battered wagon was reasonably tough, took the knocks with good grace, and they eventually debouched onto a gravel road.

Scott was of middle height, short of six feet, and thin, almost gaunt, with lines of muscle cut in his arms and neck. His salt-and pepper hair fell to the middle of his ears, and one lock constantly fell over his left eye. His nose was long and straight, his eyes blue-gray, his skin fair, but roughened with outdoor wear.

So: left or right? Scott looked both ways, and then at the gas gauge. He had a quarter tank, and decided to take the downhill route away from the mountains, where he would be more likely to find a gas station. The gravel was noisier than the dirt road, but smoother, aside from the occasional washed-out dip. Taos, he thought, was probably off to the north, but he wasn't entirely sure of that—he had no GPS, nor a signal on his cell phone.

The landscape was dry, and warm, but not hot. Maybe upper seventies Fahrenheit, he thought, getting warmer as he dropped down the hills; bright sun, puffy white fair-weather clouds. A flock of crows was working the mountainside. Scott could never quite make out what they were doing, but they were working hard at it, whatever it was, ink spots against the blue sky. He drove with the windows down, breathing in the scents of piñon, juniper, aspen, the silver-green chamisa, and his own dried sweat.

Scott didn't know precisely where he was, but did know he was headed west, unless the sun had changed its position in the solar system. He was more or less driving into it, given the wiggles in the road, and at this time of year, it should be setting generally to the northwest. As it would be in two hours.

He thought, *A motel would be welcome . . . a martini with three olives?*

The gravel track took him up a hillside, then down again, then up even higher, with a dirt cutbank to his left and a drop-off to his right, then back down a long, steep pitch. He rounded a turn and found, to his surprise, an intersection with a real gravel road and two more fire roads.

The side of the gravel road was edged with a ramshackle brown trailer, now up on blocks, that long ago had been converted into a convenience store. No sign of a gas pump; a pickup was parked in front, another around at the back. A neon-red Budweiser beer sign glowed from one window.

Scott could use something cold: a beer, a Coke, even water. He pulled in next to the pickup, a Tacoma older than his Subaru, climbed out, stretched, and walked over to the front door. A sign above the door had two words in large hand-painted letters: "More, Store."

Above the large letters was a hand-painted script in much smaller letters which said, "Everything Costs . . ." and beneath the "More, Store," an additional script in small letters which said, "Because I have to Drive to Sam's Club to Get It."

Almost made him smile.

A lot of things in the American West almost made him smile, especially the essential emptiness. If the entire world were as empty as America between the Mississippi and the Coastal Ranges, there'd be no global warming, no melting glaciers. Earlier in the spring, he'd made a pilgrimage to the Lightning Field art installation in southwest New Mexico. The field consisted of hundreds of steel poles sticking up from a level plain, apparently designed to attract lightning strikes from passing thunderstorms. He found that only vaguely interesting, but he was gob-smacked by the night.

There was no light but that from the stars. No moon, no artificial light sources within dozens of miles, and dry, crystal-clear skies. He spent hours staring at the Milky Way as it turned overhead, the stars dozens and hundreds and thousands of light-years distant, but right there in his face . . . think of all the life out there, thriving, finding a place under different suns. And think about Gaia's death spiral, the end of life on Earth.

THE CONVENIENCE STORE:

As he stepped toward it, a bulky Hispanic man in a battered straw cowboy hat walked out, carrying an open bottle of Corona, nodded, and said, "Hey," and Scott said, "How are you?"

The man slowed and smiled and said, "You English?"

Scott: "Yes, I am."

"Don't hear that accent around here, much," the man said, "You're a long way from home, buddy."

"America's my home now," Scott said.

"Hope you like it. It's a nice place, mostly," the man said, and he went on to his truck. Scott pulled the screen door open and stepped inside. A radio was playing an old Lynyrd Skynyrd tune, "Sweet Home Alabama," and dust motes floated in sunlight coming through a west-facing window.

The old trailer had been hollowed out into three separate sections: to his right, a counter, a tired-looking Indian woman behind it, and a rack of cigarettes. To his left, the main body of the store, perhaps fifteen feet long, featuring racks of snack food, warm beer, and soft drinks. A formerly white, now yellowed, refrigerator stood in one corner and had the words "Cold Drinks" written on the front with a Sharpie. Further back, a closed door had "Private—No Restrooms" written on it. The place smelled of beef jerky, overripe bananas, and nicotine.

The woman behind the counter took a cigarette from the corner of her mouth and asked, "How y'doin'?"

"I'm doing well enough," Scott said, though he also might have chosen among a variety of approved Americanisms he'd picked up in the past year: "Okay," or "Doin' good," or "Just fine." But none of those were how he felt. He was doing well enough, but no better. "Would you have cold beer? Or a soft drink?"

"In the fridge," the woman said, poking her cigarette toward the refrigerator. As Scott walked back to it, she asked, "You English?"

"Yes." He walked back, opened the refrigerator door, found a mixture of Miller Lite, Coke, Pepsi, Mountain Dew, Dr Pepper, and a few tall bottles of Mexican Coke. As an Englishman, Scott thought Miller Lite tasted like beer that had been recycled through somebody's kidneys. He took a bottle of Mexican Coke, for the sugar load, closed the refrigerator door, and returned to the counter.

"What're you doing way the hell back here?" the woman asked around her cigarette. And, "Four dollars."

"Driving around," Scott said. He pushed a five-dollar bill across the counter.

"On vacation?" she asked.

"I work down at Los Alamos," he said.

One eyebrow went up, a physical ability which Scott recognized as a scientific mystery, as yet unsolved. She said, "On them A-bombs?"

"No. Actually, I'm a doctor."

That seemed to stop her. She gazed at him, then asked, "Like a medical doctor?"

"Yes."

She put the five in a cash drawer and handed him a one. She said,

"My boy is sick. I don't know . . . maybe something he ate. Maybe we should go to the doctor, but, you know . . . insurance. We don't have it."

Scott sighed, but didn't show it. Instead, he asked, "What are his symptoms?"

She shrugged. "He's got a tummy ache. He's got a fever . . ."

Not good. Scott: "If you'd like me to take a look . . ."

"I'd love that," the woman said. "He's in back."

Scott popped the Mexican Coke's bottle cap on a counter-mounted bottle opener, took a swallow, and followed her past racks of snack food to the door in the back. She pushed through to a small living space, a bathroom and two tiny separate rooms on either side of a living/dining/TV area. One of the side doors was open, and she gestured to it. A young boy was lying awake on a narrow single bed; he wore a pair of shorts and a tee-shirt and was barefoot. His face, in the dim light, appeared to be on fire.

Scott said, "Hi, I'm Lionel. I'm a doctor. I understand you're sick."

The boy, who appeared to be nine or ten, said, "Hurt."

Scott reached out and put his fingers on the boy's forehead: too hot, way too hot.

"Where does it hurt?"

The boy touched his belly, lower right, near the waistband of his shorts. Scott used the fingers of his right hand to press softly the place where the boy had touched himself. The kid lurched up and blurted a long "Aaaahhhh. Awwww . . ."

Scott was used to the pain of children. He turned to the woman and asked, "He's had some nausea? Has he thrown up?"

"A little," she said. "That's why I thought maybe it was something he ate."

Scott shook his head. "I don't believe that's it. Your boy has appendicitis and it's somewhat advanced. We need to take him to a hospital. Right away. Do you know where the closest one is?"

"Taos," she said. She was frightened. "But no insurance, we always been healthy . . . I don't know if they'll take us."

"They'll take you. They have to," Scott said.

The woman said her pickup rode rough, so Scott suggested they drop the front passenger seat of his Subaru, and that the woman lead the way to the Taos hospital in her truck. Scott picked up the boy, who groaned and squirmed against him. His dark eyes were pools of pain, but he didn't cry.

The trip down through the mountains and then up the High Road to Taos took forty-five minutes. Twenty minutes out, Scott checked his cell phone and found that he had a bar and honked his horn until the woman pulled over. Scott stopped behind her, and as she hurried back to the Subaru, he explained what he was doing: "Calling the hospital."

When he had a nurse at Holy Cross on the line, he identified himself as a visiting physician, that he had a ten-year-old boy suffering from acute appendicitis, an emergency intervention was needed, and that they were on the way. He asked that a surgeon be notified.

Twenty-five minutes later, they delivered the kid to the emergency room and waited as he was wheeled away; a while later, a surgeon appeared and introduced himself and confirmed what Scott had suspected. To the woman, the surgeon said, "We have to operate on your son. We need to get his appendix out. The operation is fairly routine, but if the appendix is burst, there could be some follow-on problems . . ."

She gave her permission for the work. The woman clung close to Scott as she asked, "He isn't going to die?"

"He should be fine," the surgeon said. "If we'd waited any longer, it could have been tricky. But, I think we caught it."

They talked about that, then the surgeon turned to Scott. "You're British?"

"Yes."

"Where'd you go to med school?"

"Oxford."

The surgeon nodded: "Heard of it," and he went away to scrub up. Almost made Scott smile again: "Heard of it."

Then the paperwork and the question about insurance. The woman in charge of payments explained that there were some costs that could be reduced, that the woman might qualify for other aid, and Scott grew exasperated and said, "Listen. Get whatever Mrs. . . ." He didn't know her name and he looked at her and she said, "Bernal . . ."

Scott said, "Learn what Mrs. Bernal can afford to pay, and what assistance she can get, and then put the rest on my Amex card. Do you take Amex?"

The payment lady said, "Absolutely. We take everything but chickens and goats."

SCOTT PRIED HIMSELF away from the hospital and Mrs. Bernal a half hour later, when everyone was satisfied that he was willing to pay the bill for the boy's operation; and he could no longer tolerate Mrs. Bernal's appreciation. He climbed into his Subaru without telling anyone where he was going, or how to reach him, found a Days Inn, and got a room for the night.

He hadn't slept well in his tent and he didn't sleep well in the motel, despite a two-martini dinner. He wondered, in the middle of the night, why he'd worked to save the boy, and a fragment of his Oxford undergraduate education popped into his mind, courtesy of the Soviet dictator Joseph Stalin.

Stalin said, Scott recalled, "The death of one man is a tragedy. The death of a million is a statistic."

And that was it, wasn't it?

The death of the boy would have been a tragedy. The death of a million, or five billion, would be a . . .

Number. And a necessity.

1

Letty Davenport's apartment complex had a swimming pool filled with discouraging numbers of square-shouldered men with white sidewall haircuts—even on the black guys, unless they were called black sidewalls; who knew?

They all had big bright wolf teeth, gym muscle, and questionable sexual ethics; and their female counterparts were much the same, the major differences lying in how much butt-cheek was exposed, which, in one case, when the young woman climbed out of the pool, was like watching the moon come up over the Potomac.

They were soldiers, mostly, attached to the Pentagon, just a couple miles away.

Five o'clock on an August afternoon, too hot to be inside, where the barely adjustable air conditioning blew cold damp air on everything; so Letty dozed in the webbing of her recliner, a copy of *The*

Quarterly Journal of Economics covering her face. Beneath that, pressing against her nose, was a paperback version of J. D. Robb's *Celebrity in Death*, which Letty estimated was the fortieth of the *In Death* novels she'd read.

While not as prestigious as the *Journal,* the Robb novel was distinctly more intelligent and certainly better written; but, a girl has to maintain her intellectual status with the D.C. deep state, so the *Journal* went on top.

Some passing dude she couldn't see made a comment about legs, which she suspected was directed at her, but she ignored him, and was still ignoring him when the phone on her stomach vibrated. She groped for it, and without looking at the screen, pressed the answer tab and said, "Yeah?"

Her boss said, "This is your boss. I'm putting you on speaker." Other people were listening in; a modicum of respect was required.

"Yes, sir?"

"Can you get out to Dulles in the next three hours and forty-one minutes?"

"Uh, sure. Where am I going?"

"London. Well, Oxford. A guy will meet you at Dulles's United gate with a packet including the job, your tickets, and a hotel reservation. The return ticket's open, probably won't take you more than a day or two."

"How will he know who I am?"

"He'll have seen a photograph."

"Can you tell me more than that?" Letty asked.

"Not really. You know, the phone problem." He meant that that phone call wasn't secure, so whatever the problem was, security was an issue.

"How about dress? Standard business casual?"

"That will do. You can't take your usual equipment." He meant, *gun*. "I'm told by one of the gentlemen here that Oxford has some nice places to run, so you might take running gear."

"Thank you," Letty said.

"Three hours and thirty-nine minutes, now, according to my infallible Apple Watch," said Senator Christopher Colles (R-Florida), who was actually, if not technically, Letty's boss. He hung up.

LETTY TECHNICALLY WORKED for the Department of Homeland Security, but in practice worked for Colles, who was chairman of the Senate's Committee on Homeland Security and Governmental Affairs. He claimed to have the DHS secretary's nuts in a vise, possibly because of the secretary's governmental affairs. However that worked, when Colles spoke, the DHS listened.

Letty didn't exactly have what preppers called a bug-out bag, but she had something close: selected clothes in her closet hung in dry-cleaning bags, waiting to be packed, and a man's large dopp kit containing the cosmetic and medical necessaries, ready to go. She added her running gear, passport, and the Robb novel.

She traveled with a forty-liter Black Hole duffel from Patagonia and had learned to roll her dressier clothes into tube shapes, still wrapped in the dry-cleaner plastic, so they'd be fresh-looking and unwrinkled when she got to her destination. Frequent travel does teach you things, mostly about packing.

Forty-five minutes after Colles's call, she was out the door to a waiting cab; twenty-five minutes after that, they rolled up to Dulles, and five minutes after that, she ambled through security with her

DHS credentials and passport and made her way to the United gate. A young man, but older than she was, with a spray of acne across his forehead and an annoyed look on the rest of his face, walked up to her and asked, "Davenport?"

"Yes."

He handed her a manila envelope, thick with the paper inside, said, "Don't lose it," and walked away. Far too important to be sent with an envelope to meet a woman younger than he was, and it showed in his body language. Nothing to be done about that.

Letty found a seat, opened the package, extracted a thin business envelope with her air tickets. She put that in the front pocket of the duffel bag and moved on to a much thicker report on a Dr. Lionel Scott, a British subject now somewhere in the United States; exactly where, nobody knew.

Under the binder clip that held the report together was a folded piece of notepaper with the names, addresses, and phone numbers of three of Scott's friends in Oxford. She was to inquire as to what they might know about his whereabouts and activities, and whether any of them were in touch with him. A final instruction from Colles was scrawled at the bottom of the sheet: "Wring them dry."

Letty checked her watch: she had time before the flight, so she settled down to read.

LIONEL SCOTT WAS a doctor, first of all, a graduate of the Oxford medical school. After graduation, he'd done two foundation years, somewhat the equivalent of American medical residencies, then three more years studying viral and bacterial diseases in humans. Later, he'd joined Médecins Sans Frontières—Doctors Without Borders—

and had spent nine more years working in Bangladesh and Myanmar in Asia, and Uganda, Guinea, and the Democratic Republic of the Congo in Africa.

He'd left Médecins Sans Frontières for health reasons, had returned to England, where he spent a year at the London School of Hygiene & Tropical Medicine, then moved again, this time to the United States, where he'd worked for a year at Fort Detrick in Maryland, at the U.S. Army Medical Research Institute of Infectious Diseases (USAMRIID). Although still technically employed at USAMRIID, he was temporarily working at Los Alamos National Laboratory in New Mexico, and had been for almost a year.

He had gone missing from there.

The mention of both USAMRIID and Los Alamos rang alarm bells with Letty, and she thought, *Uh-oh*.

She checked the time again and took the iPad out of her duffel, read about the Fort Detrick installation and about Los Alamos. Detrick was known as the primary research facility into diseases that might be weaponized by an enemy, which was why it was run by the Department of Defense. That job made sense; Scott was an infectious disease specialist with a lot of time in the field. She couldn't pin down why he would be at Los Alamos, which was known for creating the plutonium pits from which thermonuclear weapons were manufactured.

She read further into Scott's biography: he'd been treated for what was called nervous exhaustion after his last assignment at Cox's Bazar in Bangladesh with its refugee camp Kutupalong, home to nearly a million occupants. He'd also been treated for a recurrence of malaria that he'd originally contracted in Africa, and tuberculosis.

A note from a Médecins executive credited ". . . Dr. Scott with saving quite literally thousands of lives though his work with TB patients."

Altogether, Letty thought, an admirable human being. Now, just past forty, and apparently recovering from his various health problems, he'd vanished. Since he'd had extensive contacts with scientists developing atomic weapons, and other scientists doing what was called "gain of function" research on viruses—a euphemism for "making more deadly"—a number of high-ranking functionaries further up the bureaucratic ladder than Letty had also said, "Uh-oh."

HER FLIGHT WAS called, and after waiting for what seemed like eight or ten priority boarding groups, she worked her way halfway down the plane and took her aisle seat next to an overweight man in the middle seat, who'd already seized both armrests—not because he was a jerk, but because the seats were too small.

Unlike the man in the window seat, who was already squirming, she was small enough to survive the flight. Letty, at twenty-five, was dancer slender, perhaps because she did YouTube dancer workouts, along with weight work and a daily run. As she was settling in, pushing her carry-on under the seat in front of her, the window-seat man, who wore a clerical collar, leaned around the man in the center and said, "I wonder if we'd all be more comfortable . . ."

After some negotiation, they shuffled.

Letty, in making her application for sainthood, took the middle seat, with the obese man moved to Letty's aisle seat. With the big man leaning a bit into the aisle, they all had arm rests; when the plane was in the air, the priest on the window took out a laptop, typed a few words, turned the screen toward Letty and nudged her.

She looked: *"Thanks. You saved my life."*

She took the laptop, typed, *"Say a prayer for me."*

He smiled, took it back and typed, *"I certainly will."*

During the seven-and-a-half-hour flight to London, Letty read through the rest of Scott's biography, finished *Celebrity in Death*, and got five hours of sleep. Forty minutes before landing, she lined up for the over-used lavatory to pee, wash her face, brush her teeth, jab a travel-sized anti-perspirant in her armpits, run a comb through her hair, and generally get her shit together.

Letty walked off the plane a half hour after the wheels touched down—the fat man gave her a confident smile and asked if she was staying in London, and she said, "Nope."

She skipped a tram that was jammed to capacity and walked what seemed like a mile through a lower-level tunnel to baggage claim; since she hadn't checked any baggage, she breezed through the "Nothing to Declare" gate, heading for the LHR train station.

As she walked through, a man called, "Letty Davenport!"

The man looked, Letty thought, London stylish: summer-weight dark wool suit, silk tie, shoes that appeared to be spit-shined and probably made in Italy. He was handsome, in a weather-beaten way. Tall, thin, with almost-blond hair worn a bit long and mussed, and with the muscles of an Iron Man enthusiast. He was early thirties, she thought. *No wedding ring. Why had she noticed that so quickly? She had a boyfriend, didn't she?* A duffel sat by the man's feet, much like Letty's, but of oiled canvas, rather than plastic.

She stopped, and he stepped up to her, awkwardly pushing his duffel along with one foot, and showed her an ID card: "Alec Hawkins, MI5. I'll be traveling with you to Oxford. To clear the way, should the way need clearing."

"Didn't say anything about that in my instructions," Letty said.

He nodded: "That's why we're called the Secret Service. Nobody tells anyone anything."

"I thought it was MI6 that was called the Secret Service," Letty said.

"I suppose that's possible. Does anybody really know which is which?"

That made her smile. "You have a car?"

"God, no. Takes forever and no place to park," Hawkins said. "We'll be on the train; two trains, actually. Give me your bag and follow on."

She gave him the bag and followed on, to the express train to London's Paddington Station. "How'd you know it was me coming through the gate?"

"I was notified that you'd gone through passport control and United informed us that you had no checked baggage, so I knew you'd be through quickly. And we have many, many photographs of you, including several with blood on your face. That's really quite charming, for such a looker."

She let that pass. "Are you armed?"

He frowned. "No, of course not. What would I do with a gun?"

"Shoot a terrorist?"

"There are other people assigned to do that," Hawkins said. "I suppose I could kick one; or perhaps I could fashion a makeshift knife with my identity card and slash them with the edge. It's quite sharp."

"Kill them with a rolled-up magazine?"

"Nooo . . . that's beyond my skill set, I'm afraid. Perhaps I could show them a copy of the *Daily Mail* and embarrass them to death."

They arrived on the sparsely populated train platform, with no train in sight. Hawkins said one would be along shortly. Letty asked,

"Is this escort service some kind of punishment for something you've done? Or . . ."

"No, no, I volunteered. Get out of the office, visit the old haunts at Oxford. Went to college there, actually. Balliol, modern history. Quite an interesting place. Hotel on expenses, of course."

"So it's like a vacation."

"Mmm . . . yes. Especially if we can stretch our stay to two nights. I wouldn't think we'd get much done today, especially with you jet-lagged."

"I feel fine," Letty said.

He looked down at her. "Especially with you jet-lagged."

"Ah. Girlfriend or boyfriend?"

"I leave it to you to guess," he said, flashing a smile.

And she thought, *Hmm*, but didn't vocalize it, and she didn't think it was a boyfriend.

THE TRIP TO London's Paddington Station took twenty-one minutes; Paddington itself was a chaotic human anthill, but Hawkins guided them through, bought two first-class tickets to Oxford—"On expenses, of course, you were too jet-lagged to travel with the hoi polloi."

"Naturally. Are you always this cheap?"

"Not cheap. I prefer to think of myself as savvy," Hawkins said. "Also, should there be any old Balliol acquaintances about, I'd prefer that they see me in first class, or getting off first class."

"Mmm."

"What?"

"I'm looking for an English phrase that you would understand," Letty said. "You're being very charming; are you chatting me up?"

"A bit. And making a Washington acquaintance for when I take up my assignment there. If today's chatting-up is unsuccessful, perhaps you have girlfriends."

"When will you go to Washington?"

"If nobody fucks things up, which is usually a vain hope, next January."

An approaching train was announced with, first, a wind-like sound, a distant tornado, then a nearly cataclysmic rattling, which ended with a train parked in front of them. Hawkins had positioned them so they'd be next to the first-class cars when the train stopped, and they got on board.

THE TRIP TO Oxford was quick, an hour long, with one stop at Reading, pronounced Redding. The land around them was a brilliant emerald green, farm fields and woods, with water here and there, not unlike Iowa, with some large differences. The farm fields, as an example, were like jigsaw pieces, rather than rectangles. Beef cattle and hogs seemed to be absent, though there were sheep; no tree stands for deer hunters.

Letty and Hawkins exchanged a few personal notes: he'd been divorced, three years earlier, but had survived financially: his ex-wife was a partner in her father's London real estate firm, and well off, so spousal support had been unnecessary.

"After university, I spent four years in the army, then moved to MI5. In the army, I was gone quite a bit with one thing or another, Afghanistan mostly, which helped keep the marriage together. When I was at home, we weren't nearly so happy."

Letty told him that she did, in fact, have a boyfriend, but that they were "on hiatus," and had been for four months, and the longer the hiatus continued, the less likely they were to get back together. "I like him well enough, but we've discovered that both of us are going to do what we're going to do, despite what the other one thinks. So, that's difficult."

Hawkins also told her that he'd read her MI5 biography. "I have to say, having read your history and seen the photos, you very much take after your father. The dark hair, the blue eyes; the resemblance is striking."

"I'm adopted," Letty said.

"Yes, I know. Still."

AND THEY TALKED about the assignment. The three persons on her list were all at home—none were traveling, and MI5 had made sure that all three were available for interviews.

"Two are quite straightforward," Hawkins said. "One of Scott's tutors in biochemistry, Ann Sloam, became quite close to him; a fellow medical student, another close friend, Donald Carr, later took up a position with John Radcliffe Hospital and remains there. We will meet him today at lunch, in a café at the Ashmolean Museum; the hospital itself is a couple of miles from there. The third, Madga Rice, is apparently an on-and-off lover who may have had some . . . mmm . . . effect on Scott's personal philosophy. She has a shop in Oxford."

"Very efficient," Letty said. "Maybe we can talk to all three of them today."

"I doubt it, given the fact that you're jet-lagged," Hawkins said. "I thought we'd stop first at the hotel, which is expecting us. We have an early check-in. Then we'll walk to the Ashmolean."

2

Hawkins carried their bags through the warm muggy crowds of Oxford to the General Elphinstone Inn, a red-brick and thatch building that lost part of its charm when Hawkins told her the thatch was synthetic PVC. They had rooms on the second floor, which was also the top floor, up a wide wooden stairway; each room had a bronze door knocker shaped like a rearing horse, whose hooves would hammer on a bronze plate.

Letty dropped her bag at the end of the double bed, used the bathroom, rinsed off her face. She looked tired, she decided, peering into a mirror. Eyes tighter than they usually seemed, nape-of-neck hair a little stickier than it should be.

The shower looked inviting. She'd taken Hawkins's phone number and called him: "How much time do I have?"

"Half an hour?"

"Call me when it's time."

The shower was fine: water hot and heavy, then, for one minute, cold and bracing. She got dressed again, brushed her teeth, lay on the bed, which was board-like, propped by the lumpy pillows, looked at the notes she had on Dr. Donald Carr. Like Lionel Scott he was in his early forties, but was a surgeon, rather than a disease specialist. He'd written well-received papers on burn care, published in the journal *The Lancet*.

Okay. She'd be dealing with smart people, which wasn't always the case, or even usually.

Hawkins called her at one o'clock: "Meet you downstairs in five minutes. It's not a long walk, and we won't have to run. Which reminds me: I was told that one of the . . . conferees . . . in Washington suggested that you might want to bring running clothes with you. Did you do that?"

"Yes, but I'm too jet-lagged to run today."

"Of course. I was thinking in the morning."

THE STREETS OF Oxford were jammed with people, most noticeably busloads of pre-teen school students. Small shops lined the walks near the inn, replaced by larger, heavier buildings as they approached the Ashmolean, an imposing pillared structure of a whitish-tan stone. Once there, Hawkins told her they were still early and led her quickly through a treasure box of confusing rooms filled with archaeological bits and pieces from the countries England had once ransacked. They got caught up in a case of Middle Eastern relics until Hawkins checked his watch and told Letty that they were now running late.

"He'll forgive us. Carr and his wife go on archaeological expeditions to the Middle East and Egypt. I'm sure he understands the attraction of these things. May have dipped into the Mayan ruins out your way, once or twice," Hawkins told her, tapping the glass on a display case.

Carr was waiting for them in the rooftop café. He was sitting at the far end from the stairway, vacant tables around him, with a glass of iced tea and a plate of baked falafel. All around them, the slate roofs of Oxford.

Hawkins recognized Carr from his files—Letty from Google Images—and Carr got to his feet as they walked up. He was a tall man, balding, pale-faced with large hands; he was wearing a blue suit and a white dress shirt, without a tie.

As he shook hands with Hawkins, he said, "I hope this is not unhappy news about Lionel. I've had too much of that over the years."

"How so?" Letty asked, as she took a chair.

"Oh, you know . . . the malaria, the TB," Carr said. "He once suffered a rash of boils under his arms and between his thighs, probably from bacteria exacerbated by sweat and chafing from his clothing, and possibly from the chemicals in Third World laundry detergent. He was quite interested in the phenomenon, but I don't think he ever got to the bottom of it."

"Sounds awful," Letty said.

Carr nodded. "Knowing Lionel made you believe in the ten plagues of the Bible. He broke both arms in a car rollover, but that was years ago. I know he was shot at in Africa."

"An amazing career," Letty said.

"Indeed. What has happened now"—he looked at Hawkins—"that would interest a famous American investigator and an MI5 agent?"

"I'm famous?" Letty asked.

"I looked you up on the Internet," Carr said. He pushed the plate of falafel her way, and she took one. "So . . . after the bridge in Texas, and a top-secret fuss in California, I'd say yes, you're famous, at least in some quarters. Why the interest in Lionel?"

"He disappeared," Letty said, chewing.

"Oh, no. I hope foul play isn't involved."

"We don't know what's involved at this point," Letty said. "We'd just like to find him."

"Might have gone walkabout, eh?"

"I don't have all the details, but as I understand it, his home seemed more abandoned, than prepared for a trip," Letty said. "There was nothing left in the refrigerator, the garbage had been taken out—the empty can was still sitting in the street—not much left in the way of clothing or personal care stuff. Like he left deliberately, but didn't notify anyone at his job that he was leaving. One day he was there, and the next day, gone. Not kidnapped, gone."

"Oh, dear. That doesn't sound like Lionel," Carr said. "With his experience in the Third World, he was always meticulous in telling people where he was going, and how long he'd be gone. Even when he was visiting here and was going down to London for the day."

"When did you last hear from him?" Hawkins asked.

"Mmm . . . two months ago? Something like that. Routine email, catching up." A waiter appeared, and they ordered burgers and iced tea. When the waiter went away, Carr looked back at Letty. "He was at your Los Alamos laboratory, working on an artificial-intelligence program as applied to medical statistics. He was quite adept at maths. Always was. He was interested in using mathematics as a way to get at intractable diseases."

"Like how?" Letty asked.

"I'm a surgeon, not an expert on pathogens. Chatting with

him—my wife and I had a small 'welcome home' party for him when he came back from Bangladesh, before he went to the States—he was discouraged by the prospect of individual vaccines given to children to prevent diseases like malaria. He said children were being produced faster than the vaccines could keep up. And that was true for a range of diseases."

Letty: "What was his solution to that?"

"He didn't have one," Carr said. "That's why he went to America. When we were chatting at the party, he wondered, speculatively, what would happen if we could engineer a communicable virus that 'ate' malaria parasites but didn't harm humans—or a communicable virus that would kill mosquitoes but not humans. If that was even possible; and if it would be possible to spread such a thing worldwide. A virus that would starve if it had no parasites to feed on, or mosquitoes, so in a way, would be self-eliminating after doing its job."

"Sound like it would be worthwhile and would explain why he was both at Detrick and then at Los Alamos," Hawkins said.

Carr leaned over the table, his nose pointed at Letty: "Here's the thing. When Lionel returned from Bangladesh, he was rather severely depressed. My wife has had depressive episodes, so I recognize the symptoms. Lionel's mind wouldn't stop working but was caught up in cycles that he couldn't repress. I believe he consulted with somebody in America about medication."

Letty: "Depression . . . that could lead to self-harm."

Carr nodded: "If he has really vanished, that would be my thought. My fear. A man intent on harming himself wouldn't be too worried about who knew he was gone. And a polite man—Lionel is polite—would clean out the refrigerator, so no other poor soul would have to clean up the mess."

"But he took his clothes," Hawkins said.

Carr leaned back: "Yes. That's difficult to explain, if he was intent on self-harm. A person intent on suicide might not be fully rational about anything . . . take some clothes in case you don't do it."

They talked for a while longer, ate burgers, and Carr agreed to forward to both Letty and Hawkins the emails he'd received from Scott. "It's a dreadful violation of privacy, though the emails don't contain anything especially private, especially personal, that you don't already know."

"We appreciate that, and will treat them as confidential," Letty said.

CARR HAD TO return to the hospital, and Hawkins said they should check on the second person on their list, Magda Rice, who had a shop within walking distance and was also expecting them.

"Interesting that all the people we want to interview live here in Oxford," Letty said, as they wound their way through the crowded streets.

"Most of Scott's adult life in England was here, his social life," Hawkins said. "He came from York, which is up north. His mother died while he was in medical school. I believe he is estranged from his father, but I don't know why. His parents were divorced; perhaps he took his mother's side."

A cyclist clipped close to Letty's shoulder, Hawkins saw him coming and caught her arm and pulled her closer; the cyclist got by and Letty said "Thanks," and Hawkins kept a hand on her perhaps longer than was necessary; not that it felt uncomfortable.

Rice's shop was an easy amble from the Ashmolean, a tiny closet-sized space on Cornmarket Street that smelled of a nostril-tingling incense. Not exactly a head shop, but it was over in that direction, with tarot cards, astrology books, crystals, a shelf of natural herbal supplements. A beaded curtain separated the front and back rooms.

Rice was a short cheery woman with curly red hair, a complexion that was pink and nearly transparent, with an upturned nose and large, curious blue eyes. After introductions, she took them behind the bead curtain to a table with four chairs, and said, "I'll have to run out if customers come in . . . would you like iced tea?"

They would, and she poured it from a glass pitcher that she took from a refrigerator that had a poster advertising an "ayahuasca retreat" in Peru.

"Did you do that?" Hawkins asked, nodding at the poster.

"Yep. I had the contents of my stomach coming out from both ends, and the experience was distinctly disappointing. Low-rent LSD, is what it was," she said. "I do like the poster—the jungle, the birds, and so on. I get a better high from the poster than I did from the shit they fed us."

Letty told her about Scott's disappearance, and she said, "God, I hope he's all right. When he was last here, he worried me. He tends to have dark views of humanity, but he was darker than ever when he got back from Bangladesh."

"If he was planning to hurt himself, would you expect him to give you some sort of signal?" Letty asked. "Some kind of summing-up, a reflection on whatever your relationship was?"

She thought about that, and then said, "I hadn't considered that, but now that you bring it up . . . yes. Definitely. We were long-term lovers, you know."

"I'd wondered," Hawkins said. "The people who sent us to you seemed to hint at that."

"Oh, yes, it was quite sexual," Rice said. "Though, I have to say, that except with me, I don't think Lionel was especially sexual. But with me, he was like a teenager getting his first lay. Better for me than anything I get from my husband."

Letty: "You're married?"

"Yes, but I don't let him live with me," Rice said. "Rather a rough man—not violent, you know, but he's a builder. Rough edge to his tongue, as well as his hands. All about keeping his building crews in line. That's not for me, not all the time. Lionel was a welcome change."

"Do you have any clue why Lionel would voluntarily disappear?" Hawkins asked. He told her about the condition of Scott's house.

She looked down into her lap as she shook her head: "No. There was that darkness. But . . . Wait."

She stood up, stepped through the beaded curtain, and returned with a small wooden box. She touched a light switch, and the room went dim, with the only light filtering through the bead curtain. Rice sat down and opened the box. Inside was a deck of oversized cards, wrapped in a piece of heavy silk.

"Let me ask the cards," she said.

Letty glanced at Hawkins, who winked at her. Rice was busy shuffling the cards, which had an intricate gray-and-white design on their backs. She began flipping the cards over and arranging them on the table, twenty cards in all, in a five-sided figure. The cards were done in shades of black, white and gray, and the faces showed crows of all sizes, threatening in some cases, portentous or witnessing in others.

When Rice was done with the arrangement, she peered at them, then said, "Well, he's definitely alive, but . . . I've never seen a spread like this one. It's absolutely calamitous. Look at the key cards . . ."

Her hand flashed across the spread of cards, touching five of them. "Three cards of the major arcana on just five points—the Tower, the Devil, the Hanged Man. That's astonishing, both for the simple fact that there are so many of them, and they are so threatening. And two minor arcana cards, the Ten of Swords and the Ten of Wands. All five key cards suggest something terrible will happen . . . or is happening already. The Tower brings destruction, the Devil brings evil, or bondage to evil ideas and deeds. The Hanged Man suggests depression in some readings . . ."

The Ten of Swords card showed a dying man lying face up on the ground with crows picking at his entrails; the Ten of Wands showed a strange stork-like man or animal with a huge crow on its back. "The Ten of Swords means the end of the line; the Ten of Wands is a person suffering under an intolerable burden. Because of the question I asked, that person is Lionel," Rice said.

She had suddenly gone stone-faced, her formerly transparent and pink features congealing into something witchlike. Letty felt an involuntary chill run up her spine, and when she looked at Hawkins, he was staring at the cards and no longer winking.

Then Rice sighed and pulled the cards together in a pile, and with a practiced turn of her hands, stacked them and wrapped them in the silk cloth. Looking between Letty and Hawkins, she said, "Lionel is alive. That's the best news."

That was all they got from her, other than some reminiscences about her history with Scott that pointed in no particular direction.

After the tarot reading, back out on the street, Hawkins said,

"Well, that scared the shit out of me. Complete bollocks, of course, but she did it well."

"The smartest man I know—a computer wizard and a semi-famous painter—does the tarot. He says he uses them as a gaming device, to suggest ways of thinking out of the box. But my dad, who is not superstitious about *anything*, says that the guy's cards sometimes tell the future."

"More bollocks," Hawkins said, and he walked a few steps ahead of her. "She's just a ginger witch."

Letty smiled at his back. He'd told the truth about one thing: the reading had unnerved him. She said to his back, "You're really a great big pussy."

Over his shoulder: "Quiet, you."

Letty trailed Hawkins for a block or two, amused; he was really quite attractive, she decided. He eventually turned and said, "Snit over. Let's get a glass of tea somewhere."

"I'm tea'd out," Letty said. "How about coffee?"

The found a near-empty café down a narrow alley, got tea and coffee, and what Hawkins called biscuits but turned out to be cookies. When they were seated, Hawkins said, "My parents are high churchy and, mmm, somewhat conservative and superstitious. Some of it stuck with me. I don't like walking past cemeteries in the dark. There may be no such thing as ghosts, but why take the chance?"

"I'll admit that tarot reading was the tiniest bit creepy," Letty said.

"The tiniest bit," Hawkins confirmed. "Now, I've told you about my superstitions, so tell me something about yourself that you don't like other people talking about. Or knowing about."

Letty pursed her lips and looked out toward the street, then said, "My natural mother was a terrible alcoholic. Drinking would have killed her, if she hadn't been murdered first. Anyway, working in D.C., I'd go out for drinks with girlfriends, after work. One drink. A year ago, it was getting to be three drinks. One night last winter, with a special friend, we were really rolling along and it got to be six drinks and I was drunk on my butt; but it felt too good. Like anything was possible. You get stupid ideas and think you can pull them off."

"A few steps over the line, then," Hawkins ventured.

"Exactly. I now will have two drinks in one night, and no more. Never. For the rest of my life. I'm afraid there might be something genetic in the whole alcohol thing. I believe I have the discipline to pull off the two-drinks limit."

"I believe you," Hawkins said. "It's a pity in a way. I was planning to pour alcohol into you tonight and attempt to take advantage."

"Not gonna happen," Letty said.

"The drinks, or taking advantage?" Hawkins asked.

"Let me think about that," Letty said, shrugging. "Right now, I want to finish the coffee and take a nap. The travel is starting to get to me."

Hawkins looked at his watch and said, "Why don't you go take your nap, and I'll book a table somewhere close-by for . . . 7:30?"

"That should work."

LETTY DIDN'T GET much of a nap, because when her head hit the pillow, her body clock was telling her that it was eleven o'clock in the morning, and she'd had a cup of ill-considered coffee. At 5:30 she finally went away, to be jolted awake when Hawkins called: "Time," he said.

"Ten minutes."

She jumped in the shower for one minute, re-dressed, brushed her teeth, thought about it, and put her toothbrush and a travel-sized tube of toothpaste in her purse. Hawkins was waiting at the desk, and they went out on the street, which was cool, with a soft dampness in the air.

The café was small, no more than a dozen tables scattered across one stoned-floored room and a patio, with dark wood walls. It smelled of something Letty thought might be a meat-and-vegetable stew, or pie. Somewhere close by, somebody was listening to Miley Cyrus's "Flowers."

They sat outside and watched passersby and talked about nothing until the food came, and Hawkins told her about studying at Oxford and his job, she told him about Stanford and working for Senator Colles and the Department of Homeland Security, and about the shootout at the Pershing bridge.

"When I killed the guys in the pickup, I was covered with baby blood and snot and poop and I'd handed one dead baby up through that bus . . . I confess I felt nothing for those guys. I shot them to pieces. Good riddance."

"Blood and snot and baby poop . . . everything you need for a lifelong nightmare."

"How about you in Afghanistan?"

"I spent most of my time on an American military base, looking at surveillance photos, trying to make sense of reports coming in from the field. I'd look for a nexus of Taliban activity and try to predict where the nexus would next show up, so a hunter-killer formation would be anticipating them."

"How did that work out?"

"I was rather good at it. I'd spend hours looking at maps and combat histories and what I thought of as . . . pressures on the Taliban. Affinities. Like high- and low-pressure systems in the weather. As much mass psychology as anything else, I suppose."

They both had a glass of wine with the meal, and after they'd finished, by common consent stopped at a hole-in-the-wall bar for Letty's last drink of the day, a margarita.

"Tired?" Hawkins asked.

"Actually, I'm wide awake. It's about four o'clock in the afternoon in Washington."

"So what will we do for the rest of the evening?"

Looked at him, then closed one eye, considered—he looked so hopeful—finished her drink and said, "Heck with it. Your room or mine?"

HAWKINS HAD BEEN married right after graduation, at twenty-two, and had remained married for six years, and so had a level of sexual experience—excellence?—gained from a three-times-a-week routine, at least when he was at home. Letty hadn't encountered that with her sexual history of three young bachelors. Hawkins was, as she'd suspected, a horndog.

At two in the morning, she sat up in bed, stretched, and said, "That was nice. I better be going."

"What? No, no, no. In my experience, an early-morning fuck is just the thing before a run. Gets the blood circulating," Hawkins said. "You brought running clothes, yes? So, that's settled."

She eased down beside him and said, "You talked me into it."

Hawkins went to sleep six minutes later. He didn't snore but did make some heavy breathing sounds and occasionally muttered a word or two. When she was sure he was asleep, Letty got up and retrieved her bikini briefs and pulled them on, then got back into bed. The underpants made her feel a little more secure.

She'd never before done a one-night stand, despite a number of invitations, and even though this was apparently going to be a two-night stand, she was . . . uneasy. About what she was doing, and about what Hawkins thought and felt about her.

She knew, for sure, that she liked him a lot. Way too early to think she was falling in love, but he was smart, handsome, funny, and sexy, which overall was a nice combination. Yet, the sense of unease persisted. Was this really her, basically naked in a bed next to a totally and undeniably naked man she hardly knew?

Well . . . yes.

With that decided, she went to sleep, and the next morning, fully cooperated not in one, but two early-morning fucks, one before and one after a three-mile run along riverside tracks that Hawkins knew by heart.

"Our interview with Ann Sloam is after her tutorials this afternoon," Hawkins told her, as he snuggled up against her. "I cleverly scheduled it later in the day so you'd have to stay another night. I plan to show you the virtues of the Reverse Cowgirl Laydown . . . unless you're already familiar with it."

"I don't believe so, though I can sorta imagine it," Letty said.

"It's better than you can imagine," he said. He got up, still talking, bouncing naked around the room. As far as she could tell, he had virtually no body shyness, which was a good thing.

THEY HAD A late, slow, comfortable breakfast, and spent the morning visiting Hawkins's old haunts. They spent more time at the Ashmolean, examining the archaeological exhibits, and poked their heads into the Bodleian Library, which was nothing short of intimidating. Letty pronounced it too aristo for study, though it was nice to look at.

THEN IT WAS time for the final interview.

Ann Sloam was two days short of seventy-five, according to Letty's briefing packet. She lived in a narrow three-story stone town house on a backstreet not far from the heart of Oxford. "This is unexpected," Hawkins said, looking down the line of well-kept homes. "Tutors are generally . . . mmm . . . not fairly paid. Not well paid, for what they do. This house is beyond the means of an average tutor. I would expect that in this location, it could go for well in excess of a half-million pounds."

"An estimate left over from the ex-wife?"

"Yes, I would have to admit that's true. She could talk real estate twenty-four hours a day. And often did. We'd be in bed and I was working as hard as I could and she'd moan, 'We can take care of the cat odor.'"

So, did he think about his ex-wife a lot? But wait: wasn't she the one who'd mentioned ex-wife?

ANN SLOAM HAD curly steel-gray hair and stooped shoulders, but a bright smile, a youthful step. She opened her door, looked at Letty and said, "I imagine you're the young lady from the United States."

"Yes, I am," Letty said. "I appreciate your talking to us."

"I'm happy to. I'm very worried about Lionel," she said, as she stepped back from the doorway. Letty and Hawkins looked into a comfortable sitting room with a large television hung from one wall. She pointed them at two overstuffed chairs, while she sat on a sofa. "Lionel is suffering," she said.

Letty: "I understand that he contracted several diseases in his work . . ."

Sloam waved that away. "He has handled those—though not without serious physical discomfort. The suffering I was referring to, though, is psychological. He is in a bad way."

"Tell me," Letty said.

Sloam sighed, and looked at the ceiling, gathering her thoughts. "You know that I was his instructor in biochemistry. He did two years in biochemistry before he began his medical studies. Even as he was doing that, he continued with me, as a tutor."

"So you knew him well . . ."

"Quite well. He was a bright young man, perhaps a bit short of what I'd call brilliant, but certainly bright enough." She put an index finger over her lips and tip of her nose, as though to hush herself up, then took the finger away and asked, "What do you know about the Gaia hypothesis?"

Letty shook her head: "Almost nothing. I studied economics. I mean, I've heard of it."

"So let me start with a bit of background on Lionel . . ."

Scott had grown up with devoutly religious parents—their divorce notwithstanding—and for years had gone to church services most days of the week, Sloam said. Scott carried that background to Oxford, where for his first two years at university, he continued to attend religious services on a regular basis.

"He lost his religious faith along the way, during his medical studies," Sloam said. "There were too many tensions, he told me, and he resolved those in favor of science. Still, he needed *some* kind of faith. Something to live for, some bigger purpose."

The one that tempted him was the Gaia hypothesis, Sloam said, the belief that the earth itself was a living organism that had grown and protected life itself for billions of years. He rejected the idea at first, because it seemed contrary to the general acceptance of Darwinism—that life is a competition between organisms, and the fittest survive. The Gaia hypothesis suggests the contrary, that while competition does occur, the overall thrust of life is cooperative, when you look at it from a long enough perspective, and a large enough time frame.

"All right," Letty said. "But he rejected that?"

"He did at first, as I said, but over the years, his views began to change, especially as he became more and more involved in the struggle to defeat disease in the Third World," Sloam said. She plucked at a knit on the sofa, then scratched at it, thinking. "What he thought he saw was that there had once been a kind of balance . . . a cruel balance, but perhaps a necessary one . . . that used disease to limit the human population. With his work, he saw that balance being destroyed. He came to the belief that when nobody died early, when procreation was allowed to run wild, that we would inevitably reach a state where sheer population would destroy Gaia."

Letty said, "A lot of people . . . think that is already happening."

Sloam nodded. "Global warming. Humans can defeat it in some ways—something as simple as air conditioning could make a hot world tolerable for many people, especially the rich. Temperatures in the Middle East and even in the southern parts of the U.S. now rise to levels that would be intolerable without it."

Letty agreed. "I've seen a study that says if the power grid in Phoenix, Arizona, failed during a midsummer heat wave, more than 800,000 people would need emergency assistance and perhaps seventeen thousand would die. We already have rolling blackouts in some parts of the Southwest during heat waves. So . . . things are becoming fraught."

"Yes, indeed they are. Perhaps we could control the indoors, but how do you air-condition the outdoors?" Sloam asked. "How do you air-condition forests and farmland and oceans? Can't do it. We can air-condition ourselves until our arses freeze, but we can't get along without food."

"So Dr. Scott is doing what? Looking for a cure?"

"I don't know exactly *what* he is doing," Sloam said. "I know that he spent a lot of time working with children, so many children, in central Africa and Bangladesh. I know that he began to study advanced maths, statistics. He told me once, a few years ago, that we might have to go to an enforced one-child policy, like China tried, to drive the population down."

"Put all women on the pill?"

"Well, that would be one way, perhaps . . . although, culturally, in many places, children are the guarantee of elder care, and the more children you have, the more guarantee you have," Sloam said. "I know he researched the possibility of government programs that would pay women *not* to have children, but that, it seems, would be a dead end. To get payments high enough to be effective, we'd have to spend not trillions of dollars, but hundreds of trillions of dollars. Won't happen."

"So he was looking for other solutions?"

Sloam stared at Letty for several long beats, then she said, "I have this . . . dreadful . . ."

A long silence, still staring, until Letty asked, "What?"

"The very last time I saw Lionel, he said that he was going to the States to study more biology, and to study numbers. He told me that if you examined Gaia as a scientist, one thing that became apparent was that humans are analogous to a virus on the body of the earth. You need to find a cure for the virus. If you could knock the virus down—not eliminate it, but just knock it down, as has been done with AIDS and Covid—Gaia would survive."

"You mean . . ."

"I don't know exactly *what* he meant," Sloam said. Again, she seemed to be groping for words. "But after Covid . . . you see, Covid went everywhere. We really couldn't stop it. It killed millions of people, but we have billions of people, so overall, no change. But suppose it had killed billions of people? Suppose it killed five billion people? More than half the power generation is unneeded. Half the cars are gone. Half the houses don't need heat in winter. Global warming stops, is even reversed. Gaia is saved."

Letty blurted: "Oh Jesus Christ!"

THERE WAS MORE about the Gaia hypothesis, but as soon as they'd left Sloam, Letty looked up at Hawkins and said, "We both need to phone home."

"Yes. Back to the inn, my girl. Can you still reach your senator?"

"I can. I have to."

"I'll write something tonight, and hand it in tomorrow after I put you on your plane. I expect it will be taken to the director general himself. This may be far-fetched . . . but what do I know?"

"You think you can get right to the director?"

"I'm, mmm, somewhat fair-haired," Hawkins said. "I'll at least be listened to."

IN HER ROOM at the inn, Letty called Colles's office, and after some delay, was switched through to him.

"Did you locate him?" No names to be mentioned.

"No, but I had a tarot reading that said he's still alive . . ."

"You're joking."

"I'm not. That came from a hippie ex-lover who has stashed her husband somewhere off the premises. But—we have the phone problem," Letty said. "I don't want to get into detail about an interview from this afternoon. We need to meet at your office as soon as I get back. If there aren't any delays, I can be there by four o'clock tomorrow afternoon. And Chris . . . call my father. He needs to be at the meeting. He has a friend in the Marshals Service named Rae Givens, she should be there as well, and their boss at the Marshals Service, his name is Russell Forte." She paused, and then said, "Here's some double-talk for you, because of the phone problem. The relevant person's supervisors at the two facilities where he worked in the U.S. need to be there, too. Get them on airplanes. And anyone else who needs to know. Billy Greet, for sure."

Greet was an upper-level executive with the Department of Homeland Security, and had worked with Letty on other investigations.

"Why your father?" Colles asked. "And this Givens person?"

"Because of what they do." They hunted.

"Ah. This doesn't have anything to do with the tarot?"

"No. This is much more serious," Letty said. "Much more serious than what happened in Texas two years ago, or California last year. Way more important."

"Don't tell me that," Colles said.

"I'm telling you that."

"Four o'clock tomorrow. I'll clear the decks and get everyone here. I hope you're right about the seriousness of this thing, and we don't look like idiots and have to apologize and send everyone home."

"No. You hope I'm *not* right about this," Letty said. "Because if I am . . . well—the phone problem."

HAWKINS AND LETTY spent most of the night talking about the Gaia concept, looking up and making notes on Scott's publications and academic credentials. They still made time for the Reverse Cowgirl Laydown, along with a few other biological experiments. Hawkins delivered Letty to LHR at ten o'clock the next morning for the noon flight, pressed her against a pillar for a last kiss and said, "God. I hope this *isn't* the last kiss. In the catastrophic sense of the word."

"Could we be making too much out of what we've heard?" Letty asked.

"Pray that we have," Hawkins said. He took several backward steps, holding her eyes, then turned and disappeared into the crowd, a tall lanky man in a hurry.

Eight people waited in Senator Christopher Colles's office. One of his assistants had delivered a box of donuts and a cooler of Cokes, Diet Cokes, and iced coffee; two paunchy scientists had each taken two donuts and Colles had taken an iced coffee.

An air of impatience hung over the room like a third-rate rap song.

Blond, slender, sunburned Billy Greet stood in a corner with her arms crossed, eyes drifting between Colles and Deputy U.S. Marshal Lucas Davenport; Lucas, a heavy-shouldered man, dark hair touched with gray, hands in pants pockets, was perched on the sill of Colles's only window. Like his daughter Letty, he took books with him when he traveled; in this case, a battered copy of Martha Grimes's thriller *Send Bygraves*, which he'd read perhaps fifteen times. He finished a familiar verse, slipped the book in his jacket pocket, turned to look out the window, and wondered out loud, "Where the hell is she? It's almost five o'clock."

"Plane was late. We know she's on the ground," Colles said. "Traffic is getting heavy."

"She could have called us," Lucas said.

"Not about this, apparently," Colles said. "Which is worrisome."

Deputy U.S. Marshal Rae Givens, a tall, muscular black woman, lounged on a fuzzy beige sofa, a big, well-padded black canvas bag by her feet, along with a TUMI suitcase. She'd arrived twenty minutes earlier, had gotten a hug from Davenport and a handshake from Colles, who said, "Lucas and Virgil Flowers tell me you're the cat's pajamas."

"That's true, though both of them lie a lot, so you have to take that into account," Rae had said.

Lucas had asked, "You bring guns?"

"Of course." She'd touched the black bag with a toe. "Amazed I could get them in here."

Russell Forte, Lucas's contact in the Marshals Service management, had come over from Arlington and was leaning on a credenza, looking at his phone.

GREET SAID, "MAYBE Letty stopped at her apartment to pick up her Sig. She's not happy if it's not in her pocket." Greet looked like an Oklahoma rancher, not a ranking Homeland Security executive; Letty's Sig was a sub-compact nine-millimeter handgun.

Colles: "If she stopped at her apartment, I'll kick her ass. We're too important to keep us waiting for that." He glanced at Lucas: "With your permission, of course."

"You got it," Letty's father said.

The two scientists had been sitting in a conversation cluster, eating their donuts and brushing powdered sugar off their jackets. They were both soft, bespectacled, and balding. Victor Sims was a group director with USAMRIID, the U.S. Army Medical Research Institute of Infectious Diseases. Harold McDonald held an equivalent job at Los Alamos National Laboratory. They'd both been supervisors of Lionel Scott when he worked at their respective laboratories.

"What do we know about Scott that I haven't been told?" Rae asked.

"We can't find him," Greet said. "Letty is on her way here to tell us why we need to find him."

"Dead or alive," Colles said. He looked at Lucas: "Unless your daughter has messed this up."

"She doesn't mess things up," Lucas said. He stepped over to the cooler, took a Diet Coke, unscrewed the top.

"What'd Scott do?" Rae asked.

Colles: "We don't know if he did anything . . ."

HE STOPPED TALKING as the door popped open again, and Letty stepped inside, carrying her travel bag. She looked tired and aimed a shaky smile at the room: "Hey, Dad, Chris, Russ. And you must be Rae . . . Hey, Billy." She put her bag down, walked over to Lucas and gave him a hard squeeze. "How's Mom?"

"She's fine, where have you been?"

"In traffic hell."

Colles introduced Sims and McDonald, asked, "How was the

flight?" and without waiting for an answer, asked, "What's going on? And everybody, find a seat."

Letty stepped to one side of the office, turned to the room, and said, "I worked with an MI5 officer in England. We were working last night, doing computer searches. He continued to do that while I was in the air, and I spoke to him from Dulles. Since Scott is a British citizen, Alec has access to his passport and credit cards. Scott's credit cards haven't been used for a month. However, ten months ago, he traveled to India, and seven months ago, to Uganda, using his credit cards. That's all we know for sure, about that. But, there are some indications . . ."

"Like what?" Colles asked.

"Let me tell you a little about Scott and what's called the Gaia hypothesis . . ."

She spent a minute outlining the Gaia hypothesis and Scott's possible conversion to the view, to his idea that humans are essentially viruses on the body of Gaia, and to his history of depression.

"Gaia's pretty much nonsense," Sims said at one point, and McDonald nodded.

"Makes no difference," Letty said.

"What do you mean?" Sims asked. "If it's nonsense . . ."

"Doesn't make any difference whether it is or not, if Scott thinks it's real," Greet chipped in. "Where are you going with this, Letty?"

"Alec, Alec Hawkins, the MI5 officer, couldn't find anyone who could tell him what Scott was doing in either India or Uganda. He did find a person who Scott contacted in Uganda. He said Scott represented himself as a doctor with Médecins Sans Frontières. He was, at one time, but not at that point. He'd left the organization, but still had credentials," Letty said. "Bottom line, he misrepresented himself. But Alec, you know, who is a smart guy, ran India and Uganda against a list of disease outbreaks at the time Scott was traveling, and compared that to hotel charges on his Visa card. There was no outbreak of anything in Uganda worse than the usual background diseases, but . . ."

She rubbed her forehead, and Lucas said, "C'mon. What?"

"Uganda apparently has a high incidence of the Marburg virus among its fruit bat population," Letty said. "There's a cave in a national park that's full of fruit bats and is a well-known source of Marburg. Alec found that Scott used his credit cards several times in Kisenyi Village, which is right next to the park."

Colles: "He was researching fruit bats?"

Sims: "He was researching Marburg. If you had the right permissions, credentials, you could sample bat tissue . . . Senator, this isn't good. Marburg is ugly, nasty stuff."

McDonald: "Yes, it is. It's closely related to Ebola, which is perhaps more famous."

Colles went back to Letty. "Okay, so what . . ."

"Alec looked into his India trip. His credit cards indicate that he checked into a hotel in Hyderabad, which is in the southern part of the subcontinent. Very close to the state of Maharashtra. Which, at the time Scott was traveling, was the site of one of the worst outbreaks of measles in the world."

Sims, "Oh, shit."

Colles: "What, Vic?"

Sims scratched his head, thinking, and Letty prompted him. "R-number. Do that first."

Sims looked at her, said, "Yes," and to the group, "The R-number of a disease is the number of people, on average, that an infected person would be expected to pass the disease on to. If a disease has an R-number of 1, you'd expect the infected person to transmit the disease to one additional person. The R-number of Marburg would be . . . well, almost zero. That's why we can contain it when there's an outbreak. Not many people get infected."

"So that's good," Colles said, looking around the room.

"It was difficult to calculate an R-number for COVID, because of complicating factors like the rapid development of vaccines, the fact that some people who had it showed no symptoms, that some strains were more infectious than others, and so on, but it was estimated to be between 3 and 6," Sims continued. "That is, an infected person would be expected to pass the disease to something between three and six other people, on average, among a population with no immunity. That number was high enough that we had a worldwide pandemic, starting in a medium-sized Chinese city. We couldn't stop it. Going by official numbers, it killed perhaps seven million people; unofficially, we all know it killed a lot more, perhaps twenty million."

He looked around the room. "Measles has an estimated R-number of 15 to 18. In other words, it is something like three to six times more infectious than COVID. If an . . . insane man, or group . . . were adept at viral research, it might be possible that they could bind the pathogenic load from Marburg to a measles virus. If you could give the Marburg pathogen the measles R-number . . ." He threw his hands in the air.

Colles: "How dangerous?"

Letty: "Nobody knows exactly how dangerous Marburg is. It has killed up to eighty percent of its victims in some outbreaks. In others, it's more like thirty percent. If you had a fast, worldwide pandemic of Marburg, and it killed thirty percent of those who caught it, you could lose . . . two and a half billion people? If it were eighty percent, you might kill six and a half billion? Out of a total of eight billion people."

The assembly gawked at her. Colles asked, "Why in God's name would you do that?"

"Some Gaia people—and I'm talking about a small subset—think the earth is in a death spiral," Letty said. "That everything is going down—plants, animals, humans. Getting rid of a bunch of humans might stop the spiral. In fact, some of the people I've been reading about think that's the only way to stop it."

"They're nuts," Colles said. "Carbon sequestration . . ."

"Ask yourself how that's working," Letty said.

"Given some time . . ."

"Some of the Gaia people—and some serious scientists, for that matter—think it's already too late," Letty said. "A woman, a biochemist who was Scott's tutor years ago, at Oxford, put it right out there, and it's been haunting me ever since. Kill half the people, you only need half the energy production, burn half the oil, need half the cars, you only chop down half the trees for lumber to build houses . . . Gaia is saved. In a year."

"Jesus Christ," Colles blurted.

Letty: "That's exactly what I said. *Exactly.*"

McDonald spoke up. "At Los Alamos, Lionel was studying the patterns by which infectious diseases spread. That's what we do there—work with numbers. We're trying to figure the best ways to interfere with the spread of something like Covid. How do you knock it down, how you surround it and isolate it. Of course, that information would be valuable, invaluable, to a person who was trying to *spread* a disease."

"He spent some time studying viral gain-of-function research at the fort," Sims said. "He didn't do actual experiments, but he's certainly familiar with the techniques."

Lucas asked, "What does that mean? Gain of function?"

"It's . . . mmm . . . research into increasing a pathogen's ability to become more infectious, or more virulent, or both. We've pledged never to use it, but we need the research in case somebody else does. We need to know how to detect the pathogens and hopefully stop them. The thing is, if you're looking for a WMD, this kind of research is much, much cheaper than, say, building a nuclear weapon."

McDonald: "And more deadly."

"Could one guy do it?" Lucas asked.

Sims shrugged: "With the right knowledge and equipment and access to the pathogens . . . possibly." He looked at Letty. "And this young woman is telling us that he might have been trying to access the pathogens. Now he's disappeared."

COLLES STOOD UP and turned to Greet: "Billy: You need to set up a working group now. Today, tonight, tomorrow. You've got the hammer. You'll need to provide information and physical support—plane tickets, cars, expense money—to Lucas, Rae and Letty, and anybody else who needs to go out there. They'll be going to Los Alamos."

Greet said, "We really ought to bring the FBI in. But they leak like crazy."

Colles rubbed his nose and then said, "Do what's best. I don't know what's best, I'm pulling this out of my ass. We can't have leaks: people will freak out."

Letty: "So what? If we plaster Scott's face everywhere, maybe he'll turn up tomorrow."

Greet: "If it gets in the media, it would distort the hell out of the hunt for the guy. You'll have law enforcement bureaucrats doing what they always do best, which is cover their asses, and of course the media will make it seem like we're facing certain doom. And Scott will be warned we're coming."

"Not only that," Lucas said. "If the guy has the viruses, and finds out we're coming, and he hasn't yet pulled the trigger, it might inspire him to do that. Even if we decided to put his picture everywhere, we don't know that he's acting alone. If he has accomplices, they could go on the run. We wouldn't even know who we're looking for."

"Okay, but couldn't we put out an ordinary, or a little more than ordinary, FBI missing persons alert?" Colles asked. "Get Scott's photograph out to cops? We don't have to tell anyone that he's planning to kill the world."

Greet nodded: "We could probably do that, if we're careful. Maybe get them to use the TRAK network, put a little extra spin on it."

Lucas: "When we find him . . ."

Greet: "Kill him. Kill him if you have to. Because if he's suicidal and has made this new virus thing and infected himself, he's a walking weapon of mass destruction. Don't tell anyone I said that."

Colles: "That seems premature, Billy. We don't want to talk about murder, not yet."

"Not murder—it's self-defense. For the people who approach him, and the whole world, for that matter."

Lucas turned to Sims: "This . . . binding of viruses . . . that's not something you can do with a Crock-Pot and a microwave, right? He'd need a specialized lab, he'd need PPE, he'd need, what? Tell me what? What would he have to buy, where would he get it? If we can find that, his sources, we can find where they shipped it to."

"I'll get my people working on it—they're all cleared for top secret. We'll get you a list, tonight. Get me your cell number and email," Sims said.

"Get it to Billy, her group will be controlling this. We'll be in the field."

And to Letty, Lucas said, "Call up this Alec guy: we need Scott's credit cards, phone numbers, anything you can get. By now, he must have an American driver's license, if he's been in the States for years . . ."

Colles: "Screw a phone call. Let's get him over here. Worse comes to worst, maybe he could talk this Scott down out of his tree. Oxford guys, that's sort of like the Masonic lodge, right? Secret handshakes, special neckties, all that."

"I'll call him," Letty said. "Maybe we could get somebody higher up to request him." She was looking at Colles: "Think the Secretary would do it?"

Colles bared his teeth, said, "He's surrounded by weasels who'd leak the President's atomic war codes if they thought they could make a buck out of it. But, I think we have to. I'll call him, ask him to make a request to MI5. He'll listen to me. I'll make it clear that if anything leaks from his office, we'll reserve a room for him at the supermax."

"He'll try to take it to the President," Greet said.

Colles nodded: "Probably. He never misses a chance to go to the White House. Gets a boner just thinking about it. But the Oval Office can be reasonably tight when it wants to be. Nobody wants a nationwide panic in the year before a national election."

"When you talk to the Secretary, tell him that you've worked with me before and would accept me as his nominee to head the search," Greet said. "I know enough people who could do the research and still keep the secret."

"Rae, Lucas, you okay with this?" Colles asked.

Lucas held up a finger: "When we find Scott, do we need biohazard suits? Does somebody need them? Are there biohazard teams inside the government who could deal with this if they had to, if he's either infected himself or other people or has actually started spreading the disease? I don't know this stuff. I only know what I've seen in movies, and that's all sci-fi bullshit."

Greet: "We can cover all of that and get you what you need. The information. I'll be talking to you on an hourly basis. But we need to get you on-scene. Like tonight. I'll check with the Air Force and see if we can get a plane out to Kirtland Air Force Base in Albuquerque."

Lucas shook his head: "The bureaucratic bullshit around that could take forever. Use your clout to get three business class seats on a commercial flight to Albuquerque. I'll put them on my Amex. That'll expedite things, and I can try to claim expenses later."

Greet nodded: "Probably a better idea."

McDonald: "What if it *is* all sci-fi?"

Colles: "Then we lock Mr. Scott in a quiet, secure hospital, send in the shrinks, have a couple beers and a few laughs, and pretend this meeting never happened."

Greet asked Letty: "From what you know, what are the chances that this is real?"

Letty shrugged: "I believe the potential is there. It's very likely he's been looking at sources of measles and Marburg. He has an academic history in biochemistry and in infectious disease control, and he has spent time looking at viral research at Fort Detrick, and at Los Alamos studying the mathematics of viral spread. Could be innocent, I guess . . . but I don't think so."

Greet moved to the door: "Senator Colles—I'm going over to the

DHS right now, get my group going. If you could call the Secretary, bring up my name, and suggest he talk to the President while keeping his mouth shut around the office. When I see him, I'll recommend that he keep the weasels out of it. And I'll get this what's-his-name from MI5?"

Letty said, "Alec Hawkins."

"I'll get him on the way."

Letty nodded: "Great. Alec has some useful skills."

Dark of the moon, dark of his mind. Monsoon clouds blocking starlight.

Sitting on the back steps was like having a rug thrown over your head. Lionel Scott allowed himself one cigarette a day, an act of defiance. The goddamn liberals agreed tobacco was going to kill you but didn't have the balls to do anything meaningful about the fact that the whole world was dying in front of their eyes.

America was the third biggest consumer of coal, hooked into it like a Texas meth junkie. China was worse, the biggest burner of the stuff, followed by India. The guilty libs barely bothered to talk to those countries, because that would be bigoted and white-centric. Besides, didn't we burn all that coal in the twentieth century, so how can we expect them to do anything different?

Because we didn't know back then, not really, that we were killing Gaia. We thought she'd go on forever.

But they know now, and do it anyway . . .

He wouldn't expect the right-wingers to do anything, here in the USA, or in Europe, or anywhere else—they had their own belief system, and one of their beliefs was that God had anointed the internal combustion engine and the air conditioner as holy things, even if Gaia was choking to death on their fumes. As the saying went, you could sometimes talk to crazy, but there was no dealing with stupid.

THE ACRID SMELL of the Marlboro swirled around him, pleasant, reminiscent of the old days when he believed that something might be done. Now the choices were so narrow that they'd have to choose between horrific cataclysm on one hand, and certain death on the other.

He took a last drag on the cigarette and ground out the butt beneath his boot; yet he sat, for a while, in the peace and quiet, reluctant to go inside.

Then Catton came to the door and whispered, "I can't get George plugged in again, I can't find a vein."

"All that fat," Scott said. He put his hands on his knees and pushed down to help himself to his feet. He was tired, maybe terminally tired, he sometimes thought. But he couldn't stop now.

He followed Catton into the house and into a bedroom where George Smithe lay on a single bed. He was too big for it, a two-hundred-forty pounder, but hardly aware, sweating, burning. The disease would take ten pounds off George, which made Scott almost smile at the thought: the Marburg Vaccine Diet, a ten-pound weight loss in ten days, or your money back, if you were alive to collect it.

Scott sat on a box next to the bed, got the saline lead and slapped George's arm until he saw the vein coming up. When he had it, he plugged in the catheter, and the drip began flowing. Not hard, for an experienced doctor. Catton had no experience except what he'd given her, a sixty-year-old trust-funder working as a nurse in what was almost a charnel house.

They had three people on beds, in two bedrooms. Catton and two others were back on their feet. They'd had one death, and Scott thought that was all they'd have. The three still on beds, including Smithe, had made it over the hump; although they all smelled as if something inside them was rotting. He had vaccinated them with an attenuated Marburg virus, run through mouse models until the virus weakened enough that it might no longer kill a well-cared-for human.

They'd been wrong with Morton Carey. But Carey had been a drug user and had weakened himself. Carey had died five days after the injection, and they'd carried his body up the mountainside after midnight and buried him there, marking his grave with a heavy red stone.

Of the three still bedridden, Smithe was in the most danger. The others could talk again, though they were still too weak to sit up. Scott had seen so much death in his forty years that he'd become inured to it—and when he thought about the prospect of Smithe dying, and though he actually liked the man, he tended to think most about the problem of hauling his dead-weight corpse outside and burying him, what a pain in the ass that would be. How would they even get him through the back door?

So he was pulling for Smithe . . .

When he was sure the saline line was working, he stood and went out to the kitchen where Catton and the two recovered . . . patients?

What were they, exactly? Gaia patriots, maybe? How about criminally insane accomplices?

Danielle Callister was an almost pretty, heavily tattooed blonde who'd been the first to come back, after Catton. She had an engaging smile, and direct eyes, but sometimes said shockingly sincere things about her parents, her siblings, and ex-lovers. She had a reputation as an earth-radical, a tree-sitter, who'd punched more than one cop.

Randall Foss was a short man with a bullet head, but quick, intelligent, good with computers and numbers. Of all of them, Scott himself excepted, Foss saw most clearly what was about to happen with Gaia. Foss was also their designated cook, and tonight, they were having fish sticks with French fries and copious catsup: fish and chips, more or less, accompanied by a fine Mosel Riesling, chosen to enhance the flavor of the fish sticks.

As for Catton, as Scott stood at the kitchen door, looking at her and at Callister and Foss . . . Scott slipped into a flashback.

THEY WERE AT Catton's house in Santa Fe with her lifelong companion, Jane Shepard, in the library. The library contained books on art, on literature—Catton had published a novel with a small Minnesota press—on Native American culture, on weaving and photography and mustang rescues, and, lately, on Gaia. Catton had a lot of enthusiasms, burning bright with each of them, but after a while, moving on.

Gaia was the latest, and she'd met Scott at a gathering of environmental activists in Santa Fe, which had numerous gatherings of environmental activists, usually for the purpose of fund-raising. She had instantly caught on to Scott's radicalism, his disdain for the usual remedies, which he dismissed as "nice ideas, but practically unachievable," and the fund-raisers as "collecting cash to provide jobs for hapless do-gooders."

At this particular moment, the moment of the flashback, Catton had told Shepard about the plan to rescue Gaia. Shepard had not just disagreed, she'd freaked out, screaming at Catton, weeping, staggering around the library like a drunk.

Catton was screaming back, no tears there: she was the one with the money, she was the one who could get along without the other. Then Shepard, eluding Scott's efforts to separate the two women, had slapped Catton, hard, knocking the other woman off her feet.

Catton had crawled across the floor, to steps leading down to a basement area that contained a television room, a bathroom and a storage area. She'd gotten back to her feet, and she'd said to Shepard, in a calm, muted voice, "I'm so sorry you did that, Jane. Give me a minute, please."

She'd disappeared down the stairs, presumably to the bathroom, and Shepard had turned to Scott, pleading with him to give up any idea of injecting Catton and others with his makeshift vaccine . . .

And Catton appeared at the stairs, saying again, "I'm so sorry, Jane."

Shepard turned to her. Catton was holding a short black rifle. Shepard said, "Don't be ridiculous . . ."

Catton shot her twice in the chest, the spent shells flipping out of the gun like popcorn out of a hot pot. Shepard died quickly, on the black brick floor, her blank gray eyes open, staring up at a crystal chandelier.

Catton had turned to Scott and said, "So you see, I'm that committed. We should get up to the ski valley and start the injections. I had the things you wanted delivered, the futons . . ."

And Scott had thought: *This is real, now.*

He thought it again, standing in the doorway to the kitchen, looking at the three survivors. They'd left Shepard in the basement of the Santa Fe house, wrapped in a blue plastic tarp. Catton had said, "I'd be amazed if she were found in six months. By then, one way or another, it won't matter."

And it wouldn't.

Vaccines or no, they were all dead, when the world found out what they'd done.

FOSS HAD GOTTEN up to pull the fish sticks, which were on an aluminum cookie sheet, out of the oven. He turned around with the sheet in his hand and saw Scott standing in the doorway, and asked, "What do you think, boss? George gonna make it?"

"If his weight doesn't kill him," Scott said. "He's a leading candidate for diabetes."

"Gotta die sometime," Foss said. "So, shit and chips?"

Almost made Scott smile: "That's about right. Fish sticks should be universally condemned as a crime against humanity."

Catton turned her head to him: "I wish you hadn't said that; the crime against humanity thing."

They all sat silently, then the tattooed lady, Danielle Callister, said, "Ah, well."

And Foss said, "We've got barbeque sauce if you don't want catsup."

The fastest route to Albuquerque went through Atlanta from Reagan National. Greet got them on scattered seats in the business class section, and since they wouldn't be able to talk much on the plane, Lucas, Rae, and Letty mustered in a sparsely used gate at National to talk until the first flight boarded.

Lucas said, "We gotta get that MI5 guy here soon as we can. We need to know if Scott has friends in the States and where they're located. Greet says Scott hasn't left the country, legally, anyway. Any old Oxford pals here in the States anywhere? He could be in Key West or Alaska by now, even driving. We need phone numbers."

"Scott's supposed to be very smart—he's gotta be using burners," Letty said.

"Yeah, but if we can get a number . . . burners only work if you throw them away. If you keep using one, or even have it turned on, we can track it."

"Your friend Billy needs to get us his driver's license and car registration information," Rae said to Letty. "We can do that, but not in the air. That should be waiting for us when we get to Albuquerque. I don't think there are any serious airports without license plate readers. We need to know if he's flown anywhere since he disappeared. We need phone numbers for the people who can check the readers."

"I'll call her now," Letty said.

"And call your MI5 guy," Lucas said. "It should be what, eleven o'clock there? He should be up."

Letty walked away to do that, leaving Lucas and Rae to talk. Greet picked up on the first ring: "You on the plane?"

"Not yet. I have some information requests from the, uh, marshals."

"That's okay, you can say, 'Dad.'"

"And Rae, too." Letty gave her the list, then asked, "Are you moving?"

"Yes. The Secretary's on his way to the White House. He got it, he's taking it seriously, and he's excited. He won't get to the President, I don't think, but he'll get to the chief of staff. He gave me the go-ahead to set up a working group. I'm getting them together now, and he'll be reaching out to the director of MI5 tomorrow morning," Greet said. "But I've got some unpleasant news, too. It turns out we don't really have biological emergency response teams, as such. We've got all kinds of studies, we've got the gear, we've got designated people. But we really don't have a *package*. FEMA is scrambling around trying to get everything together, but real immediate support . . . I don't know. I have the Secretary screaming at the FEMA director, so there's that." FEMA: Federal Emergency Management Agency.

"I'll pass that on to the others. I'll call Alec in a minute. He may have already talked to his director."

"Okay. You should be boarding the plane in twenty minutes or so. Call me when you get to Albuquerque. I'll still be up."

Letty called Hawkins. His phone rang three times and Hawkins asked, "You find him?"

"No, just getting started. I've got a list for you. Stuff we need from MI5."

"Give it to me. I spoke to the director, a rare pleasure, I have to say. We're setting up a working group here, led right from the top. I'm on my way to Albuquerque at the crack of dawn. I'll pass your list on before I go."

She gave him the list, and he said, "That's easy enough, we've actually already talked about most of these items. By the by, I got Scott's emails from Dr. Carr. No help there."

"Damn."

"Yes. I had some hopes. So. With any luck, I'll see you tomorrow night."

"My father's on the task force. I didn't mention our . . . friendship."

"Should that be a concern? I mean, I know he's heavily armed, but you're practically a spinster."

"Thank you. I'll treasure the comment," Letty said. "But you, and he, share some, uh, personality traits, so he'll figure things out. If he gets too paternal, I'll tell him to back off, but, you know, I love him."

"I will tread with care," Hawkins said.

"Not too much care."

He laughed: "No. I can promise you that."

SHE WALKED BACK toward Lucas and Rae and found a thickset man with glasses and a wide-brimmed canvas hat staring at them from the aisle. He looked heavily harassed. She asked, "Can I help you with something?"

He looked at her, his pasty white indoor face bobbing up and down for a second or two, and then he asked, "Are you Letty?"

"Yes. Who are you?"

"So that's Lucas Davenport and Rae Givens?"

"Yes . . ."

"I'm with USAMRIID. I'm supposed to go with you to Los Alamos to look for a virus lab."

"Uh, who sent you?"

He had an envelope in his hand with some notes scratched on it: "My boss, but the request came from a Billy Greet? I don't know him, but he's with Homeland Security, and my boss sounded scared to death, so he must have some serious clout?"

"Actually, Billy's a she," Letty said.

"Yeah? I thought Billys who were shes spelled it B-i-l-l-i-e," he said.

"Well, she's originally from Oklahoma, and maybe they don't spell so well out there," Letty said. "What's your name?"

"Walter Packer." He stuck out a hand to shake, and when she took it, realized he was missing the middle, ring and little fingers on that hand, leaving her with nothing but the index finger, thumb and a wad of scar tissue to hold on to.

"Come on over and meet the others . . ."

She led him to Lucas and Rae, who were looking at a notebook on Rae's lap. When they came up, Lucas immediately spotted the damaged hand and after Letty introduced him, Lucas asked, "You mess with fireworks when you were a kid?"

"Actually, I made some C-4 when I was a kid. I made my own chemistry set with ordinary farm chemicals. I can't recommend it."

Rae: "So you're a scientist?"

"You need a PhD to get in the scientist club. I've only got an MA, all-but-thesis at this point, so I'm a technician." He sighed and dropped his shoulders, said, "I checked all my stuff. I had to lie about some of it."

"Like what?"

"I have a pressurized air tank in my bag. It's not obvious, so I didn't tell them. Maybe it won't get there and I can go home."

"You afraid of Marburg?" Rae asked.

He held up his mangled hand. "Ask the hand," he said. "The hand has opinions about high-risk activities. Especially the ones you're sent on at the last minute by sauerkraut-eating bureaucrats."

"We know them well," Rae said. "With that attitude, we'll get along fine."

"They have a Cinnabon place here?" Packer asked, looking around.

"If they do, get me one with extra frosting," Rae said.

THE FLIGHT TO Atlanta was quick, the layover short. Since they couldn't talk, they all tried to get some sleep on the three-hour flight to Albuquerque, with mixed success. Lucas had trained himself to fall asleep, when necessary, and got more than two hours; Rae got less than two hours. Letty got a restless hour and spent time reviewing the notes that she'd made with Hawkins. Packer spent the time staring out into the dark, his lips moving silently, as if in prayer.

THE ALBUQUERQUE AIRPORT was compact, with a bag-rattling brick floor that seemed an odd choice for a place that had thousands of bags dragged over it every day. Greet had reserved three compact SUVs for them, with reservations at a Holiday Inn Express in Santa Fe.

"I thought you'd probably have to go places separately, so I got three cars," she said, when Letty called her from ABQ. "The drive up to Los Alamos looks tricky, and you won't get out of Albuquerque much before eleven, so I decided to put you in Santa Fe, which is half-way up to Los Alamos. There's a Hampton Inn in Los Alamos, you can check in there tomorrow if you need to. It's only about a forty-five-minute drive from Santa Fe to Los Alamos."

"Okay. Did you hear back from the Secretary?"

"Yes. He talked to the chief of staff, like I thought. Depending on what you guys get in the next couple of days, they'll bump him up to the President. Or not."

"Alec Hawkins should be in Albuquerque tomorrow night; I'll co-ordinate with him. Things were a little thin at Hertz, you might want to make some calls so he'll be sure to get a car."

"I'll do that in the morning, when we're talking to MI5," Greet said. "Be careful driving tonight; I know you're tired."

"Uh, we collected a Walter Packer in Washington."

"Excellent. I was afraid he wouldn't make the plane. He'll have to car-share with one of you."

Letty passed the conversation on to Lucas and Rae.

"Straight up I-25 to Santa Fe, let's not try to convoy. Meet at eight tomorrow, we'll get breakfast and figure out what we're doing," Lucas said. Letty found it mildly irritating that Lucas assumed he was the leader of the pack, but said nothing.

Yet.

PACKER COLLECTED THREE checked bags, including one the size of a Prius. He found that his gear was intact and rode north with Rae.

Letty was the last one out of the car rental area, found her way to I-25 north. Ten minutes got her out of Albuquerque, running fast in the night. I-25 was three lanes wide for the first few miles, dropped to two lanes after going through a major intersection. She could see a wide band of house lights in what seemed to be miles to her west, and her iPad map suggested that the houses might be lining the far side of the Rio Grande. She quickly left that area behind, and was plunged into the kind of darkness you only saw on interstate highways in the rural Midwest or intermountain West.

An hour out of Albuquerque, she climbed a long, winding hill, pushing through the deep-dark; and when she topped the hill, saw what looked like a huge bowl of diamonds shining below, the lights of Santa Fe. I-25 at that point was running almost due east; following the map app, she got off at Cerrillos Road, driving north into the city. She couldn't see a lot, but between the highway exit and the Hampton Inn, she saw a lot of car-related businesses, dealerships, car washes, tire stores, auto parts stores; and fast-food restaurants, mostly closed.

Nobody else was in the motel lobby when Letty arrived in her SUV, so she checked in and went to bed. She was back up at seven o'-clock, looked at her email. Hawkins was in the air, flying directly to Denver, and would connect with a commuter flight into Santa Fe. Letty sent an email to Greet to update her on Hawkins's plans to go into Santa Fe instead of Albuquerque. It was nine o'clock in Washington and Greet was in her office: Letty got a thumbs-up in fifteen seconds, and a "good hunting."

That done, she met Lucas and Rae in the lobby, and they went for a thirty-minute run, and at eight, they were all out in the parking lot. Rae said, "I found a place that looks like a deli, more or less on the way, if you want to follow me and Walt."

Santa Fe, what Letty could see of it, was a little junky, but then, they were driving an old main-entry road which would be a little junky in any small city between the Appalachians and the Coastal Ranges. They got a table at the deli, pancakes and sausage and Diet Coke and coffee.

As they ate, Lucas said, "Letty, that scientist guy, McDonald, won't be back from Washington yet, but he's set you up to go to the lab and interview the people who knew Scott the best. Rae, Walt and I will go over to Scott's house and tear it apart. The Los Alamos Police Department is sending a cop over—they should have a search warrant this morning. They've already been into the place but haven't searched it."

"Then . . . what'd they do?" Packer asked.

Rae: "It was a welfare check—they looked around and made sure he wasn't dead in there."

"The thing that I don't really understand is how you could do this virus research at home," Lucas said. "I just haven't . . . I mean, could you actually set up a virus lab in your bathroom? Where would you get all the stuff you need?"

Packer rolled his eyes, and said to Rae, who had her phone sitting on the tabletop, "Call up eBay."

She did that, and when she nodded and said, "Okay," Packer said, "Put in 'electron microscope.'"

She did, and a few seconds later said, "Whoa. There's quite a selection. Starting at less than fifteen thousand dollars, going up to . . . I find one for $116,000."

Packer said, "Put in 'biological safety cabinet.'"

She did, and found dozens of them for sale.

"That would be the heart of your lab, if you knew what you were doing, and of course, Scott does," Packer said, spearing a link sausage. "You'd need some other stuff, like a freezer and glassware, maybe some isolation cages for mice, but believe me, it's all there on eBay, and would be delivered to your front door in brown paper wrappers. Sealing up a virus lab seems like it'd be a complicated process, and it is, if you do it to government standards in a place that will be used for years. But you could do a quick and dirty but effective job with stuff you get at Home Depot. All of it is made easier if you're willing to take risks, as Scott apparently is."

"It just gets better and better," Letty said.

Packer put down his fork. "I'll tell you something else, for you skeptics. A Chinese company set up an illegal virus lab in California and they were messing with stuff like HIV. It's all over the 'net, if you want to read about it. Put in 'illegal Chinese virus lab California.' You'll see. If they could do it, Scott could do it."

"Better and better," Letty said.

THE DRIVE NORTH to Los Alamos took forty minutes. Letty had never been in northern New Mexico, and the landscape was new to her, and different than she'd imagined. Once outside of Santa Fe, the highway cut through a harsh high desert, tan dirt spotted with piñon and juniper, with the Sangre de Cristo range of the Rocky Mountains looming in the background. They passed three Indian casinos and a marijuana outlet, along with various adobe houses and businesses in various stages of disrepair.

They turned west, away from the Rockies, toward Los Alamos, the three cars running in a loose convoy this time, now climbing toward the Jemez Mountains, which were actually the rim of a gigantic volcanic caldera. Stuck on the side of a cliff wall, they drove past an expansive canyon, then up a milder slope into Los Alamos. They passed an airport, with a couple of small prop planes tethered inside the fence along the road. They'd mapped out their destinations before leaving the diner, and now Lucas called Letty and said, "See you later."

"I'll probably be done before you are, I'll come up and meet you there."

GREET HAD SET UP a meeting at the National Laboratory Research Library, which was convenient for the people Letty was interviewing, and wouldn't require any special clearances. She was stopped at a checkpoint, and a soldier in camo looked at her driver's license and Homeland Security ID and waved her through. She found a parking spot outside a parking structure next to the library, got her briefcase, and walked inside.

The library study area was large and quiet—silent—with only a few people sitting at the collection of study desks. No books in sight. At the front desk, Letty was directed to a conference room across the floor. Three people were waiting for her, two women and a man, sitting around a conference table with a collection of Starbucks cups.

Letty stepped inside, shut the door and began, "Hi, I'm Letty Davenport with Homeland Security . . ."

One of the women asked, "Has Lionel done something?"

Letty put down her briefcase and said, "We don't know. We have some people who'd like to find him, including some friends. We're worried about his mental situation. He's had some problems and we're hoping he hasn't harmed himself."

The man said, "There are rumors that he might have been involved in some . . . troubling research. Is that true?"

Letty: "I honestly can't tell you. Basically, we're just trying to figure out what happened to him. We hope we can find him and he's all right, that he's gone off on a hiking trip or something."

And she thought, *McDonald has already talked, and he's not even back from Washington.*

Then they introduced themselves: the man was Dan Carpenter, the women were Sandra Bowers and Katherine Maynard. They all worked with the Statistical Sciences Group and were the mathematicians who most closely worked with Scott. They were dressed like academics, without style, unless you were an academic.

"LIONEL DOES HIKE, mountain bikes, likes to ski," said Bowers. "He hasn't had much experience with mountains, outside of ski slopes in Switzerland. None at all with desert mountains. I warned him not to go out there alone. If you don't know what you're doing, you can get hurt."

"How?" Letty asked.

"This time of year, you can become dehydrated and that can leave you disoriented. You can fall, break bones. There are rattlesnakes out there, you can get lost . . . Lionel, most of the time, doesn't even wear a hat."

THEY SPENT MOST of an hour talking. Scott enjoyed mountain biking, often going solo, and not just around Los Alamos, Letty was told. He would seek out trails around Santa Fe, to the southeast, and Taos, to the northeast. He'd occasionally shown up for work with scrapes and bruises from falls—which Maynard suggested happened often enough that he might well have killed himself. "He said he wasn't reckless, but he was."

He didn't date at the lab, as far as any of them knew; he was distantly friendly with everyone but wasn't known to socialize. Carpenter said he'd seen Scott having dinner with a woman who owned the town head shop, Tarantula Cards, and Maynard said she'd also seen him with the woman. Letty got the woman's first name, Rose—nobody knew her last name—and the location of her shop.

"It's a small town. If you live here long enough, you wind up knowing most of the shops and the people who own them," Maynard said.

Letty asked if Scott might use weed or other drugs, since the woman ran a head shop. "We don't have a recreational marijuana store here," Carpenter said. "I never saw any sign of drug use . . . I mean obvious drug use. I wouldn't know a subtle sign, I guess."

LETTY ASKED ABOUT the possible application of the statistical studies to methods of spreading a disease, rather than determining how to slow the spread. Bowers said, "We're not so much about . . . mmm . . . the *practice* of slowing the spread of a disease, as trying to find out exactly what factors determine *how* it spreads. What slows it, what allows it to spread more quickly. That information might allow other groups to better fight the spreads of an epidemic."

"Interesting stuff," Letty said. "How did Lionel contribute?"

"He was more a student of the work, than a contributor," Carpenter said. "He would step through our models as we developed them, to see both how the model was built—in the technical, software sense—and also, what the models might be able to predict, or reveal."

"How capable was he with the math? With the software?" Letty asked.

"He was competent," Maynard said.

"One of his tutors at Oxford said that he was bright enough, but perhaps a bit short of brilliant," Letty said.

Carpenter and Maynard nodded, as if that was a reasonable assessment, but Bowers shook her head. She said, "That's unfair, I think. There are probably eleven thousand people in the U.S. with IQs of 160 or higher, which is sometimes used as a marker of genius. Most of those eleven thousand are working in places like the post office or the agriculture department or they're dentists or work for investment companies—routine, everyday jobs. Are they geniuses? I wouldn't say so, because they don't do much with their IQs. Lionel did things. Right from the time he was a college student. He excelled in college, went to one of the best medical schools in the world, and then devoted himself to saving lives in the Third World. Thousands of lives, by one account. Whatever his IQ, I think that qualifies him as a genius. He was not only very smart, he formed his intelligence into a weapon to fight disease."

Carpenter looked at Letty and said, "That's why you're here, isn't it? Lionel has run off the rails somehow. He's joined up with a bunch of Gaia freaks and they're off to save the world."

Letty, going bureaucratic: "I'd ask you to keep that kind of speculation to yourself. To all yourselves. Where did you hear the word 'Gaia,' if I might ask?"

"Lionel used to kick it around, in conjunction with some of our global models," Carpenter said. He added, "If we talk about it, you'll do what? Put us in jail?"

"You all have top secret clearances or better, so you know what that means. This is a highly classified matter. I'll tell you that I was in a meeting in a U.S. senator's office yesterday, and a supermax was mentioned. Not in a kindly way."

Carpenter said, "Whoa! What exactly do you think he's doing?"

Letty looked at each of them directly, in turn, then said, "I got brief vitas on the three of you, and all of you have top secret clearances because of the way you move through the labs here. I'm going to share with you something that I perhaps shouldn't—but something the three of you might be able to plug into your models. I'd ask you not to share it further on, with others in your group, without calling me. I would then have that person cleared through DHS and the DOD. Don't share it in advance of clearance."

"We can do that," Maynard said, and the others nodded.

"I'll say it again, to be sure you understand. If you talk about what I tell you, you'll be fired and could be prosecuted."

They looked at each other, then all nodded again.

Letty said, "It's possible that Scott is trying to determine whether it's feasible to cleanse the earth, Gaia, of what he considers to be a disease that will destroy Gaia, that disease being humanity. It's possible that he will try to do that—and maybe has done it—by loading the Marburg pathogen into a measles virus. Or something like that. I don't understand the mechanics of it."

All three looked horrified—which frightened Letty as much as anything she'd yet encountered in her research of Scott. "Do you believe that's possible?" she asked.

"We're not biologists, we're mathematicians," Bowers said. "But we know about Marburg, we have some numbers there, and we know about measles, we have those numbers. If somebody came up with a carefully considered scheme for transmitting the measles virus, you could have a very fast-moving pandemic. An unstoppable pandemic, faster and more thorough than Covid."

"Maybe," Carpenter objected. "We have an effective measles vaccine and can manufacture it in mass quantities very quickly . . ."

"What if he did gain-of-function research on measles to defeat the current vaccines?" Letty asked.

"That would be problematic," Carpenter said.

"Even if we could manufacture vaccines for eight billion people, and it was effective, how would we distribute it?" Maynard asked Carpenter. "That's a huge problem that hasn't had enough study. There's no way to do fast mass distribution in most of Africa, South America, the Middle East, Southeast Asia . . . not fast enough. Most cases, Marburg kills in eight or nine days."

Bowers had taken a small spiral notebook out of her purse. She wrote in it for a minute or so, passed the note to Letty, who read two short lists: (1) LAX, Kennedy, Houston, Miami. (2) London, Shanghai, Singapore, New Delhi, Cairo, Lagos. "If you did those, simply had a person infected with a measles virus spend a few hours in each airport, you'd have a pandemic in days. In my opinion, if the Marburg-measles hybrid was effective, you could have a worldwide panic when the death counts started coming in."

Carpenter cocked his head sideways, read the list, and said, "I might add Frankfurt, Hong Kong, and Cape Town to the list. But no matter, Sandy's right. Several people could create an unstoppable pandemic before anyone caught on, if they knew what they were doing, and of course, Lionel does. Their technique would matter."

"How?" Letty asked.

"One almost unstoppable way would be for a group of people to infect themselves with Marburg-measles, knowing they would probably die, and then travel through those cities," Carpenter said. "Unstoppable because they wouldn't be seen to be carrying anything dangerous. But, if it's possible that they simultaneously developed a vaccine that would defeat the virus, and vaccinated themselves, they could spread the disease by carrying virus cultures and releasing them in those airports. That would be more difficult, but a few people could hit that whole list of airports in maybe . . . two days? Three days?"

They all sat with their own thoughts, until finally Bowers said, "I can't believe Lionel would do anything like this. There must be some other explanation. This is monstrous; he's not a monster."

"Think about what cults have done, what Hitler and Stalin and Pol Pot did. All in the name of logic and progress," Maynard said. "I think he *could* do it."

7

Scott had purchased a home when he arrived in Los Alamos, Lucas had learned from Letty's research the day before. That had surprised his coworkers, because homes were expensive, even not-so-good homes, and because his tenure there was expected to be short.

He'd bought one anyway, telling the lab workers that he'd spent two decades overseas, banking a decent salary, spending almost nothing, and "It's time I actually had a place of my own."

When Lucas, Rae, and Walter Packer arrived at his address, off Ildefonso Road, they found a white Los Alamos cop car parked in the street, with a cop inside, reading his phone. He saw them getting out of their two SUVs, put the phone down, and climbed out.

They introduced themselves—the cop's name was Tom Miranda—and he had a key. "The first time we came in, we didn't want to bust the door, so we had a locksmith open it for us. He made a key in case we had to come back."

Lucas looked up at the house, which was perched above the street. A flat-roofed, brown-boards-and-stone construction, with a tuck-under garage at one end, it looked like it was stuck in the 1960s, except for a solar power array on the roof. A flagstone walk led to the front door. They went up single file, Packer trailing, and the cop opened the door for them.

"I can stay or I can go, whatever you want," Miranda said. "I'm not doing much."

"Then stick around," Lucas said. "Extra eyes are good when you're doing a search."

"What are you looking for?"

"Scott is a mystery," Rae said. "We're wondering if he might have walked out into the mountains and killed himself. Or let himself die. If he did, he might have left a note, or something. Maybe on a computer? Or a thumb drive? We don't know."

The interior smelled like carpet dust, and little else.

They began with a slow walk-through, looking for anything obvious. The house had three small bedrooms with a single bath, which didn't appear to have been updated since the house was built. One of the bedrooms had been converted to an office, with a desk and a side table to hold a Canon printer. The printer was still there, as was a printer cable leading back to the desk, where it had apparently been plugged into a laptop, now missing.

The walk-through didn't turn up anything. A short stairway in the kitchen led down to the tuck-under garage. Miranda dropped down the stairs, returned a minute later: "Empty garage, an empty workbench with a couple tools on a pegboard, plus two wall-mounted batteries for the solar. That's about it."

Lucas started working through the kitchen, while Rae and Packer did the bedrooms.

Scott's bedroom had sweatshirts and a sweater, two pairs of heavy jeans and a pair of high-topped boots in the single closet, cold-weather clothing apparently not needed wherever Scott was going. A short shaky chest of drawers was empty, and when they pulled them out, they found nothing hidden under the drawers.

Lucas found pots and a cookie sheet, along with cheap plastic dishes, glasses, and stainless steel silverware, half of it still in a Target sack, in the kitchen cupboards, but nothing hidden. The under-sink wastebasket was empty, as was the refrigerator, including the freezer compartment.

The kitchen cabinets were hung on the walls, their tops a foot below the ceiling. He stood on the kitchen counter to look at the tops of the cabinets, and on one of them, found a twentieth-century pellet pistol grimy with dust. Nothing else of note.

The office had been cleared out, nothing there. The third bedroom apparently hadn't been used for anything and had no furniture. The living room had an inexpensive collection of big-box-store furniture, a couch, two easy chairs, a couple of rickety end tables, a smallish television.

As they were pulling the cushions off the couches, Miranda got a call and had to go. "Got a fire. Set the locks and pull the doors shut when you leave," he called, as he hurried out the front door.

They were done in an hour and a half. Lucas went down to the garage and looked it over—no mountain bike—and he, Rae, and Parker walked around the yard, which turned out to be nothing more than a yard. The three of them walked back around the house together, through the open garage door, and started up the stairs. Packer was trailing again, and as Lucas got to the top of the stairs, Packer called, "Why does a work bench have casters on it?"

Rae: "What?"

Packer, at the bottom of the stairs, said, "I'd think you'd want a work bench to be immobile."

Lucas and Rae dropped back down the stairs. The work bench had begun life as a four-drawer chest of drawers, probably made in the first half of the twentieth century. It appeared to be sturdy, but not expensive, and had two or three coats of paint on the drawers and the sides. Two four-by-eight sheets of three-quarter-inch plywood, screwed together and painted brown, made a practical top.

The drawers were empty, but why the wheels?

Lucas gave the chest a shove, and it moved: a little stiff, but not too. He maneuvered it away from the pegboard on the wall behind it, where a half-dozen tools hung from brackets. "The tools . . . nobody ever used them," Rae said, looking at a crescent wrench.

The pegboard went right to the floor behind the bench, which was odd.

Lucas grabbed one edge of the pegboard and pulled; it was solid. When he pulled the other edge, it opened like a door, on hinges hidden on the opposite side. Behind the pegboard was a regular door, which looked as though it had been there since the house was built, with both a tuck-under garage *and* a basement.

Lucas tried the doorknob. It turned, and Packer said, "Excuse me," and shouldered past Lucas. He pushed the door open, and they peered inside, catching reflections off glass. Packer stepped forward, fumbled for a light switch, found one, turned it on, then snapped, "Back up! Get out of here!"

He backed out of the room as Lucas and Rae hurried outside. Packer said, "It's a lab. I need my gear. We'll need photos, and we'll need to seal it off best we can."

Lucas muttered, "Holy shit," and Rae said, "Maybe we ought to stand further back."

"In the street," Packer ordered. "I was inside, so stay away from me. Rae, get your stuff out of the truck, in case I need a vehicle. Leave the keys on the front seat."

When Rae had her gear bag out of the SUV, Packer pulled his own bags out, unzipped the biggest one to reveal a group of plastic packages, which he began opening. He pulled on a white Tyvek-like suit that covered his entire body, including his feet.

A backpack held a compact air tank, and another bag a breathing apparatus, and yet another an iPhone. He put it all together, then said, "I'm going to the doorway, and I'll make some photos. I'll send them back to the fort. I won't be going deep inside, and I should be okay, even if there's some Marburg around. But we can't take a chance. Stay away."

When he had the respirator on, he went back to the garage and as Lucas and Rae watched, went through the hidden door and began making photos.

Rae: "Boy's got some balls."

Lucas: "Yes, he does. I didn't see that."

When he was done with the photography, Packer sent the photos to Fort Detrick and left the phone inside the basement. Then he stepped backwards out of the lab, into the garage, pulled the lab door closed, took some sticky tape from another of his plastic bags, and sealed the door.

Outside again, he shouted at Lucas and Rae, "That blue bag . . . it's got a what looks like a fire extinguisher in it. There's a long wand beside it that you have to screw in. Go get that and screw in the wand."

Lucas did that, with Rae watching. When the two pieces were screwed together, Packer called, "You need to stand back twenty feet or so, pull the trigger on the tank, and hose me down."

Lucas sprayed him with a yellowish liquid, until he was soaked and dripping wet. Then he sat on a stump and held up the soles of his boots, and Lucas sprayed those. Five minutes later, they did it all over again.

And five minutes after that, Packer took off the hood and the respirator mask and called, "You guys . . . you better talk to whoever sent you out here," he said. "I'll talk to my people at the fort, get a full team here, if they've got one together. You have to stay away from me and away from the house."

"Got it," Lucas said. "What all is inside there?"

"What we were talking about at breakfast—the whole eBay collection of lab equipment. Looks used, but functional. One thing I didn't recognize but could be an electric kiln, and maybe they used it to burn contaminated stuff. One big thing: they did have cages for mice. They might have been trying to attenuate the virus, which means they were looking for a vaccine. They might not be doing the suicide thing."

"What are the chances that one of us is infected?" Rae asked.

Packer said, "Low. Very low. Measles virus can live on surfaces for a couple of hours, Marburg for a few days. Scott's been gone a lot longer than that. But if this guy is genuinely nuts, maybe he built a booby trap of some kind, released some virus media when the door opened. I didn't see anything like that, but we can't take any risks if he's actually made some of that hybrid shit."

AS LUCAS AND Rae walked to Lucas's SUV, Letty arrived. Lucas pointed her down the curb and when she got out of the truck, said, "We've got a problem. There was a hidden lab."

"Ah . . . no."

Lucas told her what Packer had found, and added, "I'll call Russ at the service, and we need to call Greet and Colles to fill them in. You should do that."

Letty nodded, and said, "Security circle is getting pretty big, Dad. Gonna be hard to keep a cap on it more than a couple of days. And . . . what about Walt?"

Lucas turned to look at Packer, who was on his phone. "Walt wants us to stay away. From him, and the house, both," he said.

"What about you and Rae?"

"We didn't get inside the lab," Rae called. "Walt did, twice. He thinks we're all probably okay, because viruses aren't long-lived and we disinfected him with a spray thing. But . . ."

"But . . . hidden lab. Scott wasn't making cheese in there," Letty said. "Did you find anything else? In the house?"

"Not a thing, except the lab, which we can't get into yet," Rae said.

"So we have exactly nothing to work with," Lucas said.

Letty: "I didn't get much, either, but there's one more woman I have to interview. There are some hints that she might have been his only friend here. His longtime lover back in Oxford ran what was something like a head shop, and this woman actually *runs* a head shop, so that could be a link. I stopped at the shop on the way here, but the place was closed."

"Closed like . . . she might have gone away with him?" Rae asked.

Letty shrugged: "Big sign in the window, 'Closed.' I wanted to get over here, see what was going on, so I didn't dig around. I'll go do that."

"Then go," Lucas said. "In the meantime, Rae and I'll be standing around with our dicks in our hands."

"That doesn't actually apply . . ." Rae began, but then, "Never mind."

LETTY HEADED BACK toward the downtown area, leaving Packer, Lucas, and Rae on their phones. On the way, she called Billy Greet and filled her in on the lab discovery. "All right, this is ratcheting up," Greet said. "The Secretary's probably at lunch . . . when you talk to this woman, call me and tell me what she says. If there's more I need to pass on to the Secretary."

The drive took Letty across a long bridge over what looked to be a bottomless canyon, through some improbable road-design curves, and finally down Trinity Drive, then over a block to Central Avenue. Tarantula Cards was in a dying strip mall off Central, in between a shoe repair shop and a Little Boy used-book store.

She parked in front, got out, cupped her eyes against the window and tried to look past the 'Closed' sign, but the interior was too dark. She could see furniture shapes, but nothing was moving. The bookstore looked as closed as the card shop, and when she tried that door, it was locked.

She saw a man behind the counter in the shoe repair shop, almost went inside, but at the last minute, turned away and went back to her truck. On the way to Dulles, she'd stopped at her apartment to pick up some working clothes, her gun and gear bag. Now she opened the gear bag and took out a cloth shoulder satchel and dropped her battery-powered lock rake inside it.

Leaving the SUV where it was, she noted the address on Tarantula Cards—suite 8—then walked to the end of the strip mall, around the corner, and down the alley in back. The back of the building was punctured by a line of paint-peeling metal doors. She found "8" on a door in about the right spot, looked around, slipped the rake's pick into the lock, looked around again, and pulled the trigger.

The rake made a high-pitched rattling noise, which she muffled by wrapping the shoulder bag around it; and the lock turned. A minute after she got to the door, she was inside. She pulled the door shut, found a light switch, and turned on the lights.

She was in a near-empty, windowless room. A freestanding metal rack along one wall held a half-dozen boxes with open tops. She looked in one and found a jumble of paperback books, all apparently used, and feared for a moment that she'd broken into the wrong store.

She left the rest of the boxes for later—all were dust-covered, none looked promising—and walked down a short hallway past a small bathroom with a sink and a toilet, to a closed door. There was a light switch next to the door, and she turned off the lights behind her. She opened the door as slowly and quietly as she could, and found herself looking into a small office, and down another short hallway, into the shop itself.

She exhaled in relief—she was in the right place, Tarantula Cards, and it was unoccupied. There was an open door separating the office from the shop, and the front windows provided a dim illumination in both the shop and the office.

She walked through the office and into the shop. Despite its name, the place was a head shop, with very few cards. The were no drugs in sight, but there was a selection of glass bongs, a rack of Zig-Zags, books and magazines about the benefits of weed and other hallucinogens.

She went back to the office, closed the door between the office and the shop, and turned on the lights. The room held a chipboard desk, the surface lightly patinated with dust, and on the desk, an older Apple iMac computer with a printer to one side.

Letty turned on the Mac, which asked for a password. She went through the desk, looking for random words on pieces of paper, but other than personal contents—floss, sunburn lotion, a bottle of Scope, a fingernail clipper, miscellaneous drawer junk—she found nothing that resembled a password. She pulled out the drawers, looking for something hidden, without luck.

Like Magda Rice's shop in Oxford, there were psychedelic-style posters on the walls of the office, most showing drawings, paintings, or photographs of overly healthy marijuana plants. Her eyes were caught by one centered on the desk, called Terra Mater, which the poster translated for you: Mother Earth, in Latin. The poster showed a mature, slightly heavy woman in a Roman robe, sitting in a garden, holding a cornucopia.

The three lab employees she'd interviewed that morning thought the shop owner's name was Rose. Letty stared at the poster, thinking that Rose (if that was her name) must have looked at it for hours. She typed "TerraMater," "Terra Mater," and "terramater" into the Mac, and was rejected all three times. She tried "cornacopia," was rejected, looked down at the keyboard, wrinkled her forehead, got out her phone and typed in "cornacopia," and found that it was actually spelled with a U, not an A.

She typed in "cornucopia," and the Mac opened up.

SHE WENT TO the email search function and typed in "Terra Mater" and got nothing. "Gaia," though, got fifty-three hits. She went on to "Scott" and found forty-two more incoming emails, and sixty-three outgoing.

She got on her phone and called Lucas. When he answered, she said, "Remember that lock rake you gave me for my birthday?"

Tentatively: "Yes?"

"I'm in the shop. It's been closed for a while—everything has dust on it. But. I managed to get in the back door, and then into her computer, and found a whole bunch of emails to and from Scott, and more about Gaia. If the printer works, I'm going to start printing them out. I think you and Rae should get over here."

"Packer is suggesting we might not want to have close contact with people . . . you know, like you."

"But he thinks there's almost no chance you're infected because the virus dies after a few days. It's a risk I think we take," Letty said. "We need to go through this shop, and through this computer, and do it in a hurry."

"Ahhh . . ." Lucas said, then, "Give me the address."

She gave him the address and added, "Park in front, come around back. The door marked '8' will be open."

"Of course it will be," Lucas said. "While we're on the way, why don't you call Greet and see if she can get one of those 'top secret' judges, whatever they're called, the FISA judges, to give us a search warrant. Just in case we need one." FISA: Foreign Intelligence Surveillance Act.

"I'll ask."

"We're on the way," Lucas said.

Letty called Greet and told her that she needed a fast search warrant. "This woman who owns the place, Rose, I think her name is, isn't in the shop, and the shop looks like it's been closed for a while. She may be another lover, and she may be with Scott. We gotta get inside."

"You're not inside now?" Greet asked.

"Of course not," Letty lied. She trusted Greet more than most bureaucrats, but the trust never got to a hundred percent. "Get me the warrant. This is critical. I'll wait at the front door."

"Right," Greet said. Because while she was a bureaucrat, she wasn't stupid.

LUCAS AND RAE showed up fifteen minutes later, entering through the back door as Letty was printing out emails. Letty gave them the ones that were finished, and Lucas said, "Take a break from the emails for a minute. Go to her browser and find a history."

Letty went to Safari, clicked on "history." They scrolled down through at least a hundred Internet hits, including a dozen in the most recent grouping that said "Santa Fe—Google Maps." Most of the dozen were apparently only selected seconds apart, focusing on a house on Camino del Monte Sol.

The precise address was on the image and Rae said, "We need to go there."

"After we finish here," Lucas said. "There's a lot of stuff to sort through."

"It would be nice if we haven't left before we get the search warrant," Letty said. "You know, in case somebody's looking at my phone location."

Rae and Letty took turns reading the emails; a dozen emails in, they'd determined that the woman's name was Rose Turney, and that Turney almost certainly knew what Scott was up to in the lab, although neither she nor Scott put any details in type.

"It's all like, 'with what happened last night,' or 'since I last saw you.' They never come out and say what he's doing," Letty said. "The closest they come is when Rose asks about 'progress.' She gets back an email saying, 'Talk tonight? Pizza?'"

"They're being careful. Like crooks, like the Mafia," Rae said.

Lucas was going through a plastic box of paid bills and found receipts for Verizon and two Visa credit cards. He wrote the phone number and the Visa numbers in his notebook, and said, "We need to get these to Greet as soon as we have a warrant."

THEY WERE STILL working when Greet called and asked Letty if she had her iPad with her.

"I do," Letty said.

"See if you can find a Wi-Fi. I've sent you the warrant."

"Thank you. I'll get it and go in," Letty said.

"Right. Don't let the door hit you in the eye," Greet said.

Letty smiled: "I'll be careful."

Hooking into Verizon with the iPad, Letty went to her email, found the warrant, dragged it to the desktop and opened it. "There it is," she said to the others. "We're legal to go in."

"You make me proud," Lucas said.

AN HOUR LATER, Rae said, "Look in her documents file. See if you've got a file called TSCI."

Letty looked, and said, "Yup." She clicked on it and found an invoice from a biological supply company. "Anybody know what biological reagents are?" Letty asked.

"Sounds scientific," Rae said. "Ask us about reloading ammo. Or windage."

"Print it out," Lucas said. "Packer will want it."

"Assuming he doesn't die of a strange disease," Rae added.

"As long as I'm sitting here," Letty said, and rattled across the keyboard and brought up the Zillow real estate site. She entered the address of the Santa Fe house, and a minute later said, "Wow. Three-point-one million. The inside looks really nice."

Lucas stepped over to look. "Says it's off market, so those must be the original sales photos. That was what . . . eight years back?"

"Probably a rich left-wing trust-funder who provided the funding for the lab," Rae said. "You know—when he wasn't at his drum circle."

"You think you're being funny, but you could be exactly right," Lucas said. "I'm done here. We got the house in Santa Fe, we know that Rose was hooked up with Scott and knew what he was doing, and she's been gone for a while, so might be with him. Easier to find two people than one. Letty, talk to Greet. She might have to go to the FBI, but we need to see Rose's credit cards and get those phone records."

"As soon as I'm finished with the Gaia files," Letty said. There were fifty-three of them, most of it chit-chat about Gaia, Gaia books, Gaia websites, and people who linked up personally through a Gaia website. One of the emails was from a woman that Rose referred to as a newbie, who said she must have gotten the link wrong, because nothing happened when she put it in. Rose sent her the link, which was simply a long list of numbers, letters, and symbols. Letty copied the link, pasted it into the browser, and popped up on a Gaia dark website.

She clicked through it and found emails for members. "They all go to Gmail, so I suspect that they're all secondary emails that could be hard to trace back to the owners. Except, of course, I have a friend at NSA," Letty said.

"Call him up," Lucas said. "Or her."

"I'll ask Greet to do it," Letty said. "They'll track these Gmails in about two minutes. It's gonna be a long list, so if we find anything suspicious, we'll need more people working with us."

She read some of the posts at the website, and said, "Okay, these people are nuts. They're talking about ways to cleanse Gaia, and viruses are mentioned."

Rae: "We sort of knew that, right?"

When they were as done as they were going to get, Lucas said, "Let's get down to Santa Fe and jack up this richie left-wing trust-funder pal of Rae's."

"I'll call Greet on the way and ask her to find out who owns the Santa Fe house and what they know about them, and get them to that website," Letty said.

"Ask her to get some of Packer's people down here to go through the computer. Leave a note on the password," Lucas said. He took a last look around. "C'mon. Let's get out of here. This whole Marburg thing is giving me the willies. You might be dead, and not know it."

Billy Greet found an empty meeting room at the end of a Homeland Security corridor and hastily filled it with tables and computers, then brought in a carefully chosen six-person team to provide support for the people working in New Mexico.

Before getting a desk, Greet had spent years in the field, doing serious, complicated nuts-and-bolts work, sometimes dangerous, sometimes not. It amused her, in dealing with Letty and Lucas, that she had once had dealings with one of the Davenports' best friends, Virgil Flowers, a Minnesota agent for the Bureau of Criminal Apprehension. Neither of the Davenports knew that, and Flowers didn't know Letty's friend Greet was the mystery woman he'd met in rural Minnesota, tracking a terrorist. Greet didn't plan to tell them.

When she moved inside and out of the field, she rapidly climbed through the bureaucracy, landing, at a reasonably young age, at the circle of professionals just below the top political ranks of the department.

High enough that she could walk into the Secretary's office without an appointment, when she needed to do that; the Secretary was vaguely aware that she had some kind of influence with Senator Christopher Colles but wasn't quite sure of the dimensions of the relationship, and hadn't asked, in case it turned out to be sexual. With this case, the Secretary had made a brief appearance in the temporary workspace, suggested that more personnel might be needed, but Greet told him that for the work they were doing, six was adequate for the time being.

"We're doing online research and financial support, and if we get too much larger, we'll start risking leaks," she told him. He'd walked down to the meeting room alone, without his weasels, and she filled him in with what the New Mexico investigators had found.

"We have a secret lab, and at least two people are on the run," Greet said. "The marshals and our DHS investigator are on their way to a new site in Santa Fe. The DOD is sending a biological attack team from Detrick out to Los Alamos. They are in the air now and will be there in three hours."

"DHS still has overall control?" the Secretary asked, betraying a bit of bureaucratic anxiety.

"Yes. Everything comes back to us," Greet said. "That could change if somebody decides we need to bring in the FBI, which would be a mistake. This is fast-moving, and both the FBI and the DOD are somewhat slow-moving."

"Yes. I've spoken to the President's chief of staff again, and I'll be going back to the White House at six o'clock," the Secretary said. "I'll make that point with him. I'll call you from the car for the latest updates."

"I will have something prepared and formatted for your phone, if you'd like to see it in type."

The Secretary nodded: "Do that. We want to be right up to the minute, and we'll want the White House to know that we're all over it. That bringing in another agency would slow us down."

"That will be clear in the context of what I'll send you," Greet said.

The Secretary reached out a non-sexual fist so they could bump knuckles; they did that and he left. A young woman researcher saw it, grinned at Greet and said, "Score."

GREET CALLED LETTY to tell her that the Santa Fe house was owned by a sixty-one-year-old single woman named Clarice Catton, who was apparently the heiress of a no-longer-extant chain of tire stores in Georgia.

"She supports environmental causes both nationally and around Santa Fe, gave a big chunk of land to the Nature Conservancy. The newspaper article about it mentions a companion named Jane Shepard, which probably means they're gay, for whatever that means. We're checking on her financials."

She said that all the information requests from Letty, Lucas, and Rae were being answered piecemeal as the DHS researchers came up with them. "We're sending it to you as fast as we get it. We haven't truthed all of it, you're getting it raw. By the way, Scott no longer owns a car. He sold it a month ago."

"A lot happened a month ago," Letty said.

"Yes." Greet pushed Letty for more news—"Some nugget from the

Santa Fe site to feed the bureaucracy," not later than 3:30 Santa Fe time. "The Secretary is going back to the White House and he wants to be up to the minute with what's happening in Santa Fe. If you find Scott or this Rose Turney woman . . ."

"Don't count on it," Letty said. "What about that other stuff I asked you to get? Turney's credit cards and . . ."

"Working on it," Greet said. "I spoke with your contact at NSA—I hate that bitch, but she's good and she's on it. I'll call when we've got it."

LETTY WAS DRIVING alone, Lucas and Rae following. The third SUV had been left in Los Alamos with Packer. Her phone's navigation app took them off the highway as soon as they got to the edge of Santa Fe, then through a twisting complication of streets to Camino del Monte Sol, and up a hill to the target house.

The house was a tan adobe, like most of the other houses on the street, with a short parking space both in front of, and behind, a black steel gate. There was no garage and no car.

They managed to squeeze both SUVs into the parking area, and Lucas, Letty, and Rae walked through a turquoise-painted entry gate into a heavily landscaped side yard and followed flagstone steps to the front door. The door looked ancient: carved, gray wood. On a closer examination they could make out a figure in the wood that might have been the Virgin Mary standing on a snake. A fully modern doorbell waited on a wall beside the door. Lucas pressed the doorbell. They heard it ringing, but no one answered, nor was there any sound or sense of someone moving inside.

Letty looked at the lock and asked Lucas, "You think the rake would get us in?"

"I don't know . . . it looks solid."

Rae said, "There's probably another door on the other side of the driveway gate . . . Maybe the lock's not so solid on that one."

They went back to the driveway as a man was passing with a German shepherd on a leash. He stopped and called, "Looking for Clarice?"

Lucas: "Yes. We need to talk to her. Have you seen her?"

"No, I'm wondering if she's out of town. I walk Nugget here twice a day and her car's been gone for at least a couple of weeks. She usually tells us before she goes so we can keep an eye on the house. If there's anything I can do for you?"

His attitude, when he made the offer, suggested that if they said they didn't need his help, he might be calling the cops when he got out of sight. Lucas stepped closer and took his ID out of his pocket and showed it to the man and said, "U.S. Marshal. We're hoping she can give us some information about friends of hers up in Los Alamos."

The man seemed to take a mental step back, but then said, "Clarice knows everybody, so it's not surprising that she knows people in Los Alamos. She even mentioned playing golf up there."

Lucas nodded. "We're a little worried. I'm gonna jump that gate, see what's on the other side."

The man went on his way, down the hill with Nugget, and Lucas jumped the gate. As a marshal, he knew the gate should have a release pin that would allow it to be opened even when electronically closed: he found the pin, pulled it, and Rae pushed the gate open.

There was another door behind the gate, but it had the same locks as the front door. A short exterior stone stairs went down to the backyard, and around to a lower level where heavy twin doors looked in on a library. More good locks. Rae made a cup with her hands and looked through a window.

She said, "Wow. Wouldn't you know?"

"What?" Lucas walked over to her.

"Right there by the fireplace doohickey, the black poker thing."

Lucas and Letty went to another window, cupped their hands around their eyes, and looked in.

Letty said, "A shell. Looks like . . . what? A .223?"

Rae: "Yup. There's another one by the low bookshelf."

"Look at the fringe on the rug, right in front of the fireplace," Lucas said. "See that?" A wide oriental carpet with a white fringe occupied the middle of the floor, with a bowl-shaped stain on the fringe.

"I can see the stain," Letty said. "I'm not sure it's blood . . . it could be spilled wine."

"Yeah," Lucas said. "Maybe somebody got a red wine glass shot out of her hand."

A NEW VOICE called, "Hey!"

They looked and saw two uniformed cops coming down the exterior stairs. Lucas and Rae went for their IDs, and Lucas said, "U.S. marshals. I believe we have a crime scene here, a federal crime scene. I'm declaring this off-limits to everybody."

"Yeah?" The lead cop, and the younger of the two, dropped a hand to his service pistol.

Lucas said, not being funny: "Don't pull that gun."

"Yeah? If I do?"

"Then you'll experience a critical medical emergency," Lucas said.

The older cop said, "Back off, Kenny." And to Lucas: "We'll stay while we check your ID."

Letty: "Call the Department of Homeland Security and ask for Deputy Undersecretary Billy Greet. Tell the operator that you're calling about the Los Alamos investigation."

"Do it from the street," Lucas said. "This is a security situation and I can tell you right now, you don't want to know about it."

The younger guy said, "Is this about space aliens or something?"

The older cop got in again: "Let it go, Kenny. We'll have somebody from downtown make the call." He looked at Letty: "Billy Greet. Homeland Security. The Los Alamos investigation."

"That's right."

Kenny: "Wul, what's the number?"

"You don't want to get that from me because I could be bullshitting you," Letty said. "Look it up yourself. It's easy enough."

THE OLDER COP got Kenny moving, and when they were back up the stairs, Letty called Greet and told her about the cops. "We need them scared and obedient," Letty told her. And "Honest to Jesus, one of those guys was dumber than a bucket of lug nuts."

"I can handle that," Greet said. "If you check your email, you'll find a list of where Rose Turney has used her Visa cards in the past month. The latest was four days ago at an Albertsons Market in Taos."

"Then they're still around. Now: you wanted anything new from Santa Fe. We're at the house, looking in through the windows. There are spent .223 cartridge shells on the floor, and what could be a bloodstain on a rug."

"Uh-oh. I'll call the Santa Fe police chief, maybe get a couple of his smarter cops there, in case you need local badges to keep people away. Or get in the house."

"Tell them to come in an unmarked car," Letty said.

A LOW STONE wall crossed the back of the yard, with an oversized Russian olive tree throwing shade on it, and the three of them got into the shade and sat down. Letty took out her phone and started reading through the raw material sent by Greet's researchers.

Ten minutes later, two plainclothes cops showed up, identified themselves as Ramon Martinez and John Wiggs, and took a seat on the wall.

Wiggs: "Should we even ask?"

Lucas: "I don't think so."

Martinez: "I gotta tell you, it makes me nervous that you've got a crime scene, and you're a marshal, and you're not going in there. Somebody might still be alive and need help . . ."

"That doesn't seem likely," Rae said.

"Still, you haven't gone in, and you could. And when the first patrolmen were here, you mentioned Los Alamos and said this was a security situation. If I say a word, and it's involved in some way, could you wiggle your ears at me? Like a secret signal that nobody will even know about?"

Lucas said, "I don't know. Say the word."

"Plutonium."

"There's no plutonium involved in any way, shape, or form," Lucas said. "Or as far as we know, anything else that's radioactive."

Wiggs: "You promise?"

"I do," Lucas said.

Wiggs: "Thank God for that."

Rae stretched, exhaled, and said, "It's a lot worse."

Wiggs: "Ohh . . . shit."

Rae: "Don't tell anyone. We can't let anyone go in there, for any reason, until we get clearance from Washington."

Wiggs: "Ohh . . . shit."

Lucas: "You got it, brother."

THEY SAT FOR a while, increasingly restive, waiting to hear from Washington. Letty had gone to sit at the other end of the stone wall, to talk on her phone, and eventually Wiggs asked, "That young chick. It looks like she might have a gun in her pants pocket."

Rae: "Yes, she does."

"She's the best pistol shot I've ever known," Lucas said.

Rae: "Says her father."

Wiggs to Lucas: "You're her father?"

"Yup."

Martinez: "When I first saw her, she looked kinda familiar. I thought she might be from town, here."

Rae: "Remember the girl on the Pershing Bridge?"

Martinez: "Really? I knew I'd seen that face."

Wiggs laughed: "Boy, she sure shot the shit out of those guys."

Letty took a call, listened, clicked off, got up and walked over. "Alec Hawkins, the MI5 guy, just landed in Santa Fe. I'm going to get him. He wants a ride-along, instead of driving on the wrong side of the street. There's not much for me to do here. I think Alec and I should go up to Taos."

Lucas nodded, glanced at the cops: "You get a sniff of . . . our guy . . . call. Don't go after him yourself until we hear back from the . . . fort."

"I will." She looked at the two Santa Fe cops. "My Dad was trying not to give you any information."

"He did it well," Wiggs said. "For my part, I'm glad he did. I don't think I want to be involved in this."

LETTY LEFT. FIFTEEN minutes later, Greet called Lucas and said, "They're talking at Fort Detrick. Trying to figure out what to do, what the exposure is. They said they'd get back to me, no longer than a half hour. You gotta be patient."

"I can be patient for half an hour," Lucas said. "But push them. We need to get up to Taos before it gets dark. Taos is more than an hour away . . ."

"I'll push them," Greet promised.

The half hour passed, Lucas and Rae talking with the cops, reading their phones, and walking restlessly around the lower yard.

Lucas was about to call Greet when Greet called. "They've got a committee arguing about it. Bottom line is, most of them don't think there's a problem if you go in, as long as you don't mess with anything that looks like lab equipment. If somebody got shot, it is what it is, but it's not infectious. I wouldn't touch the bloodstain, if that's what it is. It's your call."

Lucas said, "Fuck it. I'm going in."

"THIS IS NOT the brightest idea," Rae said. "But I fully support it. We don't have the time to screw around. If there's anything inside there, we need it now."

Rae looked at the Santa Fe cops and said, "The Marshals Service is always looking for qualified applicants to work in task forces."

Wiggs said, "Uh, no."

To Lucas she said, "We should kick the front door, where nobody can see it. It looks like an antique, so it'll kick easier."

"Then let's do that," Lucas said.

Martinez said, "We'll wait in the yard. If there's anything we can do for you, you can holler."

"Or scream, if that's what it's all about," Wiggs said.

THEY TROOPED BACK up the exterior stairs, walked past the cars and around the house, to the ancient front door. "Try not to kick the Virgin," Rae said.

"Thing looks so rotten I'm afraid my foot will go right through the door," Lucas said, taking a step back to get a better kick at it.

Martinez, who was standing well back, with Wiggs, said, "You know, sometimes . . ."

Lucas kicked the door and rebounded, saying, "Ow, ow, ow . . ."

Martinez: "As I was saying, sometimes these old carved doors on richie-rich houses are cut-down door faces, glued on the actual door, which is a big piece of oak. Or steel. Like this one."

"Glad you told me before I broke my knee," Lucas said, limping around in a circle.

Wiggs said, "Let me get my door opener."

Lucas said, shaking out his leg, "That hurt all the way up to my neck."

"Throw some dirt on it and quit bitching," Rae said.

Wiggs came back with a ram and handed it to Lucas. "Try this."

The ram was three feet long with two circular handles on top, and probably weighed forty pounds. "Why would you have this in your car?" Lucas asked.

"About ninety percent of the people in Santa Fe are old," Wiggs said. "They fall in the shower or they have a heart attack, and they've got their cell phones but they can't get to the door to unlock it."

Lucas nodded: "Okay. Well . . ."

He took a long step and powered the ram into the door next to the knob, and the door broke, but didn't open; a second swing knocked it open. Martinez and Wiggs had stepped back, and Wiggs said, "We'll leave the ram with you. Yell if you need help."

LUCAS AND RAE stepped carefully inside, and Rae said, 'This makes me nervous as shit. This might be the scariest entry I've ever made."

Lucas: "Think about all your entries and tell me it's still the scariest."

A few seconds later, she said, "Okay, I thought about it, and yeah, this is the scariest. How do you shoot a germ? How do you dodge one?"

They moved slowly down the entry hall toward an arch with a lighted window on the other side of it. Before they got there, another hallway intersected, going both left and right. Right would lead toward the back to the house, where the spent shells were.

They went left and found a big bedroom with a king-sized bed and an en suite bathroom, smelling of body wash and perfume. On the other side of the hall was another bathroom, much smaller, a powder room that smelled of an herb candle. At the end of the hall, they found an office with an antique two-sided partners' desk, an office chair for each, and a closed laptop on one side of the desk.

The walls were covered with photos of two women together, and apparently for much of their lifetimes. There was also a framed, hand-painted Gaia poster on one wall, and on another, what Rae thought was an original, framed Toulouse-Lautrec poster of a nude woman pulling up a stocking.

Rae knew about art. She put her nose two inches from the poster and said, "Somebody's got serious money."

"Let's clear the rest of the place," said Lucas, who wasn't much interested in art or other people's money.

They went back to the entry hall, toward the lighted window, and found a French château-look kitchen that felt old but cleverly hid modern ovens and a refrigerator, a microwave, and coffee-making equipment behind antiqued doors. Back out of the kitchen, to the intersecting hallway, they went toward the front of the house and found a dining room, with a side hall back to the kitchen, and a balcony conversation area that looked over the library and the spent .223 shells.

A two-foot-square oil painting hung in the conversation area, and Rae took a look and said, "My God. It's an O'Keeffe."

"What's that?"

"Georgia O'Keeffe, you illiterate boob. That's probably two million bucks hanging there."

"Okay." Lucas was looking down at the shells. "I think we're safe up here," he said. "Maybe."

"Possibly," Rae said. "But we gotta go down."

They took the steps to the lower level, eased up to the rug stain and Rae said, "Yeah, it's blood. It's on the floor, too. Old, dry."

"Don't get close," Lucas said. "Things dry fast here."

Another set of steps, not visible from the window they'd been looking through, continued down to an even lower level. They took the steps, looked to their right around the corner: a home theater. To their left, another door. Rae opened it and peeked inside, and said, "Oops."

Lucas looked: what was almost certainly a body lay on the concrete floor, wrapped in a blue plastic tarp. "Back up," he said.

Rae backed up: "It's been here for a while. Barely even smell it. From the size of the shoulders, I'd say it's a woman."

"Okay, okay. Shut the door," Lucas said. "Let's just say she was shot and get out of here and up to the office and dig around. See what we can find. Fire up that laptop."

Rae never got a chance to fire up the laptop. She opened the lid and found a piece of paper with a handwritten note in red ink.

She said, "Get a load of this!"

Lucas came around the desk to read over her shoulder:

AUGUST 1,

I hope this note is never read and I just put it in the shredder. Clarice is meeting Dr. Lionel Scott of Los Alamos, and his girlfriend, here this afternoon to talk more about Dr. Scott's plans to save Gaia. Clarice hasn't given me details, but I fear it involves something dreadful. Dr. Scott is a researcher into viruses, and he has convinced Clarice that he has the solution to world overcrowding and global warming. It's like she's joined a cult and Dr. Scott is God. They are planning to go to our Taos place for an experiment of some kind. Clarice has been very angry with me because I won't hear her out on Dr.

Scott's program, and I'm afraid she is now planning to leave me. She said that Dr. Scott can't allow me to "opt out of the program," whatever that means. I don't even know what the program is, but I suppose I will hear about it this afternoon. I'll leave this note in case something awful happens.

— JANE SHEPARD

"We need to call Greet and find out where this Taos house is," Lucas said. "And we need to go there."

"Letty's on her way," Rae said. "Call her. Now, before you call Greet."

ALEC HAWKINS WAS leaning against the wall outside the Santa Fe airport's baggage area, giving off, Letty thought, a Eurotrash vibe, although he wasn't smoking anything. He had a briefcase slung over one shoulder, and another waxed canvas duffel by his feet, bigger than the one he'd had in Oxford. Must be a British thing, she thought. The airport was a mess, with new construction going on, but Letty threaded her way around the problem area to the curb, dropped the passenger side window and shouted, "Hey!"

Hawkins, wearing a blue linen jacket, a cream-colored tee-shirt, sunglasses, and what were probably Italian jeans, lifted a finger, threw the duffel in the back seat, and put the briefcase on the floor in the front, climbed into the passenger seat, pulled her toward him and kissed her.

Letty kissed him back, and when they separated, Hawkins said, "I'm unfortunately happy to see you."

As she pulled away from the curb, Letty asked, "Why unfortunately?"

"Because I live in London and you live in Washington and I really need to see more of you," Hawkins said. "I last saw you, what, two days ago? I've been pining."

"Really," Letty said. They headed out the entrance road. "I don't think I've ever been pined for."

"I'm sure you have been, even if you didn't know it," Hawkins said. "Anyway, what are we doing?"

"A woman traveling with Scott used her credit card at a supermarket in the town of Taos four days ago," Letty said. "We are now on our way to Taos."

"Where is that?"

"About an hour and a half north," Letty said.

"Will we be meeting law enforcement there?" He reached across the seat and rubbed the top of her head.

"Probably not. We're trying to keep the cops out of it for the time being, because cops talk," Letty said. She filled him in on Billy Greet's working group, about finding the hidden laboratory in Los Alamos, and the cartridge shells in Santa Fe. "My father and another marshal are waiting for the go-ahead to enter the house. They'll call if they find anything relevant."

He squirmed in his seat, adjusting himself, and Letty asked, "You tired? Hungry?"

"No, we ate on the plane. Terrible food, mostly fat and sugar, so I shouldn't be hungry for several days. However, as we got closer to Santa Fe, I began mentally reviewing our bedroom time in Oxford, and now of course . . . you're right here. At this moment, I have an erection you could drive nails with."

Letty nodded: "Okay. Well, I'll keep an eye out for a construction site. They're always looking for carpenters."

THEIR ROUTE NORTH took them along the same highway as Letty had taken to Los Alamos—the casinos, the weed merchants—but they continued straight at the Los Alamos turnoff. They passed through another small city, through a slow-moving construction zone, then along the Rio Grande. Here it was a boisterous, roiling river, powering through a V-shaped canyon, rather than the turgid, muddy stream it was further south.

Hawkins said, at one point, "Not like Oxford. On the train to London, you could see maybe a half mile. This . . ." He waved at the passing landscape. "I believe some of those mountains could be fifty miles away."

"The exact opposite of Oxford," Letty said. "Dry as an iron, brown, rough, in places you can believe that you're in an abandoned country. A lot prettier than West Texas, though. Where I spent some time."

"And here, largely poor," Hawkins said, looking out at a collapsing shack.

"With some very rich spots, especially in Santa Fe. I just left a house that I was told sold for three-point-one million," Letty said. "Maybe it'll sell for less now, if there's been a murder there."

"It would in England," Hawkins said. "Although ghosts can sometimes be monetized."

THEY WERE STILL well south of Taos when Lucas called. He told her about the body and note and said, "We're trying to get a fix on the house where they were going. Rae and I will be at least an hour behind you, maybe more. I'll get you an address if I can, but do *not* go into it on your own. You can scout it, but do *not* go in. The dead woman is probably named Jane Shepard, and she was probably murdered by her partner or by Scott. That's a nice little pistol in your pocket, but don't jump into a shoot-out. That won't work against an AR. Rae has got a bag full of heavy stuff if we need it."

"We'll wait for you," Letty said. "Get us the address."

"Is the MI5 guy with you?"

"Right here, listening," Letty said.

Lucas asked, "MI5 guy—are you armed?"

"No, I'm not. I've been in the military, Afghanistan, and have carried weapons but not used them against active targets. I'm afraid I'll have to rely on you Americans for fire support."

"Good to know," Lucas said. "We've got a few things to do here with Santa Fe police, and then we'll be on our way."

Letty hung up, and Hawkins said, "An AR is one of your famous black rifles."

"Yes. Except they're not all black. They're not supposed to be full-auto, either, but some of them are converted. Then we have a thing called the bump stock, which essentially makes them full-auto. Either way, they can seriously mess you up, so try not to stand in front of one."

"I will try to avoid doing that." Hawkins fished his briefcase off the floor, and said, "The information I have is, for the time being, mostly useless, in terms of actually finding Scott. We tried to discover the current locations of his classmates and other friends from Oxford and from his work with the Doctors Without Borders group. There are a number of potential contacts, but they are scattered all over the country. A few of his medical school classmates, meaning people in his year and the years above and below his, are now practicing medicine in the States. As far as we know, none in New Mexico. They're mostly in New York, Florida, or California. The London group is continuing to reach out to known friends and acquaintances for telephone numbers."

"He hasn't used his credit cards?"

"No. Not since he disappeared. It makes me wonder if he is still alive."

"He's alive—I believe he is," Letty said.

"So do I, actually, because of one more piece of information we came up with—it's possible that Scott was infected with either Marburg or Ebola when he was working in Uganda. A nurse who was briefly at the hospital where the patients were being treated, said he was there, first as a doctor and later as a patient, and of course, he survived. Marburg and Ebola are closely related. And if you have one, and possibly if you have had either, you may have some level of immunity to one or both. Like if you had a previous case of Covid, you'd have some immunity, even to later strains."

"If he has had Marburg, and that's what he's trying to spread, then he might not be one of the people who dies from it," Letty suggested.

"Exactly."

They were mulling that over when Greet called. "I've got that Taos address for you—I already talked to Lucas, and he'll be on his way with Rae as soon as they can get away from the Santa Fe house. The Secretary called from the White House for an update. I told him about the body in Santa Fe and it looks like he's going in to see the Big Guy."

"Whatever," Letty said. "I have another piece of information . . ." Meaning Scott's possible immunity to Marburg.

Greet had already heard it: "We got that from the MI5 working group, which mirrors ours. That was the next thing I was going to tell you."

"I wonder if he's tried to make some kind of vaccine to immunize these women he's traveling with? Clarice Catton and Rose Turney," Letty said. "The letter that Rae found said that they were going to Taos to do some experiment."

"I'm counting on you to find that out," Greet said.

ON THE OUTSKIRTS of Taos, they passed an adobe church set well back from the road, surrounded with what looked like a primitive shopping mall. As they passed, Letty said, "I've seen pictures of that church. I think that's the one. If it is, it's one of the most famous churches in America. Photographers, painters . . . back in the thirties and forties, they were all making pictures of it."

"Really. What's it called?"

"I forget," Letty said. "Maybe Francisco something something."

"Not exactly Chartres, hum?"

"No, but there've probably been more miracles there, than at Chartres," Letty said. "Lots of miracles, in New Mexico."

Hawkins said, "I hope. We may need one."

IN SANTA FE, Lucas told the two cops that Catton's house should be isolated until a special team working at a Los Alamos site could come and check the place out.

"So how grim is this situation, the bug you're looking at? Some kind of germ warfare thing?" Wiggs asked.

Lucas: "We didn't say it was a bug."

Wiggs: "Gimme a break. The way you guys are acting? It's either radiation or a bug, and you said it wasn't radiation and I don't see any Geiger counters. I'll keep my mouth shut, but what are we talking about?"

Rae looked at Lucas, who shrugged, and then at the cops, and said, "Keep your mouths shut, okay? It's bad, but we think it's confined right now. I don't even think it's here. The woman in there was shot, not diseased."

Martinez: "I'll buy that. We'll do what you say: isolate the place. But we need to be talking to this Los Alamos team, we need to find out when they'll get here."

"We'll have them call," Lucas said. "It'll be soon, I think."

AS THEY WALKED back outside, Rae looked to her left, down the slope toward the lower level, and said, "Shed." A garden shed sat at the side of the yard, still on the upper level, encircled by lilac bushes, where it had been out of sight from the lower-level wall where they'd been waiting. "We should stick our heads in there."

"We gotta hurry," Lucas said.

They went to the shed, opened the door, and found a variety of garden implements. A stack of metal stakes lay on the floor, with small signs attached. The signs were face down. Lucas turned one and found a security alarm warning.

"Ah, goddamnit." He looked back at the house. "Probably a silent alarm. If it goes to this security service, and then a cell, they'll know we've been here. It's a trip wire. Didn't see a camera."

"Nothing we can do about it," Rae said. "Call it in, let's get on the way to Taos."

They walked back to the house and Lucas looked at the doorway for a camera; nothing there. Then he looked at a phone pole outside the surrounding wall, and there it was, pointed down at them.

"They could even be looking at us," he told Rae. And as he looked up at the camera, he gave it the finger and said, "Hello there, motherfuckers."

Rae: "Keep moving."

Back in the SUV, Lucas called Greet, and she said that one of her researchers would call the security service and find out what kind of alarm system the house had. "Maybe they canceled the service."

"If they did, it wasn't long ago," Lucas said. "The dirt on the stakes was fresh. And if the security service goes to a cell phone, get the number."

"One way or the other, we're on it," Greet said.

Scott and his crew were scattered all over hell and gone when Clarice Catton got the alarm on her phone. She punched in a password and got a camera image of two men standing in her yard. The front door was open, and they were peering into the house without getting too close. The two men looked like cops, but were in plain clothes, so they could have been investigators from anywhere.

"They're onto me. They're going to find Jane's body," Catton said to Rose Turney, staring at her phone in horror. "If they do, if they've done any research at all, they'll find out about the ski valley house."

Turney: "Whose body?"

"Never mind." Catton had forgotten that nobody knew about Jane except her and Scott. "We've got to evacuate, we've got to hurry. I've got to call Lionel."

She got Scott on the phone, told him about the men in her house, and the open door. "They're some kind of investigators . . . we've got to get out of there. We've got to evacuate. There are all kinds of state records with my name on that property."

Scott never seemed panicked, which was a good thing, because Catton was high-strung, and sometimes was.

"All right," he said. "I need time to think. Where are you right now?"

"We were about to go into Walmart."

"Forget the food, but go in and buy those camping mattresses we looked at. I will call you back in a few minutes, I want to talk to Randy and Danielle."

"Call us!" Catton said. "Why did we leave Jane, that was . . ." She was going to say, "stupid," but Scott was gone.

The two women got out of Catton's Lexus and hurried across the parking lot, went straight to camping equipment and bought three plastic-covered foam mattresses, the kind you'd buy if you were camping from your car. They were carrying them out to the Lexus when Scott called back.

"We need a car that isn't your Lexus—I mean, besides Danielle's, that's too small," he said. "Go over to Enterprise and rent an SUV. Have Rose drive your Lexus to a motel with a back parking lot and leave it there. You follow her in the SUV, and after she's dropped off your car, drive her over to Western Adventure and rent a recreational vehicle. We've already gone through the whole rental process with them, so she should be able to get it quick. We'll need it to move the sick guys. Then get back here, fast as you can. We'll start packing up and burning paper. Probably can't clean up all the fingerprints, but we'll try to at least make it harder for them."

"If they know who I am, they'll probably check my credit history," Catton blurted.

"Use the Amex card. I've noticed it sometimes takes a while to get the charges posted."

"All right, I can try," Catton said. "I'm still looking at my phone, the camera, and they haven't gotten out of my house yet."

"Then get up here! Get up here!"

They hurried, rented a Cadillac SUV at Enterprise, an RV at Western Adventure, and dropped the Lexus behind a motel. As fast as they were moving, it still took an hour and a half before they got back to Taos Ski Valley. When they got there, they found that they couldn't get the recreational vehicle all the way up the slope to Catton's chalet. They left the RV in a lower parking lot, which was mostly empty in the middle of summer, and took the Cadillac up the hill.

WHEN SCOTT BEGAN researching possible associates for his Gaia cure, he searched Gaia sites of the dark web and began filtering names and personalities. One he found in Los Alamos, less than a mile from his home. Rose Turney was convinced Gaia was dying but hadn't bought into Scott's cure until a romance had developed between them. And though it quickly slipped away, she'd been convinced, and was still with him.

Clarice Catton was also close by, one of the more radical Gaia enthusiasts he'd found on a Gaia dark website; she had already been vociferously arguing that the only cure was a drastic reduction of the earth's population.

The other six were from all over the States: New York, Georgia, two from California, one from Minnesota, one from Alaska. The first five to show up in Taos were Danielle Callister, who drove from Portland, Oregon; Randall Foss, who flew in from Indianapolis after liquidating everything he owned that was worth anything; and Morton Carey, from St. Paul, Minnesota. They'd gathered at the Taos Ski Valley, which was mostly deserted in the summer, along with Turney and Catton. The five were given Scott's improvised vaccine. Four had survived, Carey had not, and had been buried up the mountainside from Catton's chalet.

Three more volunteers had shown up later and were in the process of recovering from the vaccine. When Foss had asked if Marburg was actually worse than the vaccine, Scott had chuckled and said, "Mmm, let me see if I can remember the American idiom: that vaccine isn't a patch on the ass of unfiltered Marburg."

Foss had said, "Lord almighty."

THE THREE RECOVERING volunteers were too weak even to sit up, although all three were now talking coherently. Still, they would be difficult to move, and after Catton's alarm, simply lay on their cots and watched as Scott, Callister, and Foss scrambled around the chalet packing up clothes, medicine, medical equipment they would need later, suitcases they'd need to travel.

Everything that was burnable and not needed was fed into a gas fireplace. The three men were put in adult diapers and redressed. They called Catton every fifteen minutes or so for status reports; when she and Turney showed up and told the people in the cabin that they were unable to get the RV up the hill, they improvised hammocks out of bedsheets to move the three men.

When everything was ready Scott, Foss, and Turney moved the men one at a time, first out to the SUV, which they drove down the hill to the parking lot where the RV was, and then into the RV, checking to make sure that they were unobserved.

The men were in pain and groaned and at times cried out as they were moved. Nothing to be done about that. After carrying the men through the back door of the RV, they placed them on the camp mattresses that Catton and Turney had bought at Walmart. Saline racks were set up next to each bed.

As they were doing that, Catton and Callister were spraying Windex on any surface they thought might hold a fingerprint, wiping it down with paper towels, and throwing the towels in the fireplace. When they were finally done, with last-minute touches to doorknobs and locks, they took a last look around.

"No room for the goddamn bike," Scott said, looking at the mountain bike stacked in a corner.

"I don't think you'll be biking much in the near future," Catton said.

"I wiped it all down," Callister said. "No prints."

"Still, it was the most expensive thing I ever bought for myself that wasn't absolutely necessary," Scott said wistfully. "Three thousand dollars."

"Three thousand?" Foss said. "Wow. I never would have guessed."

"Not that much, really," Scott said. "You can easily spend nine thousand on a bike and you see them all over the place in Los Alamos and Santa Fe. I felt like a pauper on mine."

Foss shook his head: "What kind of fucking morons would spend nine thousand dollars for a bike?"

AND AFTER THE last look, Scott said, "We better get moving. They could almost be here by now, if they know about Clarice's chalet. Clarice can drive the SUV, and Randy and I will ride along. Danielle will follow. Rose can follow us down the hill in the RV. Then she turns north, and we turn south, and stay in touch."

They'd decided that Turney would try to find campgrounds to park in until the three men were fully recovered, which shouldn't take more than four or five more days. From there, they'd go wherever seemed best: Denver, possibly, or Salt Lake, or Las Vegas or Phoenix. Those going south would head for the nearest airports, to spread the viral media. They all had genuine passports under different names, but with real photos and real drivers' licenses to back up the passports. That had taken three careful months for Scott to accomplish. He'd started by renting an apartment in a large complex with poor mailbox security; by spotting people who lived in the complex and had never been abroad and who seemed unlikely to go, at least in the short term; by getting their birth certificates sent to the apartment building and stealing them; and then by submitting passport applications with photos of the Gaia saviors.

The driver's licenses were a little more complicated, but not much. After spending time in some risky Santa Fe bars, he'd found a man who could get them. He'd been told that in any state where there was a large illegal population, there'd be at least one legitimate employee of the DMV who would be selling real licenses. They'd cost him a thousand dollars each of Catton's money, but then, it was Catton's money.

As they were walking out, Catton said, "You know what? I'm going to take my rifle. I'll leave it with Rose, she can throw it in a river somewhere, in case I survive, and someday have to answer for Jane. I mean, they don't know who killed her . . ."

"Who's Jane again?" Turney asked, as she took the rifle.

Catton ignored the question and asked, "You know how to use this thing?"

"Oh, sure," Turney said. "I'm from New Mexico. We've got a real nice shooting range in Los Alamos, and not a heck of a lot else to do."

10

The address that Letty got from Greet, for a Twining Street, didn't exist in Taos, but there was a Twining Road in Taos Ski Valley, which was twenty miles farther north. Letty and Hawkins agreed that was probably the address they wanted—why would a woman with a multimillion-dollar house in Santa Fe want another one, only an hour and a half away, in a smaller town? A ski resort made more sense, although, Hawkins said, "You can't always tell with rich people."

They stopped at the Taos supermarket where Rose Turney had used her credit card, cornered the manager, and Letty showed him her DHS identification and used her iPad to show him a blown-up driver's license photo of Turney, and a blown-up passport photo of Scott.

The manager didn't recognize either one of them, but he called his cashiers over, one at a time, and a woman named Karen Benton said she recognized Turney, who she said had been in at least twice. "She was a friendly sort—you know, chatty. She was asking about the town and all." She hadn't seen her that day or the day before. She didn't think Scott had been with her.

"She's not a regular—what'd she do?" the cashier asked.

"She's a missing person," Letty lied. "If she's okay . . . then we're not so worried. She didn't mention where she was staying?"

"Nope. Not to me."

The store had a Starbucks, and they got a coffee and a tea, and from the bakery, a plastic box of four cherry turnovers. "Ah, more fat and sugar," Hawkins said. "Just what I needed to keep the waistline growing."

"I haven't had anything to eat since breakfast," Letty said. "I may eat all four. And you're about as fat as a rake."

"What'd you have for breakfast?" Hawkins asked.

"Sugar and fat."

BACK IN THE car, Hawkins said, "Okay, we're definitely on their trail, and they're probably up at this ski valley." He added, "If Turney's infected . . . that supermarket . . ."

Lucas called from Santa Fe: "We've got a problem. We checked a shed and found some security service signs, which look like they'd just been pulled out of the ground. There was a camera on a phone pole we didn't see going in. It's possible there was a silent alarm. If it went to a cell phone, they may know we were at the house and that we're coming after them."

"That's called stepping on your dick," Letty said to Hawkins.

Lucas: "What?"

"I'm explaining American idioms to the MI5 guy," Letty said. "What do you want us to do?"

"Hang on there. We'll all go up to the ski resort together. I keep thinking about that rifle—we know they're willing to use it, and Rae and I have armor. Also, Greet is checking on the security service and cell phone alert."

"We'll be at the Albertsons Market, right on the main drag at the south end of town," Letty said. "Or around there. I'll get some satellite overheads of the house on my iPad. And, a cashier at the Albertsons says Turney's been in, but she hasn't seen her in the past couple of days."

"I don't know what that means. Anyway, we're rolling, see you in an hour and a half," Lucas said.

"Or a little longer," Letty said. "They're rebuilding part of the highway, it's gonna slow you down. We were almost two hours coming up."

AT THE RECOMMENDATION of the supermarket manager, Letty and Hawkins drove to the center of town and found a parking place in a public lot a block away from the plaza. They wandered around for a while, stopping at a bookstore, where Hawkins bought a tourist guide to New Mexico. Since it was August in New Mexico, and Hawkins didn't have a hat, Letty bought him a pale straw Panama hat in a men's store and caught him admiring himself in store windows.

"Forty-five dollars," Hawkins marveled. "A hat like this, in London, would cost at least a hundred pounds, and maybe more."

The plaza was surrounded by low adobe or adobe-look buildings, mostly selling stuff that nobody needed. Half of the grassy park of the plaza was torn up, another construction site.

"Maybe you could volunteer," Letty suggested.

"No, in this heat, I've wilted," Hawkins said. One side of the plaza was largely used up by a La Fonda Hotel, which looked pleasant. Although, he said, "We could check in there. We've got at least forty-five minutes to wait."

"Check in for forty-five minutes?"

"Not going to take me long. Don't know about you," Hawkins said.

"You're taking some things for granted, Alec," Letty sniffed.

He smiled and said, "No. The way you kissed me back, I don't think so. Let's face it, you *want* the Hawkins."

He said it just right and made her laugh. He added, considering himself in the hat, "Do you suppose they have a cowboy boot store here?"

"Cowboy boots wouldn't go with the hat . . . but I'd be amazed if there wasn't one somewhere in town," Letty said.

They'd passed a couple of empty storefronts and Hawkins nodded across the plaza at one of them, that still had a sign advertising cowboy stuff. "Apparently their cowboy store closed. A shame."

GREET CALLED: "I talked to Lucas a minute ago. There *was* a silent alarm, it did go to a cell phone, and we've got your witch at the NSA trying to figure out where the phone was."

"So they may be running again," Letty said.

"Yes, but we needed to know what was at that house," Greet said.

When Letty got off the phone, Hawkins looked at his watch: "We better get back to the Starbucks. Your father should about be here."

As they walked back to the car, Hawkins said, quietly, "Two observations from vast experience: if you have two rock and gem stores, or even one store selling seashells, in any given location, you're in a tourist trap. Also, any place that advertises museum quality art doesn't have any museum quality art."

"Have a lot of seashells, do we?" Letty asked.

"A sufficient number, at any rate," Hawkins said. "My parents put them in the garden."

THEY GOT BACK to the Albertsons Market as Lucas and Rae were getting out of the SUV to stretch.

Lucas came around the back of the truck and asked Hawkins, "Where'd you get that hat?" and Letty said, "Easy, there. I bought it for him, and he looks terrific." To Hawkins, she said, "Dad's a clotheshorse. He'll have a hat like that by the end of the week."

"That's true," Rae said.

They all got coffee, looked at a map to the ski resort, and Letty called up a satellite view of the target house. A vibration between Hawkins and Letty got Lucas looking at him, and he eventually said, "Alec, glad to have you, but I don't know exactly what you're doing here."

"My MI5 colleagues are researching Scott's background, trying to pinpoint anyone who might be helping him. People he's known in the past, who are now in the States. We're also talking to the French DST, about contacts in Médecins Sans Frontières who might be here. I'm working as the liaison for that—passing information to people I trust on the ground. And since Scott's British, you know . . ."

Lucas nodded, said, "Okay." He glanced at Letty, who could read his mind, and who ignored him, and he added, "You guys lead."

Back on the road, they fought their way through more road

construction and a tourist traffic jam, then drove north out of town, across a broad scrubby plain with mountains on both sides and up ahead. A few miles out, they branched to the east on a highway that cut across farmland and then into another small town, Arroyo Seco.

As they left town, Letty looked out the side window and said, "Wowsa. Look at that."

"What?"

"It's a marsh," she said, looking out the driver's-side window. "Look at the cattails. Last thing I would have expected out here. I used to run a muskrat trapline in a marsh like that . . ."

There was little transition into the mountains. One moment they were on the plain, then up onto a plateau that looked down into a valley that appeared to be full of vacation houses, and then into a narrow mountain canyon that climbed toward the ski valley. Sheer gray stone walls rose hundreds of feet above them, while a creek ran down the hill to their right, the source of the water in the cattail swamp.

They met only two or three cars coming down from the ski valley, and then two more as they drove past a sign announcing that they'd arrived. The ski village was below them to their right, a jumble of condos, hotels, bars, ski shops, mostly closed for the summer. A ski lift ran up the mountain, and was moving, but they couldn't see anyone on it.

They were on Twining Road, which widened into a parking area. A shiny blue-gray motor home had been sitting motionless at the end of the open space, as they crossed it, but rolled forward, toward them, as they approached, and Letty moved over for it.

As they passed, Hawkins swiveled in his seat and shouted, "Wait! Wait! That was Rose Turney driving the bus! That was Turney!"

"What!"

"Turney!"

Letty snatched her phone out of the SUV's center console, punched "favorites" and Lucas's number, as she was doing a fast unstable U-turn. Lucas came up immediately and she shouted, "Turney is in the bus. Rose Turney in the bus."

Lucas followed her through the U-turn, and they caught the motor home, which looked like a slicked-up but shorter version of a Greyhound bus, in two hundred yards. Letty pulled behind it and then beside it, the bus accelerating as she closed. She could see the driver in the bus's rearview mirror, and thought it was Turney, but wasn't sure.

Twining was probably fifty feet above the main level of the ski valley, and as they came alongside the RV, Turney yanked the bus to the left, nearly driving Letty over the edge to the street below. Letty slammed on the brakes and was almost rear-ended by Lucas, then the bus lurched ahead, and finally slewed sideways, half blocking the road. The bus's door was on the far side, so they couldn't see what was happening, but then Turney stepped out from behind the hood with a rifle and Letty screamed, "Holy shit!" and "Get down!" as Turney began firing at them.

Two slugs tore through the SUV, making a *chack* sound as one of the slugs poked through a window, and Letty wrenched the awkward vehicle around and accelerated away, juking back and forth the best she could, glanced at Hawkins, who was looking over his shoulder at the bus. Lucas had turned his SUV sideways in the road and he and Rae were climbing out, crouching behind the SUV, Rae shoving a thirty-round magazine into her M4.

Letty pulled in on the far side of them. Rae was now standing behind the hood of Lucas's SUV and was firing in the direction of the bus. Lucas, on his hands and knees, scrambled around the SUV and then behind a tire, and waved an urgent hand at Letty, who shouted at Hawkins, "Get out and get behind a wheel."

Hawkins already had the door open and dropped toward the ground, and Letty crawled over the center console and followed him. Hawkins scrambled behind a wheel and looked back at her and said, "I will definitely be sending a memo about this."

"That's your basic black rifle, right there, pecking away at us," Letty said, at the gunshots. Another slug hit the SUV and she said, "Hertz is gonna be majorly pissed."

She took the Sig 928 out of her jeans pocket. It was cocked and locked, and she didn't unlock it. "One AR-15 shooting at us, one M4 shooting back. Maybe two M4s, if Dad's got one. Doesn't sound like anyone got hurt yet."

The shooting stopped, and Lucas and Rae were calling to each other. Then Lucas yelled, "Letty, you all okay?"

"We're fine here," she shouted back. "The car got dinged up."

Rae called out, "I think she's on foot. I think she's running."

"Let's get the armor on," Lucas said to Rae.

Staying low, he opened the back door of the SUV, crawled inside, reached over the back seat and pulled Rae's gear bag over the seat and out onto the ground. Rae kept watch while Lucas pulled on an armored vest, then he stood up with his big Walther .40-caliber handgun as Rae armored up. As she was doing that, Letty spotted Turney scrambling up a slope of tan dirt and broken rock a hundred yards away, still carrying her rifle, and Letty shouted, "Rae, Rae, right of the bus, going up the slope."

Rae stopped buckling the armor, grabbed her rifle and slung it over the hood just as Turney disappeared into a copse of pines.

Rae said, "Shit." They'd have to run across seventy-five or eighty yards of open street to get to the line Turney had been following. Lucas, protected by the bus, jogged up to it, peeked around it, then stood on the front bumper and looked into it.

He immediately jumped off the bumper and ran back to the SUVs and shouted, "There are sick people in there. There are people on stretchers . . ."

Rae: "Ah, fuck me. What do you want to do?"

Lucas looked around, then said, "We gotta stop her. Hose down the trees where you saw her, in case she's still there. I'm going to run straight across the road, and then I'll work my way through the trees toward where we last saw her. "

"What about Letty?"

Lucas shouted, "Letty, did you hear me? There are sick people in the bus?"

"I heard that," Letty called back.

Lucas: "There'll be people coming because of the shooting. You gotta keep them back. Way back from the bus. And stay away yourself."

Letty shouted, "Go! Go!"

Lucas asked Rae, "Ready?"

Rae: "Go." She thumbed the M4 to full-auto, and hosed down the trees where Turney had disappeared.

Lucas sprinted across the road and into the trees above the short sloping shoulder. There was no incoming gunfire.

Rae: "I'm coming."

"Quick! Quick!"

Lucas was mostly behind a pine tree, with his Walther aimed at the point where Turney had vanished. Rae sprinted across the road and joined Lucas in the trees, and they began threading their way through the brush along the road.

Hawkins stuck his head up above the hood and said, "My Lord. They're going after her."

LETTY SAID, "WE need to get over to the bus. C'mon."

They jogged out from behind their SUV, to Lucas's vehicle. Rae's gear bag was open on the ground, and Letty pulled it open, found a second M4, took it out, with a magazine, slapped the magazine into the gun, and handed it to Hawkins.

"Nothing in the chamber. Look like you know how to use it. We may have to get loud if the locals want to look in the bus."

Hawkins nodded. "I do know how to use it. I'd rather not, though." He pulled the charging handle back, released it, and a round slammed into the gun's chamber.

Letty nodded. "Then let's go."

Letty and Hawkins slouched toward the bus. Lucas and Rae had moved a hundred yards through the trees, hopscotching along, one at a time as the other set up to provide cover fire if needed. If Turney was in shape, and was running hard, she'd be several hundred yards away. On the other hand, she could be lying in ambush.

Letty turned around the nose of the bus, and Hawkins, who was seven or eight inches taller than she was, stood on the front bumper, looked through the windshield and said, "Jesus: they're alive, Letty. There are three of them, on stretchers on the floor. They look like they're dying, their faces are . . . grotesque . . . but they're moving their arms and heads."

"Trying to get out?"

"No. It doesn't look like they *could* get out. They look helpless. They've got infusion bags above them, with leads going into their arms."

"I gotta call Greet. I don't know what they'll want to do."

"Catch Turney and keep people away from the bus. That's all we can do," Hawkins said.

LUCAS AND RAE had reached the spot where Turney had disappeared and found nothing but a short stretch of trampled-down weeds, then a few footprints on a dirt path. They continued along the edge of the road for another two hundred yards, never saw her again, but did find her rifle, abandoned in a patch of brush, out of ammo.

"If she got a car up here, or somebody in a car, she could be heading down the mountain," Rae said. "We need to get the state police to block the road before it branches out."

"Might be too late for that," Lucas said. "I guess we gotta try."

"If she didn't get a car, if she's up in the trees, she's got nowhere to go. It'd be a hell of a tough walk out."

A WHITE COP car sped past them, toward the school bus, and Rae said, "Uh-oh."

"Yeah. We better get back there."

The cop car stopped thirty yards short of the RV and a heavyset cop got out, stood behind a door, and shouted, "What are you doing?"

Letty had put her Sig back in her pocket and now put both of her hands in the air, one with her ID, and shouted back, "Department of

Homeland Security." She walked toward the cop, while behind her, Hawkins stood at the nose of the truck with the M4. When she got close, hands still in the air, she called, "We have a very serious security situation here. There are two U.S. marshals coming up behind you . . ."

The cop turned and saw Lucas and Rae, in their body armor, jogging toward them.

He turned back to Letty and said, "What the hell?"

"We have a dangerous situation," Letty said. "We don't know what to do. We need to talk to the marshals and figure that out, but right now, I've got to call DHS and tell them what we've got here."

LETTY TOOK OUT her phone as Lucas and Rae got to the cop and showed him their IDs. Lucas asked Letty, "What?"

"Trying to find out," Letty said. "We need to tell this police officer what the situation is. Screw the top-secret bullshit."

"I had a clearance in the Army," the cop said. He was too heavy, had curly black hair and silvered sunglasses perched on his nose; he might have been a small-town cop in Alabama. "What's going on?"

While Lucas and Rae explained the situation, Letty got Greet and said, "We've got a huge problem here, Billy. We spotted Turney trying to leave the ski valley in a motor home, an RV, like a big bus. We managed to stop that, but she had a rifle and opened up on us, and basically, she got away, at least for the time being. We're in wild country, and we didn't think we could leave the bus to chase her because there are three sick people inside, on stretchers, on the floor. We need to do something about them before we do anything else."

Greet: "Let me see if I got this. You've got three sick people, and a woman who was driving the sick people got away and could be infectious herself?"

"That's right, and we don't know what to do about her, and we don't know what to do about the sick people. They could be dying on us, and we've got nobody to go inside the bus to try to help."

"Stay out of the bus," Greet said. "Stay out. I'll get the people up from Santa Fe. There are seven of them now at Catton's house or up in Los Alamos. I'll find a chopper and get them up there."

Lucas had been talking to the cop, who was now on his radio, and Lucas called to Letty: "Tell Greet that we're trying to block the valley road. We've got a state patrol car who can get across it in a few minutes. If we're lucky, and if she grabbed a car up here, we'll be able to stop her."

Letty passed that on to Greet, who asked, "Listen, you think she might still be on foot?"

"She probably is," Letty said. "She'd have to be lucky to have grabbed a car that fast, without us seeing it. She's probably hiding and trying to figure out what to do."

Greet said, "Then you gotta get her. Gotta get her. I'll call you back in two minutes. Maybe five," and hung up.

THE COP WAS telling Lucas that there were three more cops in the village, and he could get them to cover the bus, and he would check in the village to see if anyone had seen anything like a carjacking.

He added, "That bus got up here maybe an hour ago, maybe forty-five minutes, and stayed here—couldn't go any further up the hill. Too steep and narrow. I did see a big SUV come down and stop next to it for a while. It looked like they were clearing furniture out of Ms. Catton's house."

"That's up the hill?" Lucas asked.

"Yeah, but I think I saw Ms. Catton leaving, maybe fifteen minutes ago, in a silver SUV," the cop said.

"What kind of SUV?"

The cop shrugged. "I don't know. American, I think, maybe a Tahoe or Suburban? I never saw the front or back of it. Didn't pay any attention."

"Anybody in her car with her?"

"I didn't look specifically," the cop said. "But yeah, I think there was a guy in there. Maybe somebody in the back seat, too."

"Was that Ms. Catton's car?" Rae asked.

"No, I've never seen it before. Ms. Catton drives a Lexus."

"Check with your men about a carjacking, then get them up here. Surround the bus, but don't get close, and keep people away," Lucas said. "What's your name, anyway?"

"Folks call me Tank," the cop said.

"Okay, Tank, there are three very sick people in the bus, who aren't going anywhere. If anybody comes up the road and tries to push past you to the bus, shoot them. I'm not joking about that. Some guys in white suits will be showing up to take care of them . . . and the bus."

The cop asked, "You going after her? If she's on foot?"

Lucas: "What do you think are the chances?"

Tank looked around and said, "If she didn't grab a car . . . I don't think she'd be going up, because there's nothing up there and it'd be a hell of a climb. Standing right here, we're at better than nine thousand feet. You try to climb that wall, you'd be sucking wind pretty damn quick. She's probably following the road down. Maybe thinking to grab a car along the way. If she didn't take water with her, she'll be looking for some. There are a few guest houses and a condo down the way . . ."

Lucas: "Let's get some water for ourselves . . ." Lucas turned to Rae: "Do you have a backpack in your gear bag?"

"A small one . . ."

"We need to take water . . ."

Rae: "My pack is big enough for that."

Lucas looked at Letty: "That okay with DHS?"

"Good with me," Letty said. "Alec is okay with an M4, he can stay with me, you can stay close to Rae, but we've gotta run."

Tank radioed to another cop, told him to bring water ASAP. He warned Lucas and the others that when they got down the valley, they'd lose cell service. Rae got an empty backpack from her bag, gave it to Hawkins, since she and Lucas would be wearing armor.

They had a few last warning words for Tank, then started jogging along the road, stopped for the water cop, who gave them four cold bottles for Hawkins's backpack.

The cop said, "Tank is going to cover the bus with another guy. I'm going down the road to the bottom. I'll look for her. I'll call or radio if I see her, but the canyon's weird with electronics. If I can't get through, I'll fire three shots in the air."

Letty nodded: "Do that. Don't let her get close to you. If she tries, shoot her. Don't listen to any bullshit—she just tried to kill us."

Rae: "Come on, guys, keep moving."

THEY SPREAD OUT, Rae in the trees on one side of the street, Lucas in the trees on the other, Letty and Hawkins farther up the mountainside. A dirt hiking trail ran parallel to the road for a while, before slanting uphill. The trees and brush were not as dense as they would have been in a well-watered forest but were thick enough that their sightlines were limited as they moved through.

And the chase turned rough. The ground underfoot was broken, uneven, a mixture of sand, dirt, and rock, all of it on a forty-five-degree hillside. The day was still hot, and ten minutes along the road, they were all sweating, and panting from the thin air.

They passed above what looked like a trash collection area, with heavy equipment parked around it, and Rae went down and threaded her way through it. She found a man welding a hinge on a dumpster and asked him if he'd seen a woman running or stopping a car. The man looked at her M4 and the armor, swallowed, and asked, "Should I have? I mean . . . no, I haven't."

She moved on along the road, waved at Lucas.

They were moving quickly but were as cautious as they could be. They went by a couple of cabins, both occupied; none of the occupants had seen a running woman.

Then Letty, who was higher on the mountain above Hawkins, spotted Turney struggling across a steeply pitched slope ahead of them.

"I got her," she screamed. "There! There!"

Hawkins, down the slope from her, looked where she was pointing, and saw nothing but trees. He began running, as best he could, and fifty yards along, saw Turney disappear into a clump of immature fir trees. He ran that way, shouting down to Lucas, pointing. Lucas, working through the more heavily treed verge of the road, called, "Where, where?"

"Fifty yards. Didn't see a weapon."

"What?"

"No weapon," Hawkins shouted.

Hawkins was moving faster than Lucas because he knew where he was going, and he was running downhill. Letty was coming down the mountainside a hundred yards above and behind him, too fast, dodging trees, then skidding and falling hands-first down the rock-littered slope.

Hawkins saw Turney break out of the clump of fir, running heavily toward the next clump, and shouted at her, "Stop! Stop!"

She looked over her shoulder but kept running. She wasn't fat, but looked soft, out of shape, her blond hair bouncing around a narrow face. She ricocheted off a branch, nearly fell, looked back again at Hawkins, who was closing fast, both the Davenports now well behind him.

Then Turney quit, slumped over, hands on her knees. Hawkins came up, shouted, "Are you infected?"

She looked at him and grinned. "Maybe. I hope so."

She stood up and took a step toward him, and then another.

"Stay back. We've called for help," Hawkins said. He pointed the M4 more or less in her direction.

"Aw, what's a little *Filoviridae* between friends? You sound English, you could take it back to London for us."

She was fifteen yards away and Hawkins lifted the M4 higher. "Stay back. Please stay back."

From above him, Letty, on her feet again, hands and face bleeding from the fall, still seventy yards away, screamed, "Shoot her! Shoot her, Alec! Shoot her!"

Turney was ten yards from him and she grinned again and said, "Aw, you're not gonna shoot me, Alec. You're too much an English gentleman."

She took another step and Hawkins shot her in the heart. No longer grinning, she toppled backward and died.

11

Lucas ran up the slope to Hawkins, trailed by Rae, who'd come from across the road behind him, climbing through the yellow roadside weeds. Letty got to Hawkins first. He was standing, unmoving, staring at the woman's body. When Letty came up, he said, without looking at her, "I just . . . I just . . ."

"You just did the right thing, Alec, except you waited too long." She grabbed his shirt and pulled him away from Turney. "C'mon, back up, back up, we don't know if she's got the measles thing, back up . . ."

He was stumbling backward, upslope, Letty's arms around his waist when Lucas and Rae arrived. Rae said, "She's dead." She slapped Hawkins on the back. "Well done, Alec."

"I think . . ." He was still fixed on the body. "I shot her because she scared me. She wasn't armed, I could see she wasn't armed . . ."

"Bullshit. You don't know that—she could still be armed, she could have a cloud of shit around her that we can't see that could kill the whole planet," Rae said. They all looked at the body at once: it didn't look like a threat, it looked like a bag of rags.

Lucas: "Leave her. She's not going anywhere. Maybe get one of the cops here in case some tourist comes stumbling through the trees."

Hawkins couldn't tear his eyes away from the dead woman, even as Letty tugged him downhill. At the road, Rae produced a switchblade, flicked the blade out, and cut the bark off a roadside sapling. "Straight uphill from here," she said. "Let's find a cop."

As they headed back to the ski area, Lucas asked Letty, "What they hell happened to you? You look like you were attacked by a coffee grinder."

She had a scrape on her forehead and one cheek, and the heels of her hands were bleeding. "Fell on those rocks . . . couldn't keep my legs moving fast enough. I was out of control, I saw Turney walking up to Alec, who might be too nice a guy."

She still had an arm around Hawkins's waist, and Lucas said, "Why do I think you guys might be better friends than you let on?"

Instead of answering the question, Hawkins handed him the M4 and asked, "Would you mind carrying this? I'm a little distracted here, maybe shouldn't be handling an automatic weapon."

"First time you shot somebody?" Rae asked.

Hawkins nodded: "Of course. Why wouldn't it be?"

She shrugged. "I dunno. It's actually fairly routine with this crowd."

"Not with me," Hawkins said.

Letty: "Yet another memo you'll have to write."

Now he showed a hint of a sad smile: "And it will be widely read, I can assure you." He slipped his right arm around Letty's shoulders. To Lucas: "You mentioned my friendship with your daughter. Nothing untoward is going on, Marshal Davenport. We barely know each other. She seemed stressed by this entire situation, and I merely tried to do what I could to relieve her tensions."

Made Lucas laugh, and he said, "I'm sure you did."

Letty: "I hesitate to mention it, but, uh . . ."

Lucas: "But, uh, what?"

"He has some of your . . . tendencies."

Lucas: "Hey! Stay away from my daughter."

All four smiled, then Hawkins said, "I shot her right in the heart. It was like I could see the bullet go in and come out, it was like the wind, blowing through her soul . . ."

Rae turned away from him: "Oh sweet Jesus."

WHEN THE SKI village came into sight, Letty took out her telephone, had three bars, and with the others listening in, called Greet and said, "We caught Turney and killed her."

Greet: "That's terrific. I found a chopper and three of the Fort Detrick team will be with you shortly. You gotta keep everybody away from that bus and away from Turney. Do not get close to her. What about Scott and anyone else . . . this Catton?"

"It's possible that they're still up in Catton's house, but I don't think we go in there, either. We know they've been working with the disease models and we don't know how contaminated the place might be."

"You're on the ground and have to make the call," Greet said. "Do they have a fire department up there?"

"Don't know. They've got a police department, so maybe they've got something. Why?"

"Because I'm thinking maybe we hose the house down with gasoline and burn it to the ground. If anybody runs out, we shoot them."

Letty: "Wow. Is that what Detrick wants?"

"I haven't talked to them specifically about Catton's house. This is completely unprecedented," Greet said. "I have no idea of what the legalities are, but what else can we do?"

Lucas made a "give it to me" gesture with his fingers, and Letty handed him the phone. "Billy, this is Lucas. We got important stuff out of Catton's Santa Fe house. There might be important paper in her house here. I'd hate to burn it before somebody takes a look."

"You've got a point. The second group of Detrick people brought a bunch of PPE gear with them. I'll see what they've got that fits you."

"That's not exactly where I was going with this," Lucas began.

"I can always order your daughter to go in," Greet said.

"Fuck you," Lucas said. "Get me a suit, or whatever else."

"On the way," Greet said.

Letty took the phone back. "Billy, we need a meeting with everybody. Maybe even the Big Guy. I'm think we need to shut down Taos. I looked at a map, and there aren't many roads out of there. We need state patrol checkpoints on all of them—don't let anyone out unless we know who they are."

"That could cause a nationwide panic. Shutting down a whole city? Not letting anyone out?"

Letty: "Billy, spend two minutes thinking about it. If they've got that hybrid virus, they could kill the world. This would be the biggest crime in human history: this would be worse than anything Tamerlane or Genghis Khan ever did. We can't let them get out. Once they're out . . ."

Long silence: "I'll go to the Secretary."

"There's no time. Put up the checkpoints—that will probably turn these assholes around if they try to get out of the city. We've got to keep them contained."

TWO MORE MINUTES, and they ended the call. The four of them continued up the hill for a while, with nobody talking, until Rae said, "You know, Lucas, I could take a look in the house . . ."

Lucas: "Nope. This is on me, Rae."

Letty: "I don't think . . ."

Lucas: "I'm the oldest. I've lived the longest."

Hawkins: "Ah . . . Jesus."

TANK TURNED OUT to be the chief of a four-man department. He said that nobody had tried to get off the RV, and the cop who'd gone down the hill to look for Turney had found a state police checkpoint at the bottom of the hill.

"Don't have to block the canyon anymore," Lucas said. "The woman's dead. We skinned the bark off a tree a half-mile down the hill, she's right up the mountainside from there. Nobody can be allowed to go near the body. I don't think anybody will because it'd be hard just to find her. Just in case . . . where's your fourth man?"

"He was asleep and he's on his way. I'll put him down by that lady's body."

"Tell him to climb far enough up the hill that he can see her body, and not go any closer," Rae said. "This is scary shit, man. Guard the bus until some federal biological people get here. They're in a helicopter and on the way, should be here anytime."

Letty: "We need to get up to Catton's house."

Tank pointed up the parking area and said, "That dirt road goes up the hill to her house. Steeper'n hell, the last part of it. You could make a ski run out of it. There's a big stone building on the right side of the road as it goes up. Her place is maybe three or four hundred yards higher, after the road goes to one-lane. It's a red house with black trim, two stories, concrete block lower level holding up a chalet-style house. The windows are black, that black glass. It's the only place like it on the road."

Lucas said, "If it's only a few hundred yards, we should walk up . . ."

"I wouldn't. It's a real climb," Tank said. "There are some places to park up there, you'd be better off driving most of the way, then walking the rest. You'll be close to ten thousand feet when you get there. If you're not acclimated, you'd be panting like golden retrievers."

"All right," Lucas said. He handed the M4 back to Hawkins. "You got your shit back together?"

"No. But I can function," Hawkins said.

Letty swatted him on the butt. "Let's go scout it out."

THEY PILED INTO Lucas's SUV, leaving Tank guarding the RV, drove up the steeply pitched dirt road to the stone building on the right. They could see a point ahead where the road narrowed and decided to leave the SUV outside the stone building.

"If it's got black windows, we won't be able to see inside," Hawkins said. "Might have to break in."

Letty: "Let's wait until the Detrick people get here. There's no rush now—if there's anyone in there, they can't get past us."

Rae: "I agree," and Hawkins nodded.

They found the house, and settled in to watch, with Rae and Lucas on one corner, looking down the east and north sides, and Letty and Hawkins on the opposite corner, looking down the west and south sides. They were hooked together with their cell phones, which were now working well off the village phone link. They'd been sitting, watching for twenty minutes when they heard the helicopter coming in.

Letty called Lucas and said, "I should go down and talk to the guys on the chopper. Tank doesn't know enough to fill them in."

Lucas: "Go."

Letty stood up and said to Hawkins, "I don't think there's anyone in there, but if you have to . . ."

"I will. I can," he said, with another gloomy smile.

"See you in a bit," she said. She reached out to stroke his cheek. "You're gonna be okay."

They'd been sitting on a rock above the house, and she hurried down to the road, then jogged past the stone building to the RV. The chopper had circled the village, and as she got to the bottom of the road, she saw it hovering over the wide parking area, between her and the RV.

Tank was standing on the other side, holding his hat on his head, like people do when a helicopter is around. She could see the pilot looking down at her, and her phone rang, and when she answered it, a man said, "My name is David Underwood. I'm in the helicopter and I was told that a young woman would be meeting us. Is that you running down the road?"

Letty said, "Yes. I'm coming. That RV has three people in it, alive, but I believe they're suffering from Marburg or the effects of a Marburg vaccine. Or it could be a Marburg-measles hybrid."

"Okay. Then we're in the right place to set down?"

"Yes. I'll be there in one minute."

A MINUTE LATER, the helicopter, which had the name "Firehawk" on the side, was on the ground, the prop whining as it wound down. Two men and a woman were clambering out. Letty jogged up and said, "I'm Letty Davenport, DHS. We've got the body of a woman down the hill who was inside the bus with the sick people, and not wearing anything protective—no protective clothing."

"How sick was . . ." the woman began.

Letty: "We don't know. We shot her. She's dead."

"Ah. Then I guess we won't know how sick she was."

Letty nodded. "We've now got three people watching another site up the hill, which we think they were using as a hospital before they evacuated. Doesn't look like anybody's inside. It's possible that some of them made a run for it and got out before we could close the roads."

"That's not good," one of the men said. To the woman, he said, "Marta, get your bag on and check the people in the bus." And to Letty: "You better do something to find the people who got out."

"We're doing that now, DHS is. I've recommended that the state police and local cops set up checkpoints on all the roads out of Taos. We've got photos of two of them. Don't know how that is going. We were told they left in a big American SUV, could be a Tahoe. If the cops encounter any resistance, they've been told to kill them."

The man nodded: "Yes. If this is real. And it looks like it is, from what we could see at that lab."

"The woman we shot . . . We don't know what to do about the body. We've got a cop watching it from a distance, so nobody gets close," Letty said. "This other site, that might have been a hospital—what do we do about that? I mean, we got guns, but we don't know what to do about the viruses."

"If the body's being watched from a distance, that's about the best we can do for a while," the man said. "We've got more people coming from the Los Alamos lab site, we'll handle the body later. About this other site, the hospital site . . ."

"I can take you up to it . . ."

He said to the other man, "Danny, let's get the stuff out and get up there."

FIVE LARGE DUFFEL bags and three hard-sided cases were unloaded from the helicopter, and the men took one bag each, while the woman unzipped another, and began taking out what looked to Letty like the large dry-bags she'd used at a Minnesota canoe camp as a teenager.

The men picked up their bags and said, "Let's go—lead on."

"We should take our other car . . ."

They loaded into the SUV Letty had been driving, Letty looking back at the woman, who was mostly inside what looked like a white plastic suit. On the way, the men introduced themselves as David Underwood and Danny Moscowitz. Underwood was tall and gaunt, like a serious runner. Moscowitz was square and muscular, maybe a wrestler. Letty sketched in what they'd done since Los Alamos that morning, and Underwood said, "You've been busy. This car's got . . . bullet holes."

"Yeah." She told them about the shoot-out. "A rough day. We've been scared. We don't know what the heck we're doing."

"If what we're being told is correct, being scared is the right reaction," Underwood said. "Marta has actually worked in a hospital in Guinea with Marburg, but not this hybrid that people are talking about. I hope to hell the people in that RV are willing to talk. If they've got Marburg and nothing else, we can deal with it. If it's this hybrid . . . then I don't know."

"My boss back in D.C. has suggested the best thing to do with the house, the hospital house, is throw a Molotov cocktail through a window and burn it to the ground."

"If there's nothing in there that we need, I'd agree," Underwood said.

Moscowitz was looking up the mountainside to the left: "That would take out the virus, but that's a hell of a mountainside. This place is drier than dust and the fire would run up there in two minutes. Those pine trees would go up like napalm."

"You could burn down this whole goddamn forest, from Taos to the Colorado line, and it would be better than turning that hybrid loose," Underwood said. "If there is a hybrid."

They rode along for a little while, then Letty said, "I gotta remember to check if there's a fire department."

LUCAS, RAE, AND Hawkins hadn't seen anything moving around the house. Letty introduced Underwood and Moscowitz, and Underwood told Lucas, "We've got an extra-large for you. Self-contained air, and lets you breathe, but not for long."

"There could be virus all over the suit," Lucas said. "Are you going to spray me?"

"Yes. How'd you know about that?"

"We sprayed Packer up in Los Alamos."

"Okay. You'll have a half hour inside if you don't get excited and start breathing too hard. Danny will be with you, taking samples and bagging them."

"What will you be doing?" Lucas asked.

"I'll be out here hiding behind a tree, in case one of these marshals needs instructions about whether to shoot you or not."

Moscowitz deadpanned to Lucas: "Dr. Dave's too high up the bureaucratic chain to risk. Of course, if we screw this up, he *could* get crucified."

THE PPE SUITS were made of what looked like a combination of plastic and paper and were white and crinkly. Lucas and Moscowitz got some privacy behind the house, got down to their boxer shorts, and pulled the suits on. In the three minutes they were dressing, Lucas was already getting hot.

"No air conditioners on the house, that we could see," Lucas said.

"Good. They haven't been blowing the interior air outside," Underwood said.

Lucas asked Moscowitz: "Do you do this a lot?"

Moscowitz: "This is my eighth or tenth time. Of course, the others were simulations."

"So . . ."

"Yeah. We're both virgins."

"Ah, man."

Lucas's suit had a hood with a face plate that slid over the respirator mask. Moscowitz and Underwood showed him how the respirator mask fit, and how the hood sealed. They turned on the air, Moscowitz got several of the transparent dry-bag look-alikes and asked, "You ready?"

"Yeah, and I'm hot. Let's go."

LETTY AND RAE came around the house, Letty gave Lucas a squeeze and said, "Try not to breathe in." And, "When you talk, you sound like Darth Vader."

The back door was locked. They walked slowly around to the front, keeping the suits clear of anything that might snag them. They tried the front door and it opened. With the others standing well back, Lucas and Moscowitz stepped inside and shut the door behind them.

They were in an entry with knotty pine paneling on the walls and a closet to their left. Lucas led the way out of the entry into the living room, where they found eight single mattresses on the floor, all of them with saline bag hangers next to them. Several of the mattresses were stained with what Lucas thought might be body fluids, including blood.

Moscowitz: "Stay back from all of that and do what you need to do. I'll start taking my samples here."

He began unpacking his dry-bags. Lucas watched for a moment, then crossed the living room to the kitchen, called back to Moscowitz, "Nothing here except dishes, but some of them haven't been washed if you need samples."

Moscowitz: "Probably won't be necessary."

Lucas walked out of the kitchen and down a hallway, opened a closet, found both men's and women's clothing, then moved on to a recreation room with an oversized television, the floor crowded with couches and easy chairs, and three wheelchairs. A mountain bike was leaning against a wall. One of the wheelchairs showed a stain that could be blood. Lucas passed that on to Moscowitz and continued through a doorway to a smaller room fitted as a home office, with a gas fireplace in the corner. The fireplace shouldn't have had ashes but did: a lot of paper had been burned in it.

He probed through it with a barbeque fork and found nothing but the burned corner of a passport, but all the personal information it had contained was gone.

A desktop computer sat on a table with an office chair in front of it. The back of the computer had been opened, and where there should have been a hard drive, there was an empty space with a dangling connector. Scott and whoever he was with had apparently been torching evidence, although the most damning stuff—the mattresses—had been too big to burn, or they hadn't had time.

A spiral stair went up to a second level, and when Lucas got to the top of the stairs, he found the trashed remnants of a cheap flip phone. The phone, he thought, was almost certainly a burner, and probably the phone that the security service called when he and Rae went into Catton's house in Santa Fe.

The top floor consisted of four bedrooms and a bathroom, and two of the bedrooms had saline stands. The stands had been pushed into corners, as though they'd been finished using them.

The house, Lucas thought, was distinguished by one thing: there was almost no paper with writing on it. No notes on refrigerators, no matchbooks with the name of a bar, no photos with revealing scenes in the background, nothing. It must have all gone in the fireplace, or it had been taken by the fugitives.

He went back downstairs, and walked through the bathroom, found nothing of interest, walked out to the single-car garage, saw nothing of interest until he opened a trash can and saw glass at the bottom. There was a garbage bag sitting on top of the glass, and he carefully lifted the bag out, and looked at the glass more closely. It didn't look like ordinary glass, it was heavier and curved.

Moscowitz was sealing samples into the transparent dry-bags, and Lucas called, "When you got a minute?"

"Be right there."

Moscowitz came lumbering out of the living room, said, "We've got another ten or twelve minutes."

"Look in the garbage can."

Moscowitz looked, and said, "Okay, those are sealable media vials, sort of like old test tubes but with secure seals on top. If you're going to move virus samples, you put them in those tubes, then you'd put those tubes in a secure container to move them."

"So they're moving virus?"

"They could be moving virus," Moscowitz said. "They could have virus samples in easily broken glass containers that they could move through airport security without touching off an alarm."

They dumped the can so Moscowitz could take pieces of the glass for examination. Lucas ripped open the garbage bag and found garbage. He prodded it with his toe, scattering it around the garage floor, and a pen rolled out. He said, "There we go. We got something."

Moscowitz looked: "What is that? A pen?"

"Not just a pen. An insulin pen," Lucas said. "You better bag that. They're traveling with somebody who needs insulin."

"So they're gonna need a drugstore?"

"Well . . . if they're out of insulin. But some of these last a month," Lucas said. "But the other thing is, it's got a prescription code on it."

"Ah. If it doesn't belong to one of the people in the bus . . ."

"Yeah, there's that."

Moscowitz: "You should get out of here. I'll collect the pen and I'll be another few minutes. I've got a bigger air tank than you . . ."

Lucas moved out, stopping only to look in another closet, which had a couple of pieces of clothing, some shoes, and a vacuum cleaner. To Moscowitz, he said, "There's an ocean of DNA in here. We could use it to pin down who all was here . . ."

"Only after you catch them. To tell the truth, I'm not exactly sweating a trial," Moscowitz said.

"Okay, but we're talking about burning the place. Before you leave, if you could spend one minute looking in the showers, the bathrooms, for hair . . . bagging it."

"I'll try. Now, you go."

LUCAS WENT OUT the front door where Rae, Hawkins and Underwood were waiting at the bottom of the steps. Underwood was holding the sprayer tank and said, "Stop right there."

Underwood sprayed him with a faintly urine-colored spray that left Lucas soaked from his head down to the soles of the suit's booties. When every cranny of the suit was soaked with the amber spray, Underwood had him sit on the steps and stick his feet out, and then sprayed the soles of the booties. Underwood looked at his cell phone, where he had a timer running, and said, "You've got another six or seven minutes, on the air. Sit right where you are. I'm going to hose you down again in three or four minutes."

Lucas remained on the steps, dripping the fluid, until Moscowitz shouted, "I'm coming out."

Lucas moved down onto the house's driveway, still dripping, and watched as Moscowitz went through the spray routine. Then Lucas was sprayed again, and they all stood around, and then Moscowitz got the spray a second time. Lucas got a beeping signal that his air had gone on reserve, and Underwood helped him out of the suit. A few minutes after that, Moscowitz was out, and his baggies, which had been soaked when he was, were put in a steel case and locked up.

"Off to the fort, soon as we sample the men on the bus," Underwood said. "They've actually got an F-18 waiting for it in Albuquerque."

Lucas looked around. "Where's Letty?"

"The young woman?" Underwood asked. "She's back down at the bus. She's talking to Marta on a radio link, and calling what Marta says back to the fort. We've got a couple more docs on the way, but they need Marta's word right now."

Lucas: "All right. Let's go figure out what we're doing . . . and I need to talk to DHS myself."

"About shutting down the roads?"

"Exactly. And we need you and Danny to chip in." Lucas turned to Moscowitz. "Tell David about the glass things . . . the vials."

Moscowitz nodded at Underwood. "They're moving something. We found a broken hundred-milliliter transport tube with a screw-on cap. I collected it. Probably not their only one."

Underwood chewed on his lower lip for a few seconds, then said, "Shit."

12

Lionel Scott was sitting in the passenger seat while Catton drove the rental Cadillac fast down the canyon from the ski valley. Foss sat in the back; there wasn't much talk, but there was tension. Callister was following them in her own Subaru, which, except for the model year, was virtually identical to the one Scott had owned. They were all essentially stuck up a long pipe, the canyon road, and until they got out the bottom, they could be easily jammed up.

Foss looked out the back of the Cadillac and said, "I still don't see Rose. I hope nothing happened up there."

They were near the bottom of the mountain when one of their burner phones rang. There were six phones, bought at separate times in separate places. They were all in the center console, and it took Scott a few seconds to fish out the right one.

He looked at the screen and said, "Rose" and pushed the speaker button and said, "Yes?"

Rose was screaming. "They're on me! I've got the gun! They're all over me, I can't, I can't . . . I'm going out there . . . In the parking lot, they got me . . ."

She didn't hang up, but they heard the clunking sounds as she ran down the steps of the RV and seconds later, the first of the gunshots as she began firing Catton's rifle at the enemy, whoever he, or they, were.

"The people who broke into my house," Catton said.

"How far are we from the bottom?" Scott asked.

"Five minutes . . ."

"Gotta hurry . . ."

"What about Rose?" Foss asked.

"Can't help her," Scott said.

THE PHONE WAS still connected, but they heard nothing but rifle fire, and then a clatter from an unknown cause, then heavy breathing and Rose gasping, "I'm in the woods, I'm running . . ."

"Who are they? How many of them?" Scott asked.

She didn't answer, but the phone remained connected, and the Cadillac burst out of the canyon and onto the plateau over the deep valley full of houses and Catton said, "Arroyo Seco in one minute . . ."

Then Rose again, on the phone. "I'm walking, I can't run anymore. They're gonna get me, one way or another, I had to leave the RV . . . I shot at them, tried to kill their cars to slow them down so you could get out . . . best I could do."

"Hide," Scott said. "Climb high and hide. Keep the phone and hide. They can't find you if you get deep into the brush up there."

"I feel like my heart's going to blow up, too high up here . . . I can't run, I can't climb . . . Gotta . . . They got the other three, they got the RV, never saw them coming until they were right on top of me . . ."

She went away again, and they heard more thrashing sounds, apparently Turney fighting her way through the forest. That continued for several minutes, then Turney cried, "I'm throwing the phone away."

And she was gone.

From the back seat, Foss said, "They'll make her talk."

Catton said, "They can't do that, there are laws . . ."

"If they know what we're doing, and they apparently do, there won't be any laws that apply to us," Foss said.

Catton said, "We're coming into Arroyo Seco . . ."

"If we go north, there's only one road, and if they shut it down, we're trapped," Scott said. "We could go West on 64, across the gorge, there are back roads out there, but you can see the car for miles, if they have a description. And the gorge bridge is easy to close off—one car could do it."

"If we go south, into Taos, there are police," Foss said.

"Gotta go someplace," Catton said. She was hunched over the steering wheel; she was shivering with the intensity of the situation. Not afraid, but fierce. "We need a decision, quickly."

They all thought about it, then Foss said, "That house we looked at . . . been on the market for a while and it has a garage."

They'd first thought to set up their vaccination site in a rental house in Taos but decided Catton's more isolated ski valley house would be safer.

"Good, Randy," Scott said. And to Catton: "We'd get the car out of sight, in case they find your credit card, which they will do, sooner than later. If anyone saw you driving down the hill, and they're up there, they'll be looking for a Cadillac SUV. There's no reason to think they know about Dani or Randall. You and I can stay out of sight, with the car. Dani and Randall could scout around for us, if need be."

"What if the real estate woman comes around?" Foss asked.

"She said something about not seeing the place for a month," Catton said. "If she shows up, we'll have to deal with it."

"You mean, kill her," Foss said.

"We capture her, we capture her," Scott said. "We keep her tied up. We can't hide for long, anyway. We'll have to get out in a night or two or three . . ."

"If she does show up . . . we could use her car," Catton said.

There were implications to that: if they took the woman's car, then something final would have to be done about her. Maybe they could tie her up, lock her in a closet, call the police from somewhere and tell them where she was.

Subscript: Or kill her.

"Taos, then?" Catton asked.

Scott turned in his seat to look at Foss. "I think it's the best chance."

Foss was looking out the window, thinking about it, worrying, and then he turned to Scott and nodded. "Taos," he said. "We gotta call Danielle."

Scott did that, explained their thinking, and Callister agreed with the decision to go to Taos.

THEY WERE STILL fifteen minutes out of town but had no idea of how long they had to get to the hideout. Catton tended to think in terms of dozens of black-uniformed federal agents swarming the town from their federal helicopters. Foss thought that the federal government was so useless that they were probably dealing with a couple of bureaucrats and a few sheriff's deputies and local cops.

They took the main highway going south, made it quickly to the edge of town. Catton knew her way around Taos, turned west just inside the built-up area, and circled around to the south, and then back east, on city streets. The house they looked at wasn't quite tumbledown, but was thoroughly neglected, probably one reason it hadn't been rented. They crossed the main highway, found the cross street they were looking for. The house was surrounded by a coyote fence, made of six-foot bark-on sapling poles, and was dark; they pulled into the driveway, Callister behind them.

Scott jumped out to lift the metal garage door, which the real estate agent had told them was manually operated. Scott had it up in a minute, and when Catton had the Cadillac inside, he dropped the door behind it; Callister pulled her Subaru onto a gravel patch behind the fence, out of sight from the street.

Catton said, "Well, we're here, for what it's worth."

Callister said, "Better than being out there."

The door between the garage and the house was locked, but the door was hollow and Foss kicked it in. They got their bags from the vehicle, carried them inside, which was furnished, but just barely. Two beds in each of two bedrooms, a couch, two battered and stained easy chairs, with what might have been one of the original flat-panel TVs, barely three feet across, sitting on a rickety table. What looked like an antique floor lamp stood in one corner of the living room and when Scott tried to turn it on, nothing happened.

No power.

"We're camping out," Callister said, looking around.

"That's okay, we couldn't risk any kind of light anyway," Scott said.

Foss opened one of his bags, took out a laptop and turned it on. "I can see a couple of Wi-Fi signals," he said. "If I can get on one . . ."

"That would help," Scott said. "It'll be dark soon. You and Danny could walk out to that supermarket we passed. What was it? Smith's? Pick up enough food for a couple of days."

Catton began, "If the feds swarm the place, the town . . ."

They spent a half hour talking about possibilities, and then one of the phones rang. Scott had put them in a briefcase, and he snatched the case off the floor and shook the phones out and picked up the one with a lit screen.

He turned on the speaker. "George?"

"We're stuck in the RV," George Smithe said. His voice was weak, unsteady. "Rose is gone. She shot at somebody and they shot back, so it must have been police and she might be dead. A helicopter came in . . ."

"I told you," Catton muttered.

"I'm talking to the others, and we're going to tell them the excuse, like we planned," Smithe said. "We're gonna blame it on you, Lionel."

"That's just fine, that's what we agreed," Scott said. "I'm not going to make it through this anyway."

"The glassware is still locked in the box up by the driver's seat, we can blame that on Rose . . ."

"Do that," Scott urged. "Rose is out of it."

"I can hear people talking, I think they're coming. I better turn this off."

Scott: "Give them the excuse, George, but don't give up your names. You could tell them that Clarice is dead and buried up the mountain somewhere. Like Carey. Tell them that you don't know where she is, but that Carey is straight up the mountain under a red rock. That'll make them believe you're telling the truth about Clarice. If they put . . . pressure on you . . . give them my name and Clarice's. They must already know those."

"I can do that, I think," Smithe said. "Don't have much left here . . . somebody's coming. I'm gonna go. Good luck, guys, get it done."

He was gone, and Foss said, "We need to wreck those phones, now, the ones we used."

Scott: "Yes. I saw a brick in the garage, we can beat them to death. I'll go do that now."

SCOTT WENT TO do that, and Foss got a 'net connection using his personal cell phone as a hot spot—"Not a problem. No reason I couldn't be a tourist."

Scott came back with a handful of shattered plastic and electronics, and said, "Put 'Taos' in Google and see what comes up."

Foss did, and a lot came up, but it was all history and advertisements for motels and useless crap. Nothing about any police action. They renewed the search occasionally, and nothing relevant came up.

The night seemed to creep up on them. Foss became worried about using his cell phone as a hot spot: "If they really know what we're doing . . . and if one of the guys gives up my name . . . they'll sic the NSA on us. I don't think we can use any electronics. Those fuckers have been doing surveillance on Americans for seventy years."

"Then we should stop," Scott said.

"And sit here in the dark," Callister said.

Catton: "A very small sacrifice when you consider the goal. And Randall is correct in his fears." And then, "I wonder if the toilet still works?"

"Unless it's electric," Scott said. "You can find out by trying any of the water taps."

She disappeared into the gloom. Scott and the others heard the water come on, and then the bathroom door close.

In the quiet of the old house, Scott thought about prospects and possibilities: the authorities would certainly have his photo. He might obscure things by continuing to grow a beard . . . and when he thought that, it occurred to him to create some kind of disguise.

He said to Callister and Foss, "We need food and some other things. We'll make a list. You two could walk out to that supermarket we saw. It's not far. Besides food, I'll want you to look around and see if they have hair coloring. I want to change my hair color to something darker. Or red, perhaps. If they have any hair clippers, and some disposable razors. I'm thinking we could shave Clarice's head."

"Why?"

"So we can make her into a cancer victim who's doing chemo. They must know that Clarice isn't a cancer victim . . ."

"How about if I bought a pink ribbon so we could make a breast-cancer ribbon?" Callister asked. "That tends to make people not look at somebody too close because, you know, she's . . . sick."

"Even better."

"And a Covid mask," Foss added. "Breast cancer victims who've lost their hair are immune-suppressed and have to worry about Covid. With a shaved head and a Covid mask, nobody would recognize her."

"That's creepy," Callister said.

"We're way past creepy, Danielle," Scott said. "If you could find those things . . ."

They heard the toilet flush. Catton emerged from the bathroom and said, "I heard you talking. Did something happen?"

"No . . . but I'm afraid you have breast cancer and have lost your hair," Scott said.

"What?"

13

Letty stood thirty feet from the RV and watched as the woman, Marta De León, climbed out of the bus, carrying a black metal box that might once have held extraordinarily expensive cigars. She put the box on the ground and called, "There's a safe bag with a green strip around the top. I need you to get the big red canister out of it."

Letty did that. She attached the sprayer wand and, following De León's instructions, hosed her down.

"Try not to get any on you," De León said. "Hold it out at arm's length. It's not dangerous, but it is staining."

In a few seconds De León was dripping amber fluid from head to toe. When she was thoroughly soaked, she waddled to a decorative stone at the side of the parking area, sat down, and lifted her feet so Letty could spray her soles.

"Now I need you to spray the box. I'll turn it over with one of my feet . . ."

That done, they waited four or five minutes, then did it all over again. After another short wait, De León began to strip off the once-white suit. She was wearing yoga pants and a tank top, now soaked with sweat.

"Need a drink," she said. "I smell like a gym sock."

"We've got water bottles," Letty said. She got one of the bottles supplied by the cops, handed it to De León, and asked, "What do you think?"

De León turned to look at the RV, then back to Letty. "I believe all three people in the bus have Marburg, or Ebola, or an adverse reaction to a vaccine. They claim they were paid to take part in a biological experiment and didn't understand how bad it would be."

"Probably lying," Letty said.

"Probably," De León said. "Because if this is the real deal, they're all going to get the death penalty. Anyway, they say two of the experimental subjects died—they're both buried up on the mountainside. One of them, a woman named Clarice, they don't know exactly where. They said she was older and was the first to die. She was buried by Lionel Scott. The second man, whose name they didn't know, was buried straight up the mountain from the back door of the house they were in. They said Scott put a big red stone on the grave, and he might have done something similar with Catton. Built a cairn."

"How many are loose?"

"Wouldn't say—claimed they didn't know. Nobody knows any last names. Scott insisted on that as a security measure, but it didn't apply to Catton and Scott, because they were the recruiters."

"Did you believe them?" Letty asked.

"No. They were lying about some of it, and maybe all of it," De León said. "The red stone thing would probably be checkable."

"How sick are they?"

"They're sick, but they're not going to die. They're already on the rebound, they'll be walking by the end of the week."

"Are they infectious?" Letty asked.

"They say they aren't, but they don't know for sure."

"All right. I'll pass this along to the DHS working group."

De León said, "The box." She looked back at the box, sitting in a drying puddle of the amber virus killer. "The box contains twenty transport tubes, glass tubes. They contain some sort of culturing media. I'm not a virologist, I don't know exactly what it might be, but it could be the virus that they were planning to release. We need to get it to Detrick. Quick as we can."

LETTY STEPPED AWAY and called Greet. As she was filling her in, one of the Detrick crew turned a big translucent bag inside out, and De León picked up the metal box and held it out. The Detrick crewman rolled the inside of the bag over it, so the box was inside without ever touching the outside. He sealed it, carried it away from the RV, and put it on the rock that De León had been sitting on.

Greet listened to Letty's report, then asked, "Has another chopper come in? A second one?"

"Not yet."

"We need everything you can get off that bus and fly it straight back here. We should know more by tomorrow: Detrick has staff standing by, to work overnight when we get the material."

"What do we do with the people in the bus?" Letty asked.

"That's up to the Detrick team. I suggest we leave them where they are, in the RV, so they don't contaminate anything else. Bring in food and water. We need IDs on them. And, you know, if they die, they die."

"I'll get one of the bio team to go in and try to get the IDs," Letty said.

"Your father and this Moscowitz guy found an insulin pen in a garbage can, still with a prescription label on it. We're checking to see who it goes back to," Greet said. "I'm told we'll know within the hour, so that should give us another name . . . unless it's somebody on the bus."

"Okay. What about closing down the roads out of Taos?"

"The state police have set up checkpoints," Greet said. "We're told they've got all roads covered, and they're all looking at photos of Scott and Catton, though if Catton's dead . . . Anyway, they've got photos of Scott, and they've been told that he's suspected of being a serial child killer, so they're taking it seriously. Let's hope that the insulin pen gives us another name and another photo."

As they were finishing the conversation, another helicopter was coming in, and circled overhead, kicking up dust. Letty told Greet, who said, "Get the stuff from the bus and turn the chopper around. You gotta get that moving."

"We will. I'll call you when they're off."

THE HELICOPTER LANDED, disgorged two more men and two women, and another pile of oversized duffel bags. At the same time, the five people at Catton's house came back down to the parking lot, having locked the empty house behind them. When everybody knew what everyone else had done, the samples collected by De León and Moscowitz were placed in the heavy duffels, along with the box of glass tubes from the bus.

Underwood, leader of the Detrick team, said, "We need to take samples in the bus, and we need to do it now, so we can ship it with this load."

Tank, the police chief, had watched the proceedings from a distance, and now walked up and said, "Everybody? It's gonna be dark in a couple of hours, and when the sun goes down, it gets dark real quick. What are we gonna do about Ms. Catton's house?"

Lucas said, "They cleaned the place out before they left. If Danny doesn't need it for more samples, I say burn it."

Tank: "You could start one hell of a forest fire . . ."

Lucas: "Okay, burn it carefully."

Underwood said to Tank, "We don't have to do anything right now. I think you people . . . with guns . . . should watch the place overnight, and by tomorrow, we'll have decided what to do."

Tank: "I'll talk to the fire chief and the forest service . . . I'll have my guys take turns sitting on the house overnight."

"Do that," Letty said. "The working group in Washington thinks we should leave the sick people on the RV, bring in food and water, get their IDs if we can. Which means we'll have to put more people inside the bus, right now, and we've got to hurry."

LUCAS ASKED TANK, "When you saw the SUV leaving . . . you said you thought Catton was inside."

"I believe it was her. She was driving. She's got long silver hair down on her shoulders, and that's what the driver had."

"Maybe she's not dead," Lucas said.

"If she's not, then the people on the bus are still cooperating as part of the conspiracy," De León said. "We need someone who can get harsh with them. We need to tell them how the vaccine won't save them now—that if anyone dies from a release of the Marburg, they'll be tried for murder, found guilty, and executed."

Lucas said, "Aw, hell. Give me another suit."

Hawkins, who'd been standing on the edge of the circle, behind Letty, said, "I should do it. I interview would-be terrorists from time to time. Threaten them, get unpleasant when I have to. I know how to do that, and I have an Oxbridge accent . . . which their boss had. Psychologically, that could work for us."

All the people with guns looked at each other, and Lucas said, "When you're right . . . I mean, be my guest."

14

A second doctor, named Suzanne Lasch, would be getting on the bus with Hawkins. Before suiting up, Hawkins went to his suitcase, dug around, and came back with a device that looked like a cell phone. "Fingerprints," he said.

Lasch, a thin woman in her forties, said, "Show me how to use it, if it's simple. Then you won't have to touch them. I have to anyway."

"Okay." He showed her—it was simple enough, press a finger against a screen, and the pressure would trigger an internal camera to image the fingerprint and store it. They would take images of both thumbs on each man. When the prints were stored, they could be transferred to a cell phone with Bluetooth.

When she understood it, they suited up. Lasch went first, spent a few minutes checking temperatures with a no-touch infrared thermometer, then took blood samples from each of the three sick men.

After each sampling, she carried the syringe to the RV's door and dropped it into a non-penetrable bag that was immediately sealed.

That done, she told the sick men that she was going to take a "differential blood pressure," and made the thumbprints, and the print recorder was passed out the door into a transparent isolation bag. Hawkins, working through the transparent plastic of the bag, transferred the prints to his cell phone and used his messaging app to send them on to Letty, who sent them to Greet.

"I need one of those fingerprint gizmos," Letty said.

"If you can afford to buy me a Panama hat, you can afford one of these," Hawkins said. "They're dirt simple and dirt cheap."

She got in front of him and poked him in the chest: "When you're in there . . . easy does it."

THE RV WAS large, but not as big as a Greyhound bus—maybe half that size. Both sides of the interior were lined with gray leather-look couches, with a compact kitchen halfway down the length, and a bedroom in the back. The sick men were lying on thin plastic camping mattresses, on the floor between the couches, rather than on the couches themselves. They wore what looked like hospital scrub suits, and when Lasch checked, found that all three were wearing adult diapers. The RV stank of intestinal gas and sweat.

All three men were awake and aware.

Hawkins, in an isolation suit, boarded the bus and squeezed past Lasch, not touching, and made his way to the bedroom and began pulling open drawers, which were empty, and a storage closet, which was not. Inside were four mid-sized suitcases, stacked atop each other, and four smaller carry-on flight bags, and a purse.

He pulled them out and lay them on the bed. None of the suitcases were locked, and inside, he found travel gear for three men and a woman, and in each, dopp kits full of the usual travel items—toothbrushes with travel-sized toothpaste tubes, travel-sized deodorant containers, fingernail clippers, travel-sized bottles of Scope mouthwash, and a tube of Frizz Ease, a hair cream. The three suitcases with male clothes also contained disposable razors and travel-sized cans of shaving cream.

The items in each dopp kit were identical, except that those with male clothing had the shaving gear. After thinking about that, Hawkins realized that they'd probably all been bought by the same person at the same time and were chosen so the traveler could make himself or herself look as respectable as possible—no body odor, no fly-away hair, no terrible breath, no beard stubble. The stuff was intended to groom the wearers for TSA eyes at the airports.

The rest of the contents of the suitcases was more variable—men's clothes in different styles and sizes in three of them, women's clothes in the fourth, but again, all of it bland, respectable-looking.

None of it meant much, except for the conclusion that everything had been carefully chosen, as part of a well-thought-out plan. He picked out several of the grooming items—those with hard sides, that would hold fingerprints, carried them to the front door and handed them off to one of the Detrick crew, who was waiting with an isolation bag. "More possible fingerprints," he said.

Back at the closet, he went through the four carry-on bags, and found a U.S. passport in each one. The first one he looked at belonged to a Sandra Klein, but had a photo of Rose Turney, taken recently: she looked exactly as she had an instant before Hawkins had shot her in the heart. A wallet held what looked like a real New Mexico driver's license for Sandra Klein, again with Turney's photo.

He found more passports and wallets in the other travel bags, and each of the wallets contained a correct-looking New Mexico driver's license and a matching passport.

The documents named the men on the floor: John Brickell, Rory Long, Cameron Johnson, all probably fake. Hawkins stood over them, one at a time, checking their faces against the photos in the passports and driver's licenses, then carried the documents to the RV entrance door where more collection bags were waiting for him. He dropped each of the passports and licenses into separate transparent bags, which were immediately sealed. The bags were big enough that the passports could be opened and manipulated without breaking the seals.

Using the radio, he told those outside the bus that he thought the passports and licenses were "real, but with fake names and photos. We need to check the names and addresses to see if there are real people behind them, and if they are active accomplices. We should do that as quickly as possible."

"I'LL GET THE names to Billy," Letty radioed back. "See what pops."

Finished in the bedroom, Hawkins worked his way through storage areas in the rest of the bus, not finding much except a rental agreement for the RV; the signature at the bottom of the page was illegible.

Lasch had been interviewing the three men about their physical symptoms. All three showed what appeared to be bruised faces, and the one she was examining complained of lower stomach pain, made worse when she gently pressed his stomach. He told her that he and the others all had had episodes of diarrhea, which was why they were wearing diapers. The worst pain, he said, was in the muscles of his thighs, both quads and hamstrings, in the joints of his elbows, shoulders and fingers, and in what felt like his internal organs.

His eyes were clear and his voice was shaky, but understandable.

When Lasch moved to the man in the middle of the three, Hawkins sat on the couch next to the head of the first man on the floor and began lying. "I'm a friend . . . well, a former friend . . . of Lionel Scott. We were classmates together at Oxford. We were on our college rowing team for two years, and after graduation, I went on to a career in the military. Because of our relationship, the British and American governments sent me here to talk to his . . . associates . . . in this experiment. I need to ask you some questions . . ."

The man on the mattress claimed that he knew nothing of an effort to spread a disease; he said that Scott was attempting to find a vaccine that would be effective against Marburg and Ebola, and that the three of them were volunteers in the experiment. "Volunteers, but we got paid ten thousand dollars up front. I needed the money, and he said it would be safe, so I signed on."

Hawkins shook his head: "We know that's not true, Cameron," he said, using the name in the man's passport. "I just looked through the passports with the fake names. We have compiled a lot of evidence that you knew exactly what was going on—why else would your friend Rose have opened fire on us this morning?"

"I, I don't know. I did hear gunshots, but I didn't know what was happening . . ."

"Rose was shot to death on the hillside here, by one of the investigators," Hawkins said. "She's dead. I have to say, as politely as I can manage, that you will be, too. Dead, that is, and fairly soon. We don't have the death penalty in Great Britain, but you certainly do here in the United States. And, my friend, if you don't begin cooperating, you are going to be strapped down to a table and given a lethal injection, not too far in the future."

"But I don't know anything . . ." the man wailed.

"You know some things," Hawkins said. "You know how many people were in the car that went out of here ahead of you. How many were there, Cameron?"

One of the other men, overhearing the question, called, not loudly, but clearly, "We have the right to remain silent, we have the right to an attorney . . ."

Lasch turned to look at Hawkins and moved so he could see the face of the man who had called out.

"Those rights have been suspended by order of the President," Hawkins lied again. "Just as Americans do have a right to free speech, you do not have the right to shout 'Fire' in a crowded theater. In other words, those rights are not absolute. In the face of the critical problem you have created for us, you no longer have the right to remain silent, or to have legal counsel. In fact, if you don't cooperate, it has been hinted that some very impolite men will take you to a dark place and ask the same questions, and they will not take no for an answer."

"You mean torture," said Rory Long, the middle man. He appeared to be the strongest of the three.

"I mean interrogation," Hawkins said. "Enhanced interrogation, as you Americans call it."

"We've already held up with the Marburg vaccine in us, so waterboarding isn't going to scare us," Long said.

"Marburg vaccine made you sick. Enhanced interrogation will do far worse things to you than Marburg, far worse than waterboarding. And it will still keep you alive for the lethal injection."

"You can't—"

"I can't, but the people waiting outside this bus certainly can," Hawkins said.

He looked down at the man named Cameron Johnson. "Cameron, how many people were in the car?"

Johnson called, "Rory . . ."

"Do what you have to," Rory Long, the middle man, said. "Nobody told us anything about torture."

Johnson, his face red, still burning with fever, said, "There were three. I don't know their names. Their whole names. There was Lionel Scott, and a woman whose first name was Marsha and a man named Carl. We weren't supposed to reveal our last names to anyone, even each other."

"You're still lying to me, and I'll have to report that," Hawkins said. "We have video confirmation, and eyewitness confirmation, that Clarice Catton was in the car."

Johnson's eyes widened fractionally, and he said, "Clarice is dead. We were told she's dead. That she was buried. We were in her house, but we never saw her after she got sick. Are you sure she was in the car? Marsha was in the car . . ."

Rory Long backed him up. "Maybe Clarice is alive, but you couldn't prove it by us. She was an older lady with gray hair . . . but we were given our injections and were already sick before I saw her that one time, and she was sicker than we were, and later we were told she died and was buried up the mountain. If you have video and eyewitnesses, you're probably seeing Marsha, who is also older with gray hair."

Hawkins moved closer to Long, so he could talk to both Long and

Johnson at the same time. He pressed them on whether the measles-Marburg hybrid virus had been successfully created and tested, and both Long and Johnson said they didn't know about a hybrid. He eventually left them and went to the third man.

JOHN BRICKELL, A large man, probably the sickest of them, had nothing to say at all. "Leave me, I'm dying," he groaned. "I want to die now. I want to die. I can't . . . the pain . . . I can't."

Hawkins looked at Lasch, who shook her head. She didn't say it, but she was clear enough: he wasn't dying. Not yet, anyway.

Hawkins said, "Dr. Lasch, I suggest that you let him go, if he's dying. We don't have the time or the medical supplies to waste on people who can't help us. It would be a mercy to let him go."

"You're right," Lasch said. "I can pump him full of analgesic, hydrocodone, that'll keep him unconscious and more-or-less comfortable until he passes."

Brickell turned his head to Lasch, "You can't do that. You're a doctor, you're supposed to treat me. Get me well."

"I don't believe I can get you well. I will be keeping you as comfortable as possible with the supplies we have . . ." She worked through her bag and produced a syringe and a bottle of transparent fluid.

Brickell said, "Wait, wait. I'm a human being . . ."

"Who's trying to kill five or six billion other human beings, including hundreds of millions of children," Hawkins said.

"Wait . . ."

Hawkins: "How many people are running, Brickell?"

Long said, "Keep the faith," and Brickell turned his head that way, then back to Hawkins and muttered, "Three."

Long: "Goddamnit."

Hawkins said, "We know it's not three. I'm going to ask you again: how many? We have an idea of how many, from searching Catton's house. If you lie again, I swear to God, I'll pull Dr. Lasch out of here, and you'll be left to stew in your own shit. No more treatment. No more nothing."

Johnson groaned, and Long said, "You can't . . ."

Hawkins: "The number . . ."

Brickell: "I, I . . . four."

"So Catton is alive, well, and in that car."

Brickell didn't speak, but nodded, then looked away.

"For your own good, for treatment, you have to tell us," Hawkins said. "Do you have the Marburg crossed with the hybrid measles virus, or were you made sick by a vaccine?"

"Only the vaccine," Brickell said. "It's crude, but Lionel believes it works. He used it on himself first, and then on Clarice. One person died from the vaccine, he's buried above Clarice's house. We're not infectious."

"Yeah, I believe you, you fuckin' homicidal maniacs," Hawkins said, letting the disgust seep into his voice. "You're safe, but billions of people were gonna die when you hauled those tubes of virus media into airports . . ."

"Gaia's dying, Gaia's dying," Johnson called from the other end of the line, his voice high and not quite whining.

"And you think that justifies killing more than half the people on earth?" Hawkins asked.

"Yes, we do. All the people on earth are going to die unless the global warming is stopped. It's too late for any conventional methods," Long said. "You and your fascist friends are killing billions more than we would. All you're doing is . . . nothing. Letting Gaia die. You can give me an injection. I don't care. I don't want to be here when Gaia dies."

Hawkins went back to Brickell, the weakest of the three. "What airport were you supposed to go to? You can tell us, because you're obviously not going to it."

Brickell: "Miami, with a stop at Atlanta, and then on to Rio. I was supposed to release virus in the international gates of all three airports."

Long: "Goddamnit, George, shut up."

Hawkins, looking down at Brickell: "So George is your real first name? And you all know the names of all your accomplices?"

After hesitating, Brickell nodded. "First names. Not last."

"Where was Rory going?"

"I don't know where anyone else was going," Brickell said. "Lionel gave us separate assignments. We weren't supposed to talk about them with each other, so we couldn't give them away if we got caught."

Hawkins moved up beside Long: "Rory, if you cooperate . . ."

"Go away."

Hawkins moved to Cameron Johnson: "Cameron, you're not going anywhere. You could tell us the airports you were supposed to infect."

Long called, "Cameron, if you tell them, they can eliminate those airports from their lists, and figure out where the others are going."

Hawkins said, "There are hundreds of airports, Cameron—and if you talk to us, like a civilized human being, that will carry weight at your trial."

Johnson turned his head to the side and said, "Help me . . . just help me."

"Honestly?" Hawkins said. "We're afraid to help you. We're afraid you're infectious and will give us Marburg. If this so-called vaccine kills you, well, it kills you. Tough luck."

"Then screw you, you fuckin' monster, let us die," Johnson said.

HAWKINS WENT BACK to Brickell. "It's hard to believe that Lionel would launch this plan if he hadn't tested the hybrid virus on someone . . . did he do that?"

Brickell turned his head from side to side, his tongue flicking in and out like a snake's; his face was swollen, red, and one hand crept across his stomach and seemed to squeeze a bit and he said, "Hurts. They didn't say it would hurt this much."

Hawkins nodded, and said, "Okay." He reached down with one gloved hand, his fingers rigid, and jabbed Brickell in the stomach, hard, and the man tried to scream but not much came out but a gasp of breath and a groan, and saliva, and Hawkins jabbed him again. "I can't think that your pain will amount to much compared to the pain of millions of children who have the raw Marburg . . ." And he jabbed Brickell again, and this time harder, and the man did manage to scream and tried to roll.

Hawkins pushed him flat again, and snarled, "John: was there a test?"

"Don't . . ."

Hawkins jabbed him again, harder still. He snarled again and let Brickell hear the coarseness: "I can do this all day. This is what I do."

"Ahhhh . . . Please . . ." And Brickell farted, a long, loud expulsion of gas that seeped into the RV's air and Long said, "Ah, my God, you're killing him."

Hawkins: "So what?" He turned back to Brickell: "John? George? Whatever it is?"

"There may have been a test," Brickell said, groaning. "I heard Lionel talking to Clarice about a Lamy test. I don't know what a Lamy test is, but it was a test of the virus."

"The hybrid."

"Yes."

Hawkins looked at Lasch, the doctor: "What's a Lamy test?"

"Nothing I've ever heard of," Lasch said.

Hawkins asked the other two men, who shook their heads, and Long said, "I never heard of anything like that."

LASCH, WHO HAD been watching the interrogation, said to Hawkins, "You're low on air. You should hear a beeping sound when you go on reserve. I just heard mine."

Brickell: "You're not leaving us here?"

"Yes, we are," Hawkins said. "The doctors will be coming to look at you, from time to time, but this bus isn't going anywhere until we get confirmed analyses of your illnesses. If you start feeling better, don't even think of trying to escape: you will instantly be shot to death. There are people outside this bus who think they should be allowed in here now to shoot each one of you."

Long: "You can't do . . ."

Hawkins: "Yes, we can. What did you expect, given what you're trying to do? We've got dragnets out for the others, and they're to be shot on sight."

Long: "You can't . . ."

"Yes, we can. We will. We already have."

Hawkins heard the reserve-air alert, the beeping sound, and said to Lasch, "We should go."

15

Outside the bus, and out of the isolation suit, Hawkins told the others what he'd gotten in the interviews. That there were four people on the loose, that they were no longer sick, they undoubtedly had vials of the hybrid virus, that they were planning to contaminate international airports around the world.

They said the four were in one car, but Hawkins thought they were lying about that. "When we were driving up the canyon, I remembered seeing a silver SUV going down, a big one, and there was another car right behind it, and I had the feeling they were connected. They denied it in there, in the bus, but I think they were lying."

Letty used her iPad to Google "Lamy Test" on the Wiki and found that the test was given to diagnose a dreadful childhood disease called Maroteaux-Lamy syndrome that led to distortions of the internal organs and skeleton. Few untreated victims survived past adolescence, and even with treatment, life expectancy was greatly shortened.

"What the heck does that have to do with Marburg?" Rae asked.

"I dunno," Letty said. She looked at Hawkins: "You sure you got the name right?"

"That's what he said. Try different spellings."

She tried Lamey Test and Lamie Test and didn't come up with anything that seemed relevant. She'd typed the words in quickly, but then, in frustration, typed "Lamy," with one finger, into the Google field, but before she could type in "Test," Google suggested several possibilities and the first one was "Lamy, NM."

She looked at it and said, "Jeez. There's a Lamy, New Mexico. You think they could have tested the virus on a town?"

"Where is it?" Lucas asked. Letty entered the name in a map search field, and it came up with a tiny town south of Santa Fe.

"Three hours from here," she said. She looked at the helicopter. "Unless we flew."

Underwood said, "It's heading down to Albuquerque to deliver our bus samples to the jet. That'll take forty minutes or so . . . it could probably have you in this Lamy in an hour."

"Could it drop me off on the way, and pick me up on the way back?"

"I'll ask."

Before they did anything else, they called Greet, who approved sending Letty and Hawkins to Lamy on the chopper.

After absorbing the other information that Hawkins had gotten from the sick men, Greet said, "We'll get pictures of Scott and Catton to airport security for every airport in the country, and Canada and

Mexico. We'll do that right now, paper those places by tomorrow morning. But you can't let these people get on a plane."

And they heard her calling to somebody there with her. When she came back to the phone, she asked, "How are the checkpoints working?"

"We don't know," Lucas said. "We're still at the ski mountain."

"Get down to Taos where you can talk to the cops," Greet said. "Be careful about what you say. We're walking on the edge of a panic."

Lucas: "You should tell airport security to send officers into all the areas outside all the departure gates, before anyone goes through security. If Scott and the others see extra security precautions, they could try to contaminate people headed overseas, when they're still outside the security lines."

"We'll get that going," Greet said. "But God help us if they've gotten out of Taos. They could already be in Albuquerque. Heck, they could already be in Phoenix or Denver or Dallas-Fort Worth, if they got a plane out of Santa Fe."

"I've been thinking about it, and I believe they're still with us," Lucas said. "If they were in the cars that Alec noticed, they wouldn't have had time to get all the way to the north-south highway. We choked off the exits pretty quick. I believe they're hiding in Taos, or around Taos. What's the incubation period for measles? Or Marburg?"

"Prodrome averages eleven days or so for measles . . . that's first symptoms, but can be as little as seven days," Greet said. "With Marburg, it's shorter, two to seven days on average."

"So our problem is, if they're cornered, and if they can even spread the disease in Taos, and stay in hiding, and people go streaming out . . . I mean, Covid started in a single Chinese city. Taos is a tourist town, there are people here from all over the country. They'll be flying home, and since there aren't any big airports nearby, with direct flights, a lot will be flying through hubs."

"I'll put that on our pile of nightmares," Greet said. "You've got to kill them before they do that, before they figure that out."

The biological response team had loaded the samples into the Firehawk and Letty said to Lucas, when he got off the phone, "Alec should come with me. There should be two of us to ask questions, and you and Rae will work best with the cops."

Lucas nodded. "Yeah." He turned to Rae: "What do you have in extra handguns?"

"Got a decent Ruger .357."

"Perfect. Give it to Hawkins, and let's get them on the way."

Hawkins was shaking his head, but Lucas said, "Take the gun. You needed one earlier today, and you came through. You might need another, and I don't think you'd want to be carrying that M4 around town."

"No, but I don't think . . ."

Letty said, "Take the gun, Alec. If we get in trouble, you can hand it to me."

HE TOOK THE gun, a five-shot revolver, with a box of ammunition. He'd fired pistols in the Army, at firing ranges, but wasn't familiar with a revolver. Rae gave him a thirty-second lesson, said, "That's about all you need. Point it, pull the trigger and keep pulling. No safety to worry about. The trigger's gonna feel really stiff compared to an auto-loader, so unload it and try it out. Letty can tell you anything you need to know."

As they were getting on the chopper, Greet called again and said, "I told them to drop you off on the way, instead of going to the airport first. Won't slow them down by more than five minutes, and you'll get to this Lamy place in daylight."

And with that, they were on the helicopter and gone, Letty and Hawkins with their bags, and one of the biological team members to handle the sample packs; a crew chief sat in the back with them. With a clatter and a groan, the Firehawk climbed over the lowest of the mountain peaks and then swooped down over the Taos plain.

They couldn't talk much, even with the doors closed. Hawkins unloaded the .357 and dry-fired it a dozen times, while the biological team member watched with a worried look on his face.

"I'd feel more confident if I had seventeen shots instead of five," Hawkins shouted at Letty.

"Basically, all you need is one," she said, and smiled at him.

"Okay, Wild Bill."

THE CHOPPER HUGGED the Sangre de Cristos to their east, following the Rio Grande rift, overflew Santa Fe, picked up I-25 and followed it to a junction of another highway, followed that one, then broke left and descended toward a beat-up-looking village on a set of railroad tracks.

To the west, a white-orange sun was dropping toward a low blue range of mountains, the same range that held Los Alamos.

"Got a police officer," Hawkins said, peering out a side window. Letty leaned over him to look and saw a police car in the parking lot of what might have been a railway station. The car's flashers were working and a cop was standing beside the car. The chopper circled down toward it, finally landing in a patch of dirt across the highway from the station, in front of a restaurant. The crew chief pulled the door back and they picked their bag up and bailed out, under the turning helicopter blades, into a storm of dust.

They ran away from the chopper toward the cop car, and when they got to the cop—a state police officer, as it turned out—the helicopter lifted off again, in an even bigger storm of dust.

When it was gone, and the dust was beginning to settle, and they could hear again, the cop asked, "Who are you guys, anyway? And what do you want?" And to Hawkins, "Is that a gun in your pocket?"

THE MOST IMMEDIATELY salient fact about Lamy was that it seemed to be deserted. The tiny town was located in a valley, and though the sun was still above the horizon on top, down in the valley, shadows were getting deep.

A shabby railroad depot sat beside the tracks. Signs in the windows said that the station was unstaffed, although the Amtrak trains still stopped there from time to time to pick up passengers. The passengers apparently had to wait on benches in a covered outdoor space adjacent to the station. There were a number of abandoned and obsolete old railroad passenger cars, and a couple of old engines, sitting on unused sidetracks, but with no sign of anyone around them.

The restaurant across the road from the depot was dark, and a sign in a window said that it would not reopen until the middle of August, still several days away. There was a house sideways across the street from the station, but there were no lights on.

LETTY TOLD THE state cop, "We need to talk to somebody here. Anybody. Could you drive us around? We saw some houses from the air . . ."

The cop, whose name was Jerry Wright, conceded that he could do that, and that after they were done in Lamy, could even drive them back to the Santa Fe airport so they could rent another car.

"Great! The ones we rented this morning got all shot up," Letty said.

"Say what?"

She explained, telling a few lies along the way.

THEY DROVE OUT a dirt road—Wright was unfamiliar with Lamy and since they couldn't hook up to a cell tower or a Wi-Fi system, they had to go along by following their noses—until they saw lights in an adobe house on a rough side street. The house turned out to be fairly nice, and when they knocked on the door, a woman answered through a speaker beside the door.

"Who is it?"

"New Mexico State Police and two federal government officials," Wright said.

"Back up a little bit so the camera can see you better."

They looked up and saw a tiny camera poking through a hole in the wooden trim above the door. They backed up, and the door popped open and the woman, holding a dog the size of a healthy rat, asked, "What's going on?"

Letty: "Have you been aware of anyone in the community suffering from a life-threatening illness in the past month or so?"

"Nope. Nobody sick here."

"No rumors of a serious illness?"

"Not that I heard. There's not much place to hear stuff. Everybody works in town or doesn't work at all. If you come out here, you kinda stay to yourself."

"Okay." Letty took a step back, clicked on her iPad and showed the woman photos of Scott and Catton. "Have you seen either of these people?"

The woman looked at the photos, then tapped the photo of Scott: "He might've come through. In an old Subaru? I only saw him through the car window as we passed, so maybe it wasn't him. But somebody that looked like that came through here, mmm, several times. Haven't seen him for a month or so, at least."

"Thank you. Who else might have met him? Do you know where he seemed to be going?"

The woman didn't, but said, "You oughta talk to Carol-Ann Oaks. You go down to the bottom of the hill and turn left and go, mmm, maybe a half mile, and you'll see a house with yellow shutters. Carol-Ann keeps her ear to the ground."

AS THEY WALKED back to the patrol car, Hawkins asked, "Didn't Rae get the make of Scott's car?"

"I think so," Letty said, "She said he sold it, and I think she said it was a Subaru, but I'm not sure about that. I can call her."

"Heck, I can get it in two minutes," Wright said.

At the car, Letty showed him a shot of Scott's driver's license, and Wright got on his radio and called in a request. He got an answer back in three or four minutes: "A 2013 Subaru."

"There you go," Wright said.

Hawkins: "We need to find out who he was visiting."

"Maybe Carol-Ann Oaks can tell us," Letty said.

THE HOUSE WITH yellow shutters was a wood-frame, unlike the other houses they'd seen—they'd all been real or simulated tan adobe—with a corrugated red-steel roof. A gray-haired woman was in the side yard, working a flower garden with a hoe and a garden hose, and turned to look when the patrol car's headlights swept across her.

Letty led the way across the front yard to the garden; the hose had been turned off at the nozzle, but hissed at them when they passed, like a fifty-foot-long snake. "What happened?" the woman asked.

She agreed that she was Carol-Ann Oaks; Letty identified herself, Hawkins, and Wright, and asked her the question about life-threatening illnesses.

"Haven't heard about anybody being sick, but . . . I haven't seen Joe Cross for a month or more, and I usually see him most days. He lives over on the other side of the tracks, but he comes over here to take pictures and so on. He's a hobby photographer. Black and white only. I thought about checking on him . . . but I didn't."

She went in the house, came back with a spiral notebook, put it on the hood of Wright's patrol car, and drew a complicated map of the back-country roads around Lamy, and pinpointed Cross's house. She looked at Letty's photos of Scott and Catton, touched Scott's photo and said, "He came through here quite a few times, starting last spring, right up until a while ago. I can't tell you how long, exactly."

"Was he on the road to the Cross house?" Hawkins asked.

Oaks nodded: "Yes. Could have been going there, but I don't know if he did."

THEY GOT BACK in the patrol car, followed the dirt trail along the railroad tracks, crossed them, followed the dirt track on the other side until they got to Cross's driveway. The driveway was marked with a white ten-gallon bucket from Home Depot that was filled with sand and said "Cross" on the side, in hand-lettered black paint.

The driveway disappeared through anonymous shrubbery, and they followed it two hundred yards or so, and found what looked like a prefabricated farmhouse, or cabin, with a red steel roof like the one on Carol-Ann Oaks's house, and an attached garage. An open-front machine shed stood in the back and they could see a compact Kubota tractor and a Kubota utility vehicle parked inside.

The house was dark and felt abandoned. Hawkins banged on the door and tried the doorknob, but it was locked. The back door was locked, and looking through the windows, they couldn't see much at all inside, except the expected furniture. They could see a yellow Jeep in the garage, but it hadn't been moved for a while—there was a layer of dust on the short concrete apron outside the garage door, but there were no tracks in the dust.

Night was coming, and Wright got a Maglite from his car; they poked around the machine shed without finding anything of interest until Hawkins noticed a drag harrow, sitting behind the building, that looked like it had been recently used, with loose dirt on the chain and frame.

"Odd time of year for that, you'd use it in the spring. Any rain at all would have knocked the dirt off," he said. They were losing light, but Wright spotted what seemed to be a patch of barren earth a hundred feet or so behind the shed, that circled around piñon trees.

"Why would you do that?" he asked.

Letty was looking around at the sparsely vegetated earth—yellow weeds and some short wildflowers between piñons. "If you'd dug a grave, in this dirt, it'd look a lot like a grave and for a long time. Maybe . . ."

"Nice to have an optimist with us," Wright said to Hawkins.

"I saw some rebar in the shed," Letty said. "C'mon, we gotta hurry."

They each got a rebar stake from a pile in the shed and hustled back to the disturbed ground. Walking in a line, they began pushing the rebar into the disturbed surface. Underlying the dirt was a layer of caliche that would stop the rebar; but halfway across the circle of harrowed earth, Wright hit a soft spot and pushed the rebar rod down a full two feet.

"Damnit, I wanted to go home—but there's something here. Or not something. I'm not hitting the caliche."

They probed the soft area and found it grave-like in shape—or a little more than one grave, a little wider. Wright suggested that they call the Santa Fe sheriff's department and get some crime scene lights and help digging.

"We're going to need a lot more than that," Letty said. "We need to get to a place where I can make a cell phone call."

Lamy was in a deep desert valley south of the town of Eldorado. They left the Cross house, drove out the road past Oaks's house and up the valley wall to the highway from Eldorado. It was now fully dark. Letty had Wright pull to the shoulder of the road, and she and Hawkins walked away from the car to make a call to Greet.

She was still at her desk, though it was close to eleven o'clock in Washington.

Letty told her about the possible grave site. "Scott was here, apparently frequently, until about a month ago. We think he might have been visiting this guy, the guy hasn't been seen for weeks, the house looks abandoned, and if it was an experiment that killed Cross . . . it probably would have been a test of the full hybrid virus. I can't think of any other reason."

"Then we need to have the Detrick crew do the excavation to see if there are bodies there," Greet said. "We're flying more people out now—a military crew this time. They'll be there in the morning."

"People in Lamy know we were asking about Cross," Letty said. "Do we watch the place overnight, or just leave it? I mean, I gotta get some sleep sooner or later. This has been a heck of a day."

Greet: "I'll get you a car at the Santa Fe airport and a couple of rooms in Santa Fe. Have the highway patrol guy sit in the driveway until we can get somebody there to relieve him—probably another highway patrolman. Warn him not to go near the possible gravesite."

"All right. Though we're so far out in the sticks I doubt that anybody could find the grave . . . if it even is one. And they're called the state police here, not the highway patrol."

"Do what you think is right—I have confidence in your judgment," Greet said. "By the way, Barbara Cartwright should be landing in Albuquerque about now. She's bringing her sniper rifle in case we need a stand-off shot."

"That's something I hadn't thought of, but should have," Letty said. "I had lunch with her last week, which seems about six months ago."

"I'll get her a car and put her in the same hotel you're in, probably that Holiday Inn you were in before," Greet said. "She should be in Santa Fe in a couple of hours, and we can figure out in the morning where she should go next."

When they got off the call, Hawkins asked, "Who's this Barbara?"

"CIA. With their Special Activities Division. Don't tell anyone. She's a friend of mine, she was with me last year in the California situation."

"Ah. The one nobody can talk about."

"That's the one."

WRIGHT WAS LEANING against the patrol car when they got back to it, and asked, "How did the secret phone call go?"

He was smiling, big square white teeth, but didn't seem especially happy.

Letty: "Listen, Jerry, I don't want to ask you to do this without knowing the problem—but you can't tell anyone. If you do, you could create a panic. This is a top-secret situation . . ."

"Aliens?"

Hawkins frowned: "Why would you think that?"

"Because this is New Mexico," Wright said. "You know about Roswell?"

Hawkins: "Yes, but . . . No, this is not about aliens. A disturbed individual—an Englishman—may have contrived to create a hybrid virus. He may have combined a very infectious measles virus with one of the deadliest viruses known, much, much, much worse than Covid. His intention is to kill off most of the world's population to save the world from global warming and other population effects."

Wright didn't respond for a moment, then said, "That sounds crazier than aliens."

Letty nodded: "Yes. If that's a grave back there, it's possible that there are some infectious bodies inside of it. A team from Fort Detrick will be excavating the area tomorrow. Detrick is where the Army does germ warfare research."

"What if there are no bodies? If it's just a soft spot?"

"That'd be a good thing," Hawkins said. "Though we'd still need to know what Scott was doing in Lamy."

Wright said, "What you really need is to have somebody with a gun sitting in Cross's driveway overnight to make sure nobody gets curious about what we were doing there and goes sneaking around."

Letty nodded: "Yes."

"So I'll run you to the airport in Santa Fe, talk to my dispatcher, and then get back here and sit," Wright said.

"We'll try to get you some relief during the night," Letty said. "Don't tell your relief what we told you. Just tell him to sit."

"Don't worry about a relief," Wright said. "I'll grab some cheese crackers and coffee and get back here. I've slept in my car before. I'll wait until your team gets here."

WHEN THEY WERE off the shoulder of the road, Wright turned on his flashers and siren, and they made the run to the airport at a hundred miles an hour—five miles out to I-25, on what Wright said was one of the more dangerous highways around, down the interstate to another divided highway going north, and then into the airport.

An SUV was waiting for them, and Wright, still with lights and siren, headed back to Lamy. Letty got a text from Greet: they'd be staying at a Holiday Inn Express.

Hawkins: "Two rooms. I really don't wish to presume . . ."

"One would be enough," Letty said. "But we don't have to tell anybody that."

"Excellent. I need to call home. It'll be a little after six in the morning, there, but there'll be somebody on the working group desk. You should call your father and find out what's been happening in Taos . . ."

16

Lucas watched Letty get in the helicopter and kept watching until the chopper disappeared behind a mountain.

"She'll be all right," Rae said. "She's enjoying herself. Though she wouldn't admit it."

"That Brit has his eye on her," Lucas said.

Rae laughed: "You think? And maybe something other than his eye?"

"I'll worry about it later. We should get down to Taos, talk to the cops—and maybe call Greet on the way," Lucas said. "We need more of your SOG guys up here. Not so much the hunters, more the kicking-in-the-door guys."

"Greet's got them cranked up and ready to go—we need to say the word."

"We can say the word on the way. Which SUV is least shot-up? We'll give the other one to the Detrick team."

THEY MADE SURE the Detrick team had a fix on the four locations they knew about at the ski village—the RV, Turney's body on the mountainside, Catton's house, and possibly a body in a grave up the hill from Catton's back door, with a red stone on it—and had a plan to work them.

They gave Underwood Greet's direct number, and told him to stay in touch with her, so that everybody knew what was going on. They transferred Rae's gear bag and all the luggage to the SUV Letty had been driving, but before they left, Underwood said, "Ah, Lucas. Give me a minute."

They walked off to the side away from the others and Underwood said, "I get the impression you're directing the law enforcement traffic here."

"Me and Rae," Lucas said.

"My people back at Detrick are scared to death," Underwood said. "They've been looking at what Scott was doing there, the details of his work. They believe that he could very well have created this hybrid virus—that's after Packer turned in a full report on the lab in Los Alamos. They haven't been able to test the hybrid virus yet, but given what Packer is pulling out of the lab, the equipment and so on, they think he completed his experiments."

He continued: "And from what we've seen in Catton's house and the bus . . . and with Alec's interviews in the bus . . ."

"He's got it," Lucas said. "The hybrid virus."

"Yes. I've got an MD, but I've never practiced—I veered over into research—but I've talked to a lot of field people, doctors, who've dealt with Marburg and Ebola, treating it, and they say it's the worst,"

Underwood said. "The very worst. All us Detrick guys can do is research it—but you law enforcement people have to stop it. You have to kill these people, Lucas. You have to make sure the virus doesn't get loose. If it gets loose, it'll be worse than any world war we've ever had. You gotta stop it, man."

Rae shouted, "Let's go!"

"We'll give it our best shot," Lucas told Underwood, as he took a step toward the SUV.

Underwood hooked Lucas's arm, stopped him. "'Best shot' might not be good enough," Underwood said, holding on. "You have to do *anything* to stop it. Anything! Anything! I'm looking around and I'm not seeing enough cops, enough planning, enough fear. It's like this is just another problem, but it's not."

"Well . . ."

Underwood jabbed Lucas in the chest, hard. His eyes were hard, like black marbles: "Do you have kids?"

"Sure, four, including Letty."

"If this gets loose, go home and wrap your arms around them, because some of them, maybe all of them, are gonna die," Underwood said. "They're gonna die right in front of you, begging for help and there won't be a fuckin' thing you can do about it."

"I . . ."

"Lucas: this is it! This is it!"

Lucas shook him off, took another step back: "I got it."

"I hope so. Because you guys are about the only thing standing between us and a calamity."

Lucas nodded. "I gotta get going."

Underwood stood in place, looking after Lucas as he walked over to the truck and got in.

Rae asked, "What was that all about?"

"The guy's freaking out," Lucas said. "Now he's got me freaking out. Christ, this whole thing seemed like a little bit of a fantasy, a movie. Then Underwood . . . I mean . . . gonna watch my kids dying right in front of me, nothing I can do about it . . ."

"Now I'm freaking out," Rae said.

They drove down the canyon and hit a state police checkpoint at the bottom; the two patrolmen looked at their IDs, asked them what was happening, but Lucas told them he didn't know exactly—that there was a government team at the top of the mountain that might know more. One of the cops said that every road out of Taos was being covered, and that there were some serious traffic jams going south and west.

"What's west?" Rae asked.

"The Rio Grande Gorge Bridge. We're not letting anyone across it, we're routing them back through town if they want to go south. If we let them across the bridge, they could get lost on the back roads," the cop said. "I'll tell you what, there are a lot of pissed-off people out there."

They continued toward Taos and Greet called again. "I got another name—a Randall Foss, who is diabetic. We got the fingerprints from the bus, and none of them go to anyone named Foss. There's a Randall Foss who was fingerprinted for TSA airport clearance four years ago, from Indianapolis, and the insulin pen goes to a pharmacy in Indianapolis. He's divorced, quit his job as a computer programmer at a steel fabrication plant two months ago. We'll hit Foss's house, pick up the ex-wife. We'll have more records coming in, and NSA is looking at his online contacts and his phone. We've got decent photos. I'll email them to all of you."

"Then we probably know three of the four people in the car, or two cars, if Hawkins is right," Lucas said. "We'll be talking to the Taos cops in twenty minutes. I'm hoping we'll have some kind of a net on the streets in an hour or two."

"I've spoken to the Taos police chief, he's expecting you, and he's pulling in all his people. He seems competent enough. They've got an action plan in case of something like a school shooting," Greet said.

"Did you tell him the problem?" Lucas asked.

"I left the details to you, you'll have to feel him out a bit, see if he'll panic. I told him it was a critical national security problem, that it was still being treated as top secret, and that they should give you whatever you want. He might need a little further encouragement, but I got his attention."

Rae: "Billy, we need more marshals. I've got four particular guys that I'd like to see up here . . ."

"Give me the names and they'll be on the way in an hour. We've got a jet on the runway at Alexandria," Greet said. "Also—on my own, I'm sending you a woman named Barbara Cartwright. Letty worked with her last year, and they're friends. She's an operator with the CIA's Special Activities Division. More importantly, she's a sniper, and she's bringing her main weapon, in case you need to stand off from someone. She's got a green light to take out anyone you designate. She's in the air, she'll be in Albuquerque any time now."

"Holy cats: you must be building some serious clout back there," Rae said.

"We are. The Secretary sat down with the President and people from the National Security Council. They worked through it, and got some casualty estimates from us and the DOD. The Big Guy freaked and told us we could have whatever we need. *Whatever we need.* And if we run into any bureaucratic interference, he would personally straighten it out."

"Well, okay," Rae said.

A MINUTE AFTER Greet rang off, Rae got an alert on her iPad, and when she opened it, found four photographs of Randall Foss, including a passport photo. A note from one of Greet's researchers said that the passport photo was definitely of Foss, but the passport had been issued under the name William R. Price with an address in Santa Fe.

"I don't like this at all," Lucas said. "They've got real passports under different names. Another thing that Hawkins got right. And if those germ vials are pure glass, they could walk through airport security with the vials on their bodies and not set off any alarms."

"If there are real people behind the passports, I wonder if they're cooperating? Or if the names were simply stolen?"

"You'd just need to find people who'd never left the country, and a way to get at their mailboxes. I wouldn't be surprised if every one of them went to an apartment house with crappy mail security."

"What about their New Mexico driver's licenses?"

"Virgil and I worked a deal in San Diego," Lucas said. "A cop there told us that you could go to any border state and find somebody who was selling valid driver's licenses. The real thing, run off at night, right at the DMV. And New Mexico is . . ."

"A border state."

AT TAOS, THEY wound through a confusing jumble of streets to the police station, which would have been almost unfindable without their cell phone navigation apps. The station was adobe colored but wasn't trying too hard to look like actual adobe. Rae took her iPad with her, and they went inside, talked to a woman behind a heavy glass window, and were led back to the chief's office.

The chief was a midsized dark-haired man with a brown mustache, spade beard, and blue eyes, which made him look a bit like the last Russian czar. Rae introduced herself and Lucas—the chief's name was Christopher Mellon—and they all shook hands and settled into chairs around his desk.

Rae: "Do you have any idea of what's going on?"

"I know we've got a heck of a mess with the state police stopping every car going out of town. We can't handle the calls we're getting. What are you doing?" Mellon asked.

Rae: "Have you ever been in the military?"

"I was a targeting analyst with the Air Force," Mellon said. "Enlisted, not an officer, but I did have to go through an SSBI."

Rae turned to Lucas: "Background check. Same as the one for top secret, but not SCI. We're probably SCI now, but . . . we gotta trust some of these people."

Mellon: "What's SCI?"

"Sensitive compartmented information," Rae said.

"Never heard of that," Mellon said.

Lucas said to Rae, "You're right. He's got to know. His cops are going to be looking for these guys."

Mellon was confused: "What the hell is going on?"

Rae and Lucas took turns explaining the problem, including what had happened up at Taos Ski Valley that day, and what had been found in Los Alamos and Santa Fe.

Mellon: "You don't think these four are infectious . . ."

"No. But, given what they're doing, they're fanatics—or just plain nuts," Lucas said. "Taos is a tourist town. You've got people here from all over the country, and probably all over the world . . ."

"We do," Mellon agreed.

"If these guys see that they're about to get busted, they could deliberately break open these tubes, these vials that they're carrying, to try to infect anyone who gets close," Lucas said. "If they do that, and those infected people are allowed to go . . . wherever, to travel through hub airports, the situation could get completely out of control."

Mellon ran one hand through his thinning hair. "So what . . ."

"They can't be allowed to do that," Rae said. "I don't know exactly how to put this, but . . . if you see them . . ."

"Kill them," Lucas said. "If you can. Don't give them a chance. Then stand back, way back. Ideally, we'd locate the four of them, and take them all out at once. If they've separated, and they may have, all trying to get out in different ways, then we may have to take them one at a time. Kill them one at a time."

"Man, is that even legal?" Mellon asked, wide-eyed.

"We don't know. We're doing the best we can," Rae said. "We've killed one of them, we've captured three more sick people, we've seized some of these vials supposedly full of virus. They're on their way to Fort Detrick's virus lab to get looked at . . . but we're cutting across a lot of legalities."

Lucas: "It's like this. A guy is standing in an auditorium full of people and he's holding a bomb that will kill everyone in the place. You've got a sniper. Do you kill him before he can trigger it? Or do you call a judge to discuss the legalities?"

Mellon nodded: "Pull the trigger. All right, what do you want us to do?"

LUCAS: "I DON'T know what I want you to do, because I don't know anything about Taos. And I'm not really great at organizing big groups of people, anyway. Rae could do it, but we need her on the street. *You* need to figure this out. You need to get a couple of your best guys in here and figure out what's possible with what you have."

"We can do that," Mellon said. "After I talked to that Billy Greet person, I got most of the force headed over to city hall, next door."

While Lucas and Rae waited, Mellon called a sergeant and a patrol officer, both off duty but on the way to city hall, and told them to get to his office as quickly as they could. Mellon's two selected cops showed up in less than ten minutes. One was wearing shorts and a tee-shirt, the other still in uniform.

They were briefed and they both agreed that what the marshals wanted them to do to the other town cops was crappy: the one named Tom was most reluctant to go along.

Lucas: "If we tell them what the real situation is, some of them will try to get their families out of town. Their families will want to get other friends out, and pretty soon we'll have a panic and people will be running all over the place, trying to get out of town on four-wheelers and probably airplanes and even walking out."

The cops looked at each other, and one nodded.

Lucas: "That'll make it a lot easier for these assholes to get out. If they get out, then it's possible that all those people will wind up dead. Along with the rest of us."

"This is like the hydrogen bomb of diseases," Rae said. "People will try to run, but it won't help."

"If we do this, we won't be able to work with our guys anymore, they won't trust us," the one named Louis said.

"If this works out, you won't have a problem. If it doesn't work out, you *really* won't have a problem, because there's about an eighty percent chance that you'll be dead," Lucas said.

"I don't even believe that," Tom said.

"You know who does believe it?" Rae asked. "The President. If you want us to do it, we might be able to set up you guys to talk with him. But that would be like, tomorrow. Right now, we need you to help organize the rest of the police force and find these people."

"You don't even know that they're here," Tom said.

"If they're not, then we're really and truly screwed," Lucas said. "But we think they are."

The two eventually agreed to go along, which was a relief, because the rest of the police force was already waiting in the city hall.

Mellon said to the two cops, "All right: how do we do this?" and Lucas and Rae stepped back.

IF THEY'D TRIED to stop the gang in almost any other city, they would have failed—but Taos could be jammed up. Only a single highway went north, and that was already blocked. To the west was the gorge of the Rio Grande, an unpassable canyon except at the Gorge Bridge and another obscure bridge several miles downriver, both of which could be easily blocked. To the east were the Sangre de Christos, with only a single highway going across the mountains, also easily blocked.

Things got more complicated going south, but the number of realistic exits from Taos could be jammed with fewer than a dozen state police and Taos cop cars, and the state police already had all of them covered, and were enhancing the checkpoints with traps—a hidden state police car would let traffic go through, but if any approached a checkpoint and then tried to turn back before they got to the checkpoint, they'd be run down and pulled over.

To avoid the possibility of panic—that most of the Taos cops would try to evacuate their families if they were told about the virus—Mellon and the other two cops agreed to go with the serial killer story, enhanced to create a Charles Manson–type gang of four people, two men and two women. The cops would be told that the gang would try to flee Taos and had to be stopped before they got to larger cities where they could vanish in the crowds. All the cops would have photos of the three known faces.

Once all the exits from Taos were solidly jammed up, the remaining cops would be placed at key intersections, checking vehicles, while others called around town, setting up a network of trusted people who would be asked to contact more well-known and trusted townspeople to ask about strangers hiding out in a car, or holed up in a house, or visiting friends.

"They're going to have to eat, no matter where they are. From what you guys say, two of them must know that we have their faces, so they'll have to have food brought in by the other two," Mellon said. "We know one of those faces, but they won't know that we know. I'm thinking we have to cover stores, supermarkets, gas stations, take-out places . . ."

"And we have to get them to move . . . make them think that they can, and make them think that they have to," Lucas said.

"How are we going to do that?" Mellon asked.

"Tomorrow morning, we go public with the serial killing gang," Lucas said. "Get Scott's and Catton's faces out there, on TV, on the internet. We won't tell the media that we have that third face, hoping that they'll send him out to scout around . . ."

"We don't deal much with TV reporters up here," Mellon said.

"The woman who's coordinating this whole thing is a big shot in the Department of Homeland Security—she can handle the media," Lucas said.

Tom, the uniformed skeptic, said, "I'm starting to believe you guys. You got three alive but maybe dying?"

"We do," Rae said. "If you'd seen their faces—they look like they're . . . rotting. Rotting alive. If you'd seen that, you'd believe for sure."

WHEN THEY'D HAMMERED OUT what they thought was the best available plan, they moved over to the city hall wing to brief the rest of the police force. Mellon introduced Lucas and Rae, and Rae made the basic pitch, while Mellon gave out assignments, with alerts and ideas to come back to Mellon, Tom, and Louis, who would pass the word back to Lucas and Rae.

If any of the four fugitives were spotted, they were not to be approached: that would be left to the marshals. When asked why, Rae explained that they needed to take all four of them, and if they'd separated, and one was spotted, that one might lead the marshals to the others.

"These are the worst people you can imagine," Rae told the gathered cops. "No matter how long you're cops, you'll never meet anyone worse. If they try to resist, we'll kill them."

The chill in her voice got the cops glancing at each other; some of them, Lucas thought, were figuring out that something was going on, and that they didn't know what it was, but it wasn't serial killers.

An hour after they'd arrived in Taos, Lucas and Rae watched the Taos cops streaming out of the place, heading for their assignments.

Lucas, watching them, muttered, "This is fucked up."

"It's what we got," Rae said. "We ain't got no more."

THEY UPDATED GREET, who told them that the first batch of samples from the ski valley were at Detrick, and the lab was taking them apart. Letty called, told them about the possible grave in Lamy, and that they were heading to the Holiday Inn.

Lucas told her what was happening in Taos. "It's gonna be a mess."

"Of course it is," she said. "I'm going out to the grave site tomorrow; they're sending some of the Detrick people out there with us."

"Hold your breath," Lucas said. And, with a certain tone, "You better get some sleep."

She said, "Yeah, I'll do that."

Lucas: "I knew that goddamn Hawkins was up to something."

"Shut up."

Rae started giggling, the first time Lucas had ever heard her do that, and he finally said, "Rae . . ."

She hiccuped, and said, "I can't help it . . ."

THEY WENT OUT on the streets.

Nightfall made everything worse. Crowded streets, glaring lights, arguments at checkpoints, families with kids who had no place to stay.

Lucas and Rae separated, moving between checkpoints, talking to the cops, chatting with civilians on the street.

Too many of them were tourists who were trying to get out of town and determined to do that. And too many were allowed to leave, in Lucas's opinion, judgment calls by the cops. The cops were careful, but they only needed to make one mistake.

As he was walking between checkpoints, he took a call from Underwood. "We've covered Turney's body, we're keeping the captives in the bus until we can get a full decontamination crew here, which should be here by tomorrow morning. Danny and I are going to head down the hill in case we're needed there in Taos."

"Good. If they're here, we'll need you. Bring one of those docs and those white suits, just in case."

LUCAS AND RAE ran into each other at a midtown checkpoint, and Rae said, "Feels hopeless."

The words had no more than gotten out of her mouth when Lucas took a call from Mellon, who asked, "Where are you?" and when Lucas looked up at the street signs and told him, the chief said, "We got a solid hit. You're about six blocks away . . ."

They got directions and jogged the six blocks to a checkpoint with a line of cars waiting to go through. One of them, a Chevy Equinox with a Hertz look to it, had been pulled out of line, and a man and a woman were standing next to it, with a cop.

When Lucas and Rae came up, the cop said to the couple, "Federal marshals . . ." and turned a thumb to the couple and said to Lucas and Rae, "These folks are from New York . . . they got a place in Telluride and came down for the week . . ."

The woman said, "David and Niki Levy. We had an Airbnb place and were leaving to go back to Telluride . . ."

Her husband took it up, the words tumbling out: ". . . and we saw this couple walking down the street and they asked us if we knew where the Smith's supermarket was, and we did, and we told them where . . ."

Niki Levy: ". . . When we got to the checkpoint this police officer showed us the pictures and the man . . . I mean, we saw him. It was him. Oh my God, it was him for sure . . ."

David Levy: "No doubt about it, it was the guy we talked to. They're going over to Smith's. This was ten minutes ago."

Rae: "What did the woman look like?"

Niki Levy: "My height, maybe . . . middle thirties? Blondish . . . dishwater."

David Levy: "Thin, white blouse, jeans . . . Nice looking, I guess, maybe a little tough, tattoos, like she might know about Harleys."

Lucas asked the cop, "How far are we from Smith's?"

"Two or three minutes if you run; one minute in the car. You gotta cross a highway . . ."

"We'll run," Rae said, "We don't want a cop car around if we can avoid it . . . Point us . . ."

The cop pointed and they began running, the Levys and the cop looking after them. On the way, Rae said, "Go in separately."

"Yeah."

"Pull your shirt out," she said. "I can see your gun."

"Yeah."

"If they're together, I'll be looking at the woman. If they don't spot us as cops, we could trail them . . ."

"Okay. Slow down for a few seconds before we go in," Lucas said. "Catch our breaths . . ."

They caught a break in the traffic and ran across the highway; the parking lot was crowded with cars and pickups, and they kept as many as they could between them and the supermarket's front windows.

Rae: "You okay?"

"Yeah. I'm going in."

Lucas took a breath, walked through the door and turned to the right.

Foss was right there, just through the checkout counter, holding two big brown grocery sacks. He locked eyes with Lucas and dropped the sacks and shouted, "No!"

17

Darkness inside made it worse.

Scott, Catton, Foss, and Callister were lying on bare mattresses in the two bedrooms, or sometimes sitting in a circle on the living room chairs and carpet, afraid to let any light hit a window, in a house that was supposed to be empty. The only illumination, in a shut-up bedroom with a blanket over the only window, came from a laptop screen, and it wasn't enough. They hadn't had anything to eat except two shared power bars, and the stress from the flight down the mountain, along with hunger, cranked the anxiety.

Foss had gotten online through an unprotected Wi-Fi at a neighbor's house. A website told them that the Smith's supermarket closed at midnight. After some talk, they decided the best time to shop would be between nine and ten o'clock—late enough that there'd be fewer people around, but not so few that they'd be memorable.

"They must have my face and Clarice's too," Scott told Foss and Callister. "You two should walk over, get enough food for a couple of days."

"I could drive over in my car," Callister said. She added, "If they don't have our names, my Oregon license is still good . . ."

"Better to walk," Scott said. "They'll be going over every car; there'll be checkpoints everywhere. And if you're both in the car, and if they know one of you . . ."

"Okay."

"And get some water, and maybe some bottled tea," Catton said.

"Stay together, hold hands. Look like a couple, taking a stroll. That's less suspicious than a lone guy walking in the dark," Scott said. He was making it up as he went along. "Separate just before you get to the store—if they're watching the store, and they stop one of you, the other might have a chance to call us and let us know. Or get away clean."

"Do we take our flasks with us?" Callister asked.

Scott said, "Not in the safe boxes. Use the fanny packs."

"The fanny packs were supposed to be . . . an attack thing," Foss said.

Scott: "I think we're there, Randy. If a cop approaches one of you in the store, if you know you're done, break the flasks. Maybe something will come of it. A supermarket late at night . . . we'd get a few people, and with any luck, some of them would be leaving town."

Foss: "The viral footprint . . ."

"Would be small, but the Covid footprint was small to begin with. The Chinese became aware of a few people with pneumonia, and from there . . . boom."

Callister: "Boom."

THEY LAY AROUND, talking sporadically, Scott did some pushups, Foss joined in, and Callister started rattling along about death.

She said, "I thought I might die if we did this. I thought I might be killed by angry people, in revenge. I thought I might die from the vaccine. I didn't care. But then I got through the vaccine, and I feel good, better than I've felt in years. Now I don't want to die."

"The vaccine works! The vaccine works! You have had Marburg, the exact same form that's in the flasks," Catton said. "If we can get it out, you'll live in a world that's been saved, instead of one that's doomed."

"I know, I know . . . I wasn't scared when I thought I might die, but now I am. I can't help it," Callister said. She'd wrapped her arms around her knees and shivered.

Scott, on the floor, rolled up on his side, propped his head with one hand, and said, "This project . . . our project . . . is the most important thing in the world. Right now, the four of us, here on this carpet, are the most important people in the world. If we're successful, people will try to hunt us down and kill us, but there'll still *be* people. If we fail, a hundred years from now, or two hundred years . . . the planet will be a barren rock."

"I don't actually believe that," Foss said. They all looked at him, and Catton tilted her head as if she couldn't believe what she'd heard. "What?"

"If we don't do this," Foss said, "We'll experience a great extinction . . ."

"We already are—the extinction is underway," Catton said.

"Yes, I *do* believe that," Foss said. "But as the planet begins to die, the chaos among humanity will be much worse than anything *we're* planning. There'll be wars, there'll be plagues, mass starvation, the systems will break down and maybe we'll get knocked back to the Stone Age. Or maybe not the Stone Age. Maybe the steam age. Or 1950. Then again, maybe Lionel is right about humanity—it might go extinct. I personally think there will be survivors. People. Even if the worst happens, and humans disappear, I believe there'll be life in the oceans. Whales, sharks, fish. There'll be plants, and insects, maybe enough mammals to give the world a new start. I mean, humanity may or may not end, but I don't think the planet will. I don't think it'll be a barren rock. I think Gaia will have enough left to . . . regenerate."

Scott: "You hope. We all hope."

Foss: "Yes. I hope what we're doing is saving humanity along with the rest of the world, so that humanity will have learned the lesson: you don't kill Gaia. You preserve it at all costs."

"I believe all that, but I still don't want to die. Here on the floor, I feel like a hunted animal. Like a rabid dog," Callister said, and a tear trickled down a cheek.

"Are you sorry you got in?" Scott asked. He simply sounded curious, rather than angry or resigned.

"No, no, I got in and I'll stay in. But there are some . . . regrets."

"Yes, of course there are," Scott said. "If there weren't, you'd be insane."

FOSS AND CALLISTER planned to walk to the store between nine and ten but wound up leaving a little after eight o'clock because they couldn't stand being in the house any longer. Couldn't handle the desultory talk, the darkness.

When they were gone, Catton said, "They'll be okay."

"If the police don't have their photos," Scott said. "When I was at Fort Detrick, I talked to intelligence people from time to time. I was astonished at the level of surveillance the American government has developed—and I was told that the UK government is several steps further down that road. I lost touch out there in the refugee camps. I didn't know how far things had gotten."

"That somebody broke into my house . . . and so quickly. I can't imagine how they did that," Catton said.

FOSS AND CALLISTER held hands as they walked to the supermarket. That felt unnatural, because they were the two members of the group who were furthest apart in temperament. Callister was impulsive and emotional and intuitive, somebody who was headed for a cult, Foss thought. Callister saw Foss as a cold, calculating, overly rational, overly intellectual computer nerd. They had one thing in common: they both needed a hand to hold on to, so they did that.

The street they were on was rough, broken blacktop with potholes filled with gravel when they were filled at all. And it was dark, the street narrow with trees hanging low overhead. They had to make two turns to get out to the main street. Five minutes from the hideout, they encountered an athletic-looking gray-haired man and a slender dark-haired woman loading luggage into a car. Foss asked, "You guys wouldn't know where Smith's market is, would you?"

"Sure, we've been there." The man nodded and pointed: "You go straight ahead to the highway, it's right on the other side. Can't miss it. Maybe a five-minute walk."

Callister smiled and said, "Thanks. The streets here are so confusing."

"Not going to get better," the woman said. She had what Callister thought of as an East Coast accent. "There's something going on. The police have all the roads blocked going out of town. I'm told they interview every single person before they let you out, and they've got wanted poster and pictures, and it's taking forever."

"Hope it's not something awful, some criminal on the loose," Callister said. She hugged herself and pretended to shiver.

"But it's bound to be," the man said.

FOSS AND CALLISTER said goodbye and strolled away. When they were out of earshot from the couple, Foss took out a phone and called Scott: "We talked to a couple trying to get out of town, but they said the police have all the exits blocked with checkpoints and they're looking at faces."

"All right. Don't bump into a checkpoint. You don't want them seeing you running away."

Foss shut the phone down and a minute later they got to the highway and saw the supermarket across the street. Foss said, "Look."

Callister looked to her left; a half-mile away, at another traffic light, they could see a cluster of cop cars with the light bars flashing, and a two-block line of cars trying to get through.

"Gotta get across," Foss said, dropping Callister's hand. "I'll slow walk—you go on ahead. Stay away from me inside."

THEY GOT A green light and crossed the highway, Callister walking ahead. She went inside, tried not to look around too much, but saw a dozen shoppers around the cash registers, more moving in the back. They hadn't talked too much about what she should buy, but since they had no power, and were operating in the dark, they were essentially camping out.

She put a three-dollar burlap shopping bag in her cart, to make it easy to carry heavier loads. Okay, what would she take on a camping trip that was reasonably healthy and vegetarian? She shopped carefully, bought bottles of coffee, ready-to-eat carrots and apples and oranges, sourdough bread, honey spread, cheese and crackers, peanut butter and jelly . . . and a Covid mask for Catton . . .

She was moving slowly through the store, hyperaware of the sounds around her, voices, anything that might be an alarm—she heard nothing like that—and slowly began to loosen up.

Foss came in a minute behind Callister, moving fast. He saw Callister down one aisle, and avoided her, hurrying on, throwing a variety of no-cook food in his shopping cart: bananas, grapes, packs of sliced cheddar, pepper jack and Swiss cheese, three boxes of crackers, sliced deli chicken and sliced ham, mustard, potato chips, peanut butter and bread, bottled tea and bottled water, a box of plastic knives.

Five minutes in the store and he headed toward the check-out counters. The cashier was a little slow, and he tried not to show his impatience. When it was all totaled up, he handed the cashier two fifty-dollar bills, got change, picked up the paper shopping bags, and turned toward the exit.

The cops were right there.

He instantly recognized them for what they were, a big guy, blue eyes on him, a black woman behind him, the black woman already with a gun in her hand.

He shouted "No!" and dropped the bags and reached around his hip for the fanny pack and the glass vials of liquid virus media.

The white cop shouted "Hands! Show me hands!" and reached inside his jacket . . .

But Foss went for the fanny pack and dragged it around his hip and yanked on the Velcro strip that kept it closed, and the ripping sound that it made as he pulled it open was the last thing he heard in his life . . .

Because Rae shot him in the head.

CALLISTER WAS LOOKING at yogurt when she heard a man scream "No!" and she was at an angle to the check-out counters and she twisted that way and saw a picture that froze in her mind, a tableau of Foss and a check-out woman and three or four other people and two of them were looking at Foss who reached for his fanny pack . . .

A black woman shot Foss in the head and Foss threw up his hands and went down and a heavy-set checkout lady jerked toward Callister and Callister saw that her face was covered with what must have been Foss's blood . . .

A woman screamed "Shooter!" and then somebody yelled something else and people began screaming and running through the store and a man shouted "Active shooter!"

There was another shot, and then another, and without even

thinking about it, Callister picked up her bag and stumbled toward the back of the store, the heavy bag banging on her hip, where a store employee in a blue apron spread his hands and bellowed, "What the hell?" and Callister screamed "Shooter, active shooter!" and the employee turned and ran through a swinging door into the back and she followed, saw an outdoor light and went that way. She dropped off a loading dock and ran into the dark . . .

"NO!"

Lucas saw Foss drop the bags and realized that the other man was going for a fanny pack and that the pack contained either the virus vials or a gun, and he went for his gun but Rae, who was a step behind him, already had her weapon up and she stepped to the left and fired and Foss went down.

People began screaming *Shooter!* and Lucas went for his ID and badge case and began shouting "U.S. Marshals, U.S. Marshals," and Rae joined in, "U.S. Marshals," but the store had dissolved in chaos with people screaming, and a man came out of the water aisle holding a pistol in both hands and Rae shouted, "Gun!" and Lucas swiveled toward the man with his badge and shouted "Marshal" but the man pulled the trigger on his gun and it jumped in his hand, the bullet missing everything, and Rae shot him in the chest and he went down.

Lucas said, "Ah, shit!"

Rae: "Who is he, who is he?"

"Don't know . . ." He ran toward the wounded man with Rae still shouting, "U.S. Marshals, U.S. Marshals," and Lucas knelt over the man, who looked at him with eyes gone hazy gray and Lucas kicked the man's semi-auto across the aisle. The wounded man was wearing an overshirt on top of an olive drab tee-shirt that said, "FREEDOM" in block letters. Lucas pulled the overshirt open and looked for a fanny pack—or anything—and found nothing.

He punched up the police chief on his cell phone: "We've got two down at the Smith's supermarket, one dead, one wounded. We need an ambulance here RIGHT NOW!"

Rae, with her gun in her hand, stooped over the dead man, Foss, reached back into a hip pocket and produced a switchblade and cut the fanny pack strap that went around the dead man's waist. She saw no signs of wetness, liquid, on the outside of the fanny pack, and pulled it free of the body and left it on the floor.

The screaming had stopped although there were people in the parking lot calling back and forth, and two cop cars rolled up to the store and the cops hurried inside.

Rae called to them, "We've got a wounded man, we need to transport him . . . ambulance coming?"

"Called for one, should be here in a minute," a cop said. "What should we do?"

Lucas was still kneeling next to the wounded man and a woman poked her head around a corner of the aisle and asked, "Are you really a marshal?"

"Yes."

"I'm a doctor. Should I look at this man?"

"That'd be great," Lucas said.

She did, then shook her head and said, "Better wait for the ambulance. Can't help him here. Don't think he'll die. What'd he do?"

"He was a hero," Lucas said, looking down at the man, a hand-sized puddle of purple blood leaking out from under his shoulder. "Unfortunately for all of us."

CALLISTER, IN A panic, kept running until she couldn't run anymore, unaware of the bag hooked over her arm, though it was heavy, and when a side-stitch finally slowed her down, gasping for air, she put the bag on the street and took out her phone and called Scott.

Scott answered instantly, but she found it hard to speak, and she said, "Minute . . . minute . . . gimme a minute . . ."

Then, "Randy was shot in the store, he'd dead! I think he's dead, he was shot in the head! I ran. Whatever phone he called you on, you should get rid of it."

"Ah, no. Are you sure?"

"I saw him get shot! I saw blood all over a woman's face! Yes! I'm sure."

Scott said, "You are unbelievably brave. To get out and warn us. Can you get back here?"

"Yes. But the phone . . ."

"Do you have enough light to take the battery out of your phone?"

"Uh, I think so, there's a streetlight . . ."

"Take the battery out, then bury the phone, if you can. Doesn't have to be deep, but underground so nobody can stumble over it."

"I can do that."

"Do it. I'm destroying this phone, now!"

THE SUPERMARKET WAS empty, except for Lucas, Rae, and one of the cops. Lucas looked down at the fanny pack that Rae had dragged off Foss's body and said to Rae, "We gotta look. We gotta know if any of that shit got out, if we might have a problem. You should back up."

"I could . . ."

"Rae, back off."

She backed away.

Using a plastic knife from a box that Foss had in his grocery sack, Lucas lifted the flap on the fanny pack. He could see the tops of five of the test-tube shaped vials. "Looks intact," he said.

He used a pack of cheese slices to pin the top of the fanny pack to the floor, and eased out one of the vials, still using the plastic knife, and then the others. None of them were broken. He could see a pinkish liquid inside the tubes.

He exhaled, stood up: "I think we're okay."

18

Lucas called Greet and told her that Foss was dead and that he hadn't released the virus. "He was buying a lot of food, enough for four, so now we know that they're still here."

"Okay, okay. We might have some leads that will get us to the woman we haven't identified. The NSA is analyzing the phone calls of all the people whose names we know, looking for a woman they've all called and who suddenly stopped using her phone, and who might have been involved in Gaia stuff. They tell me they've got a candidate and they're looking for photographs."

"Need them as soon as you can get them," Lucas said. "We've got a store video, but Foss and the woman he was with apparently split up before Foss walked into the store. From the commotion after the shooting, she probably knows he's dead. The couple who spotted them in the street said they were holding hands, so . . . If you can get me a face, I might be able to confirm it, if she came into the store before or after he did."

"I'll push it. Our sniper is on the ground on her way to Santa Fe, she should be hooking up with Letty any time now."

"Have Letty send her up here tomorrow morning. I don't think much more is going to happen tonight, though the cops will keep the pressure on."

LETTY AND HAWKINS had just gotten out of the shower at the Holiday Inn when someone began banging on the door. Hawkins looked out the peephole and saw a magnified turquoise eye looking back at him. The owner of the eye stepped back and resolved into a tough-looking young woman who said, loud enough to be heard through the door, "Open up."

Letty: "That's Barbara."

Hawkins, buck-ass naked, cracked the door, still on the chain, peered out and said, "We're indisposed."

Cartwright: "How indisposed?"

"Somewhat. I'm without any clothing whatsoever."

"Sounds interesting, but not compelling. Anyway, I'm going down to an IHOP."

"What's an IHOP?"

"Pancakes."

From the bed, Letty called, "Barb: we'll come with you. We're starving. Go brush your teeth or something. Comb your hair. Clip your fingernails."

"I'll wait. Impatiently. Knock on my door. I'm in 212."

THEIR HAIR WAS still damp ten minutes later when Letty and Hawkins knocked on Cartwright's door. When Cartwright answered, she had a wicked-looking rifle in her hands. She turned back to the bed and gently placed it in a hard-sided rifle case. "Making sure it hadn't got bumped," she said. And, looking at Hawkins, "Who's the guy?"

Letty introduced Hawkins, explained the MI5 connection.

"Sounds like you guys weren't letting any grass grow under your feet, relationship-wise," Cartwright said.

Letty: "Should I mention your LA courtship?"

"Not entirely necessary," Cartwright said. And to Hawkins, "Does everybody call you 'the Hawk?'"

"Actually, nobody does, but I like it," Hawkins said. And he repeated the words a few times, as if tasting them. "Hi, I'm . . . the Hawk. Hello, Hawk here."

"Shut up, Hawk," Letty said, as they walked down to the elevators. "This has been a day."

Cartwright: "Yeah? Shoot anyone?"

Letty gave her a quick "Don't go there" headshake and said, "Uh, Alec did. He's having a little trouble with it."

"Perhaps more than a little," Hawkins said.

"Well, man, I'm sorry," Cartwright said. "What were the choices?"

"None," Letty said. "You know the story so far?"

"Your Billy Greet caught me up on most of it," Cartwright said. "She didn't mention that Alec was the shooter this afternoon."

"It was a woman, and she was unarmed, middle-aged, and very close," Hawkins said. "I shot her with an M4. In the heart."

Cartwright: "Yeah, well, that happens. Better with a gun than a knife, where she takes fifteen minutes to suffer and bleed out while you're sitting around reading your iPhone. Gun's quicker."

"Jesus, Barb, take it easy," Letty said.

"That's okay, I've heard the talk, in Afghanistan. I just wasn't the . . . subject of it," Hawkins said.

Cartwright asked him where he'd been in Afghanistan, and when he told her, mentioned that she'd passed through the same base a couple of times. "I sorta came, and then I went."

"Having solved somebody's problems," Letty said.

"Sometimes," Cartwright said. "Not all the time."

CARTWRIGHT DROVE THEM to the IHOP, which she'd spotted while checking out the territory around the hotel; she'd checked the territory around the hotel because she always did that. At the IHOP, they got menus and Hawkins asked, "Are link sausages the same as bangers?"

"More or less," Cartwright said. "I'd recommend the blueberry pancakes, but I'd also stay away from the whipped cream. And what's this about a body out in the weeds?"

They spent an hour in the booth, talking and eating; Letty and Hawkins were famished, and expected the next day to be as rough.

"We have at least four people out there, probably in Taos, but not a clue to exactly where, or what they might be doing," Letty said. "What scares everyone is the possibility that they've already turned the virus loose."

"If they have, we'll hunt down every one of them before we die," Hawkins said.

"If that ain't a fact, God's a possum," Cartwright said, poking a fork at him.

Hawkins frowned, turned to Letty for a translation, who said, "She's from Texas."

THEY WERE GETTING ready to leave when Greet called: "Rae and Lucas killed another one of them, the Foss guy. He was buying a lot of food at a supermarket, too much for one guy. He was in the store alone but was seen earlier with a young woman with tattoos, so we're pretty sure they're all in Taos. We know Foss and the woman walked to the supermarket and we know one place they passed as they were walking, so we're narrowing down search parameters."

"Then we all need to get up there," Letty said. "Our state cop can show the Detrick guys where the body might be in Lamy. That doesn't seem as time-crucial."

"I agree. Get some sleep, and get up there early as you can," Greet said.

When they'd ended the call, Cartwright said, "Sunrise is a little after six. Let's get up at six, get up there by seven-thirty or eight." She knew when sunrise was, because she always knew that, and where to sit so the sun wouldn't be in her eyes, or reflecting off the objective lens of her scope.

"See you at six o'clock," Letty said. "Maybe we can hit the IHOP again."

BEFORE LETTY AND Hawkins got in bed, Letty called Lucas and when he answered, said, "Just getting ready for bed. Billy says you guys killed Foss."

"Yeah. We're still there, at the scene. A supermarket. We're waiting for Underwood and the Detrick crew to show up and handle the body."

"We're coming up early tomorrow," Letty said. "Should be there by eight. We'll let the Detrick team figure out if there's a body buried in Lamy."

"All right. We've got more marshals coming in from Louisiana. Should be here any time."

"Excellent. We need all the help we can get."

"Let me talk to the MI5 guy for a minute," Lucas said.

"Hang on," Letty said, and she handed the phone to Hawkins.

He said, "I'm here."

"Yeah, that's what I was worried about," Lucas said. "See you tomorrow morning. Sleep tight."

He clicked off and Letty smiled at Hawkins: "He can't help himself. He's a cop."

"He's teasing me now, is what he's doing."

"What did you think of Barb?"

"Just that."

"What?"

"She's a barb. You know, like a sharp, steel, well-curved harpoon." He paused, then said, "However, not totally unattractive."

"Yeah, tell me about it. She's sleeping with the best-looking computer genius in Los Angeles."

"That sounds like a story."

"It is, but we're not allowed to tell it."

AS LETTY AND Hawkins drifted off to sleep, Scott, Catton, and Callister were working through the same analyses that the cops had gone through.

"I don't know exactly how they got Randy's ID and photo, but I'd bet that cell phones were involved somehow," Scott said. "Damn it all, I didn't see this happening. We should have gone to Dallas or Los Angeles to do the vaccines. We didn't need the isolation up at the ski valley. We could have done an Airbnb in a major city and if trouble showed up, we could have gone right out to the airport . . . or driven to another major airport. No way to seal off Los Angeles or Dallas."

"Water under the bridge," Catton said.

"What do we do now?" Callister asked.

"You got out of the store, so they apparently don't know your face yet. But they will, and soon," Scott said. "I can see them doing facial recognition runs on the supermarket surveillance video, and phone analyses of calls that we all made to you and comparing the faces that come up with the cell phone numbers. That must be how they identified Rose and Randy."

"Danielle should run," Catton said, looking at Scott. "The Santa Fe airport only goes to about three places, but they're all major airports—Phoenix, Dallas, Denver. If she can crack a vial in the airport, the virus could make it to three hubs. If she can get down to the Albuquerque airport, she's got that ticket for Dallas early tomorrow."

Scott: "I agree."

Callister: "What if they don't know my face, but they know my car from the ski place?"

Scott: "Then . . . You'll know at the checkpoint. They'll be all over you. Put one of the vials between your feet on the floor of the car. If they jump you, crush it with your foot. Then surrender. Put your hands in the air. You'll be okay, but you'll infect everyone who handles you."

Callister dropped her face, looking between her legs, said, "Oh, God."

Catton said to Scott, "The cars might be a problem, but this house is for sure. Randy and Danielle were seen, what, six blocks from here? When they talked to the couple on the street?"

Scott: "Yes, but, where'd we go?"

"To Marilyn's," Catton said. Marilyn Wong was the Realtor who offered to rent them the house. "We know she lives alone. She's single and her own boss . . . maybe nobody will expect to see her tomorrow. She lives at the other end of town, and she'll have a car . . ."

Scott looked at her: "We'd have to kill her."

Catton said, "Listen to yourself. Why are we even here?"

Scott licked his lip, then nodded. He turned to Callister: "Danielle. You think . . . you could do this? Make the run to Santa Fe and Albuquerque in your car? If they don't know your face, they probably don't know the car."

"You mean . . . right this minute? I'm pretty fucked up right now."

Scott: "I don't know if it's true, but I've always read that the body's lowest time in the day, the time when it's least alert, is between three and five o'clock in the morning. That's when we send you out."

Callister nodded and said, "All right. Go at three o'clock. I'll go with you to Marilyn's."

THEY TOOK EVERYTHING they had—food, luggage—and loaded it back into Callister's Subaru. Scott said, "Get the gun out," but Catton answered, "Can't shoot her. Her neighborhood's too dark and quiet. Somebody would call the police . . . give me one minute."

She walked out the back door and came back with a rock the size of her fist. "I saw it when we looked at the house. There's a little stone johnnie out there."

Callister: "I used to make those, when I was hiking up in the Cascades."

"What's a stone johnnie?" Scott asked, puzzled.

"A little stack of stones that people put up to mark waypoints along wilderness trails," Callister said. "Now people just put them in their yards."

"All right, I've seen those," Scott said. "But what are you planning to do with a rock?"

"I'll threaten her with the gun, tie her up. If she tries to fight or scream, hit her with the rock."

MARILYN WONG LIVED in another of the ubiquitous adobe-look houses in a neighborhood at the north end of Taos. They stuck to backstreets going over, and saw two checkpoints at a distance. Wong's house was distinguished by an extensive flower garden with masses of multicolored zinnias and a dozen dinner-plate-sized sunflowers.

"Let me lead," Catton said. She led the way up the front walkway with her stone and pushed a lighted doorbell button. A moment later, a woman's voice, from a speaker next to the door: "Who is it?"

"Marilyn, I'm terribly sorry to bother you at this time of night, but this is Clarice Catton. I came to talk to you with Dr. Scott about renting a house. We've run into a really difficult situation and we thought you might have some ideas . . ."

The door popped open and Wong, dressed in a pair of black silk pajamas, said, "I understand the police . . ."

What she understood, the group never found out, because Catton struck her in the forehead with the rock, a sound like a sack of sand being dropped off a ladder. Wong collapsed on her back. Catton stepped over her, stooped and hit her twice more, and was about to hit her a fourth time when Scott caught her arm and said, "Clarice . . . enough."

He pushed past Catton, bent over Wong, whose head was misshapen like a deflated volleyball. He felt for a pulse in her neck and shook his head. He looked back at Catton, whose eyes were glittering like a leopard's, and it occurred to him, not for the first time, that Catton was mad as a hatter. Mad in a medical sense: something far beyond the rational or calculated. "She's gone. Let's get inside."

They stepped inside, trailed by Callister, whose face had gone paper-white. Catton, her nose twitching with the scent of fresh blood, pulled a revolver out of her pocket and hurried through the house, making sure it was empty.

Scott and Callister watched her do it: it hadn't occurred to them it might be needed. When Catton came back, she said, "All clear," and "Marilyn was on her computer. It's still running, so we're online if we need to be."

"Okay. Great," Scott said. He went to one knee, lifted Wong's body in his arms, carried her to a family room—shook his head, they might want to watch television—then to a powder room, where he lay her on the floor, checked her pulse again, then backed away and closed the door.

To Callister, he said, "I'm sorry you had to see that."

"She needs to toughen up," Catton said. "We're not doing anything that's not necessary."

"She's fine as she is, she's a smart, sensitive human being," Scott said. He wrapped Callister in his arms, hugging her for a long ten seconds, whispered, "You are great," into her ear, then backed away and said, "Let's see if they're looking for us. The news should be on."

The news came out of Albuquerque, and the talking heads got to Taos ten seconds into the broadcast. "We are told that there's a major police action taking place in Taos, and that cars are being stopped at police checkpoints all around the town. According to a police officer we talked to, who didn't want to be named because he wasn't authorized to talk to the news media, they are searching for a man and a woman believed to be involved in a child sex ring, and that some of the children may have been murdered."

Photos of Scott and Catton came up.

"We don't yet have names for the people being sought, but police say that they are armed and dangerous. If you have seen either of these individuals, contact Taos police immediately by dialing 9-1-1. We will be enlarging on this breaking story as soon as we have further information."

Catton said, "Well, there goes my hair."

Scott said to Callister, "They don't have your photo."

"I should still go at three o'clock?"

"I believe that would be best."

THEY'D LEFT THE Subaru in the driveway, and now looked in the garage and found a blue Nissan SUV and a black Jeep with oversized tires. Catton backed the Nissan into the driveway, and Callister drove the Subaru into the garage, to get it off the street and out of sight.

When the garage door was down, Scott, unsure of what should come next, simply nodded when Catton said, "We should eat."

Scott and Catton poked at the vegetables and fruit and ready-to-eat vegetarian groceries in Callister's sack, then Scott looked in the refrigerator and found a mound of frozen microwave food, including chicken pot pies intended for an oven, and packs of microwave mushroom risotto. Catton had never cooked, she said, so Scott and Callister figured out Wong's oven, and put in two of the pot pies; the risotto would wait until the pies were done.

FOSS HAD BEEN designated to get razors and hair color from the supermarket, so they didn't have that. Catton went into the master bath, and found that Wong had pink disposable razors, the kind women use to shave their legs. Scott went to look, and when he came back, he found Callister on her hands and knees, cleaning up a blood puddle where Wong's head had landed on the floor.

"Oh, Lord, let me do that," he said.

"No, no, I got it," Callister said, scrubbing furiously. "I'll throw the paper towels in the garbage. Not that it'll make any difference to anyone."

"Do you think you could help Clarice shave her head? I don't think I'd be good at it," Scott said.

"I guess. But . . ." She shook her head.

"But what?"

"She enjoyed doing that. Killing Marilyn."

Scott said, "Clarice is . . . what she is. She's valuable and committed. We can't do this without her."

"Okay, but I'm right. She's crazier than a Marburg fruit bat. About the hair . . . the hair will take a while."

While the pot pies were cooking, Catton sat on a toilet with a towel around her neck and Callister used a pair of scissors to crop her hair to a half inch. There was some pulling that must have been painful, or at least annoying, but Catton was stoic, and sat without flinching.

She talked politics: ". . . the stupid shit approved that whole area for oil exploration, which is going to do nothing but encourage the people with the big SUVs and those ridiculous pickup trucks. How many trucks do you actually see that are hauling anything? You could buy a hybrid or an all-electric for half of the price of one of those trucks, and on the rare occasions you actually had to haul something, you could rent a truck. Save money all around, but your Bud Light boycotting asshole buddies would think you were gay or something, maybe a tranny . . ."

Callister agreed with that assessment, but shuddered every time she had to touch Catton, whose scalp seemed soft and wobbly and *nasty* to the touch, almost like a dead person's cheek. She was also moderately shocked at the words coming out of Catton's mouth; she was supposed to be some kind of aristocrat, but when Callister thought about it, she wasn't sure heiresses of tire-store chains were usually considered to be aristocrats. Maybe, she thought, Catton came on the language naturally.

WHEN THE HAIR was cropped all around Catton's head, they used shampoo as shaving cream and Callister managed to shave the rest of the hair without nicks or cuts. When they were finished, Catton used a washcloth to rinse her scalp, dried it, and then checked herself in the bathroom mirror.

"If I'd known I'd look like this, I'd have done it years ago," she said, approvingly. "My own parents wouldn't recognize me—not that my father ever recognized me anyway. He thought I was some annoying kid passing through the house."

"At least you had one, and you knew who he was," Callister said.

Catton went into Wong's bedroom and began rummaging through her chests of drawers, eventually coming up with two Hermès scarfs. "Who would have thought," she said, pleased.

When Scott called them from the kitchen, where he'd taken the pies from the oven and was microwaving the risotto for Callister, Catton walked in wearing one of the scarves and a black Covid mask. "I'm immune-suppressed: What do you think?"

"You don't look anything like Clarice Catton," Scott said. "It's strange, a complete transformation. If I were a police officer, I would look at that photograph, and then look at you, and see no resemblance whatever."

THEY GOT FOUR hours of sleep, woke to a cell phone alarm, started moving Callister to the Subaru, sputtered last minute instructions at her . . .

"I got it, I got it," Callister said. "Albuquerque to Dallas, and from Dallas to Charles De Gaulle and then, settle for a while. Lay down a patch in Albuquerque, two in Dallas, and whatever is left in Paris."

"One modification," Scott said, as he humped her suitcase out to the car. "If you get south, just outside Santa Fe you'll come to the bypass around the city, Highway 599. You'll see it, there are big signs. The 599 goes just a few blocks from the Santa Fe airport. Stop at the airport, go inside, like you're waiting for someone, lay down a patch outside the departure area, and then continue to Albuquerque. All the flights out of Santa Fe go to hub airports. If you can do that . . . that might be all we'd need. Then, just one in Dallas, in one of the domestic terminals. A gate for a Los Angeles flight, or New York, or Atlanta."

She nodded. "I can do that."

"I'm giving you two of the phones," Scott said. "We'll still have four. Use the gray phone first. I've called it, you can call me back by looking at the 'recents.'"

"Got it."

AT THREE-THIRTY, SHE was on the highway south. A mile or so out of town, she ran into a checkpoint, with thirty or forty cars waiting. She'd spent time in an earlier part of her life trying unsuccessfully to practice meditation as a way to reduce stress. For the next hour, she breathed in through her nose and out through her mouth, without noticeably reducing her stress levels.

When she was still five cars back, she took a call from Scott: "I don't know why we didn't think of this sooner, but you need to get out of New Mexico as quickly as possible. We checked American Airlines online, and there's a 6:24 flight to Dallas from Santa Fe. We made a reservation for you."

"I'm still not through the checkpoint," Callister said. "I'm still in Taos."

"How much longer before you go through?" Scott asked.

"Maybe ten or fifteen minutes? If I make it."

"You will, we have confidence in that. If you're through in ten minutes, you'll make it to Santa Fe in plenty of time for the plane. Wait until you're through security, then open one vial in Santa Fe, and save the others until you're in Dallas."

"All right. I'm moving up now, at the checkpoint. All the cars are getting through, but they're taking pictures."

"Call back when you're through."

WHEN SHE GOT to the checkpoint, formed by two state police cars with a ten-foot angled gap between them, a gruff New Mexico state cop asked for her driver's license and any other ID she might have. She dug around in her purse, produced her wallet and an Oregon driver's license and said, "I have a passport in my suitcase . . ."

"Where did you go with a passport?" the cop asked.

"I live in Portland . . . I go to Canada to ski, at Whistler."

"I thought you could get into Canada on your driver's license," the cop said.

"You can, but sometimes at the border they get pissy if you don't have a passport. Like you think they're some low-rent country," she said. "They really don't like us much up there."

The cop said, "I'd heard that," gave her a smile and handed her license back. She noticed another cop behind the one talking to her, taking a photo of her face with what looked like a sophisticated camera. “Go on through. Don’t hit my car.”

“Thank you,” she said, politely. She pulled through and in her rearview mirror saw the camera cop taking a picture of her license plate.

But then she was loose and running south.

Letty was having an annoying nightmare about going to see her putative boyfriend, Jackson Nyberg, the one she was on hiatus with. In the dream, she'd decided to tell him that their relationship was over.

The problem was, she couldn't get to the restaurant where they were supposed to meet, and talk. The dream included an insane series of mishaps involving lost office keys with her phone and purse locked inside the office, no-show Ubers, a taxi with a flat tire. During the whole ordeal, time was ticking down before Nyberg was leaving for somewhere else, far away, not specified in the nightmare.

Hawkins reached around her, groped for a breast, and used it as a kind of handle to half-roll her, and said into her nearly sleep-deaf ear, "You're kicking the life out of this bed."

"Wha . . ."

"You're kicking. You're having a nightmare."

"Oh. Yeah. Thanks."

Hawkins instantly went back to sleep because he could do that.

Letty, fighting off a recurrence of the nightmare, tried to think of something else, but kept coming back to the key question, *What was she going to tell Nyberg?* She thought about praying that Nyberg had met someone, and that he'd break up with her, but her ego wouldn't allow her to dream that. Then she imagined that Nyberg was killed in a tragic accident with a UPS truck, but . . . she didn't want him dead. Then . . .

Like an answer to a prayer, her phone rang. It wasn't Nyberg, it was Lucas and he was shouting at her: "Up! Get up!"

She sat up, poked Hawkins, and Hawkins pushed himself up to listen in.

Lucas's words were tumbling out, as if he had no time to say them: no time at all. "The woman's name is Danielle Callister. We have her photos. We've confirmed she was in the supermarket at the same time as Foss. When the Taos cops propagated the photos out to the checkpoints, they found out she went through a checkpoint at 4:40 this morning driving a green Subaru SUV. That's a little more than an hour ago. She was going south, toward Santa Fe. If that's her destination, she'll be there in half an hour. She could be headed for the Santa Fe airport, or maybe Albuquerque. If she's going anywhere other than Santa Fe, we can grab her, because she'll be on the road for a long time and we've got the make of the car and the license plate and time to set up roadblocks. We can't get anyone to the Santa Fe airport faster than you, because nobody down there has been briefed on the problem yet—to handle the possibility that she's carrying the virus, and what to do about that."

"We're going," Letty said.

"Take your iPad, I'm sending the photos we've got," Lucas said.

"We'll look for them."

She punched Lucas off and as Hawkins threw her clothes at her, called Cartwright: "Out of bed. Get your rifle. We're going. Five minutes, no more, gotta be out of here in five minutes."

"What . . . ?"

"Don't talk, just dress. Get the gun."

THEY RAN OUT of the motel five minutes later, Letty carrying Hawkins's nearly empty suitcase. They all piled into the same SUV, with Cartwright driving because she'd taken the Special Activities Division driving course. Along the way, Letty, in the back seat, extracted Cartwright's rifle, a long, monstrous camo'd weapon with an aluminum stock and stainless barrel that must have weighed fifteen pounds. She loaded it with Cartwright urging her not to touch the scope: "Don't touch it! Don't even breathe on it."

Letty snapped back, "Quiet! I know what I'm doing."

And then she laid out what they'd do when they got to the airport: "Go in slow. Fast right up to the airport, slow the last hundred yards. If she's there, we don't want her to see somebody coming in like it's a big emergency. Alec and I go in, carrying Alec's bag . . ."

"Ah, that's why you took the bag," Alec said. "Even smarter than I thought you were."

"Thanks a lot, Hawk."

"You were about to say . . ."

"We check out the waiting area, though she shouldn't be here yet. It's an hour and a half, more or less, from Taos to here, and that's in the daylight, and she's probably not driving fast, because she wouldn't want to risk being stopped by cops. So, we should be in time. Barb, I want you outside with a clear view of the front entrance."

Cartwright: "In the rifle case, the side zipper, check and see if there's a box of ear plugs and a sandbag, small sandbag . . ."

"Got 'em, got 'em."

"I'll park and set up to shoot from the back window if I have to, but that's not ideal. I'll get in the . . . holy fuck, get out of the way, you asshole . . ." She leaned on the horn. "Honest to God, give a guy a Porsche . . ."

"Don't tell that to Lucas," Letty said. "He's got two. You were saying . . ."

"I can shoot from the car if I have to, but I'd rather be high . . ." Cartwright glanced at Hawkins. "Got your gun?"

"Ah, no, it's in the room. I don't carry by default."

"It's okay, I've got mine," Letty said.

Lucas called again: "The airport opens at five for the early flights, so there'll be people there . . . How far out are you?"

"Two minutes. Barb's driving like a maniac."

"Good, that's good. How are you setting up?"

She told him about the sniper rifle and that she and Hawkins would go inside carrying the bag . . .

"You should have the photos. So. You got it, kid. Be safe as you can be. Don't let her pop the cork on any of those bottles."

LETTY CALLED UP the photos on her iPad, looked at them, then handed the iPad to Hawkins, who showed it to Cartwright, then passed it back to Letty.

They made the turn off Airport Road into the airport entrance road, past a junkyard full of wrecked cars. "You sure this is right?" Cartwright asked, "I don't see a control tower, I don't see shit, we're in some kind of slum . . ."

"Buildings up ahead . . ." Hawkins said.

"They look like machine sheds on my cousins' ranch," Cartwright said.

"This is right, we've been here," Letty said. "They're rebuilding the place."

They went past a yellow sign that said, "Santa Fe Regional Airport." A wide, low control tower appeared in the dim light, and what had to be the terminal building in the ubiquitous boring stucco brown. They were powering past a line of concrete traffic barriers, with a chain-link fence on the other side.

Cartwright: "Man, I've been in stone-cold shitty airports in North Africa, the Middle East, and Central Asia, and this is in the top-ten shitty list."

"Miss Tolerance America," Hawkins said.

"It's a construction zone," Letty said.

ACROSS THE STREET from the terminal, they could see a fifteen-foot-high cone-shaped pile of dirt behind chain-link gates. They followed the entrance road to the terminal, and Cartwright said, "I'll drop you off at the door, I'll find a spot to set up. I'll try to climb that big pile of dirt. Should be able to see everything from up there. Keep me up on your phone. I won't know what's going on, so you gotta make the call."

"We'll keep her outside the terminal—if she even shows," Letty said.

Cartwright dropped them off at a temporary entrance, and then kept moving. Letty watched as she drove halfway around the arrival loop, stopped, hopped out of the SUV, pulled open a gate, drove through and disappeared behind the dirt pile.

Hawkins said, "If she gets up there, she'll see everything coming in. Let's go inside. You have your little gun . . ."

Letty touched her pocket where her Sig was tucked inside a Sticky Holster. "All set."

"I hope Barb is as good a shot as you think she is."

"Barb . . . doesn't miss. Ever."

Hawkins picked up his suitcase and held the door as Letty stepped inside, her fingers on the gun. There were four people inside the terminal—two sleepy-looking airline clerks, and two sleepy-looking travelers, both male, sitting in chairs that lined the outer wall of the terminal. The terminal itself couldn't have been more than fifty yards long and looked more like a hallway that should have been connecting two buildings, rather than the building itself.

Hawkins said, "I'll check right, you go left."

They did that, didn't see Callister or anyone else except the clerks and male travelers, and met back in the middle two minutes later. Hawkins said, "Security isn't open yet, still dark inside the secure area. So . . ."

"Not here yet, if she'll ever be."

Hawkins leaned toward her and asked, "What do you *feel*. Is she coming here?"

The question struck Letty as odd, but then Hawkins *was* a little odd—that whole thing about the tarot reading—his bedroom skills notwithstanding. She tipped her head away from him, considering the question, then turned back and said, positively, "Yes. She's coming here."

"Crikey."

NO ONE WAS waiting at the American Airlines desk, so Letty led the way there, leaned across the counter with her DHS identification, and asked the clerk quietly, "Who is in charge this morning?"

"I am . . . I guess. The manager doesn't get here for a couple hours."

"Can we step behind the counter? I need to talk with you privately."

"I suppose. Should I call security?"

"If you can do it quietly, without bothering your travelers."

He nodded, slipped a cell phone out of his pocket, punched a button, and said, "Meet me in the break room. Uh, right now. It's important."

Hawkins said, "I'll wait here in case . . ."

Letty nodded and followed the desk clerk into the back. "Carl should be here . . . here he is."

An armed security man in a blue uniform showed up; the butt of his pistol had dust on it. "What's up?"

Letty showed him her ID. "We have a serious criminal that we think may show up here in the next few minutes. My partner and I will be hanging out near the doors . . . is there any other way in here?"

The security man shook his head. "Nope. Not for people who are flying."

"Okay. We'll be hanging by the door, but we don't want you to call attention to us. We'll try to take her outside."

"It's a woman?" the clerk asked.

Letty paused for a second, unsure of how to answer, since she'd referred to the criminal as "her." She blinked and said, "Yes . . . it's a woman. We want everybody to stay cool while we . . . apprehend her."

A wrinkle appeared between the security man's eyes: "Apprehend. I don't like the sound of that. Are you . . . is there going to be some shooting? Maybe?"

Letty shrugged and lied: "No, I don't think so. But she's desperate, and we really don't know what's going to happen."

"Your partner out there . . . the tough-looking guy . . . he's got a gun?" the clerk asked.

"No, he doesn't. We hope to do this without any violence," Letty said, which, judging from their faces, they doubted. "Maybe it'll turn out that she isn't coming this way at all."

Her phone buzzed, and she looked at it: Cartwright. "Yeah?"

"A little green SUV just rolled through the parking lot looking for a space, but there aren't any spaces because of the construction, so she went around the circle and down to the closest lot. I'm out of the truck, all set up. When she gets out of her car, I could take her."

"You sure that it's her?"

"I couldn't see her face. Thin woman driving a little green SUV?"

"Callister looks thin in the photos, but that's not good enough, not yet. There's a flight coming in and passengers are starting to arrive. Let her walk this way. Keep the phone open."

Letty dipped her hand in her jeans pocket and came up with the Sig, checked it, and said to the two men, "Be cool, guys," and walked out to the lobby. Hawkins was standing sideways to the window in the door, peeking out, watching the road.

Cartwright on the open phone: "She's parked, the car's interior lights came on."

"Okay," Letty said, and to Hawkins, "Say it again."

"What?"

"Crikey."

He smiled and shook his head: "As soon as I said it, I had a feeling it'd be coming back on me. Better than you Yanks, with your 'holy fuck.'"

"That's true."

Far down the entry road, they saw movement on the sidewalk, a thin woman pulling a wheeled suitcase with one hand and carrying a small carry-on in the other. They couldn't see her face, yet, it was a faint white oval. Hawkins said, "Yes. That's her."

"How do you know?"

"Because that suitcase and hand baggage are just like the hand baggage and suitcases I found in the RV."

Letty lifted the iPhone to her face and said, "Alec says that's her. Not a complete guess."

"Take her now?"

"Hang on a minute. We'll go outside to meet her. If we can get her to quit and keep her hands away from her fanny pack, if she's got one . . . she could give us some good stuff on where the other two are hiding."

"Like your old man said, don't let her pop the cork . . ."

"If I say 'Green light,' hit her, fast," Letty said. "I'm not going to show her my weapon at first, I'll try to talk to her."

"Ten-four, big fella."

"What does ten-four mean?" Hawkins asked, in a near whisper, though they were still inside.

"It means 'yes,' usually sarcastically, in what's called the 'ten code' that cops once used on their radios," Letty said.

"Ah."

As Callister passed under a light, they clearly saw her face, and Hawkins said, "Shit-shit-shit-shit."

"Yeah." Callister was getting close. Letty spoke to Cartwright: "Did you see her face?"

"I did. It's her."

"We're stepping outside." Letty prodded Hawkins with an elbow and said, "Let's go."

A LITTLE MORE than an hour earlier, Callister had called Scott to tell him she'd gotten through the checkpoint in Taos.

Scott said, "If you're stopped on the way down, or at the airport, we don't want you to have the phone you're on now. They might be able to pinpoint where these calls originated, so throw the phone out the window when I ring off. Both Clarice and I will try to get out of Taos today or tonight. We're afraid they could start to do a house-to-house search."

"How will you get out?"

"Haven't worked that out yet, but one of us will take Marilyn's Jeep and probably head north, or east across the mountains, if we can find a way to get there. In any case, best of luck to you, Danielle. I love you for this: you're saving the world. You're Joan of Arc and better than that."

"I hope I don't end like she did," Callister said. "You know, burning at the stake."

"You'll live forever," Scott said, and he was gone.

HIS LAST COMMENT was ambiguous, Callister thought, as she drove into the night. Live forever, like not dying? Or, live forever in the memories of the survivors of a cataclysmic plague, as one of the people who perpetrated it?

She drove south on cruise control; threw the phone she'd been using out the window. She was driving at exactly three miles over the speed limit . . . which, she'd calculated in a calmer moment, would get her there about four and a half minutes faster than if she drove exactly at the speed limit. She didn't have many calmer moments, gripping the steering wheel so tightly that her hands ached before she was halfway to Santa Fe.

She had one small city to go through before Santa Fe. She hit the lights of Española, pressed on with even tighter, grim-fisted precision through the sleeping town, careful at traffic signals, watching all of her mirrors.

Like that, for eighty miles.

Just outside Santa Fe, she diverted down Highway 599, an interstate-style bypass, rolled without incident to Airport Road, took the right and the left, found she couldn't park at the terminal, and so rolled through the drop-off area back to the first parking lot.

There, she sat for a minute, flexing her hands. One more task: she got her suitcase off the back seat, opened it, took out the fanny pack and fastened it under her blouse, which she wore loose, and above her butt. There was no metal on the pack, and the vials were glass: nothing that would show up on a routine security scan. Once she was behind security at Santa Fe, she would stay behind it anywhere she went.

She got her suitcase and the carry-on, left the car keys on the front seat of the Subaru—nearly teared up, saying goodbye to the car, a good car, a great car, her all-time favorite—then crossed the road from the parking lot, and started walking toward the terminal.

Gonna do this.

NO, SHE WASN'T.

She was twenty yards from the door to the terminal when Letty and Hawkins stepped out. Callister had had a number of conflicts with the law when she was tree-sitting, men in suits and sunglasses coming around to knock on her door wanting to know who sabotaged those Caterpillars and Kubotas and stinger-steer log trailers, who pounded those spikes into the redwoods . . .

She knew that the woman and the tall man were cops. Neither showed a gun, though the woman had a cell phone in her hand, near her mouth. Callister reached behind herself to pull the fanny pack around her body . . .

Letty reached out her left hand and cried, "Danielle, wait. Wait, please. You know . . . this is a terrible thing you're doing. This is a terrible thing . . . Stop. Help us stop it. Save yourself."

Callister shouted back at her, still pulling the strap to the fanny pack: "I know it's terrible. We all know it's terrible. But Gaia is dying. The whole world is dying, and this is the only way left to stop it. Don't help the fascists kill the world . . ."

She had the fanny pack halfway around, was fumbling with the Velcro to open it, found the tab and pulled on it.

Letty: "We need to talk . . ."

Callister's legs wobbled and her face contorted in misery and fear, and she cried out, "It's too late for all of that," and the Velcro ripped open and her fingers slipped down to the cold, slick surfaces of the vials inside.

Letty said, "Green light."

An instant later, Callister's head exploded, and her face seemed to fly off into the dark.

And Hawkins said, "Oh my God, oh Jesus . . ."

"Easy there," Letty said, though there was something grotesque about the way that bullet shattered Callister's head. Not like in the movies, not at all.

Cartwright was walking toward them, holding the rifle by the barrel, the stock on her shoulder. She looked down at Callister. Her face was flat, unmoved by the other woman's shattered skull. She said, "Hope you made the right call, girlfriend."

"She had the fanny pack open," Letty said.

"Then you made the right call," Cartwright said. She looked at Hawkins and said, "Buck the fuck up, redcoat."

"I . . ."

"Don't want to hear it," Cartwright said. To Letty: "Think we should take a peek at the vials or tubes or whatever they are?"

"No. She tried to open her fanny pack, but we killed her before she got it open. We stand back, way back, and let the guys from Fort Detrick deal with it. We should be okay if we stand back."

"Maybe. If the cops don't shoot us," Cartwright said. She was looking down the entry road.

Letty turned to look and saw two Santa Fe police cars coming in a hurry, light racks flashing into the growing dawn.

Behind them, the airport security man stuck his head out the door and he said, "I called the police." He saw the body, and asked, "What have you done?"

Not waiting for an answer, he stepped back inside the terminal and they heard the door lock snap home.

Letty said to Hawkins, "We'll meet the cops. Block the road with your body, don't let them through. We need to talk them down. They're going to be scared and probably pissed off because they're scared."

"Wonder why?" Hawkins said. Then, unexpectedly, he caught Letty by the shoulders, pulled her close and kissed her on the forehead. "You and Barb are something different entirely."

Cartwright called, "How come I don't get a kiss?"

"Just haven't gotten to you," Hawkins called back, and he started to smile but caught sight of Callister's shattered face and twisted away and said, "Oh Jesus, I can't . . ."

"Buck the fuck up," Cartwright snapped.

Letty said, "Let's go meet the cops."

THE THREE OF them walked down the road, but a few feet apart, so the patrol cars couldn't get past without running them over. Behind them Cartwright unlimbered the rifle, the barrel pointing down, but the recoil pad pushing up against her shoulder.

The cars stopped thirty feet short of them, a cloud of dust rolling out from under the wheels. Letty and Hawkins continued walking slowly forward, Letty holding out her ID with one hand. There was one cop in each car, and they both got out but stood behind their car doors, and one of them shouted. "What are you doing? What's going on?"

Letty shouted back, "Homeland Security. We need you to block the entry road, not let anyone past."

"What are you talking about? What happened to that . . ." He didn't say 'body,' but he pointed.

"We shot her. She's dead. This is one of the serial killers we've been hunting up in Taos. You probably heard about it."

The two cops exchanged some words, then looked back at Letty. "Is this one of the germ people?"

Letty: "What?"

"Is this one of the people trying to spread the germs?" the cop shouted.

Hawkins muttered, "Oh, shit. It's out."

Letty shouted back: "We can't talk about it. We need you to block the road and we need to evacuate a couple of people from the terminal. You can get there by going the other way around the traffic circle. Can you do that?"

The two cops talked again, then one got back inside his car and they saw him on his radio, and the other one called, "We'll come and get them out. Is it safe to get that close?"

"We believe so," Letty said.

"Believe, my ass," the cop called. "Why don't you go get the people who you want out of there and walk them around the circle and we'll take it from there."

Hawkins shook his head. "Oh, brother."

And the cop added, "Tell that other woman to put the rifle down."

Cartwright heard that, and she took the rifle down and shouted, "You're not very friendly."

Five minutes later, with the situation stabilized, and the two travelers moved out of the terminal and around the traffic circle to the cop cars, Letty called Lucas. He picked up, not quite groaning. "What happened?"

"You awake at all?"

"Asleep since I last talked to you."

"We killed her," Letty said.

"Aw, that's excellent. Maybe we'll save the world after all. Who pulled the trigger?"

"Barb."

"Good. Ol' MI5 seems a little shaky after what happened yesterday, and you've killed enough people for someone your age. What happened to the tubes, they okay?"

"They seem to be. She didn't get her fanny pack open, so I'm like ninety-five percent on that. We're isolating the body until somebody from Detrick gets here," Letty said.

"Okay. I'll try to get a couple more hours of sleep, I'm an old guy."

"You know about the leak?"

"What leak?" Lucas asked.

"The cops down here asked if she was the germ lady . . ."

"Fuck me with a barbed-wire fence pole," Lucas said, suddenly wide awake. "Call Greet. We may need a lot more help. The people up here are gonna go batshit."

20

If the people in Taos were going batshit, Letty was not instantly aware of it, because she was almost a hundred miles away.

When she called Greet to tell her that Callister was dead, Greet said, "You're doing well. I'll call the Santa Fe police chief—I have him on speed dial now—and get the airport covered."

Two members of the Fort Detrick team were on their way to Lamy from Taos to see if there was a body buried there. Greet said that they'd have to let that go, for the time being, and she'd divert the team to the airport.

"Now the unpleasant news," Greet said. "The researchers at Fort Detrick have been working on the virus tubes and they say it's quite possible that the reconstructed virus will perform as Scott intended. I don't understand the biology, or virology, or whatever you call it, but the virus does seem to have the infectious characteristics of measles, and it is bound to a full Marburg particle, or whatever they call it. It's scary enough that they seem fascinated, and they're talking to the CDC about getting research started into a vaccine."

The further bad news was that the CDC needed at least three committees and a middle school marching band to approve anything, so if either Scott or Catton managed to break out of Taos and release the virus, it was unlikely that a usable vaccine would arrive in time to help much.

And, she said, the Army, possibly fearful of the consequences of having allowed Scott to work at Fort Detrick, had cranked up the 93rd Military Police Battalion at Fort Bliss and put them on buses heading north. "The plan was to have them stage at Kirtland Air Force Base in Albuquerque. From there they could be in Taos in three hours, so I'm told. I told them to fuck that, send them straight in. Blockade the town—no one in, no one out, until the other two are dead. Or captured. Preferably dead."

"Why preferably?"

"This would actually be above your pay grade to know, but . . . since you can keep your mouth shut . . . it'll allow the bureaucrats further up the line to obscure exactly what happened, and who might be to blame."

"Of course, I should have known that without asking," Letty said. "Did you know the word is out that Scott's people are trying to spread a killer virus?"

"What!"

"Yeah. I'm thinking you might want to tell those MP bus drivers to lean on the diesel," Letty said. "If Scott and Catton have released the virus in Taos . . . it'll metastasize like a cancer."

"Jesus Christ! I'm out the door on my cell phone. I'm walking down to the Secretary's suite. I'll call you back."

TWO MEMBERS OF the Fort Detrick team that Letty hadn't met, Sam Dyer and Lily Rocha, showed up fifteen minutes later. Letty, Hawkins, and Cartwright had been wandering in circles around the body, trying not to look at Callister's head. The Detrick team suited up and while everybody moved farther away, carefully cut open Callister's fanny pack, removed five intact vials, and put them in a well-padded steel lockbox. The lockbox lid was sealed with antiviral tape, and the box moved to the team's SUV. Letty, because she'd already done it once, was chosen to hose down the two team members with the antiviral spray.

Out of the suit, Dyer said, "We should be safe, unless she did something crazy, like deliberately use a vial and soak herself with it. But, all the other viral packs that we captured had five vials, and she had five, all intact."

"But what do we do about that possibility that she contaminated herself?" Letty asked. "She's right on an airport road with an airport that only flies out to major hubs."

Rocha said, "It's not my call, but if I were you, I'd get about a hundred gallons of gasoline, soak her with it, and keep burning the body until there's nothing left."

"I can't do that," Letty said, appalled. "That's awful."

"Like I said, it's not my call, but that's what I would do," Rocha said.

"It's not like it would hurt her," Cartwright said, "Her being dead. But what do I know? I'm a simple Texas country girl."

"Yes, you are," Letty said. She looked around the parking lot, which was also a construction site, saw a front-end loader and asked, "What if we filled up that bucket with dirt and covered her with it, like two feet deep?"

"That would be better than just letting her lay out in the open," Dyer said.

"Call back to your team leader, what's his name? Underwood. Ask him."

Rocha looked at Dyer and said, "Call him."

Underwood agreed with Letty's suggestion. "Put a lot of dirt over her. Better than burning. We need to isolate the body if we can, so we can run tests on it. We need to see if they are contaminating themselves. If they believe the vaccine is working, they could do that, figuring if they were captured, they'd spread the disease to their captors."

The airport manager was waiting at the end of the entry road, and Letty had the cops escort him in, explained what she wanted to do.

"I don't have anyone to operate the machinery, and I kinda don't want to ask the guy who does, to come down here and risk his neck with these germs."

"Wouldn't be in any danger . . ."

"If he wouldn't be in any danger, why are we covering the body? Why not just get it out of here?"

"Well, that's . . ." Letty threw up her arms in exasperation.

"That's what I thought," the airport manager said.

One of the cops, who'd been listening in, said, "Hang on a minute," went to his radio, called someone and asked, "Is Martha still out there?"

He got an answer and said, "Tell her to come in here."

To Letty, he said, "One of our officers works part-time in her husband's nursery business. I think she knows how to run Kubotas."

Martha showed up, in uniform, and Letty pointed at an orange Kubota machine sitting on a pile of dirt and asked her if she could run it.

Martha looked and said, "That's an SVL track loader. It's bigger than what we've got, but I could figure it out pretty quick."

"Don't have a key," the airport manager said. "And Larry lives in Albuquerque."

"Should have a keyless ignition pad," Martha said. "You could call him and get the combination." She looked back at Letty. "What do you want me to do?"

MARTHA FIGURED OUT the machine in a couple minutes, did some practice runs, and then built a pile of yellow dirt on top of Callister's body, three feet high and eight feet wide, all around.

"Best we can do," Letty told Rocha and Dyer. "I'll have the cops watch it until we can figure out something permanent."

"We need to get down to . . . Lam-ee? . . . and look at that body," Rocha said.

"If there is one," Letty said. "And I think it's Lay-me."

Rocha and Dyer took off. Letty, Hawkins, and Cartwright talked to the Santa Fe chief, and Letty made a quick recorded statement for him, taking responsibility for the shooting of Callister. There was some shouting and harsh words—the airport manager warned that an American Airlines plane was coming in, and if the people at the end of the street were not allowed to board the plane, there would be hell to pay.

Letty said, "Read my lips: Fuck American Airlines."

IN THE END, it was two hours before the three of them got back to the hotel, picked up the second SUV, and made it to Lamy, bringing with them the full panoply of McDonald's junk food for Jerry Wright, who had remained on guard at what might be a grave site.

When they arrived, Rocha and Dyer were standing in a hole where the rebar had found soft dirt, and Wright was sitting on the hood of his car, watching them from a respectful distance. When Letty, Hawkins, and Cartwright pulled in, Hawkins gathered up the sack of junk food and carried it over and handed it to him.

He said, "Ah, the breakfast of champions," and to Cartwright, "I've heard about you."

"I hope it was complimentary."

"A little scary, and they didn't mention how gorgeous you are."

"Keep talking, I can handle it," Cartwright said.

Letty: "If we could break up the lovefest, Jerry . . . what happened here?"

"We dug down two feet and hit plastic. We all agreed that's a bad sign."

Dyer, thirty feet away, overheard that, turned and said, "It is a sure thing that we've got a burial. Of somebody, or something. Or both."

"Both what?" Hawkins asked.

"Both a body and medical equipment, whatever Scott would have used in his . . . experiment. We hit something that went *clink*."

DYER AND ROCHA hadn't sealed themselves into their suits, because it was already getting warm, the suits were stifling, and they hadn't yet seen anything apparently dangerous.

"Any virus in there is dead," Rocha explained, adding, "We hope."

"Gotta be," Dyer said.

They scraped and shoveled and scooped down another six inches, then had to lengthen the entire hole by a foot, eventually exposing a long wad of plastic in the shape of a huge cigar, or perhaps an insect pupa. The plastic was thick, crinkly, originally translucent but now stained with earth colors, mostly yellow.

When they'd cleared the length of the plastic, Dyer knelt on it, bent over it, and said, "Yeah, it's a body. I can see an ankle and a blue sock."

"Now we need the suits," Rocha said.

Rocha and Dyer got out of the hole, got bottles of water and drank, and then sealed themselves into their isolation suits. Dyer dug around the plastic wrap until it was all clear, then he and Rocha both worked their hands under the body, picked it up and lifted it out of the grave. They laid it clear of the excavated dirt.

Rocha got a kit from their car and they made a series of tiny cuts through the plastic, using a scalpel, and began taking slices of body tissue and placing them in individual sealable glass dishes. Samples were taken from several areas on the exterior of the body, and deep samples were taken from the liver, kidneys, intestines, and lungs with what looked like large syringes. An ordinary battery-operated electric drill was used to open holes in the skull, and brain tissue was sampled. Each opening in the plastic was resealed with antiviral tape. All of the gathered tissue samples were further isolated in metal containers, labeled, and placed in one of the metal boxes.

"On its way to the fort," Rocha said. She nodded at the still-wrapped body, and asked Letty, "What do we do with that?"

"You're the experts, but I'd put it back in the grave and cover it up until we can figure out something permanent," Hawkins said.

"I'll talk to Underwood," Rocha said.

She did, they put the body back in the hole, and shoveled dirt back on top of it. Again, they had Letty hose them down with the antiviral solution.

When they'd done that, and waited a bit for the fluid to work, Rocha and Dyer peeled off their suits and Rocha asked, "You guys hear what they're saying about that first tranche of samples from yesterday?"

"Yeah. Not good," Letty said.

"Much worse than 'not good,' way worse," Dyer said.

"You know what? I bet there are guys at the fort already looking to save some of it, to work with it," Rocha said.

"Let's not go there . . . if we want to keep our jobs," Dyer warned.

"I don't like what you're hinting at here," Hawkins said. "If I understand you . . ."

"Yeah, well, imagine you create an effective vaccine, stockpile it, and then turned the virus loose in, say, India or China or Russia . . . and when the first case came up, you started your vaccination program here in the States," Rocha said. "Lot of problems solved, if you have the right 'Murican mind-set."

"Except the Chinese or the Russians would figure it out, and the last one out the door would push the big red button and there wouldn't be a 'Murica to worry about," Hawkins said.

"There is that," Cartwright said.

Wright asked, "What are you guys talking about?"

Cartwright said, "Nothing." She batted her eyelashes at him. "Tell me again how gorgeous I am."

"Other than that, what do you want me to do?" Wright asked, looking at the two from Fort Detrick.

"We're done for now," Dyer said. "A different crew will come back and look for more bodies, but that'll probably be a few days."

"You just gonna leave the body in the hole for now?"

"No. We'll talk to your bosses about getting a regular car out here to watch it, until it can be moved," Letty said. "If you could hang in for another couple of hours . . ."

Wright nodded: "Get somebody out here as soon as you can. I'm feeling a little kicked."

Cartwright: "We outa here?"

"Taos," Hawkins said.

Letty: "We're gone."

21

Callister didn't call.

She'd had two of the burners with her, and even after disposing of one, she should have called from Santa Fe on the other. As the hours got longer, and the sun came up, Scott and Catton began to believe that something had gone badly wrong. Marilyn Wong owned a television with every channel known to mankind, but they couldn't find anything about Callister.

"They won't be showing any mercy—they can't," Scott said, wandering around the living room with his hands in his pockets. He fiddled with a turquoise cuff he'd bought when he arrived in New Mexico, a good luck charm. "Maybe she's okay. Maybe she's on her way to Dallas. Maybe the second phone didn't work. Maybe they captured her and she infected them. I don't think so. I think she's dead. I think they plan to kill all of us like they killed Rose and Randy, shot on sight. They're scared."

"I can't believe they could stop us at this point, we've worked too hard," Catton said. "We can figure this out."

"Before we can figure it out, we have to find out what the police are doing. We know they have checkpoints. If that's the end of it, we should be able to get out," Scott said. "I don't think that's the end of it."

"What more could they do? Surround the whole city?"

"If they're desperate enough, I think they might," Scott said. He dropped into an easy chair. "Get your border patrol up here, they've got helicopters and those all-terrain vehicles . . ."

"You think we're finished?"

"No. We have to work through it. We're safe enough for the time being, here in this house, but eventually, they'll do a house-to-house search. They probably don't have the manpower for that, not yet, but they will. Our primary problem is, somebody smart figured out what we're trying to do and they'll do anything to stop us. Anything."

Catton walked around the room, looked at some Hummel knickknacks on a shelf, thinking about it, walked off to a family room and looked at the TV, not for the news, but almost as a kind of meditation; some talk show out of New York, the panels of idiots laughing at the world that she and Scott were trying to end.

Scott trailed after her, looked at the TV, picked up the remote control and hit "mute." The idiots were even more informative when you couldn't hear them talk. Catton slumped on a couch, Scott took a chair again.

After a while she said, "I'm not going to make it out of here. I shouldn't even try."

Scott nodded: "Then what will you do? I'm listening."

"How many times have you been in Taos?"

"A few," Scott said. "It's . . . a little too isolated. For my interests. Los Alamos is interesting, Santa Fe is, too. Albuquerque, not so much."

"I'm here all the time in winter, and quite a few times the rest of the year. The thing about Taos is, it's self-consciously weird and always has been. Major hippie outpost in the sixties," Catton said. "That pulls in the curious. If you look around town, especially around the plaza, you realize that most of the people you're looking at aren't from Taos. They're tourists. Texas, Colorado, Oklahoma, California. The shops around the plaza are tourist shops."

"Okay. Where's this going?"

"The incubation period of measles is a week or ten days. For Marburg, it's two to five days. Right here, where we're at, we're about . . . mmm, I don't know . . . not more than a ten-minute walk from Santa Dymphna Catholic Church. It's baroque, for lack of a better word. Plaster statues of the saints. Hand-carved stations of the cross, done by folk artisans. Pope Francis gave them specific permission to continue saying the Latin High Mass. Incense, and all that. They have Masses every morning, and since the church is old and funky, it pulls in a lot of the tourists. I've had the vaccine, Marburg won't kill me . . ."

"And you go to Mass and infect everybody in the church. If you get there ahead of time, you could wipe the culture around a bunch of the pews, so people would be sitting on it." Scott cupped a chin, felt the beard sprouting there. "Since the incubation period is probably a minimum of two to five days, if we are either dead or surrender . . . they'll let the tourists out of town."

"I don't know if I'll surrender," Catton said. "I think I might step away. You know . . ." She meant to kill herself.

"They'd still have to find you, to let everybody out," Scott said. "A private suicide wouldn't help us."

"I'd turn myself in with an anonymous phone call," Catton said. "I'd rush them. Suicide by cop."

SCOTT SCRAPED HIS lower lip several times, a habit developed in his first job, in a desert in Sudan. His lip, from that time, held a particular bitterness that never seemed to go away. He'd been in the Sudan for a month when he realized the taste was similar to the odor he encountered when he walked past a nearby camel corral. The taste of camel dung; now purely psychological, but never quite gone.

"That is an amazing idea, a way to save the project," he said, eventually. "It's not what we wanted, but it would work. If you decided at the last minute to . . . not suicide . . . you could actually surrender. Let them take you. And explain us to the world. Not mention the church."

"I always liked being on television. I was, from time to time. Nothing dramatic, you know. I was on charity boards, sometimes they asked me to say something. I could PR for the apocalypse." She half smiled, thinking about it, but then the smile faded. "What about you? We know they have your face . . ."

Scott interlinked his fingers, twisted them, then said, "I can't be seen. At all. But. You know I was a mountain biker. Now I'm sorry we had to leave that bike at the ski house. But there's a bicycle shop in town. You could go there—you don't look like the photos they're passing around, not at all. You could buy me a mountain bike. The place is called the Popcycle and they've got high-end bikes. We've got cash we're not going to need . . ."

"I've seen the place, I know where it is. It's not far," Catton said. "I agree about my appearance. I startle myself when I look in a mirror. But where would you bike to?"

"However far I have to go to get past their checkpoints. I can sneak down alleys, if Taos has alleys, down backstreets in the dark, follow arroyos out of town. Ride cross-country. When I'm sure I'm past the checkpoints, I get a car and head for Albuquerque."

"How do you get a car?"

"We have your gun. You won't need it." The revolver had been Catton's house gun at the ski valley.

"Okay. But if you get a car, why not Denver or Phoenix? You wouldn't really even have to get in the departure areas, you could seed the area outside the gates, outside security."

"I can do the same thing in Albuquerque, and Albuquerque is close and fast. If they decide that I got out of town, I wouldn't be surprised if they actually begin setting up checkpoints at border crossings . . . this area isn't New York. There aren't that many roads out. If they're desperate enough, they could literally blockade New Mexico."

"When do you want to go?"

"Tonight. We're probably okay here, for now. We're comfortable, we can watch TV for any news—but you've got to get the bike."

"Great. You get out tonight. I could go to church tomorrow. Nine o'clock Mass. Huh. All right. Let's think about this—if this is the best we can do. If we don't think of anything before the bike shop opens, I'll go get you a bicycle."

They didn't think of anything better. At one point, Catton said, "We've got both of Marilyn's cars . . ."

"But they're looking for cars. Somebody might have figured out that we're either hiding with friends, or we've taken hostages and we could try to get out with the hostages' cars. The checkpoints will get tougher and tougher, knowing that Danielle got through them. Since they got the men on the bus, and Rose, they'll know we have high-quality driver's licenses. The only way Danielle could have been caught is that they must have figured out that she got through the checkpoint."

"We don't know she was caught."

"She was," Scott said. "We just don't know if she accomplished anything."

"What if she's alive, and she gives us up?"

"Then . . ." Scott grinned and shrugged. "Then, we're fucked."

AT NINE O'CLOCK, they caught a news update from Albuquerque saying that authorities had closed the Santa Fe airport, apparently after a shooting in the parking lot. Police were not releasing details, and it was uncertain when the airport would reopen.

"You were right. They got her," Catton said.

"Yes."

"I wonder if she managed to do a release?"

"No way to tell, but . . . she apparently was caught before she got inside."

Catton sighed, pushed herself out of the chair she'd been sitting in, and said, "I'll see if Marilyn had some pink ribbon or even a pink blouse. I'll make a breast cancer ribbon . . ."

"Bald head, ribbon on your lapel, nobody would even look at your face," Scott said.

On the top shelf of the bedroom closet, Catton found a plastic box full of wrapping paper, and spools of ribbon, including one that was pink. She made herself a breast-cancer ribbon that was good enough—

Lord knows she had enough friends who'd been through breast cancer. She left the bedroom, went out to the Cadillac and got her suitcase, found what she thought of as a suitable outfit—shin-length wraparound skirt, blue blouse, low heels.

Respectable, she thought. *Not a mass murderer.*

She was carrying them to the bedroom, to change, when Scott called, "Hey! Hey!"

She swerved to the TV room, and Scott pointed at the screen, where a woman in a red dress was saying, ". . . said they weren't looking for serial killers at all, but a group of people who are attempting to release a deadly virus, perhaps an enhanced version of Covid. The motive for doing this is unknown, and none of the Taos authorities will comment on the claim. Perhaps related to the claim is the fact that a huge Army convoy passed through Albuquerque an hour ago heading north on I-25, and police sources here said the convoy was made up of a military police battalion from Fort Bliss, in El Paso. Our sources say they are always warned of convoys like this in advance, because they affect traffic flow, but they got no warning this time . . ."

The report went on, based on rumors and speculation, almost all of which was incorrect, but certain to stir up fear.

"Perhaps we got a break . . . there'll be a rush of people trying to get out of town," Scott said. "It'll be chaos out there. You should go now, to Popcycle . . ."

CATTON PUT ON one of the Hermès scarves that she'd found earlier. It was light and colorful and, carefully tied, revealed a swatch of pink scalp. She added the Covid mask that Callister had picked up at the supermarket. Wearing the respectable outfit, she checked herself in the mirror, and walked to the kitchen, where Scott handed her the keys to the Realtor's Jeep.

"Watch for checkpoints . . . don't back away from one, though," Scott said. "Take backstreets if you can . . ."

"I've thought all that out," she said. "I don't need luck, I just need to focus. I'm a harmless little old lady with breast cancer."

Scott stood in a dark corner of the garage as Catton backed the Jeep out. When she was gone, he dropped the door behind her and went back in the house to monitor the television.

Catton followed a zigzag route to the bike store. She stuck to backstreets, and saw only one checkpoint, a full two blocks away. She came into the back of the store, gathered her wits and her money—she had twenty-five hundred dollars in a bank envelope, which Scott said would buy a capable bike, if nothing special.

They'd talked out what she should say to the store clerk, and when she went inside, she found two of them—one talking to a man wearing a garish "I'm a serious cyclist" Lycra suit, the other peering out the front window past an overhead rack of bicycles.

That clerk came over to her, smiling, said, "Quite a hassle out there today."

"I suppose," she said, smiling back. She didn't like being the slightly confused old woman, but she could do it well enough. "I need to buy a mountain bicycle for my nephew. He's *very* athletic and my sister says he's a good rider, but he wrecked his bike last week. My sister says they scraped together a thousand dollars to buy his last bike, which I gather wasn't exactly top-end."

She took the bank envelope out of her purse. "I brought two thousand dollars with me, straight from the bank. That's all I'm going to spend, and I hope you have a bike for that amount."

"We have some excellent bikes for fifteen hundred to two thousand," the clerk said enthusiastically. "Depending on what kind of specs you want . . ."

"I'll have to rely on you to tell me that," Catton said. "Not more than two thousand, though. Oh, I was told something about getting flat pedals, I don't know what those are . . ."

"If you come over here . . ."

THE CLERK HELPED the little old lady load the Norco Fluid FS4 in the back of the Jeep; a wheel stuck out, but would be okay. The actual list price for the bike was $1,999. After some dickering, the little old lady conceded that she had another hundred dollars in her purse, and while that wouldn't cover all the sales tax, the clerk offered to cut the retail price to the point where it all came out at $2099.

"Could you throw in a helmet and bicycle gloves?"

More dickering, and it turned out that she had twenty-five hundred dollars. The smiling clerk got it all. "What am I going to do with more money, anyway?" she asked, touching her scalp.

The clerk shied away, thought about other things, took the cash, and helped load the bike.

As he watched her drive away, he said to the other clerk and the cyclist, "That's one dead-ass old lady."

BACK AT WONG'S house, a pleased Lionel Scott wheeled the bike around the inside of the garage and said, "I like it. A lot. Did you have them check the tire pressure?"

"I had them do everything. They said it's ready to ride."

"Tonight, then," he said. "By tomorrow night, we'll have been successful, or we'll . . ."

"Be dead," Catton finished. "I'm old enough to have thought a lot about being dead. It doesn't bother me anymore."

"Bothers me a bit," Scott said.

"Only a bit?"

"Only because I'd like to know how all this worked out. If we were successful. If we saved Gaia."

22

Lucas showered and shaved, because he wouldn't feel awake and human if he didn't, and popped a Dexedrine. He and Rae had checked into another Hampton Inn late the night before, and he called her as he dug through his travel bag.

"I was waiting to hear from you," she groaned.

"I woke you up to tell you to go back to sleep," Lucas said. "I figured you'd be up soon, and you don't have to be. Shit is going on, but nothing that you have to worry about right now. Somebody leaked about the virus, things could get crazy. I'm going out to scout around."

"Then I *am* going back to sleep. Call me when you're done scouting."

As he was getting dressed, Mellon, the Taos chief, called and said, "You better get down here."

"What happened?"

"About a million cops are headed up here. MPs from Fort Bliss, ordered here by the Army. There's a rumor that the President has declared martial law in New Mexico, but I haven't heard anything directly about that, and there's nothing on the news channels except the rumor. Everybody knows about the virus, we got hundreds of cars at the checkpoints. We're holding on for now . . ."

"Jesus. When will the Army get here?"

"I took a call five minutes ago, I guess the commander is in town looking for the police station. They want to know what they need to do. And he told me a helicopter unit will be coming in later in the morning. It's like a flock of ducks landed on my head; I don't know what the hell I'm doing."

"I'm coming," Lucas said.

LUCAS HAD TO use his iPhone's navigation app again to get him back to the police department, where he saw a single military vehicle in the parking lot, and no MPs hanging around. Inside, he found Mellon talking to a lieutenant colonel named Harris Foley and a major named Anna Vincent.

When Lucas walked in, Mellon said to the soldiers, "Here he is. Talk to him."

Lucas shook hands with Foley and Vincent, and Foley said, "We need to know everything, because we don't know much except the Army chief of staff called me and the base commander during my kid's Little League game last night and jacked us up, and here we are. He said something about terrorists and a virus."

"How many of you are there?" Lucas asked.

"We think . . . think . . . about seven hundred forty of us including a few support troops. Not here yet. And we lost a couple of vehicles due to breakdowns on the way, so part of the convoy had to fall out to help them along. Then, some people were on leave, and so on. But . . . about seven hundred forty of us. We'll be staging over in a park across the highway. We have another crew coming up with tents and meal service equipment; we're eating off MREs for the time being."

"What are MREs?"

"Meals Ready to Eat. Packaged rations," the major said.

"Also known as Meals Requiring Enemas," Mellon said.

Foley smiled and said, "Ex-military?"

"Yup." To Lucas: "That guy from Fort Detrick—Underwood?—I called him, too. He's on his way, should be here in ten minutes."

Foley: "I've been told that later in the morning, we got a helicopter battalion coming in. They'll fly out of Santa Fe because they need the refueling facilities. They can stay on station up here, for a couple of hours before they have to go back for fuel. If we stage them correctly, we should always have a couple in the air."

Mellon: "There are God-only-knows how many ATVs and four-wheelers around here, probably want to keep the helicopters circling the built-up area and look for runners."

Vincent said, "The colonel and I . . . we've never seen anything like this. There's this virus . . . but what do you know about that? How do we handle it?"

Lucas looked from one to the other, nodded at Mellon, and said, "I'm sorry, I'm still a little unfocused. Yesterday was intense. To begin with, so you understand how serious this is, we've shot and killed three people attempting to spread the virus. We shot another guy, probably an innocent civilian, wounding him, who thought we were 'active shooters' in a supermarket. He had a gun and took a shot at us.

He's in serious condition at the hospital but will make it. If he was a better shot, I'd be dead and so would he. We have three very sick people confined to an RV up at Taos Ski Valley until the big brains at Fort Detrick figure out what to do with them. We don't think they're contagious, but we can't take any chances."

"But how bad is this thing . . ."

"Up to eighty percent death rate, in one outbreak. The man behind it, who's sort of a mad genius, has hitched the Marburg virus to the most infectious virus known, the measles virus. Could even be an enhanced measles virus . . . We could be talking about a worldwide plague like nothing seen before. Covid would be a walk in the park compared to this."

Foley looked at Lucas for a moment, then around the small office. "Let's get some chairs . . ."

Everybody sat.

"Quick question before we get into the details," Lucas said. "Do your guys have live ammo? Or are they more set up for crowd control?"

"We can do both," Foley said. "I'd hate like hell to have to shoot somebody."

"I understand. You'll change your mind by the time we're at the end of the briefing."

LUCAS TOLD THEM what he knew about the virus, and outlined the fundamental difficulty, which was to locate two people hiding among the seven thousand residents of Taos, and probably several hundred more tourists. He explained that they had photos, but that the allowable failure rate was zero.

"They cannot get out. They can't be allowed to turn the virus loose. If they manage to infect any number of people in Taos, we have to . . . sequester . . . those people whether they want to be sequestered or not. If we believe that a particular person or group of people may have been infected, and they refuse to be contained, we kill them."

"I don't know if we can do that," Foley objected.

"Talk to your chief of staff. If he's not important enough, we can ask the President to have a word with you."

Vincent: "Really?"

"Really," Lucas said.

"There's another problem here, Marshal," Vincent said, brushing a hand through her short-cropped hair. "Have you ever worked for a regular police department? My father was a cop in San Diego and I'm pretty familiar with civilian cops. You marshals are sort of elite . . ."

"I started on the street in Minneapolis, was an investigator with the Minnesota Bureau of Criminal Apprehension," Lucas said. "With the BCA and as a marshal, I've coordinated with police departments all over the country."

"Then what I have to tell you is that our MPs are no better qualified intellectually or emotionally to make life-and-death decisions than an average beat cop," Vincent said. "Some are solid, reliable troops. Other ones, not so much."

Lucas shook his head. "I can't help you with that. You'll have to sort them out yourselves. Put the dummies backing up the Taos cops on checkpoints, where the cops can supervise. We can use the smart people running their own checkpoints. I'm thinking we need to link your troops up to the outer checkpoints . . ."

"If you're talking about an eye-sight perimeter, seven hundred troops aren't enough to do that, not if they have to do it over three shifts," Mellon said. "We'd be talking about a thirty- or forty-mile perimeter . . ."

"Then we have to tighten the perimeter," Lucas said. "What we got is what we got."

He turned back to Foley and Vincent: "Nobody gets out, for at least the rest of today, or until we nail these two people and have made sure they haven't turned the virus loose. We can run off copies of their photos for every MP you've got. We really jam up the town. Make it so nobody can go anywhere without getting looked at. Later on, we may be talking about a house-to-house search. We have an idea of what area they might be hiding in, two of them were seen last night on the street, walking."

Mellon asked the two officers, "Have you heard anything about martial law?"

Foley shook his head. "Not yet. Have you?"

"Rumors so far. But as I understand it, if we get it, we might not have to worry about things like search warrants."

"I'll check with my CO, he can check with Washington," Foley said.

UNDERWOOD STEPPED INTO the office, looking like he'd been up all night. He nodded at Lucas, and Lucas said, "This is the guy who'll tell you why you *will* shoot to kill."

The briefing was done in an hour; Underwood was specific and adamant about the worldwide threat. Foley and Vincent were appalled both by the threat and by the problem they'd have to contend with.

Vincent said, "Look, everybody. I'm sure we can help with jamming up the town, but we need to keep some of our people, our best people, together as a fast-reaction force. If you should locate Scott and Catton, we may need to surround a whole neighborhood, and fast."

"Or worse, if we find out that they've deliberately infected a group of people, and we need to contain them," Foley added.

Underwood said, "You catch on fast, Colonel."

Halfway through the briefing, Mellon called the county courthouse and talked to the tax assessor about getting some large-scale maps for the MPs. A bureaucratic hassle erupted, which Mellon cut off by shouting, "I'll tell you what, Don, you get those goddamn maps over here in fifteen minutes or I'll have some cops come and get you *and* the maps and drop your ass off at the jail. Yeah, yeah, you heard what I said. Fifteen minutes!"

"Good work," Lucas said, when Mellon rang off.

The maps came in, they unrolled them, Foley and Vincent spread them out on a table and bent over them, and Foley said, tracing the edges of the city with an index finger, "We're not gonna be able to keep everybody in the net . . . too big and too scattered out in the countryside . . . but Lucas, you're telling me they're most likely in town. Gonna need state police and local cops, sheriffs, people with cars to start hitting some of these outlying houses to check them out, and clear the people so we can pull in the edges of the net . . ."

Vincent to Foley: "I suggest we get all the NCOs together, right now, get Captain Feather to pull them together, we'll need to distribute these maps . . . Is there a copy center around here?"

"There's Copy Queen," Mellon said. "I can show you where . . ."

THE MPS WERE better than Lucas had hoped. Both Foley and Vincent had experience deploying large bodies of troops, and in the hour worked out a deployment plan. They made arrangements to communicate with Lucas, Underwood, and Mellon by cell phone "so we won't have to fool around with radios."

Underwood told them, "When you brief your troops, you have to emphasize that they can't let these people get close to them. If they're spotted, and they try to get close, kill them. Then stand way back—way back—and call me."

When they hurried out of the police chief's office—Foley headed toward the park where the MP unit was setting up, Vincent going to the copy center with the maps—Lucas said to Mellon, "I think we got a chance. We got a chance."

"What do you want to do?"

"How many guys you got on checkpoints?" Lucas asked.

"All of them, that aren't asleep."

"Let's figure out a way to get more state police in here, to take over the checkpoints. We need to get whole shifts of them, with the MPs as the outer ring. Your guys, we need on house-to-house."

Mellon shook his head: "We can't go busting into private homes without search warrants. Not until we hear about the martial law thing . . ."

"I believe we can," Lucas said. "I'll have somebody call you on that before you can get your people together. Somebody high up."

"I dunno," Mellon said. "Even if somebody says we can, I don't like it."

"I know, I know."

LUCAS CALLED GREET: "We have a legal problem involving both the MPs and the local law officers. We're thinking we might need a house-to-house search. We need somebody high up to tell us that we can do it without warrants. Do we have martial law now?"

"There are arguments about that, the DOJ stuck an oar in. Give me a half hour to get some clarity," Greet said. She added, "The word from Detrick keeps getting worse and worse. The infectiousness is off the chart. The mortality rate can't be determined without more work."

"All right. Well, we think we've got all but two of them. The other two are cornered, but I don't know what we'd do if they decided just to infect the city."

"Don't even think about that. I'll get back to you."

"Get back to Chief Mellon and Colonel Foley," Lucas said. "They'll be organizing the searches and blockades."

"What are you going to do?"

"I don't know. I'm more useful on the street. We're figuring it out one inch at a time and I'm going to get a car and look around."

When he'd finished talking with Greet, Lucas told Mellon that somebody would be calling about authorizing warrantless searches. "I need to borrow a squad car. Something that will get me through checkpoints without having to wait."

"Not a problem," Mellon said.

THE WHITE SQUAD car reeked of hot dogs and less strongly of urine but had a full tank of gas and a light bar, all Lucas needed. He called Rae, who was up and around, told her that he'd pick her up at the motel.

"Nice ride," she said, skeptically, when he arrived. She opened the back door of the car, sniffed at the interior.

"It is what it is, as Marcus Aurelius once said," Lucas said.

"Really? He said that?"

"How the hell would I know? Do I look like a historian?"

"Okay. Well, I'm hungrier than hell," she said. She put her equipment bag on the back seat. "I brought our U.S. Marshals jackets, so maybe we won't repeat last night's little adventure, shooting a civilian."

"Wish we'd thought of that last night . . . I saw a McDonald's on the way down here, not too far from where we'll be going."

"Where are we going?"

"Around."

THEY GOT SACKS of junk food and Diet Cokes at McDonald's and turned south again. The Levys had been staying on a street called Los Pandos Road, and that's where they'd seen Foss and Callister. Lucas used his iPhone's navigation app to get him back there, and they cruised slowly down the length of the street.

Los Pandos was a leafy lane, narrow, tall trees overhanging, some of the homes well kept, others not, open grassy lots from place to place. Most of the homes had fences or walls, with the cars parked in front or the side; few of the houses had garages. There must have been a dozen streets intersecting, leading off to other streets.

"If they were walking down Los Pandos to Smith's, they probably hadn't walked too far. Probably one of these side streets," Rae said. "We need some door-knockers. We need to ask who saw a man and a woman walking down the street around nine o'clock, and where did they come from?"

"Hard to see into the street from these houses," Lucas said. "Everybody is walled up inside their own compounds."

"It's our best shot, right now," Rae said. She unzipped the equipment bag and took out her iPad, called up a map of Taos. "We could block off the most likely places with . . ." She counted. "We'd need nine or ten checkpoints to isolate the neighborhood and start working through it."

"Lot of guys . . ."

"That's just the checkpoints. We'd need a couple of dozen more to walk the streets and knock."

Lucas shrugged. "No choice. I'll call the Army guys, get them to send some MPs down here. They should be making paper copies of Scott's and Catton's faces. We'll use them for the checkpoints, get Mellon's cops down here to walk the street. Maybe . . . there are a lot of MPs, we put one MP with every walking cop . . ."

"It's a plan," Rae said. "I hope Scott and Catton haven't taken off."

NOTHING HAPPENED FAST enough. The MPs had yet to arrive, then had to be sorted out, and put on a bus. Mellon marked the points where they'd set up to isolate the Los Pandos neighborhood, and found wooden barricades at the Taos County Fair, which was getting organized, yet still two weeks away. The MPs were told not to let anyone out of the neighborhood without approval from a Taos cop.

Some of the MPs had been issued M4 rifles, and Lucas asked that they be put at the barricades, because the weapons were intimidating. The MPs were told to arrest anyone trying to get out on foot.

A dozen cops came in; the city only had about twenty sworn officers, and most of them had worked the overnight and had been dragged out of bed by Mellon.

It was early afternoon before everything was in place to begin the hunt. Shortly after the search teams began working the web of streets, two formidable-looking Army helicopters churned up the main highway, no more than a hundred feet overhead. Rae said, "We need to talk to those guys, too."

"Colonel Foley should do it for us. We basically need them circling the edges of the built-up area, looking for people trying to make a run cross-country."

Lucas called Foley, who said he'd take care of it. Then Lucas and Rae joined a police sergeant who was outlining the search to the Taos cops, and they all went for a walk.

THEY WALKED FOR six hours down Los Pandos and the streets around it. The day turned hot, and everybody was sweating and by late afternoon, everything had slowed down: half the cops were cranky with a lack of sleep, the others discouraged by the lack of results. There were shouting matches with people who were not allowed to leave the neighborhood. One man said he was "going to get my gun" and was arrested and sent to the Taos County Adult Detention Center, which was not far away, while his wife screamed at the arresting officers.

"Drunk or crazy?" Lucas asked a cop.

"I don't think she's either one," the cop said, as they watched her acting out. "She knows what she wants and damn everybody else if she doesn't get it. Same with her old man."

"Sad song of the eternally entitled," Lucas said.

One cop was attacked by a Labrador retriever, the first time that Lucas had seen a Lab attack; the cop was sent to the hospital to get the tooth punctures patched up, the dog's owner frightened and apologetic, fearful that her dog would be shot. It wasn't.

Lucas had been attacked by a cocker spaniel early in his career, and late in his career by a rare white cockatoo. The Taos cops thought the cockatoo story was hilarious, those that believed it, and most had their own animal attack stories, all dogs but one. That one was a cop who'd been bitten by a horse.

"You don't want to get bit by a horse," he said, shaking his head. "The goddamn things have teeth like steel traps and they can bite your face off."

"Your face looks all right," Rae said.

"That's because the horse bit him on the ass," another cop said. "That's not a scar you'd want to see."

LETTY SHOWED UP early in the afternoon, trailed by Hawkins and Cartwright. Lucas knew about Cartwright from one of Letty's previous investigations: CIA sniper, don't tell anyone.

In the end, they'd knocked on every door in the neighborhood, and nobody knew about Scott or Catton. There'd been no response at twenty-one of the houses, and one man they talked to said there were a number of Airbnbs in the area. Lucas called Greet about getting a list.

"I don't know," he told Rae, after they'd gotten off the phone. They were sitting on boulders in the shade of a tall deciduous tree of some kind. Letty was down the street, walking toward them with Hawkins. "The Airbnb thing makes some kind of sense, I guess. Quick way to find an empty house."

"Gotta wait for the list."

"I don't want to wait. The longer we wait, the longer they have to come up with an escape plan."

"Or decide to let it go here, in Taos," Rae said. "What do we do if they call us up and say 'We surrender' after they've turned it loose in some store we're not watching? I don't think it's politically acceptable to blockade the whole town until the incubation period is up. Can't get away with keeping people here for days. You saw what some of the people were like today—they don't even like being held up for a few hours."

"Yeah. But we can't let it get out. *We can't.* The Detrick guys . . . they're telling us we'd be way better off nuking the whole town, than letting the virus out."

"Nuking what?" Letty asked, as she and Hawkins came up.

"Nothing. They're not going to nuke the town," Rae said.

"Probably not, but I bet some asshole in Washington is researching the possibility," Lucas said.

They all thought about that, and Hawkins knocked a fly away from Letty's head and said, "You got flies."

"We all got flies," Lucas said. More silence, and Lucas said, "We're about done here. Got jack shit. Where do we go next?"

"I can answer that question," Hawkins said.

Rae: "Really?"

"Yeah. You know those twenty-one no-response houses?"

Rae: "Yeah?"

"We start kicking doors," Hawkins said. He looked out at the sun, which was sliding down the western sky. "We do it all night if we have to. Forget about warrants."

Lucas smiled and reached out a hand to be slapped: "I like the way you think."

23

The idea was not without its detractors, including Mellon and, from what Mellon had to say, the entire city council. "We're the ones gonna get our asses sued to hell and back, while you go back to slumming in Washington, D.C."

"That's my daughter. I'm from St. Paul, myself, and Rae's from Louisiana . . ."

"Lucas, I know you've been working hard all night and day, but this is over the line," Mellon said. "There's no indication that Scott or Catton were ever in any of those houses . . ."

They were still talking when four men in dark tee-shirts and khaki slacks showed up, wandering through the cops and MPs, each carrying either a pack or a duffel bag, and Rae said, "Oh my sweet Jesus: we're saved."

Andres Devlin, an average-sized, average-looking black man with short-cropped hair and an easy smile, walked up to Rae, patted her on the ass and said, "How you been, Sweet Pea?"

Rae leaned over and kissed Devlin on the lips, and said to Lucas, "You already know Andres, of course, he claims that you're his spiritual advisor; this other racially and ethnically balanced crew are Langer, Stuart, and Hoang," Rae said, pointing to them one at a time. "Guys, this is Lucas Davenport, his daughter Letty, who shot all those people down by El Paso, Alec Hawkins, of His Majesty's Secret Service, or something like that. Coming down the street there, that young lady is Barbara Cartwright, a sniper who works with an unspecified agency. We are about to do warrantless searches of twenty-one houses, which will probably get the shit sued out of all of us."

"Semper fi," Hoang said. "Who's got a ram?"

Lucas laughed and said, "I love the Marshals Service."

After more talk with Mellon, they agreed that the marshals would form three two-person teams, armed with rams borrowed from the Taos police department; Letty, Cartwright, and Hawkins would each be attached to a different team, as backup. Any of the Taos cops who were too tired to keep working would be sent home, and a fresh shift of MPs would make sure the area remained sealed.

"Get it *on*!" Langer said, and they did.

"SEVEN HOUSES EACH," Rae said, as they walked out to their first house. "I'm still tired after last night. Be lucky to get done by midnight tonight."

"Dexies," Lucas said.

"You got some?" she asked.

"Maybe. If you can keep your mouth shut."

"You're such a criminal. I don't know why I hang out with you."

Lucas, Rae, and Cartwright opened the festivities by taking down the front door of a stucco three-bedroom/two-bath that smelled lightly of mildewed paper, and, when the lights were on, showed bookcases in every room except the kitchen, but including the two bathrooms, all filled with paperbacks.

Lucas spent a minute looking at one bookcase that mostly contained crime novels, many of which he remembered from his youth. "Look at this," he told Cartwright, tapping the back of a book. "John D. MacDonald, *Bright Orange for the Shroud*. Great stuff."

She was mystified. "What? Who?"

"I forgot, you're still a child."

No sign of anything to do with Scott or Catton.

LETTY FOLLOWED LANGER and Devlin into a disintegrating concrete-block/stucco house with an open back door. The only occupants were cats who seemed to come and go, apparently attracted by a leak under the kitchen sink that left a puddle of water on the floor, slowly draining off the back stoop.

One bedroom had no bed, but did have two hundred boxes of Converse All Stars sneakers in a variety of sizes; and a hundred and ten bottles of Tide laundry detergent.

"Shoplifters," Devlin said. He ran a finger down the line of All Stars boxes. "Got my size, too."

"Probably not shoplifters. More likely truck hijackers. How are you gonna get out the door of Walmart with a hundred bottles of Tide in your yoga pants?" Langer asked.

"I've seen some women where I said to myself, 'That can't all be ass,' and I believe I was correct," Devlin said.

"FBI looks at this. We should make a note, and report it," Langer said.

Letty: "Do you really care?"

Langer: "Sure. Theoretically I do. If I don't have to do anything about it. People in my neighborhood are afraid Target's going to close because of assholes like these people."

"Maybe they just got a lot of babies and they need a lot of baby diapers," Devlin said.

"And as the kids grow up, they could use all those different shoe sizes," Letty added. "They're honest folks, thinking ahead. Way ahead. Let's get out of here."

"I'm ashamed. That hadn't even occurred to me," Langer said, as they went. "Nice, upstanding folks, taking care of their little kids."

THE FOURTH NONRESPONSIVE house hit by Stuart, Huong, and Hawkins turned out to be occupied, just not by the owner. They knocked front and back, shouted, saw not a sign of a light or heard anything like movement.

"Let's hit it," Huong said, and Stuart knocked down the front door with a ram. As they crashed into the entry, a woman screamed, and Stuart dropped the ram and jumped backwards; Huong hit the living room with a 25,000-lumen flashlight, which, if you were in it, was like standing on the starboard side of the sun.

A young blond woman was sitting on the floor; she was wearing what looked like a pajama top with horses on it, and white underpants, and a frightened look. She was barefoot.

Stuart had his pistol out and shouted, "Hands, let me see your hands," and the woman lifted her hands over her head and cried, "Don't shoot us, we didn't do anything."

And a man, out of sight, shouted, "I'm coming out with the baby . . ."

Stuart: "Come out, we want to see your hands."

A Hispanic man came out of the back bedroom, and they could see his hands, which were wrapped around a newborn who was sucking on a Binky.

Huong: "Who else is in here?"

"Nobody. Nobody," the blonde said. "We're alone."

Stuart: "Let's clear it." To Hawkins, he said, "Watch these people."

While Stuart and Huong were clearing the house—the blonde had been telling the truth, there was nobody else there—Hawkins asked, "What are you doing here?"

"We don't have anyplace to go," she said. "We knew the house was empty."

"Were you here when we came by this morning?"

"Yes. We . . . didn't mean anything. We were scared."

Huong and Stuart came back, and the Hispanic man explained that they'd been kicked out of the trailer they'd been renting when he lost his job. "This house is owned by a company from Denver. They're going to fix it up for rent. I was going to be on the work crew to fix it up, but they decided not to do it right away and so . . . no more crew. We knew it was not being used . . . we were using it until one of us got a job."

Stuart asked Hawkins, "What do you think?"

"Nothing to do with us," Hawkins said. He looked at the man and asked, "Do you know how to call the company in Denver?"

"No. The contractor who organized the work crew . . . he can."

"Call the contractor and tell him to call the company and tell them that U.S. Marshals knocked down his door, and you can fix it for . . . what?"

"Two hundred dollars?" the man ventured.

"Sounds about right," Huong said.

"And in the meantime," Hawkins said, "you'll guard the house against looters."

THE SECOND HOUSE hit by Lucas, Rae, and Cartwright showed lights. When they knocked on the door, a woman came to the door, looked at them and said, "Can I help you?"

She was so polite, and so upset when Lucas insisted that they had to clear the house, that all three of them felt bad as they left.

"Not what America is supposed to be," Cartwright said.

Huong, Stuart, and Hawkins moved on to their next house, the only one they'd seen with a garage. No answer, front or back, and they took down the door. Stuart hit the lights, but nothing came on. "No power," he said.

He added his own insufferably bright light to the mix, and they cleared the house. "Somebody's been in here," Hawkins said. "They were eating these power bar things."

"Yeah, but when?" Stuart asked.

They got to the garage last, through a door off the kitchen. Huong stuck his head in, said, "Looky here."

Hawkins looked: A large American SUV. He called Lucas. "There's nobody here, but there's a Cadillac SUV in the garage and it's got those Hertz plates we were looking for."

"No movement?"

"None. Feels dead, no recent odors."

"Be right there." Lucas turned to Rae and said, "Your boys found where they were. They're gone, but that rental car is still there."

"Damnit. They got a ride from someone."

THEY GOT TO the house ten minutes later, found a crowd of curious MPs standing around watching the marshals who were walking in and out of the house. Cartwright was sitting on a stump looking bored.

Huong walked over to Lucas and said, "We need to find the owners of the house. The neighbors say it's a couple named Jerry Wallach and his wife Katherine, who moved to Austin, Texas, two months ago, with their kids. Nobody knows exactly where and we can't find anyone who has a phone number."

"Was the house up for sale? A real estate agent . . ."

"The neighbors say there was no 'For Sale' sign. They think the Wallachs might be trying to rent it in case the new job doesn't work out, and they move back."

Letty showed up with Langer and Devlin, and they all walked into the house, which was skimpily furnished and dark—no power. There were no waste baskets, either, and wrappers for granola bars were crumbled on the floor, pushed into a corner.

"It does look like the owners were trying to rent," Letty said. "Still a few pieces of furniture . . ."

The Cadillac was empty.

A Taos cop went to his car and came back with the spelling of the Wallachs' last name, and the information on their driver's licenses and automobile registration. A call to the Marshals' office in Austin got a hunt going there.

Lucas spoke to the chief deputy marshal in Austin, who asked how the Wallachs should be treated. Lucas filled him in on the Taos background, and they agreed the Wallachs should be treated with suspicion, but were not actual fugitives.

"It's possible that Scott and Catton knew about the house and broke in," Lucas said to the chief deputy. "When Foss and Callister were spotted, they ran for it. Push the Wallachs on Scott and Catton, see what they know. The minute you get anything, call me."

"I'll do that," the chief deputy said. He added, "Hold on a minute."

A minute later he came back and said, "They haven't applied for Texas driver's licenses yet, or changed their auto registration. This could take a while."

Lucas stood, arms akimbo, in the garage. "Now what?"

There were no cars moving through the neighborhood after nightfall, none at all.

If he crouched in the courtyard, and listened carefully, Scott could hear something that sounded like diesel generators, a throbbing growl he recognized from his stints in rural Africa. He didn't know what they were powering, or where they were, but they had a military feel to them; an expeditionary force. He'd expected chaos when word about the virus got out, but that was not what he was seeing or hearing.

Back inside, Catton had settled in Wong's family room, watching television, switching from one channel to the next. Information was thin, the same news reports cycled and recycled.

"Another possibility," Catton said, continuing the options conversation as Scott walked into the room, "would be to sit tight. Maybe there won't be a search. Maybe they'll convince themselves that we got out." She was on a couch drinking red wine, most of a bottle already down.

"I don't believe so," Scott said, looking past her at the television. She was watching a sales pitch for women's products, done by a long-necked movie star whose name he couldn't remember.

"I've worked in a couple of countries where there'd be a bit of resistance, or something that the army didn't like. They'd lock down a neighborhood until they found who they were looking for. It would be like this. Nothing moving. People afraid to go out."

"I wish the news reports were better . . ."

"Nobody wants to come in. No reporters," Scott said. "The virus rumors have frightened everyone, especially the comments from the President. I don't think we'll find out what's really happening, without actually going out in the street."

He stopped talking as a helicopter went over, seemingly right at rooftops.

"And that kind of thing . . ."—he pointed at the ceiling—". . . is what's keeping people inside. The famous black helicopters. Deliberate intimidation."

The presidential comments were frightening because the President had been trying so hard to be upbeat, cheerful, reassuring, for which he was being taken to task not only by Fox News, but CNN and MSNBC as well. Although they knew little about the virus, the talking heads were asking why, if everything was so rosy and okay, was an entire town blockaded by the Army?

Their answer: nothing was okay. Nothing at all.

MSNBC had put up their producers' cell phone numbers and had asked Taos residents to report for them, something that Fox and CNN then copied. Dozens of people had apparently called in, but few knew anything—they'd seen soldiers and checkpoints, hadn't been allowed to leave town, heard helicopters flying low, but knew nothing about the virus or the people who were trying to distribute it.

CNN took a report from a man who claimed to be an MP in Taos, who told the reporter that a house-to-house search was taking place in a Taos neighborhood, and houses were being broken into by the search teams without warrants or invitations.

And yet, outside Marilyn Wong's house, all was quiet.

SCOTT HAD RESTLESSLY spent the afternoon and evening in front of Wong's computer, studying Google Maps, and especially the satellite views. He traced different pathways through town, yard by yard, inventing one route after another, looking at Google Street View, discarding them one after another.

"They can't block every street, not yet," he said to Catton. "They'll block key intersections. They won't care if you're on a street, as long as you can't get off it . . . and there'll be leaks. I have to find the leaks."

He would have one big unavoidable problem: dawn. He needed to be well out of town, and hopefully in a car, by the time the sun came up. He needed to leave late enough to avoid wakeful people, but early enough to actually go the distance on the bike. And he had to do the most difficult part of the ride in the dark.

He eventually decided that no matter what he did, there would be a strong element of risk. He spotted one narrow highway on the far west side, Highway 240, that would take him around most of the city. Along much of it, there was easy cover in roadside brush and trees, if he had to get off the road for a passing car, or if he had to go back because of a checkpoint. Logically, though, there'd be no point to a checkpoint on 240, except at the ends of it—he could put down a lot of mileage, but it would all be inside the cage.

If he took that route, he would have one major highway, 68, to cross. That was the main route south out of Taos and would be heavily guarded. There would likely be a checkpoint at the intersection of 240 and 68, but he would see that coming because of a traffic signal at the intersection.

And there, he thought, was a potential leak. An obscure jumble of neighborhood streets—they looked more like tracks in the satellite view—showed up a few blocks west and south of the intersection. He would cross the highway there. There would almost certainly be another checkpoint farther south on 68, and maybe more than one, but that was irrelevant. He wouldn't be on 68.

He was aiming for a back highway, 518, better known as the High Road to Taos, that ran from a point just north of Santa Fe through the foothills of the Rockies to Taos. He'd driven it a few times, when investigating bike trails in the mountains, and it was only sparsely inhabited. One drawback: once he was on the High Road, there'd be no turning back, and no easy way off. If somebody smart had set a checkpoint halfway down the road, he'd have a problem. There were fire roads up through the mountains, but many of them dead-ended, and he could find no official fire road maps online.

After long consideration of both the distances and his own physical condition, he decided that he would have to find a car when he was somewhere well south of Taos, but before he got to any of the small villages along the High Road. That should be far enough along the road to be outside the heaviest search area. How long would it take him to get there? By dawn, he hoped, but that might be too optimistic. Once it was light, he'd have to hide, and wait out the day, unless he already had a car.

"Find a route?" Catton asked, wandering in from the TV room.

"Penciling it out now," he answered. "I'll need a little luck to get out of town. If I can't, I'll come back and try to do what you're planning. Find a heavily populated place to contaminate. The hardest part will be taking a car. If I take one too soon, and there's a checkpoint beyond it, I'm in trouble. I might be able to slip by a checkpoint with a bike, but if I'm in a car, and they see me suddenly turning around, they'll come after me."

IN THE TEN O'CLOCK hour before he'd make his break for it, Scott searched through Wong's house, looking for supplies. He found most of what he needed, including a backpack that could be made to fit him. He put the box containing his allocation of virus vials into the pack, along with the fanny pack he'd use when he began the actual distribution of the virus. If he took falls on the bike, the box would provide impact protection.

To the pack he added four bottles of water, two packs of graham crackers, and a plastic bag full of Oreo cookies with "Extra Stuf." He made two chicken sandwiches and sealed them in Ziploc bags. He included a knife, the revolver, and a homemade first aid kit scavenged from Wong's bathroom and closet. He didn't have to worry about infection, but he did have to worry about bleeding. He put a flashlight in his jacket pocket.

They'd found a box of pasta in the cupboard, and he'd set that to simmering on the stove just before ten o'clock. He wore jeans and a dark green jacket for the ride, and ordinary hiking boots. The boots settled easily on the large flat pedals of the bike, one of the reasons he'd chosen them. He spent a few minutes stripping all the reflectors off the bike. That might spark something in the suspicious mind of a watcher, but then, there were enough idiot cyclists on the road without reflectors that he should be okay, and far less visible.

"Pasta should be ready," Catton said. "There's shredded cheese in the refrigerator . . ."

"Let's pile it on," Scott said. "The last supper."

"Not funny," Catton said.

"A little funny," Scott said. He was getting tense.

AT ELEVEN THIRTY, he pushed the bicycle to the garage's side door, strapped on the helmet, pulled on the gloves, leaned the bike against the garage wall and said, "Give me a hug, Clarice. Sending me off into the great unknown."

She gave him a loose hug—she didn't much like to be touched—and said, "Call me when you have a car and are ready to make your run."

"I don't know whether I'll have one before you leave for church," Scott said. "I don't know what's out there—it could take me a day or two to even get loose."

"Okay, then I'll call you before I go to Mass."

"Well, then," Scott said. He opened the door, pushed the bike through, and with his face barely visible in the dark, his teeth flashed, and he said, "Good-bye, Clarice."

An uncommonly cool parting for two conspirators almost certainly heading for death, he thought, but that was Clarice.

WHEN SCOTT DISAPPEARED in the night, Catton went back to the family room to watch the television news broadcasts, but it was all politics—even the virus speculation was politics. If the virus got loose, how would that effect the presidential race? If the virus got loose, would New Mexico lose a critical congressman? She should call them, she thought. Identify herself. Tell them, "If the virus gets loose, you won't have to worry about losing the New Mexico congressman. You'll have to worry about losing New Mexico. Along with California, Texas, New York . . ."

And she thought about what would happen in the morning. She would arrive early for Mass, try several different pews, spread the viral medium as carefully and as invisibly as she could. Then leave before the Mass started. If she were to be caught, she'd want that to happen somewhere else so the people in the church would have dispersed.

That was for tomorrow.

Right now, she had to pee. She got up from the couch and, without thinking, opened the door to the powder room, saw the body of Marilyn Wong. She looked at it, so still, thought *That could be me*. Tomorrow.

But, she still had to pee. She closed the powder room door and headed for the main bathroom. Afterwards . . . did she see popcorn in the cupboard?

SCOTT THOUGHT ABOUT bushmeat hunters he'd met at a hospital in the Congo. They hunted chimpanzees with rifles, nothing as crude as bows or spears, but still: hunting to eat wasn't easy. The key to success, they said, was stillness. If it was not possible or unproductive to sit still, then very slow movement was the ticket. Very slow. Step, stop. Step, stop. Movement catches the eye.

Riding through the neighborhood on his bicycle, he remembered that and took it to heart, as best he could. He stayed close to the ubiquitous walls. Stopped when he heard sounds or saw lights. Steered from one dark spot to the next, working his way through the heavily residential area around Wong's house. The dark of the moon had been four days earlier, and now a thin crescent was rising in the east. Not much light, but enough to see the surface of the streets. He had one deadline: he had to be well out of town by dawn.

WONG'S HOUSE WAS in a lane off Valverde Street. He worked his way south down Valverde, then west on a couple of narrows lanes out to Upper Ranchitos, and then he was on the highway he'd stay on for miles. The road was reasonably straight and flat, the houses spaced out from each other, and now he could risk some speed. He would be almost invisible in the dark, he thought; but only *almost*. He could hear helicopters in the distance; he'd read of border patrol helicopters using heat-detection devices to pick up warm bodies crossing the Rio Grande, but according to the television news, these were Army helicopters. Did they have heat detectors aboard? If so, he'd be a white globule on their video screens, now moving swiftly along Highway 240.

He sensed something in front of him, a movement, an animal? He dodged, but never actually saw it—a dog, a bobcat, a skunk.

"Please, not a skunk," he muttered to himself.

There were no cars for the first couple of miles; then he saw headlights coming up from behind, moving slowly, and he swerved into roadside brush, pushed through it, waited until the car had passed. A Taos cop car. He waited until it was out of sight, did another mile, maybe four minutes in the dark. A snatch of music from a house behind a screen of trees; the unintelligible sounds of television.

Another car came up from behind, with a growling engine. Whatever it was, it had a searchlight and was probing the roadside brush. He slipped off the road again, behind the thickest clump of weeds he could feel, and lay flat on the ground. The light flicked over him, the truck went on.

Another mile, and he saw the blinking lights of a helicopter, coming north toward him, but slightly off to the west. He swerved toward a house where he could see lights in the back, and stopped outside the walled courtyard, leaned the bike on the wall, and walked back and forth along it. Just another homeowner, going about some late chore. Taking the garbage out? Certainly not trying to hide in some roadside brush. The helicopter must have been a half-mile west and didn't slow. When it had gone, he was back on the bike, pedaling smoothly, picking up speed.

He made a big turn to the east, toward the Rockies, and in the distance, saw the traffic signal at Highway 68 and the flashing lights of a police light bar. Marvelous that he'd made it this far, and so easily—and as the thought passed through his mind, the bike's front wheel dropped into a pothole and threw him sideways onto the road surface, stunning him.

"Ohh . . . crap." He lay there, shaken, surprised, but apparently not injured. He stood, shook out hands, arms, and legs; he might be sore in the morning, he thought, but that was minor. He might be dead in the morning.

He'd had worse falls in the mountains, but not from something so hard-edged as the pothole. He checked the bike's front wheel, and it seemed okay. He got back on and pedaled toward the traffic signal, more slowly now. He'd gotten ahead of himself; he couldn't do that.

TWO HUNDRED YARDS from Highway 68, he diverted onto a narrow track to the south, rode two hundred yards over dirt bumps and weeds, then turned back toward 68. When he got to the highway, he could see the flashing lights of the checkpoint at 240 and 68. There were three cars at the checkpoint, as close as he could tell, and the police that he could see, small dark figures on the other side of the cars, all seemed focused on the cars. There were no cars trying to get into town.

He took a breath, rolled slowly up to 68, and crossed quickly, into the mouth of another narrow, poorly lit street. Riding in the dark wasn't getting easier; if anything it was getting harder, more disorienting. Slowing down didn't help, so he sped up again.

A half hour later, he intersected with the High Road. He checked his watch: 2:46. The sun would be up a little after six, so he had three hours to get as far out the High Road as he could. He had to get far enough out that he could be fairly sure he'd encounter no more checkpoints.

The High Road had a bike lane, which again was an irrelevancy: first, there was no traffic, and second, he had no choice but to take that road, bike lane or not. There were houses and businesses on both sides of the road, but because of the peculiar culture of Northern New Mexico, many of the houses were enclosed by the characteristic *latilla* fencing, made of close-set poles, usually at least five feet high. Even in broad daylight, residents of most of the houses wouldn't be able to see him going by on the road. Much of the road was also edged by brush and trees, blocking the view of houses from the road, and vice versa. After he'd passed the built-up area, he began climbing; an invisible man, feeling the altitude in his lungs and legs.

At the crest of one of the long, rolling hills, he stopped, got off the bike, pulled it into the roadside weeds, sat and drank water. A rare car went by, moving very fast, even for a highway. He couldn't see it well, but he thought it was civilian, not official. He forced himself to sit for fifteen minutes, then got back on the bike and pedaled south, up and down, but mostly climbing. Unlike daytime riding, he couldn't just coast down the hills; he had to brake down, keep the speed controlled.

And at five-fifteen, he ran into another checkpoint.

He could see the lights from most of a mile away, and he closed carefully. He was sure he couldn't be seen; he could barely see the cops, who were talking to a man whose car had been pulled to the side of the highway. The speeding car that had passed him farther back? He didn't know.

Steep hill on one side of him, sharp drop on the other. He pedaled slowly forward, then dropped into a dip in the road and stopped.

He was stuck, at least for the time being. He crossed the road and pushed up the bank above him. The brush was not dense: there were piñon trees all around, short, prickly, so dark green that he couldn't see them until he walked into the branches. There were dry weeds around his knees, but he couldn't see them, either; he spent a minute worrying about rattlesnakes, but then stopped worrying.

A hundred feet off the road, and sure that he was behind several layers of piñons, he put the bike down, kicked around it—snake removal—and sat down, tried to get comfortable. Handicapped by the dark, he opened the top of the backpack, fished out a chicken sandwich, took a drink of water.

Nothing to do now, but wait.

25

One o'clock in the morning, bags of potato chips, a twelve-pack of Dos Equis, a bottle of wine and plastic glasses.

The six marshals, plus Letty, Hawkins, and Cartwright, gathered in Lucas's room at the Hampton Inn to talk about what to do next. The search of the Los Pandos neighborhood had been a success only in the negative sense—they knew where Scott and Catton had been, but not where they'd gone.

Cartwright, looking around the room, said they reminded her of her team in Afghanistan, when she was in the Army—sitting on the floor, sprawled on the bed, slumped in chairs, with guns, armor, a helmet that somebody had brought with him.

Letty said, "If they're out, I think we would have heard, unless they headed up into the mountains and are hiding themselves. But if that's what they've done, with all the bulletins that are out there now, somebody will spot them."

Cartwright: "The big question, how are they moving? They had two cars that we know of, plus the RV, and you guys stopped the RV and we got Callister's car down in Santa Fe, and Catton's rental Cadillac here. So: they must have another car or are planning to get one. We've got the plates for Catton's Lexus, and everybody's looking for it. You guys got the checkpoints up pretty quick, and we know Foss was here and Callister left from here, so . . . I think they're still inside the perimeter."

"So do I, but they're planning to get out, somehow," Lucas said.

Devlin, slouched on the couch next to Rae, pointed out that there might be houses with hidden or non-obvious spaces—the eaves of houses—that would make a real house-to-house tedious and maybe impossible. "We can't watch everything all the time. We search one block, clear it, and they manage to sneak into that block in the middle of the night, kill the homeowners . . . it's whack-a-mole."

"It's a problem," Lucas agreed.

"HERE'S ANOTHER QUESTION," Rae said. "How did they find that rental house? Do they know the Wallachs? Couldn't have just been luck."

"Gotta find the Wallachs to know that," Lucas said. He had his head on a pillow, on the bed, and sat up and said, "The guys down in Austin put out a public plea on all the TV channels asking them to call. That's the best they could do. The local cops are looking for the license plates . . . they'll find them, but I don't know how soon."

"We know they're trying to get out, and there's apparently a little airport here, somewhere," Hoang said. "Could they have stuck a gun in the ear of a private pilot . . ."

"That was shut down, first thing," Letty said. "There are a couple of Army trucks parked across the runway, I've been told."

Rae: "We know he was a mountain biker . . . could he bike out?"

"His bike is still up at Catton's place. Apparently they didn't have room for it in the Cadillac," Lucas said.

Stuart said, "There gotta be bike shops in town."

Langer added, "He wouldn't actually have to ride to Denver. He'd just have to get around the checkpoints and then steal a car. He might be able to do that on a bike."

Lucas sighed: "I guess we gotta ask."

LUCAS CALLED THE police hotline and asked for Mellon, who'd gone home, but he'd left behind a sergeant to deal with virus questions. Lucas asked about bike shop ownership, and he said he'd call back.

Stuart said, "If we've got them cornered, their best bet would be to infect a large group of people here in town, and hope some of them get out to spread the virus. You guys are telling me this virus is crazy infectious. I think us guys ought to set up in all the places that will still attract crowds in town. People have to eat, so . . . supermarkets, you know. They've got this plaza here, if that pulls people . . ."

"Where else?" Rae asked.

Before anyone answered, Lucas's phone rang and the sergeant gave him two names of bike shop owners. He had addresses but no phone numbers for them. "They're also the store operators, so if Scott bought a bike, they'd probably know."

When Lucas rang off, Rae said, wearily, "Let's mount up, go knock on those doors."

"Hang on a minute," Letty said. She looked down her list of contacts and punched one, and put the phone on speaker so everybody could hear.

An extremely cranky woman asked, "What?"

"This is Letty . . ."

"I know who you are. What do you want?"

"We need cell phone numbers for two people in Taos, New Mexico," Letty said.

A frigid silence. Then, "Give me what you know about them."

Letty gave her the names and addresses, said, "That's all we've got," and the woman rang off without saying goodbye.

"That's a friendly sort," Devlin said. "I wonder if she dates?"

Made Letty smile, and Rae asked, "Why would you wonder that, my little sweetie?"

"What else we got?" Lucas asked. "Anybody?"

"I think Hoang is right—they might start looking around for crowds," Hawkins said. "We not only need us, we need the local police and the MPs to cover everything where more than five or ten people congregate. Indoors, only, I think . . ."

Letty's phone buzzed. She looked at the screen and when she answered, a man asked, "Do you have a pencil?"

"Yes."

"I have four phone numbers for you . . . the subjects and their wives . . ."

Letty took down the numbers, the man asked, "Got them?" and she said "Yes," and he hung up.

"My God," Hawkins said. "What was that, five minutes? Six minutes? That's disturbing."

Cartwright: "She's dealing with the NSA, America's crime family."

Letty called the first number, for the owner of Popcycle. The phone rang six times and went to the answering app. She hung up, dialed it again, and a man answered. "Who is this?"

Trying to explain exactly who she was would be too complicated, so she said, "U.S. Marshals Service. We are asking local bicycle shop owners if they sold any bicycles today or yesterday, especially mountain or off-road bikes . . ."

"You mean so somebody could sneak out of town cross-country?" the man asked sleepily.

"That's exactly what we mean, yes."

"Uh, we did sell a bike this morning, but it was to an elderly lady and she bought it for her nephew . . . she said. She bought a helmet and gloves to go with it."

"Did you get a name on her card?"

Pause. Then, "Actually, she paid cash. Twenty-two hundred dollars for the bike, a helmet and gloves."

Letty had her phone on speaker, and there were a couple of "whoas" and an "oh boy" from the room around her.

"What did she look like? A tall woman? Gray hair?"

"She was sorta tall, I guess . . . didn't have any hair—she was a cancer victim, she had one of those pink cancer ribbons. She was wearing a Covid mask, so I really couldn't tell you what she looked like."

Letty asked for his email, told him to stay on the phone. "I'm going to send you a photo . . . it'll be there in a couple of minutes." She retrieved her iPad, called up the photo of Catton, and sent it. The man on the phone said, "Got it. I really can't tell, I mean . . . she was bald, she had a scarf on her head . . ."

"Put one hand on the top of her head in the photo and cover up the bottom half of her face with your other hand. What do you think?"

The man said, "Yeah. Um, it could be her. It sorta looks like her."

Lucas blurted, "Ahh! He's already on the road. If he gets past the checkpoints, he'll try to grab a car."

LETTY GOT GREET out of bed—it was three forty-five in Washington.

Letty began, "I'm sorry to wake you up . . ."

"Don't apologize, just talk to me," Greet said.

"We think Scott may have slipped out of town. A woman we think is Catton bought a mountain bike at a Taos bike shop."

"Shit! Let me think about this for a minute or two. Literally a minute or two. I'll call you right back."

While they were waiting, they argued about Scott's next move, if he was on a bike. They were still doing that when Greet called back.

"Here's my thoughts. Maybe you've already covered this territory, but I'll tell you anyway. Letty, I think you, Hawkins, and Cartwright need to get down to the Albuquerque airport. Like, now. I've been looking at maps all day, and he almost has to go south, because that's where a real road network is, west of the mountains. East through the mountains, north and west we can block: he won't get through there. To make sure, I'll plug the very ends of those roads with more state cops. We've got more of them on call, they're ready to move, and I'll move them in the next hour. But, my feeling is that the logic of this will send him south. I also think that he won't be able to ride a bike the whole way—he'll have to grab a car, one way or another."

"We agree with all that," Letty said.

"Okay. If he grabs a car, and somehow gets away with it, once he gets to Santa Fe he could go in any direction he wants, but the number of roads are still fairly limited and we can block them. What we need to try to do is funnel him down toward Albuquerque. Other than Santa Fe, that's the closest and fastest airport within reach, that would meet his requirements. We need to ambush him there, as a last resort. I'll try to use the media to get him there. If we can determine what car he's using, we'll be able to stop him before he gets to the airport. But if we can't determine that, we need you guys to set a trap at the airport itself."

Lucas: "That could work. What will you tell the media?"

"As I understand it, we don't have a clue where Catton is, except that she's probably still in town. She bought that bike yesterday morning, and we've not let anybody out of town since then. That means she's holed up somewhere, and if she's looking at TV, we'll have the news people reading reports saying that we believe the two of them are holed up somewhere in town, and that we'll be starting door-to-door searches, isolating different districts in town, and that we expect to search every house in town in the next two days. We'll say that we're putting together a statewide emergency response no later than tomorrow. If Catton calls Scott with the news, or if he hears it on a car radio, that should make him think about his options. His best option would be to move fast and hope for the best, and that would be either Santa Fe or Albuquerque. We'll block off the approaches to the Santa Fe airport. Discourage him from trying to make Denver, Dallas, Phoenix, or El Paso."

"That's a plan," Rae said. "Lucas and I and the marshals team here can keeping pushing on locating Catton. The biggest problem we see is that she'll try to infect a whole crowd of people, and we won't know who they are . . ."

"You gotta find her," Greet said. "I trust you people to do that. We're all counting on you."

When Greet had rung off, they all looked at each other and then Letty said, "Barb, Alec and I need to get down to Albuquerque, I guess. We'll try to get some sleep in the airport."

"If Scott tried to sneak out on a bike, I'll bet he waited until after dark, when things had quieted down," Lucas said. "I think you've got time."

Letty: "Wish I had some Dexedrine."

Lucas: "I might find something like that in my dopp kit . . ."

Letty: "Really? I'm shocked."

"Forget about it. I've got much better stuff," Cartwright said. "If we're gonna go, we gotta go."

The phone woke Lucas. He rolled over in bed, picked it up from the bed stand. The screen said 7:17 a.m. and the call was coming in from Austin.

"Hey, this is Gary, you called last night. We found the Wallachs. They saw the media request and called us. They have a Realtor named Marilyn Wong who's handling it. She's shown it a couple of times but hasn't rented it yet. They gave us her mobile number . . ."

Lucas took the Realtor's information, yawned, sat up, decided to clean up before he went looking for her. He did call Rae, and Devlin picked up and said, "Rae's phone. Lucas?"

"Yeah, I got a call from Austin . . ."

He explained, said he could meet Rae in fifteen minutes, if she was awake.

"She's in the shower. Give her twenty minutes. I'll go tell her. You want me along?"

"Probably not necessary for the first contact . . . come if you want to."

"I'll pass . . . I'll get the other guys up, we'll go get some breakfast."

"That's fine. Probably get everybody together afterwards, figure out the next move. See if this Ms. Wong has anything."

RAE MET HIM at her motel door, yawning, equipment bag over her shoulder. She asked, "Get some sleep?"

"Yeah, I'm fine. Do McDonald's again?"

"They've got some kind of breakfast downstairs . . ."

"Yeah, but . . ."

"Gotta have those Egg McMuffins, huh? That's fine. You know where we're going?"

"Not yet. Bring your iPad."

Lucas and Rae tended to agree on food and got four Sausage and Egg McMuffins for the two of them, along with fries and Diet Cokes. They sat in the car and ate and talked about the hunt.

"I think if we don't get her today, we're in trouble," Rae said, chewing.

"If I was a cheerleader, I'd say, '*Then let's get her today.*'"

"Mr. Gloom."

"Well, what we're talking about . . ."

"Yeah, I don't like to think about it." But it was impossible not to think about it. After a moment, Rae asked, "What about Scott's whole theory? I believe in global warming and all that, but are we really killing the earth? Is it even barely possible that getting rid of half the people is the only way to save the rest of them?"

"I don't believe it," Lucas said. "I read some pop science websites, and it seems like there are a bunch of different things we could try before we go off killing half the people on earth."

"Yeah . . . maybe. I know for sure that we shouldn't kill five billion people on one guy's say-so, even if he is some kind of genius."

"Dr. Evil," Lucas said.

"But not a funny one."

THEY TALKED ABOUT mutual friends: Virgil Flowers, who'd worked with Rae undercover on an organized-crime heroin sting, and Flowers's emergence as a thriller writer, whose second novel had made the bottom of the *New York Times* bestseller list; Andres Devlin, and Rae's relationship with him, which she said had become serious; Bob Matees, who'd been shot to death on assignment with Lucas, and who'd been Rae's Marshals Service partner and best friend forever.

"Andres would like some kids," Rae said. "He'd like daughters. When he said that, I thought, 'Well, maybe.' But we've still got some talking to do."

"He's a good guy, and wicked smart, and so are you, so your daughters would be, too," Lucas said. "You wanna share your fries?"

"No."

"If you're gonna be that way, I'm gonna call this Realtor."

"So call her."

Their whole conversation, Lucas thought as he punched the Realtor's number into his phone, had a little End-of-Times feel to it.

HE GOT NO answer. Rae looked her up with the iPad, got an office number, and called that. No answer.

"It's Sunday," Rae said. "She might be sleeping in."

There were no longer phone book listings, those had disappeared in the nineties, so they didn't have an address for her. They did find an address for her office and went there. The office was closed, but did have two names listed on the window as Realtors, with numbers for work phones. The number they had for Marilyn Wong was a work phone, and possibly the reason she wasn't answering it.

They called her partner's phone, and she did answer: "Hello?"

Lucas explained who he was, and that he was trying to get in touch with Wong.

"Is there something wrong?"

"No reason to think so, but we want to talk to her about a house she's trying to rent . . ."

They got a personal cell and an address from her partner, called the number, and still got no answer. "We'll have to go there," Lucas said. "You think she could be at church?"

"Dunno," Rae said. "What would Realtors pray for? Lower interest rates?"

CLARICE CATTON CALLED Scott, and when he picked up, asked where he was. "I don't know exactly geographically, but in terms of dirt, I'm on a mountainside above the High Road, walking very slowly through the piñons."

He was speaking quietly, so she had to strain to hear, even with the volume turned up on the phone. "I ran into a checkpoint last night. I had to get off the road. I'm probably a half mile above the road right now, and walking parallel to it, pushing the bike. Sometimes, I have to carry it. When I get well past, I'll go back down, but I won't be pedaling again until dark, unless I see an . . . opportunity."

"Well, I'm up and dressed and about to eat breakfast before I go over to the church. I'm not going to use all five tubes. Three should do it, and I'll save the other two in case I see something else. They have a public restroom house here in Taos. Lots of toilets. I thought maybe . . ."

"That would be a target," Scott agreed. "Dozens of people coming and going on a Sunday. Get doorknobs and door handles . . ."

"Yes. So, Lionel. It's been a privilege to be involved in saving Gaia. It seems unlikely that we'll both make it, that we'll see each other again. Good luck with . . . the rest of your life."

"Good luck, Clarice. It *has* been a privilege."

CATTON MADE STOVETOP oatmeal with sugar and cinnamon and two percent milk, took her time with it, looked at her watch: 8:10. Time to go. Maybe the last time of her life? Maybe not. She opened her suitcase and took out a nice pair of black slacks, with a white blouse and dressy black jacket. She added the Hermes scarf, wrapped around her head with a hint of bare strip of scalp showing, and pinned the pink cancer ribbon to a lapel.

She looked in the mirror: "There," she said, satisfied. She would take her shoulder bag.

The virus vials had screw tops. She took them out of their safety box, put three in the bottom of the shoulder bag, and the other two in her fanny pack, with the tops sticking up where she could easily reach them. She added a dozen paper towels, carefully folded into absorbent squares. All that done, she thought about opening one of Wong's bottles of Sonoma Valley wine for a final glass, shook her head: no.

With a last look around, she got Wong's keys, walked out the front door, locked it behind herself—she might be coming back, if everything broke right—and started off for the church.

Nice day. Most summer days were nice in Taos, and Santa Fe, for that matter. She was only six blocks from the church, but she'd plotted out her route in advance, sticking to the narrowest lanes. The church itself was a modest structure with a rounded roof, overhung in front and back, set in a plaza with an expansive parking lot. Like many of the homes in the neighborhood, it was built of real adobe, with a real mud finish, tan with the slightest tint of orange. A white-painted wooden cross hung under the front roof overhang.

As she walked toward it, a woman went inside ahead of her. At the entrance, she took a quick look around, then pulled the heavy door open and went inside. The church was pretty—impressive—but with the modestly suffocating atmosphere she'd felt in most churches, plus the scent of burnt incense. The altar was straight ahead, perhaps a hundred feet away. She was standing in the part known as the narthex, or entryway, and to her immediate right, under a crucifix, was a holy-water font, and she thought, *Hmm.*

Moving to one side, as if to take a handkerchief from her bag, she unscrewed the top of one of the vials in the fanny pack, covered its mouth with one of the paper-towel pads, and tipped it upside down until she felt the liquid on her fingertips. She screwed the top back on the vial, then, making sure nobody was close enough to see what she was doing, she pushed the contaminated pad into the holy water font, letting it soak. She heard the door opening behind her, and she took it out and wadded it up in her hand and walked two-thirds of the way to the front of the church, and sat in an empty pew.

The people coming behind her dipped their fingers in the font and walked toward the front of the church. Catton soaked another pad with the remnants of the culture in the first vial, and when it was fully soaked, wiped it across the pew seat. She checked around again, making sure she wasn't observed, moved over a few places, and did it again.

Over the next ten minutes, she moved backwards, and from side to side, one pew to the next, surreptitiously swiping the pads over the seats. She ran out of viral culture before she got to the back pews. After thinking it over, she dug in the fanny pack and took out a fourth, one she hadn't intended to use, and continued moving back.

Time check: 8:50.

Overhead, church bells began ringing. Not actual bells, she thought, but a bells recording, broadcast over loudspeakers. Not expensive loudspeakers—along with the bells a listener got electronic spits and sputters.

More people were arriving. She took one more long swipe on a polished wood seat, and then got up, made her best imitation of a sign of the cross, turned and walked toward the back. At the holy-water font, after another glance around, she poured the last of the culture from the fourth vial into the water.

The door to the church was now open full-time, as people hurried in, passing the open door from one to another. At the door, Catton looked back past the entering crowd and tried to make a quick head count. At least a hundred, she thought, and she was sure she couldn't see all of them. She lingered, to watch them enter: felt no sympathy for the pick-up-driving, jet-riding planet killers.

And she was done. She'd walk down toward the plaza, hit the restroom building with the last vial, and then walk back to Wong's place and think about her next move. The plague, she thought, was now an inevitability. Not quite as fast and sweeping as they'd hoped, with the airport contamination plan, but it would happen.

And if Scott made it south, maybe they'd get the airports as well.

Outside the church, a heavy stream of worshippers was moving steadily toward the open door, and she stepped to the side to let them pass. Most were dressed for church, and many were wearing what looked like improvised church clothes—tourist clothes. That was a good thing: they'd be on planes tomorrow or the next day, and the plague would ride with them.

LUCAS AND RAE got to Wong's house, knocked, got no answer. Rae asked, "What do you think?"

"We gotta talk to her," Lucas said. "I guess . . . we wait?"

"She's got an alarm system," Rae said, pointing at a camera. "If we kick the door, it goes off, she sees it on her phone, calls the cops and rushes home."

"And sues us."

"I think the American taxpayer can handle it," Rae said. "You want to kick, or should I?"

"That's a job that usually calls for a man," Lucas said. "But since I almost broke my knee trying to kick a door in Santa Fe, feel free."

"Sissy."

Rae took a couple of steps back, a couple more toward the door, and kicked it at the knob. The door jamb broke, but the door held on. "One more time." She kicked it again, the door window cracked, and the door popped open.

From past habit, they both stood still, and silent, waiting to see if somebody screamed. Nobody did.

Lucas took his gun out, and held it up to Rae, who nodded, and they went inside, with Lucas leading. A pot of oatmeal stood on the stove, and the smell of it was in the air. Rae reached out and tentatively touched the metal side of the pot, and said, "Still warm. Somebody's been here in the last little while."

"Then watch yourself—what's that door?"

"Probably the garage. Let me look." Rae had her pistol out, eased up beside the door. Cracked it, listened then pushed it open. "Garage, two cars, no sign of life."

"Walk around it," Lucas said.

Rae got her gun out front and walked around the two cars, looked between, came back and said, "Yeah. They were here."

"How do you know?"

"Because there are . . . one, two, three . . . three new bicycle reflectors laying on the floor."

"Ahh . . . Let's clear the rest of the place and see what we can find. There's a suitcase over there, got clothes in it," Lucas said.

He took a step toward it, then Rae caught his arm and said, "Should we be doing this? If we think they've been here . . . what if they've contaminated it?"

Lucas thought about it, then said, "Wouldn't we be kinda small-fry? One or two people in this place . . . not that we shouldn't quarantine afterwards."

"Okay. That's a thought. Let's clear it." They took a step toward the back, and Lucas put out a hand.

"You hear people talking?"

Rae listened. "What is it? Doesn't sound like a news program."

Moving even more slowly, they checked a bathroom, got to the family room, where the television was turned off. Voices were coming from a smaller room from the right. They moved carefully that way, and Rae peeked: "Computer," she said. "Looks like a two-person TED talk. Good speakers."

Lucas was at a back door, which was locked. Nothing in the bedrooms but beds, but both had been slept in for some period of time. Then he opened a small door toward the side of the family room, a powder room with a body on the floor. "Ah man! This must be Wong. We should have thought of it sooner. Last night. Who rents houses if you can't do it yourself? A broker."

Rae took a look, said, "She's a mess. Not shot, her skull's been crushed. These people don't quit."

Lucas: "But where'd she go? Catton? Or maybe Scott's still here . . ."

"No mountain bike," Rae said.

"So where's Catton?"

"Gotta be close. That pot wasn't hot, but it was pretty warm . . ."

"Let's walk over to the . . ."

He never completed the sentence. From not too far away, church bells began to ring. They looked at each other, and Lucas said, "Oh, no."

And Rae said, "Run!"

They got outside and started running toward the sound of the bells, and Lucas said, after a few seconds, "Slow down, slow down," and he took his phone from his pocket and punched up Mellon's number. Mellon answered immediately, and Lucas said, the words tumbling out, "Catton was just at the house of a real estate agent named Marilyn Wong and there's a church near there, its bells are ringing right now and we need all the cops you got to surround the place and not let anybody out. She would have gone in early to contaminate the place and she's probably going to leave now or she's already gone, we're running there, me'n Rae. We'll try to jam it up, we need cops! And those MPs!"

And he stuffed the phone in his pocket and caught up with Rae, who pointed down a walled lane and said, "That way, I think," and then, "Shit, it's a dead end."

"But that's the church," Lucas said, pointing at a box on a rounded roof, where the bells seemed to be. "We jump the walls."

The walls were five feet high, and they went over them, ran across a yard, jumped the next fence into another yard, then jumped the last fence and came out on the plaza surrounding the church. A dozen stragglers were still going inside, hurrying now, not to be late.

And they saw Catton coming out, the head scarf, the Covid mask.

Sirens started in the background, and Catton turned toward them, and away from Rae and Lucas, didn't see them coming until Lucas shouted at her.

"Clarice Catton! U.S. Marshals! On the ground! On the ground!"

Catton turned toward them, looked at them steadily, said, "You're too late," then stepped among the last few people going into the church. Lucas kept his pistol pointed at her and ran closer, twenty yards.

Catton called, "Are you going to shoot me with all these people around? Risk their lives?"

Lucas shot her.

Rae later told Letty, "She'd watched way too much TV. You know, where the killer guy holds a hostage and cops turn their guns over? She was trying to hide behind a screen of churchgoers. Your old man got sideways to her and popped her exactly between the eyes."

CATTON WENT DOWN and the people outside the church began screaming and seemed about to scatter and Rae fired her gun in the air and shouted, "No! No! Go in the church! Go in the church!"

The panicked churchgoers froze for an instant, looking at the six-foot-tall black woman with a gun, then all turned and ran up the low steps and into the church and slammed the door behind them.

Lucas shouted at Rae: "There's gotta be another door. Run around back. Don't let anybody out. Anybody tries . . ."

"Shoot 'em," Rae said, and she ran around the corner of the church and out of sight.

The cops began arriving a minute later. When the cops got out of the first car, Lucas shouted, "We can't let anybody out of the church, and you can't get close to me. I might be contaminated. There's another marshal behind the church, tall black woman, also might be. I'll call your chief on my phone—you guys get around the church. Surround it. Nobody gets out. Anybody tries . . ."

"What?" shouted one of the officers.

"Order them back inside! If they try to run, man, woman, or child, shoot them!"

27

The cops wanted to get closer, but Lucas kept waving them back. Then gunfire broke out from the back of the church, and everybody crouched, looking, guns coming out. Rae shouted, "Warning shots, warning shots, people trying to get out."

Mellon called: "What the hell is going on there?"

"People in the church are trying to get out, but we can't let them out. I believe they're all infected: Catton was on her way out of the church when I saw her, and she said, 'You're too late.' She'd already unloaded that shit."

"What do I . . ."

"Get the Army up here, right now. That fast-reaction group they were talking about. Get them up here," Lucas shouted.

"Yes." And he was gone.

A cop shouted, "They're coming." The church door opened, and a man, woman, and two children pushed through.

"Go back inside," Lucas shouted. "Go back inside."

"We're coming out. You can't hold us here," the man shouted, and he prodded the kids forward.

"If you come out, I'll shoot you, and no doctor will want to get close. You'll just lay there until you die."

The woman grabbed her husband's jacket sleeve, and tried to pull him back inside, but he shook her off and said, "You wanna shoot kids, I guess you can."

"I will," Lucas warned him.

The woman was talking urgently to the man, and a cop, not far away, turned his head toward Lucas and said, "You shoot at those kids, and I'll kill you."

"No, you won't," Lucas said. "I am very fast and very accurate, and I will shoot you in the head."

"Wanna bet?"

"No, I don't, but I *will* kill you. Believe that. We cannot let those people out. Not even the kids."

"I got kids," the cop said. He was young, middle twenties.

"So do I," Lucas said. "But I will shoot them if they come running out, and I will shoot you."

AT THE CHURCH, the woman pulled the man toward the door, and he stepped back, then pulled the kids with him, and the door closed behind them.

Another cop shouted at Lucas, "I'm not shooting anybody in there."

"Neither am I," another cop yelled.

"If they come running out, and you don't push them back, maybe eight out of ten people in this town will die, and that includes your own families," Lucas shouted. "You think we're doing this because we like it?"

The cops were calling back and forth to each other, arguing. There was nothing more moving at the church doors, and they waited; a helicopter flew over, at altitude, and didn't slow or circle, so the pilots might not have intended to overfly the church. As the sound of the helicopter faded, a priest, wearing his vestments, came to the door, looked at Lucas and called, "We need to have a conference."

"It'll have to be by telephone," Lucas said. "Everyone in your church may have been contaminated, by that dead woman you see there." He pointed. Catton's scarf had come off, and her scalp was like a pink soccer ball in the dirt.

The priest seemed to notice Catton for the first time. "Who did that?"

"I did. I'll shoot anyone else who tries to come out. We will have some viral specialists here within the hour, to figure out what to do," Lucas said, waving his gun like a windshield wiper, wanting the priest to see it. "For the time being, Father, nobody leaves. You need to go back inside, calm everybody down, and just wait. We'll get some medical specialists here as soon as we can."

UNDERWOOD SHOWED UP two minutes before the MPs' fast-reaction force. He started toward Lucas, but Lucas waved him back. "That's Catton," he called, pointing. "I think she opened the vials in the church and is contaminated herself. I've kept everybody away from her body, but I was only about fifteen or twenty yards from her when I shot her, so . . . Everybody's got to stay away from me. Same with Rae—Rae's covering the door in the back of the church for the time being."

Underwood said, "Goddamnit! Goddamnit! Nobody got out?"

"Not so far, but these cops are really not happy about the idea of shooting anyone. There are kids in there."

Underwood looked around, shouted, "Who's in charge? Which one of you guys . . ."

A cop called, "Dascoe!"

A cop with a sergeant's chevrons on his sleeve jogged from the back side of the church, and Underwood said, "You gotta tell your guys that this is the worst. If they come in contact with any of those people, they'll have to go into quarantine. They'll likely die. And you need to back away from the church. Get your whole . . . platoon . . . back at least fifty yards."

The cops began to move back, and then the MPs arrived in a dark blue bus, with Major Vincent.

Underwood told her what had happened, and she looked at Lucas, shook her head.

"You and Underwood have to figure this out. I'm out of it," Lucas called.

Underwood, loud enough for Lucas to hear, said to Vincent, "We've got to get some fencing up. Some of that chain link, and tall, and get it up in a hurry. With concertina, if you can find it. You need to pull those tents of yours down and put them back up here in the courtyard so we can eventually start getting the people out of the church. Right now, get your MPs around the church, same circle you see with the Taos police officers, at least fifty yards back. More would be better. As far back as they can get and still see the church. I just hope to God that's enough."

"You don't know?" Vincent asked.

"No. I don't know," Underwood snapped. "We're dealing with the most infectious agent on earth and it can spread through the air. Fifty yards oughta be enough, but honestly, the best thing the Army could do, and maybe the kindest thing you could do, is drop a bomb on that church and then napalm it."

Vincent took a step back. "You're . . ."

"Not exaggerating," Underwood said. "You have no idea of what's about to happen in there."

An SUV pulled up in the street, and Underwood stepped toward it and said, "Get your people spread around. All the way out to the edges of the plaza here . . . As far back as they can get and still see what's going on at the church. And get some more guys here and start evacuating the buildings and houses out two blocks . . . get the townspeople out of here."

And, he added, "I'll be right back."

"Where are you going?" Vincent asked.

"Into the church."

LUCAS WAS SURROUNDED by a wide-open space, mostly tan dirt with high-desert plants that he would have identified as weeds. The disease problem had begun to sink in with the cops, and they'd all moved well back away from him. The MPs had spread around the church, filling in gaps between the cops; they all had rifles in their hands. Shortly after they'd gotten into place, Lucas could hear Rae shouting from the back of the church but couldn't tell what she was saying. A minute after that, she walked back around, saw Lucas, and walked up to him.

"We screwed? I mean, we, personally?"

"I don't know." He nodded toward the SUV, where Underwood was pulling on an isolation suit. "Underwood might be able to tell us a little more, but we really haven't had any time to talk. He's going into the church. Gotta hope they don't pull him apart in there."

"Gotta be a pressure cooker," Rae said, gazing over at the church's wooden door.

"Yeah. What were you yelling back there, a minute ago? I heard some gunfire. It sounded like you."

"People tried to sneak out the back. I fired a half a mag into the portico, or whatever you call it, the roof over a porch, on the back of the church. Scared them back inside."

A second man had gotten out of the late-arriving SUV and was suiting up with Underwood. Lucas recognized him as Danny Moscowitz, who'd searched Catton's ski valley house with him. When they had the suits on, and sealed, Moscowitz picked up one of the virus-killer spray tanks, and they clumped toward Lucas and Rae.

"So how fucked are we?" Lucas asked Underwood.

Underwood looked at Catton's body, then stooped and scratched up a little dust with a gloved hand, and threw it up in the air. It drifted toward Catton. "You're probably okay, if the wind hasn't changed. You need to back up more, though, and we're gonna have to quarantine you for at least two weeks. We'll figure out how to do that after we get out of the church."

"Ah, man. You think . . ."

"The measles virus can infect through air contact. So, who knows?" Underwood said. He looked at the church. "I'm wondering if I should take a pistol in there."

"Do you guys know how to shoot?" Rae asked.

Underwood and Moscowitz looked at each other, then Underwood said, "Not really."

"Then you shouldn't."

"Hope they don't lynch us," Underwood said.

They all looked toward the church as the door opened again, and the priest stepped out, with a woman. "We can't all stay here. There are more than a hundred of us, we can't stay here. People are panicking. They have children."

"Goddamnit!" Moscowitz said. "I didn't really know I'd signed up for this."

The priest shouted, "I can't hear what you're saying."

"He said, 'Go back inside.' They'll be in to talk in a few minutes," Lucas shouted back.

The priest and the woman hesitated, then went back inside and Lucas said to Underwood, "You should probably check Catton before you do anything else."

Underwood nodded, said to Moscowitz, "Let's go," and to Lucas and Rae, "Back up. Don't get too close to the cops."

Underwood and Moscowitz clumped over to Catton's body, knelt beside it, talked for a minute, then rolled the body over, her arms flopping like a rag doll's. Lucas could see that they were pulling up the back of her blouse, then looking at something else.

"Fanny pack," Rae said. "Let's back up a little farther."

They backed up, then Underwood stood and looked toward them and shouted, "Four open vials and paper towels stained by media. It looks like she was probably wiping the media on the seats inside . . ."

They talked together again, then stood, and Moscowitz picked up the antiviral tank and they started spraying Catton's body, rolling her as they did it, until she was completely soaked. Then Underwood shouted at Lucas, "Tell one of the cops to get all of the spray tanks out of the van and bring them toward you. Also, we need a big blue bag. Big blue bag. Tell the cops not to get too close to you. Not too close. Then you pick up the tanks and bags and bring them toward me. Not all the way, halfway, and we'll come and get them."

They did that—it took another five minutes. The blue bag contained a heavy black body bag. Underwood and Moscowitz unzipped it, picked up Catton's body and put it inside, then zipped it up, and sealed the zipper with tape. They used one of the spray tanks to soak the bag.

That done, Underwood shouted, "We're going in."

They walked through the church door, and more than a hundred frightened and angry faces turned toward them: men in what looked like space suits.

"WHAT A FUCKIN' catastrophe," Rae said.

Lucas: "You say 'fuck' a lot."

"Both of us have been. Because everybody may be more fucked than everybody has been fucked in the entire history of the universe," Rae said. "I don't know, Lucas. I'm not sure we can stop it."

Lucas looked around the plaza, the cops now having gotten as far back as they could, the MPs with them. "Gonna get hot. People are gonna start to get impatient. I gotta talk to that major chick."

"We got a major chick?"

"You know what I mean," Lucas said.

He spotted her, standing in a circle of NCOs, and yelled at her: "Major! Major!"

She turned her head and he waved, and she took a step toward him. Lucas took out his phone and shouted, "I'm going to call you."

He had her in his "favorites" list, tapped, it and she answered: "Yes?"

"You gotta figure out what to do," Lucas said. "You and the colonel. Nobody else has the experience. Those people inside probably have water, but they're gonna need food, and you have to figure out how to deliver it without getting anyone contaminated."

"We don't know about contamination," she said.

"You have to talk to Underwood and Moscowitz when they come out. You have to figure out how to barricade this place so nobody can escape. You need to get the food going, but there probably aren't any cooking facilities inside, so you might have to deliver microwaves. You might have to deliver diapers if there are babies," Lucas told her. "There's a Walmart here, you can probably get a bunch of stuff there. You might have to provide hospital beds, if this is gonna get as ugly as some serious people think it will. Medical equipment. You have to figure all this shit out. *You* do."

"What about you?"

"They're gonna quarantine Rae and me. We're out of it."

She said, "I'll start calling."

She rang off, and Rae said to Lucas, "Call Greet."

LUCAS CALLED GREET, who groaned, swore, and said, "This is gonna be a political black hole. Keeping a hundred churchgoers bottled up with Marburg, when half the people in the country think you should just let a pandemic burn out?"

"They won't think that when half of them are dead," Lucas said.

"Yeah, but if it doesn't happen, because we stopped it, the cynics will say that it never would have happened."

"Fuck 'em," Lucas said. "We know what we gotta do."

"I'll talk to the Secretary now," Greet said. "We'll need massive medical care out there. Dying children . . . we need a military field hospital. And all the PPE we can find."

"Maybe it won't get quite that bad," Lucas suggested. "Nobody's gotten sick yet, not from the actual disease."

"You got a dead guy in Lamy," Greet reminded him. "And that's not what I'm hearing from Detrick. They're saying it looks worse and worse, the deeper they dig into it."

"You need to talk to the Army guys out here," Rae said, leaning forward to speak into Lucas's phone. "They seem pretty effective at this kind of management."

"I'll do that. Goddamnit, Lucas . . . you're out of it?"

"Rae and I are. There are four more marshals out here, talk to Andres Devlin, he's a smart guy. I don't know where they'll put Rae and I, but . . . keep talking to me, too. I really need to know what's happening out here."

UNDERWOOD AND MOSCOWITZ were in the church for half an hour, then walked out, hurrying a bit, low on air. They used the second antiviral spray tank to soak themselves twice, with the five-minute interval in between sprays, then clumped around Lucas and Rae, keeping their distance, to their SUV, and stripped off the suits. Underwood took out a cell phone and called Lucas, fifty feet away. Rae listened in.

"As I understand it," Underwood said, "you tracked Catton here from a Realtor's house?"

"Yes. The Realtor's body is in a bathroom, it looks like she was beaten to death. I think the best thing would be to get the fire department over there and burn the house down. I don't think the house is contaminated, but I don't know. And I don't know what you'd want to do with the body—maybe bag it and bury it."

"We can handle that," Underwood said.

"What's the deal inside the church?"

"One hundred and thirty-four people, including twenty-three under eighteen, and most of those are under twelve. We put a blacklight on the pews, and we could see where she wiped the media on them. She infected at least fifteen pews, and Danny thinks he can see some red tint in the holy-water bowl. If he's right, everybody who used the holy water to make the sign of the cross is contaminated. We asked the people inside how many did that, and most of them raised their hands. We took a sample. If Danny's right, Catton did a bang-up job in there, from a killer's point of view."

"So it's bad."

"Bad as it can get. Now I'm wondering, what do I do with you and Rae?"

"Find another empty house, put us in there. We should know in ten days or so, right? Deliver food to the front porch. If we've got it, treat us, then burn the house down afterwards."

"All right. I'll have the local cops find a house."

Rae took the phone: "We'll need a TV and Wi-Fi to keep up with everything."

"Give us an hour. Why don't you go sit in the SUV? Be better than standing out here in the sun . . . and the breeze."

"Okay," Lucas said. "You got this under control?"

"Barely. Maybe. Shit, I don't know."

Rae took the phone and said, "What if we went back to the Realtor's house? We could pack up the body for you . . ."

"I don't think so," Underwood said. "If you got sick, it'd confuse the issue—is it the house that was infectious when you went in, or did you get it here, when you shot Catton? If you got it here, it'd tell us something about the throw weight of the virus."

"All right. Get us a house, then."

THEY RANG OFF, took a last look around, then walked over and sat in the SUV.

"What do you think now?" Rae asked.

"You mean about us?" Lucas thought about it, then said, "I think we're okay. I didn't think about the breeze before I shot Catton, but Underwood was right—it was blowing at our backs when we walked up there. And we were still twenty yards away. But, can't take a chance."

"It's that goddamn measles thing that's sticking it to us," Rae said. "If it was just Marburg, we could handle it. People would die, but there wouldn't be a pandemic. If it was just the measles, people who aren't vaccinated would get it, but so what? Some people would get messed up, but ninety-nine percent wouldn't. The combination . . ."

"I read once that if somebody dropped a one-megaton nuke on Wall Street, it wouldn't have much effect on Central Park," Lucas said. "You could take a nuclear war and most people would make it through. This really could be worse, if the Detrick guys are right."

"Yeah. Though I'd like to see your sources on the nuke on Wall Street."

Since dawn, Scott had been working his way along the mountainside a couple of hundred yards above the High Road. The piñons above the road were arrayed as they might be on a checkerboard, not a solid wall but a scattered design probably the result, he thought, of some kind of environmental necessity. Access to rainwater, perhaps, that kept them from growing too closely together.

If he stayed high enough, though, the checkerboard design cut off any sightlines from below. He still had to be careful about noise and dislodging rocks, especially as he passed above the checkpoint. The going was rough, treacherous, stones hiding in the weeds; the weeds pungent, like herbs, and the slope beneath his feet a slippery layer of dust and sand. He worried about rattlesnakes and he had to check every gap in the trees for sightlines that would allow somebody below to see him. The bike was a pain in the ass, pushing it along, carrying it at times, slowing progress, but he would need it again after nightfall.

At ten o'clock, it occurred to him that Catton hadn't called, and he made the same assumption that he'd made with Callister: she'd been stopped. Whether it had happened before or after spreading the viral media, he couldn't guess.

At noon, perhaps a half mile past the checkpoint, he gave it up. He'd come to an eroded gap fifty yards wide, where he could be seen from the road should a car pass, and he would make an odd, memorable sight, pushing a bike across the mountain. Then again, the gap offered a space where he could more easily get the bike down to the road after dark.

He found a shallow bowl in the dirt, made sure there were no snakes—he'd never seen one in his whole time in New Mexico, but he knew they were out there—cleared a spot, lay down. He had been wearing his helmet, and he turned it around, put it on his face with his nose and mouth out in the air. Using the backpack as a pillow, and after smoothing out a few dirt clods, he went to sleep.

He slept reasonably well, much to his own surprise; but he'd gone for most of two days with hardly any sleep at all, and he was familiar enough with sleeping in the open. He woke sporadically, readjusted himself, moved the backpack to a better position. At five o'clock, he sat up feeling stiff, stretched, yawned, stood, weaved between piñons, peed on one of them as he checked the road. Did some toe-touches. He thought about chancing the gap, continuing to walk along the mountainside, but that seemed pointless. When he got down to the road, with his bike, he could make in five minutes the same distance that would take two exhausting hours on the mountain.

He ate the last chicken sandwich, sat down again in his dirt bowl, and looked up at the sky. Nothing up there except a vapor trail, the jet probably headed for Los Angeles or San Diego. If he or any of his accomplices had been on it, the deal would be done, Gaia would be saved.

He got bored with sitting, and neither of his burner phones was a smartphone, so he couldn't browse. He lay down again and dozed. After a few cycles of dozing and waking, he felt evening coming on, cool air sliding down the mountain. He stood, leaving the bike and backpack behind, carefully walked down toward the road, feeling his way along, and made it without falling into a hole or off a hump.

There were no houses in sight, and no traffic at all. At the bottom of the slope, he carefully eased around a piñon and looked back toward the checkpoint. Two police cars were still parked across the road but were so far away that he couldn't see the cops. He could see no cars approaching the checkpoint from either direction; whatever was happening, the traffic had been choked off. That was good, he thought—this checkpoint was probably the last one.

Although he tried to suppress his impatience, in the end, he couldn't. He climbed back up the slope, pulled on the pack, and wheeled and half carried the bike down the hill while there was still light in the sky. At the bottom, he peeked around the piñon again. There was no activity around the police cars. He put his helmet on, hurried across the road, to be on the less visible side of the slight curve away from the police cars, and set off south, pedaling hard for the first ten minutes, taking advantage of the little light still left.

When that was gone, he slowed, but still moved as quickly as an easy jog, seven- or eight-minute miles. The road was not quite invisible beneath the bicycle wheels, and he pushed on, occasionally bumping onto the shoulder, ricocheting back onto the main blacktop. The road was bizarrely traffic-free. He passed a single house with a yard light, but there were no other lights, no car in the driveway, so he kept going.

HE CAUTIOUSLY PASSED a clutch of small houses fifteen minutes farther on, showing lights, but too many to risk an intrusion. He passed more houses, and even accumulations of houses, but never felt in danger of being seen as long as he was careful. At four o'clock in the morning, he was feeling beat-up, and a little disoriented because he'd spent so long straining his eyes, trying to penetrate the darkness.

He coasted, slowly, slowly down a hill, feeling for the bottom and the following rise, when he saw yellowed headlights coming toward him, and watched as they turned down a dirt track. He pedaled that way for less than a minute, and when he looked right, saw an elderly man getting out of the truck, carrying a sack toward a dark, lonely house trailer. The man fumbled out some keys, went to the trailer, unlocked a door and went inside. A second later, interior lights came on: the man was almost certainly alone.

So here it was, Scott thought. He'd been present at two murders, both by Catton. Now he was on his own. A murder—he didn't lie to himself—that had to be done. He rolled the bike off the road, took the revolver out of his pocket. Nothing to worry about with a revolver: pull the trigger, it fired. No safety, no complicated magazine. Nothing to think about but the trigger.

He kept the gun in his hand as he approached the door. The trailer had one long, low window, and he saw a shadow moving on it, away from the door. He hesitated, then knocked, not too hard. The shadow on the window stopped, was motionless for a second or two, then turned toward the front of the trailer, toward the door.

"Who is that?"

"Been in an accident," Scott said. "I'm hurt."

"I'll call an ambliance," the old man called back.

"Do you have a towel or a sheet? I'm bleeding . . ."

The door cracked open and the man looked out. Scott was standing at an angle to the door, his hand at his side, the gun out of sight, his other hand over his stomach, like he was holding himself together.

"Don't see no blood," the old man said.

"Call the ambulance but give me something I can use to hold my guts in," Scott groaned.

The door opened wider. "Where's your car? I didn't see no car coming in" and "You British?"

Scott saw the old man was holding an AK47, but pointing up toward the ceiling. He'd seen the same guns all over Africa, Russian surplus. "I am British, I might have been on the wrong side of the road . . ."

"Okay." The door came wider. The man was only three feet away. "I can get you a sheet and then I'll call . . ."

Scott lifted the revolver and shot the old man in the heart, the gunshot incredibly loud, echoing down the hillside. The man, dead before he hit the floor, fell backwards. Scott pushed inside, the door partially blocked by the dead man's feet. He dragged the body out of the way, pushed the door shut, locked it, looked for the light switches, found them, and turned off the lights.

And sat, his ears still ringing, waiting for headlights, for the cops to respond to the gunshot.

Five minutes, ten minutes . . . and nobody came.

Still in the dark, he checked the old man's pockets, found his keys and cell phone, then tugged the body to the back of the trailer, to a section walled off as a bedroom. He managed to push the old man under the bed and pulled the bedcover down to hide him further. And waited. Twenty minutes, a half hour.

He turned the lights back on, saw a long streak of blood on the linoleum floor. He got a towel from the tiny bathroom, wet it, and cleaned up the blood, throwing the towel under the bed with the old man. If somebody should check the trailer, Scott wanted the old man gone, not dead. The AK47 was there on the floor. He picked it up, thought about it, couldn't see how he could use it, and shoved it under the bed with the old man's body.

He looked at his watch: four forty. Still operating in the dark, he found the refrigerator and pulled it open. Eggs, milk, ratty-looking blocks of cheese, gray hamburger, a six-pack of Tecate beer, a bag of fresh carrots. He took the carrots out of the bag, sat on the only chair, and looked at the cell phone. An iPhone, but older. The phone wouldn't open; it would be extremely useful if he could make it work.

Crunching on a carrot, he went to the bedroom window and looked out: no lights anywhere, nobody to see a light in the trailer—he hoped. He turned on the bedroom light, pulled the old man's head and shoulders out from under the bed, arranged his head so his face was turned upward. The man's eyes were mostly closed; he thumbed the eyelids up, pressed them to hold them in place, then clicked the power button and the screen lit up. He held the screen over the old man's face, and the phone opened.

Thank you, Apple. He pushed the body back under the bed, turned off the light, and groped his way back to the chair. The phone charge was at one hundred percent. He immediately went to "settings" and changed the screen time-out to "never." He ate another carrot, and further considered his options, which had widened with a smartphone unknown to the cops; he had access to current maps. Once he got off the High Road, and past Santa Fe, he could take back roads all the way to the Albuquerque airport. The police couldn't choke off every street in Albuquerque.

A TELEVISION SAT at the back of the kitchen table, where it could be watched from the chair. Using the smartphone's flashlight, he moved the television under the table, dug around in a storage closet and found a quilt, which he draped over the table. That done, he used a remote to turn the television on, switched through the channels until he found one from Albuquerque, then crawled out from under the quilt and checked the light-tightness. With a few rearrangements of the quilt, no light escaped from the television.

Back under the table, he waited for the start of a news program; when he found one, the Taos story was right at the top.

Talking head: "The military operation in Taos continues, with more than a hundred men, women, and children locked in St. Dymphna Catholic Church, where a Santa Fe woman was believed to have spread a deadly virus. Nobody is being allowed in or out of Taos, and Army MPs from Fort Bliss are conducting a house-to-house search of neighborhoods that might hide the accused mastermind of the viral terror attack, British doctor Lionel Scott . . ."

She continued: "Reporters were not allowed to enter Taos, but KOAT has a stringer in Taos who filed this report via the Internet . . ."

Scott watched, fascinated, a reasonably well-shot video of two men in U.S. Marshal jackets kicking in the door of a house while helmet-wearing soldiers were arrayed around the house with rifles. The broadcast included head shots of Catton and Scott: Scott was pleased to see that he was perfectly clean-shaven in the photo. He'd been working on a beard at the ski village, and now had a quarter-inch of silvery facial hair. Not wonderful, but better than being bare-faced.

So the authorities thought he was still in Taos. Okay. Now, he needed to move fast. When they didn't find him, they might start spreading a wider net. He got the truck keys, cellphone, revolver and carrots, checked in both directions along the road, locked the trailer, got in the truck and started it. A slender wire stretched out of an unseen connection on the dash: a charger for the phone. He plugged it in, and with a last look around, rolled out to the highway and turned south, the iPhone's mapping app guiding him along the way.

Catton was dead. She'd infected a church, but the church was now quarantined, and nobody was allowed out. Scott rubbed his temples. Had anyone escaped from the church? The authorities didn't seem to know for sure, but most of the churchgoers were still inside, and the Army had set up a chain-link fence to prevent runaways.

It was all on his shoulders now.

LETTY AND HAWKINS, fortified with Cartwright's eye-openers, were up all night, as Cartwright slept, waiting to see if Scott showed up in Albuquerque. They passed the time by walking around the airport approaches, speculating on whether he'd try for another airport, or even another transportation nexus, like a rail or bus station.

"His problem is that everyone is looking for him," Letty said. "His face is everywhere, people are freaking out and turning in everyone with a British accent. A bus station or a railroad station wouldn't have enough people inside to risk getting turned in. An airport . . . he wouldn't have to actually get in the gates. He'd just have to contaminate the approaches."

"But he'd have to sneak away somehow," Hawkins objected. "If he was spotted in the airport, everything would be shut down and everyone would be quarantined."

"So he'll come here, but he'll try something clever," Letty said.

"Disguise himself as a nun, perhaps?"

"Maybe not a nun, but something," Letty said.

"You were right about Santa Fe. Maybe you'll be right about Albuquerque."

THE APPROACHES TO the Albuquerque airport were easily made into a vehicle trap, with the help of the state police. The approach was uphill and flattened out and actually tipped downhill at the turn to the parking garage and at the arrivals and departure areas. Checkpoints in the downhill areas couldn't be seen by the cars arriving until it was too late to turn back. A long traffic holdup might warn Scott away, but the cops were processing cars as quickly as they arrived, so there was no unusual traffic jam. There were also cops stationed inside the terminal doors, in case they should see somebody leave a car at the sidewalk and try to slip inside on foot.

As Letty and Hawkins walked through the night, or waited at the exterior doors to the baggage claim area, Cartwright found an empty space in the Lost and Found room, filled it with fake leather cushions taken from airport chairs, and went to sleep.

Nothing at all happened during the night, and the next morning, Cartwright found Letty and Hawkins slumped in chairs facing the glass doors leading outside. They were both awake, but grumpy.

"Nothing," Hawkins said. "Haven't heard anything, nobody's seen anything . . ."

"Go get some sleep," Cartwright said. "You can shut and lock the door, and it's dark inside. But, no sex in the airport. Apparently it's some kind of FAA rule." Letty and Hawkins stared at her, moving from grumpy to hostile, and she cheerfully amended, "Just kidding."

"Sex seems unlikely, whatever the rules are," Hawkins said. "We're both exhausted but still wired from whatever that dreadful drug is, that you gave us."

"I got another one that'll bring you down," Cartwright offered.

"But what happens if we take it and Scott shows up?"

"I've got another that'll bring you back up."

Letty: "Screw it. Let's go sleep."

"I'll call, whatever happens," Cartwright said.

THEY'D BOTH LEFT their duffels in the Lost and Found room, got dopp kits, and hit the restrooms to brush their teeth before going to sleep. The Lost and Found room was lockable, as Cartwright had said, and not entirely uncomfortable; they'd both slept in much worse. "I'd like to get undressed," Letty said. "But . . . if we really had to run . . ."

"I'm not sleeping in my clothes," Hawkins said. "I'll sleep badly enough as it is. If worse comes to worst, all I need is my undershorts and a gun."

"That's the old British colonial spirit," Letty said. "I'm with you."

After five minutes in the dark, Letty said, "These cushions are damp. Kinda nasty."

Hawkins muttered something unintelligible; he was already mostly asleep.

THEY WERE DOWN for four hours when Letty's phone rang. They both lurched up, and Hawkins said, "What?" and Letty picked up the phone and looked at the screen.

"It's Dad," she said. "And he knew we'd be asleep. Something's up." She poked the "answer" tab.

"What are you doing?" Lucas asked.

"I *was* asleep on the airport floor, having been up all night. What time is it?"

"Noon. I've got some ambiguous news for you," Lucas said. "Rae and I killed Catton. Actually, I did. Unfortunately, we were too close, she had already infected an entire church full of people, which we've now got surrounded by cops and Army. Rae and I are going to be quarantined to make sure we weren't infected. Never got closer than fifteen or twenty yards, and the wind was at our back, but Underwood doesn't want to take any chances."

"Details," Letty said. "Give us some details." He gave her all the details, finding Wong's body in her bathroom, hearing the church bells, drawing the conclusion.

"So if you hadn't guessed right on the bells, the world would be over," Letty said.

"Not the whole world, just part of it."

"How are they planning to quarantine you?" Letty asked. Hawkins elbowed her, and she turned the phone so he could better hear.

"They'll find a house for us, some place a little isolated, maybe out in the sticks. We'll sit there for ten days or two weeks, watching television, reading the Internet. They'll drop food for us in the yard, books, whatever. If we're clean, we go home. If we're infected, we join the folks in the church. The church is more or less being converted into a hospital."

"Ah, Jesus, that's awful. But you think you're okay?"

"We think so, and Underwood does, too. If we kill Scott, Rae and I won't be joining the champagne lunch. Neither will the one hundred and thirty-four people in the church. If Detrick is right about this thing, a whole bunch of them are going to die. So, I wanted to let you know. No sign of Scott so far."

"All right. I'd pray for you, but . . ."

"Yeah, yeah. You have more faith in pills."

"Dad . . ."

"Keep your goddamned butt down, Letty. I'll call you with more as soon as I know more."

WHEN LUCAS RANG off, Letty called Cartwright to tell her what he'd said.

"So he's infected, or might be?" Cartwright asked.

"He doesn't think he is, but he killed Catton this morning."

"Good for him. One to go . . ." Cartwright said.

Letty: "As far as we know."

"Hey. That rhymes. One to go, as far as we know."

"Great. Turn it into a song," Letty said. "I'll look for it on the Hot 100. In the meantime . . . I think I'll go back to sleep."

"Go ahead. Get as much as you can."

"Don't he a heroine, wake us up when our shift is due."

"I will do that," Cartwright said.

THEY GOT RESTLESS after four o'clock, spent some time talking about nothing, did some light necking, and then Letty said, "C'mon. Let's get up. I'm wide awake. Maybe call Dad again, see where he's at."

They dressed and Letty called Lucas, who said he and Rae had moved into a house well on the outskirts of Taos and were now officially in quarantine. "The house has Wi-Fi and a TV and some streaming services charged to the Marshals Service. Gonna catch up on my old-timey movies."

"What about the church?"

"Have you heard of the Black Hole of Calcutta?"

"Ah, man."

"When they let the real media in town, gonna get worse," Lucas said.

"Call me whenever," Letty said.

SHE CALLED CARTWRIGHT to tell her about Lucas and Rae, and that she and Hawkins were going to brush their teeth and would be around in ten minutes.

"I sent a flunky through security up to the food place to get us a bunch of food. Hope you like Chinese," Cartwright said.

"We like Chinese," Hawkins said. "Tell them to get a lot."

After washing their faces and brushing their teeth, they walked out to the baggage area, where Cartwright was stretched out on two chairs, attended by a couple of state cops. She said, "I was just telling these guys"—she poked a finger at them in turn, identified them as Ben and Tom—"how unfair it was that you two were sleeping together and I'm out here all by myself, and lonely."

One of the cops said, "And we were explaining to her that there's a cure for that."

"I know about that cure," Letty said. "The famous three inches of Ben and Tom female cure. A Minnesota cop named Flowers mentioned it."

"I'm insulted," Ben said. A couple beats. "Tom isn't."

Tom: "Hey! You're supposed to be my buddy."

Hawkins looked at Cartwright and asked, "Where'd you get a flunky? And where is he?"

"He's coming . . ."

THEY SAT IN the airport eating fried rice and orange chicken. Cartwright told them that she was still wired and planned to stay up until eleven o'clock or midnight. Unless something crazy happened, she wouldn't expect them to relieve her until eight the next morning. "If Scott doesn't get here tomorrow, I think he might have gone somewhere else, and we're all in deep-shit city. In the meantime, I'd kill for a shower."

"If you want to take a sponge bath in the restroom, we'll guard the door," Ben the cop said.

"I will think seriously about that. I have clean clothes in my duffel," Cartwright said.

"And we can check on you every few minutes to make sure you haven't drowned," Tom the cop said.

"Or even come in and help you scrub up," Ben the cop said. "Help get to those hard-to-reach areas."

"That's so thoughtful," Letty said.

Hawkins: "I hate to break up the comedy routine, but I wonder where Scott is? And what is he doing? He needs a car: has he murdered anyone yet, to get one?"

Tom the cop: "Are all Brits as cheerful as you are?"

29

Letty and Hawkins had patrolled through the night they arrived at the airport, while Cartwright slept and Scott pedaled away from Taos. Cartwright worked the next day, cooperating with the hidden cops, and scouting the airport area, while Scott dozed above the High Road and Letty and Hawkins slept.

That evening, when Letty and Hawkins finished eating their orange chicken, Cartwright suggested that they all walk the full terrain around the airport terminal. "All the way out to that street down the hill. What is it? Harvard? Yale? Princeton? Something Ivy League."

They told the cops they were going out. The evening was warm and dry, with the first stars popping up overhead. They walked the full loop around the parking lots, and talked about the possibility that Scott, if he showed up, would ditch the car and come in on foot, or even that he might hitch a ride partway in, contaminate the driver, and then leave the airport, never going inside himself. "He could do that," Letty said, "and the only way to stop it would be to close the airport. They won't let us do that, because . . . politics."

"If he did do that, he might not get the level of contamination he wants," Hawkins said. "The whole idea of going through airports would be to get the virus going to as many directions as possible, and through the biggest hubs. Somebody who only gets a touch of virus . . . it might possibly be contained."

"From what they're telling us, that's not likely," Cartwright said. "But it's true that he might be thinking that way."

The four-deck parking garage overlooked most of the airport approaches, as well as another parking area, and south to the Sheraton Albuquerque and its parking lot. A cop was stationed on the top level, and they talked to him; he had a pair of naval binoculars but said he couldn't see much of anything before the cops on the ground did, because everybody arrived in cars, and all he saw was roofs.

"All I can do is warn them if I see somebody coming in at a hundred miles an hour . . . I don't know what good that would do."

They left the cop with his binoculars, walked down the exit ramps, and eventually over to the hotel; the street on the other side of the hotel was Yale Boulevard. "I knew it was something like that," Cartwright said.

They went back to the main terminal, waited, and nothing happened. Letty called Lucas, who said he was already bored, but that he'd talked to the Army officers controlling the infected church, and that the church was now fully contained. "Whatever else happens, that is going to be awful, if the Detrick scientists are right about the virus," Lucas said. "Those people think they're fine, bitching twenty-four hours a day, threatening to sue, but a lot of them are going to die and there's fuck all we can do about it."

"Fuck all? That's British. You've been infected by Alec."

"Yeah. I just hope you haven't been."

"Dad!"

"Yeah, I'm sorry," Lucas said. "Jesus, I'm bored."

And Letty called Greet, who was as bored as Lucas. "Nothing can happen until we know where Scott is—if he's gotten out, who he's infected. Then we go nuts. Until then we stand around doing nothing and waiting for the Secretary to call to ask why we're standing around doing nothing. What are you doing?"

"Standing around doing nothing," Letty said.

As Scott pedaled down the High Road toward his meeting with the old man, and the old man's murder, Cartwright yawned and said, "I'm going to bed. If you get a sniff of anything—anything—call me."

Letty said she would.

Hawkins: "Where's Scott?"

"You already asked that," Letty said.

"Yes, but . . . where the fuck is he?"

SCOTT WAS DRIVING carefully through the darkness; the road had few straight stretches, and even some radical curves, and the lights on the old truck were yellow and weak. The last news report he'd seen on the old man's television had the U.S. Marshals Service, the Army, and the state police still terrorizing Taos, working through blocks of the town, searching it house by house, yard by yard, almost literally inch by inch. KOAT had a video of MPs probing a dumpster with ten-foot-long metal poles.

The more convinced they were that he was still in Taos, the more likely he could make it to Albuquerque. He'd been in and out of the Albuquerque airport a half-dozen times and knew it fairly well—it had occurred to him early in the work that he might use the Albuquerque airport as one of the starting points for the pandemic, so he'd spent some time looking at it.

As he drove south, he occasionally passed oncoming cars, which hinted at open roads farther south. Now, as the High Road curved down to the main highway, and as the dawn began showing on the crest of the Rockies, he diverted onto side roads, sliding completely around the city of Española. He had to take the main highway for several miles before getting off again, and then into Santa Fe through a back door. On the way, he noticed that the gas gauge, which had showed the truck had a quarter tank of gas, hadn't moved. Was it broken? How much gas did he have? Another worry.

Once in the city, he pulled into an empty parking lot to study the maps again. The main route to the Albuquerque airport would be straight down I-25—too direct, he thought, and probably well-patrolled. Once on it, he couldn't get off, at least not onto any roads that went anywhere he wanted to go.

But just as there was a back door into Santa Fe, there was a back door into Albuquerque. He'd done an early viral efficacy study on a man in the town of Lamy, and he knew how to get to Lamy, which was southeast of Santa Fe itself.

The road to Lamy would also take him to I-40, which entered Albuquerque from the east, rather than the north. Even better, from the eastern edge of Albuquerque, he could divert onto backstreets to the airport. Also: as far as he knew, nobody knew that his Lamy experimental subject had died, because he'd buried the man himself. And the man had a Jeep and lived alone. It was possible that the Jeep was still there, and he could trade the old man's beat-up truck for the Jeep and not have to worry about the gas.

He thought as he drove, and made the decision: he'd go to Lamy, then in the back door to the airport.

A half hour later he was at the intersection of I-25 and Old Pecos Trail. He turned left onto Old Pecos Trail, drove a couple of hundred yards, and pulled into an informal parking area to look at the old man's iPhone map again. Old Pecos Trail was a narrow two-lane that apparently predated I-25 but would take him to where he needed to go. He got back on the road, and thirty-five minutes later, bumped into Joe Cross's driveway; he'd seen nobody on the narrow road in but an old lady working in her garden, looked like she was pulling onions for a breakfast omelet.

And in the driveway, found himself facing a state police car, with a cop inside. "Shit, Shit, Shit!"

HE COULDN'T GO back; he groped for the pistol on the passenger seat. The cop got out of his car and ambled over, thumbs hooked over his duty belt, and Scott kept his face lowered, so the cop could see the beard but not much of his face, and rolled the side window down. The cop put his hand on the A-pillar and leaned toward the window. Scott brought the pistol up and the cop had just a hundredth of a second to flinch and Scott shot him in the face and the cop went down in the dirt.

"Now I'm a serial killer," Scott muttered to himself. There were no nearby houses, he'd learned that from his earlier visits. Still, the shot might bring some kind of investigation. He had to hurry. He got out of the car, checked the cop to make sure that he was dead; and he was. He picked the man up—he was a load—and half-staggered, half-trotted toward the house, and then behind it. He hid the body in a tight circle of piñons, then jogged back to the house. The Jeep was still in the garage. He walked around to the back of the house, opened the latch on the electrical service box, and pulled down the main switch to cut power to the house. From his work there earlier, he knew there was a cheap alarm system that went out on Cross's Internet, and that it didn't work when the power was out.

Inside, he went to the kitchen, to a conch shell on the counter, and found the keys to the Jeep. He backed the Jeep out of the garage; as he turned it, he happened to look at the spot where he'd buried Cross. The area had been excavated, which explained the cop. Whether Cross was still down there, he didn't know. He drove around the cop car to the entrance to the driveway, then hesitated . . . left the Jeep running, and trotted back around the house.

He needed one more thing from the cop.

LETTY LOOKED AT her watch: Seven o'clock in the morning. Another hour and she'd wake up Cartwright. She agreed with Cartwright that if Scott didn't show up in the next twenty-four hours or so, he'd probably gone somewhere else.

She was sitting in a chair in a doorway of the terminal, while Hawkins had gone out to patrol around the back of the parking area. People were walking past her to catch their flights, and they checked her and then the cops who were spread across the corridor behind her, looking at faces; and they hurried on. None of them, she hoped, were carrying vials of viral media. All of them, to their probable great annoyance, would be patted down at the security, and would have their baggage taken apart, to make sure that they weren't.

Letty was looking at her iPad maps, trying to figure out where Scott might have gone on his mountain bike and a stolen car. She was looking at satellite photos of all the ways out of Taos, and had talked to a state police commander about the likely targets for a car theft—an isolated house, they agreed, with not many people around.

There were a lot of those in rural New Mexico . . .

A minute after seven o'clock, she took a call from an unknown number.

"Yes?"

"Miss Davenport?"

A woman's voice, older, she thought, and almost recognized. "This is she."

"This is Carol-Ann Oaks. You stopped and talked to me about Joe Cross and then you went to look for him. There's a rumor that you and the police found that he was . . . dead."

Letty thought: *this is something*: "Yes, we did."

"That man you were looking for, in the Subaru? He drove past me a little while ago. Maybe twenty minutes, or a little more? I didn't think to call until I was sitting here eating my eggs. I was out in the garden when I saw him. I'm almost sure it was him, though he changed his Subaru for an old Chevy truck. I think he was headed for Joe's house."

"Oh my God. Listen to me carefully," Letty said. "You may have seen on television the situation in Taos?"

"I saw something . . ."

"This is the man we are hunting for. He is incredibly dangerous," Letty said. "He will kill you if he thinks you recognized him. Stay in the house, lock the doors. A whole bunch of police cars will be there in a few minutes. They may ask you to ride with them to show them where Joe's house is at."

"I will lock the doors and wait for them," Oaks said. "I have a gun and I know how to use it."

"When the police come, don't go out with the gun," Letty told her. "Don't let them see a gun. Just go out and wave at them. You have a red roof . . ."

"Yes. I will wait."

Letty never considered going to Lamy: too far away, an hour or more. She called the state police commander, told him what Oaks had said. He said, "Wait one."

She waited more than one—more like five. The commander came back and said, "We're sending everything we got within range. We have an officer there, Duane Rogers, and he's not responding, but GPS says his car's still in the yard there."

"Then he may be in trouble. The best way there . . ." She told him the best route to Cross's house, and about the old lady with the red roof who could show them the shortest way in. He said, "Our first car is fifteen minutes out. We're running without sirens. If something happened to Duane . . ."

LETTY CALLED CARTWRIGHT, got her up, and called Hawkins back from his scouting trip, told him what had happened. "It's five minutes or so from Oaks's house to Cross's. That means if it's Scott, he was there twenty minutes ago. If he . . . took out the cop . . . and is making a run for it, it's an hour from Cross's house to here. He'd be here in forty minutes or so."

"What's he driving?"

Letty shrugged: "Don't know. Maybe an old Chevy truck."

Hawkins: "He'll run into the police on his way out, won't he?"

Letty said, "I don't know. He might have to go by Oaks's house again."

"Call her," Cartwright said.

Letty called Oaks, who picked up on the first ring. "The police are on the way," Letty said. "It's possible that Scott will come back out past your place. If he does, don't let him see you at the window, but call me and tell me if he's still driving that truck. Tell me anything else you know about it."

"Old, it's dark, maybe dark brown but I don't think black, could have been old dark blue . . . I'm locked in and I've been peeking out the window since we talked, and he hasn't gone by. He could have gone by while I was eating breakfast. There is a back way out from Joe's house, a shortcut to the highway . . ."

Letty was looking at it on her iPad. "I'll call and tell the police about it," she said. "They're coming fast, should be there in ten minutes or less."

She called the police commander and told him what Oaks had said, and he promised to pass it along to the converging cop cars. "Still no answer from Duane," he said.

Letty hung up and said to Hawkins and Cartwright, "I've got a feeling that Duane won't be answering. Ever."

Twenty minutes passed and the state police commander called and said, "We're there, and so is Duane's car, but there's no sign of Duane or Scott, either one. We're gonna start walking the place."

"What about that dark truck?"

"That's still there. It's possible that he saw us coming and took off on foot."

"When we were out there, Cross's Jeep was still in the garage. I don't think anybody moved it—is it still there?"

"Wait one."

This time, Letty didn't wait one, or five, but more like ten. The commander came back: "Duane's dead, shot in the head. Found his body out in back of the house. He's got a wife and two kids."

"Jeez, I'm so sorry," Letty said. "This guy, he's a maniac. If you see him, kill him."

"That's already baked in the cake," the commander said.

"Just don't get close to the body . . . what about the Jeep?"

"Ah, shit, I called out there and the first thing they did was tell me about Duane and I forgot to ask. Wait one."

This time, it was two minutes, and the commander came back: "This Oaks, the old lady, said he had a yellow Jeep, and there's no yellow Jeep here. But it looks like there was one not long ago, because there's tire tracks in the dirt outside the garage, and the dirt's soft like dust. The tracks are still clear. We're looking up the registration information right now . . ."

Letty rang off and said to Hawkins and Cartwright, "Yellow Jeep. He could be here in the next ten minutes, if he's coming here. Alec, go talk to the main cop guy, tell him to call everybody, then you go down to arrivals level. Barbara, by the doors here. I'll get the garage."

Hawkins hurried away, Cartwright caught Letty's arm and said, "Talk to the guy on the garage roof."

Letty nodded and ran out to the parking garage, rode an elevator to the top, found a different binoculars cop eating a sandwich. "He could be on the way," Letty shouted, running toward him. "Yellow Jeep!"

The cop looked over the side of the garage, still chewing, and said, "You mean . . . like that one?"

Letty looked over the edge of the garage. A yellow Jeep had just pulled into the Sheraton parking lot.

SCOTT TOOK THE back way out of Cross's home because he didn't want anyone to see the yellow Jeep go by. The back way was rougher but just as quick; and instead of turning south on the main highway down to I-40, he crossed the highway onto a narrower road that cut diagonally cross-country toward the interstate. He was pressed with the feeling that things were coming to an end; he thought he would likely die, and only hoped that it wouldn't hurt too much when he was killed.

The airport, he knew, might be a trap. He wouldn't risk simply driving up to it, and then trying to go inside. There were two banks of elevators in the parking garage, six elevators total. He could pull into the hotel parking lot, jog across to the back of the garage, and then take an elevator between floors, never going all the way down to the terminal entry levels.

If he could get up to the fourth floor, he could ride down to three and contaminate every floor-selection button in the elevator, along with the elevator floor itself. Then he could go back up, and do it again, and again. If he could get all six elevators, he would contaminate dozens, or even hundreds, of passengers going all over the country.

If that worked, he could try the terminal itself. The terminal would be tough: that's where he'd see the resistance.

He hit I-40, turned west toward Albuquerque, rode it a short distance, got off on a backstreet to the south, found his way to Yale Boulevard. The Sheraton was right there, and he could see the parking ramp above him, and pulled into the hotel's parking area.

Life or death in the next fifteen minutes, he thought.

Life or death for him, and Gaia as well.

LETTY TOOK THE binoculars from the cop and watched as a man climbed out of the yellow Jeep. He might have sensed her gaze, because he looked up, directly at her, though she doubted he could see her clearly, half covered by the parking garage wall. When he did that, though, and she was looking straight at his face, she knew they had him.

She handed the glasses back to the cop, said, "That's him, watch him," and punched up Cartwright and then Hawkins on her phone and said, "He's in the Sheraton parking lot, walking toward the back of the parking garage. Come on, come on . . . hurry."

The exit ramps from the garage were on the back of the structure, one leading to another, and she ran down them, pausing at the second floor to look over the wall. Scott had started perhaps two hundred yards away, and was now jogging toward the back of the parking structure, and no more than a hundred yards out. Behind her, she heard Hawkins's baritone "Where are you? Where are you?"

She didn't want to shout back because Scott might hear. She continued running down the ramps to the lowest level, and punched up Hawkins on her phone: "Bottom level, all the way to the back. He's closing in."

"Wait for me," Hawkins said, his breath harsh in the phone.

She punched off and her phone rang a second later, and she glanced at it: Cartwright.

She had no time to answer but pivoted around the last of the exit ramp walls and ran out into the street behind the parking structure and Scott was right there, coming fast. For a moment he didn't recognize her as a threat and then she lifted her Sig and screamed, "Scott! Stop or I'll kill you."

Scott jerked a hand up and he had a revolver in it and he snapped a shot at her. She didn't know where the slug went, but it didn't hit her and she fired two fast but deliberate killing shots into his chest and he staggered and went down. His trail hand had been at his back: had he been trying to get at a virus vial? She wasn't sure.

She didn't want to get too close but stepped forward and then sideways toward Scott's body and was looking at his fanny pack when he suddenly came up off the ground and charged her. She got off one more shot that staggered him but he came on and crashed into her, and they went down together and she managed to pull her gun hand up and push the muzzle of the Sig under his chin and pull the trigger.

He was gone in an instant.

Then Hawkins was there, lifting her off Scott's body. Scott was dead this time, having taken four separate killing shots. Letty felt a dampness on her hands and looked at them: they were pink with fluid. She said, "Get away," but it was too late. Hawkins was looking at his own hands, which he'd used to lift Letty, and they, too, had smears of the pink fluid.

Cartwright was running toward them and Hawkins jumped up and shouted, "Stay back, stay back, we're contaminated. We're contaminated."

Letty, still a little stunned, looked at Scott's body, said, "I killed him four times, but he kept getting up . . ."

"No blood," Hawkins said. He reached down and pulled open Scott's shirt, revealing a bulletproof vest.

"He killed a cop in Lamy," Letty said. "He took the cop's vest."

Hawkins tipped Scott's body and pulled open the flap on the fanny pack: all the vials were open, two were broken, and the bag was soaked with the pink fluid. He turned and shouted to Cartwright, "Get buckets. Get buckets from the terminal. Get a cigarette lighter."

"What?"

"Buckets," Hawkins shouted.

Cops appeared behind Cartwright, and she warned them away, and they rapidly backed up, all of them looking down toward Letty and Hawkins as they stood over the body.

"Now what?" Hawkins asked.

"We're healthy. We'll make it," Letty said.

"From your lips to God's ears," Hawkins said.

CARTWRIGHT GOT BACK with four plastic buckets and Hawkins shouted, "Get closer, then throw them toward us as hard as you can, then back away."

"What are you doing?" Cartwright shouted. She got within about thirty yards, pushed the buckets together, nested inside each other, and threw them.

"Going to start a fire," Hawkins shouted back. "Did you bring the lighter?"

"Oh yeah." She pitched a Bic lighter toward them.

Hawkins picked up the buckets and the lighter, walked over to the parking garage, squatted behind a pickup and said, "Why don't you fire about four shots into the gas tank? As close together as possible, to make a big hole."

"Won't it explode?" Letty asked

"Never happens," Hawkins said.

She lay on her side, ten feet back, did what he told her to do, fired four shots into the gas tank. Gas gushed out, and Hawkins left Letty to change buckets as each one filled, as he carried the full buckets down to Scott's body and soaked it with gasoline, paying special attention to the fanny pack. They got twenty gallons on the body and the area around it, then shot up another pickup gas tank—"Pickups are best because they have the biggest tanks," Hawkins told Letty. They put another two buckets of gas on and around Scott, then found a rag in a trash barrel, put some gasoline on it, lit it with the lighter, and Hawkins threw the rag at the gas-drenched street and ran away as he did it.

The gas exploded in a fireball fifteen feet high; the heat was like an iron pressed to their faces. "I hope that will do it."

"What about us?" Letty asked.

"We have more work to do," Hawkins said. He had Letty shoot holes into the tanks of cars on both sides of the two pickups, and all the cars in between, until the whole floor of the parking garage was soaked. They set that on fire, hurrying back into the street as they did it.

Hawkins called Cartwright: "Don't let them put out the fires. We had to burn the garage because Letty and I were inside of it. We need you to drive our SUV down the ramp until you're thirty or forty yards away, then leave it. We'll be driving it up to Taos, and the church. When we're gone, you need to burn the part of the street we walked on."

"You're really that infected?" Cartwright called.

"We think we are. We have no choice but to believe that."

Cartwright: "I'll bring the SUV."

30

Lucas was not an early riser under ordinary circumstances, and with the days-long stress of the virus investigation, he was still deep in sleep when his phone rang. He ignored it once—what would they want so early, when he was quarantined, and was out of it?—but when it started ringing again, one minute after the first call stopped, he rolled over in bed, looked at the screen.

Letty calling, and she knew he slept late. He was too late to catch the second call, so he tapped Letty's number, calling her back.

When she answered, he asked, "What's up?"

"We killed Scott a half hour ago at the airport in Albuquerque. He had his vials open, and we poured about ten buckets of gas on him, and around him, and set him on fire."

Lucas sat up. "Ah, that's everything I wanted to hear. Everybody is okay, then?"

Letty didn't answer immediately, and he thought *Oh no* and dropped his feet on the floor and bent over the phone and Letty said, "That part's not so good. Alec and I both got smeared with the viral medium. We're in our truck headed for the church. We've talked to Underwood, and he agreed that's the best solution. They're bringing in all kinds of people and they're essentially building a hospital around the church . . ."

"I'm coming, kid . . ."

"No. No, no, no, you stay right where you are, goddamnit. If you're infected, I'll see you soon enough, and in the meantime, you don't want to spread the virus," Letty said. "If you're not infected, there's no reason to get close to anyone who might be. I talked to Underwood and that major, whatever her name is . . ."

"Vincent."

"I told them that if they see you heading for the church, to put your ass in jail. They told me they would."

"Letty . . ."

"That's the way it's gotta be, Dad. We've been reading everything we can find on Marburg and Underwood's reports to Detrick. Alec and I have a really good chance of getting through it. We're both in great physical condition and Homeland Security and the Army is bringing in everything they've got to treat us."

"You're not feeling . . ."

"We're feeling fine. I already talked to Mom because I was worried about how you would react, and she's going to call you in a few minutes to harangue you, so brace yourself. As soon as I get off this call, Alec is going to call his boss at MI5 and then his parents. We'll be at the church in half an hour to see what we need to do."

"Tell me what happened at the airport. Exactly."

"It actually started up in Lamy . . ." She told him the story, and about the bulletproof vest.

"There's no way you could have seen that coming, Letty. No way. I would have done exactly what you did," Lucas said.

They talked for two more minutes, then Letty said, "I've got to go, and let Alec call home. I know you'll worry but try not to worry too much. We'll be okay. See you in a couple of weeks."

RAE HAD BEEN in her bedroom down the hall from Lucas, heard voices too early in the morning, and walked down to his bedroom with a cup of coffee in her hands. The talking had stopped, but she still heard muffled sounds coming from the bedroom. She lifted her hand to knock but stopped before she did and listened again.

A chuffing sound. Something awful had happened. Maybe to Letty? Lucas wasn't crying; it sounded like he was struggling not to. What was wrong with men like him?

HAWKINS CALLED HIS office, got switched around, and eventually was hooked up with the director general of MI5; when that call was done, he called his parents; and when that was done, he and Letty rode, in mostly silence, the rest of the way to Taos.

As they approached the church, things had changed. There were military vehicles everywhere, and construction trucks. When they pulled into the church itself, they found two layers of twelve-foot chain-link fence surrounding the church, the church parking lot, then extending across the parking lot and around a long, low building that looked like—and was—an elementary school. The far side of the parking lot, probably a hundred yards from the church, held perhaps twenty new shipping containers.

As they approached the fence, four MPs looked closely at the vehicle, then stood well back, and pushed open the gate.

"We were expected," Hawkins said.

"No kidding," Letty said. Her phone rang. She looked at the screen: Underwood.

"I'm looking at you from the other side of the parking lot. You see that building on the other side of the church?"

"Yes?"

"That's an elementary school. Lots of toilets, small cafeteria, separate rooms. We've taken it over. We're sealing it up now, we're almost done. We'll use it as a hospital—the church is too limited. Because of . . . what you guys did . . . you'll get a private suite. By that I mean, a teacher's prep room with a bathroom. For now, you'll be at the church. We hope to start moving people to the school later this afternoon. The church is a mess, as you'll see. We told the people there that you were contaminated by Scott, before he was killed, but we didn't tell them who you are. Either one of you. I would keep that quiet . . ."

"We will," Hawkins said.

"Nobody's sick yet, but we expect that to change in the next day or two," Underwood said. "You two will probably get sick later. Everybody gets the best possible medical care. We've got people coming in from all over the world, right now. So . . ."

"We actually have some of the viral media on us. Is it important to get it off?" Hawkins asked.

"I don't know," Underwood said. "Most people will develop the disease from a fairly low contact with the virus—but in the cases of other viruses, a big dose sometimes means a more virulent disease. I don't know if actual contact with the stuff will make it worse, but I'd get it off first thing. There's a bathroom in the church, I'll have somebody get you in there right away. Do you have clean clothes with you?

"Yes, we have our bags."

"You'll need to change. Take everything you need into the church with you. We're going to move your truck out and burn it."

"All right."

There were two people standing by the front door in isolation suits; both had air tanks on their backs, larger than the tanks Letty and Hawkins had seen. The unusual aspect to them was that they each had pistols strapped around their waists. One of them said, "Heard about you guys and what happened. Sorry about that, but you done real fine."

He pulled open a door and they walked into the church, carrying their suitcases and equipment bags. Churchgoers were scattered around the pews as individuals by themselves, as couples, and as groups. Not as much talking as Letty had expected. A half-dozen people in isolation suits were working through the church, apparently taking blood samples or talking with the people held there.

A man in an isolation suit was standing to the left of the altar. He waved at them, calling them forward. They went that way, threading past some children in the aisle playing with hand-held video games. When they got to the man, he pointed, and said, "Bathroom through that door. Paper towels, put them in the burn bag when you finish cleaning up, along with your clothes."

THE BATHROOM WAS small, and contained a rack and a sign with "Burn Bag" on it, along with the usual bathroom fixtures, but no shower. A tall container of antiseptic soap stood next to a sink, the kind with a push-down spout. They stripped, threw their clothes in the burn bag, and scrubbed down with the soap and paper towels, washing their entire bodies, including their hair. When they were dressed again, they went back out to central part of the church, to a woman in an isolation suit who was waiting with a syringe. She took blood samples from both of them, put the samples in isolation bags.

When she was done, she said, "There's food in the back rooms, over there." She pointed, and Letty said to Hawkins, "I'm hungrier than hell."

"So am I . . ."

They went that way, found people browsing through tables stacked with fruit, cereal snacks, candy, along with four large chest freezers filled with microwave dinners. A half-dozen upright refrigerators held milk, orange juice, lemonade, soft drinks. Another long, heavy table held six microwaves.

A man was heating a pot pie in a microwave and asked, "What'd you guys do?"

Hawkins said, "We ran into one of the virus people down in Albuquerque and he splashed us with the stuff that supposedly contains the virus."

"Wow."

"We were sent up here. Cop cars front and back to make sure we didn't make a break for it."

"Well, when you're here for a while, you start to feel what's really strange about it . . ."

"What's that?" Letty asked.

"We're all, all one hundred and thirty-four of us, perfectly healthy," the man said. "For now, at least. Nobody even coughs or sneezes. I guess it's a hundred and thirty-six with you two. We're waiting to see if the disease is real, or fake."

"Has anyone said how long we might have to wait?" Letty asked him.

The microwave beeped and he pulled the pot pie out, handling the aluminum pie disk with gloved hands. That done, he said to Letty, "They say we could start seeing the Marburg tonight or tomorrow. They take these blood draws, they call them blood draws . . . and they say we got it. What that means, we don't know."

"We got Wi-Fi? Or phone access?" Hawkins asked.

"Oh, yeah, we got it all," the man said. "We still hope . . . but . . . I believe we're in trouble. Enjoy yourself while you can. I talk to my wife every hour or so. I can't wish that she was here, though to tell the truth, if she *was* here, I'd feel a lot better."

Letty and Hawkins got cereal and milk and a couple of bananas, and took their bowls out into the nave, where a line of tables had been set up along a side aisle with folding chairs. A half-dozen people were eating, and more were tapping on laptops. They sat next to the man with the pot pie, and Letty asked, "They brought in people's laptops?"

"Yeah. If you don't have one, they'll give you one—Macs, Windows, whatever you want. I asked for a big MacBook Pro that I always wanted, and it was like, *no problem*, and I had it about six hours later. The kids got video games . . ."

The man started eating his pot pie, and Hawkins leaned over to Letty and said, "This is going to be . . . dreadful."

"Yup."

WHEN THEY FINISHED eating, they watched the people in the church, got up and walked around, looking at the Stations of the Cross, the altar, the rack of votive candles, the medics in isolation suits, and soon enough, ran out of things to look at.

When the church had been sealed off, it had only been about two-thirds full, so there was plenty of sitting space in the pews. They found an empty space, opened Letty's iPad and Hawkins's laptop, read emails, and sent a few. Letty had several from her mother, Weather, and Lucas, and more from Greet and Cartwright. Cartwright was now in quarantine in a house in Taos, but not the same one as Lucas and Rae. Hawkins had three emails from his parents, and more from MI5 colleagues.

They answered the emails, as best they could—there wasn't a lot to say, and they were still in shock from the fight at the airport, and the fires. Hawkins said, "Do you think . . . never mind."

"No, what?"

"Never mind, stupid thought."

Letty started reading newspapers and spent time staring at headlines without seeing them. Hawkins went out to a series of photo blogs—he was a photo enthusiast and found he couldn't focus on the latest Leica Q camera, which he lusted after. Letty went out to a comics site and read comic strips: *The Far Side, Calvin and Hobbes, Big Nate, Non Sequitur, Pearls Before Swine, Luann, Doonesbury.* An hour later, she couldn't remember them, and read them again.

The parish priest came by, dressed in jeans, Nikes, and a Molly Tuttle tee-shirt. He tried to reassure them about the disease, and though he seemed like a good man, neither Letty nor Hawkins were interested in what God's hands might do for them.

That was how it went; hours dragging. Lucas had warned of the Black Hole of Calcutta, but it wasn't that.

There was a high stress level, but even so, it was all boring.

"Do you find it odd that we can't even amuse ourselves for a half-day, without going stir-crazy?" Hawkins asked.

"I'm too stir-crazy to respond to that," Letty said. "What I'd like to do is lie down."

Hawkins shrugged: "There's room. Lots of people are lying down in their pews. So lie down."

"I would sorta like you to be lying on top of me."

"We may have to wait a few hours for that," Hawkins said. "If Underwood comes through with his promise of a suite in the school . . ."

AT SIX O'CLOCK a man in an isolation suit came through the door with a bullhorn and said, "David Underwood here, folks. We're ready to start moving people over to the school. We don't have enough individual rooms for everybody, so some people will have to share rooms. Plenty of food, every room has a television, and there'll be a big screen in the cafeteria . . ."

LETTY AND HAWKINS walked across the parking lot with the rest of the crowd, looked out to what amounted to prison fencing surrounding the parking lot. Two dozen prison-style lights stood on metal posts outside the fence, illuminating the parking lot so harshly they couldn't look at each other's faces without squinting.

At the school, they visited the cafeteria, ate again, and found their teacher's prep room. They had it better than most of the others, who had to share two communal bathrooms, while they had their own small bathroom with a toilet and a generous sink. They also had two thick and comfortable foam mattresses, and blankets. They pushed the mattresses together, made love twice, and eventually went to sleep.

At five o'clock in the morning they heard a fuss in the hallways and got up to see what had happened. Outside, they found several people in isolation suits, talking to a man and a woman. A child, they found, had begun running a fever and had developed a headache.

One of the confined men, standing next to Letty and Hawkins, said, "It's begun. God help us, it's begun."

AND IT HAD. The toddler was still upright, but, said another observer, she was getting sicker, and quickly. They watched for a while, then went back to bed, but neither of them could sleep.

At nine o'clock, Letty called Lucas and Greet and told them about the sick child. Neither had much to say. Lucas seemed almost unable to speak; like he didn't want to hear about it.

During the day, a half-dozen more people began getting sick. They were moved to classrooms that had been transformed into medical wards. Letty and Hawkins felt fine; they got jobs moving equipment and furniture that might puncture isolation suits.

One of the docs told them that they hadn't yet seen measles outbreaks—the disease specialists thought that might take another week. But the Marburg loads were beginning to express themselves.

Letty and Hawkins worked through the first five days, doing what they could as more and more people fell ill, until the church and school—they were free to move between them, and the church was attracting people who needed to pray—began to feel almost empty. There was much weeping, and some shouted arguments, a near fist-fight between two women broken up by Hawkins and another man.

The school began to feel and smell fetid, as the inside atmosphere had thickened with intestinal gas: the victims were experiencing run-away diarrhea, and the medical people were torn between recommending high-energy food for people not yet affected, or abstention from foods to reduce the effects of the gastric upsets.

On the sixth day, Letty began to feel weak, and the weakness came on quickly. Hawkins began to go down an hour later; they were the last two, except for a medical worker who'd accidentally stuck herself with a contaminated needle while drawing blood from one of the victims. Before Hawkins started down, he helped push Letty, on a gurney, to one of the four classrooms now being used as hospital wards, three for women, one for men, because most of the churchgoers had been female.

The ward smelled so putrid that Hawkins began retching, and after containing the impulse, saw Letty settled into a bed. The medics directed him back out, so they could put her in a diaper. He kissed her before he went, put his hand on her heart and said, "I'll see you on the other side of this . . ."

Outside, he began vomiting into a trash container's burn bag, and a few hours later, when he could no longer stand, was taken to the men's ward.

LETTY HIT BOTTOM on the ninth day after the onset, and Hawkins, a day later. Everything in their bodies ached; they burned up with fever; they were barely aware of people around them, barely aware of the needles going in and out of their arms and legs. They knew that some of it was antiviral drugs, some experimental; barely aware that almost all of it was being recorded by video cameras for later review in the Level 4 labs the world around.

On the thirteenth day—she'd lost track of time, had no idea of passing days—Letty thought she recognized the woman standing over her, changing her diaper. There wasn't much in the diaper but liquid—she'd been urinating the saline and nutritive solutions being fed into her arm—because she hadn't been able to eat anything.

Looking up, she asked, weakly, "Alec Hawkins?"

"He's asking about you," the woman said. "He started to pull up yesterday."

"So he'll make it."

"Yes. So will you."

"How bad is it?" Letty whispered. "Overall."

The woman leaned close. "We're not supposed to talk about it until people are actually up . . . but I know who you are, and what you did. We've had sixty-four deaths—forty-seven percent. All the children under thirteen died. We think the dying is mostly over. Two more are on the bubble, the rest should be okay."

Letty tried to cry over the number, but was too weak, and all she could do was shake. The medic said, "Easy there . . . we're going to give you a very mild sedative to help you sleep now . . ."

And she slept.

SHE WAS IMMOBILE for the next two days; on the third day, she found Hawkins leaning over her. He was gaunt, with waxy skin, and hair that looked like it had died, all lank and greasy.

She smiled: "You look like shit."

"If I look like shit, you look like double shit. I've been talking to Lucas. He's been waiting for you to call." Hawkins held up a phone.

"Hold it for me," Letty said.

Lucas answered instantly: "You're alive."

"Yes. Alec and I are just leaving for the Bahamas, where we plan to have a lot of wild sex and get rum drinks with mimosa flowers in them."

"Ah, Jesus . . ." And Lucas began to laugh. He sounded drunk, Letty thought, out of control.

"Where are you?" she asked.

"We've been out for six days . . . no antibodies in our bloodstreams, so we were never infected. We can't find anyone outside the containment area, you know, the church and the school, who has symptoms. So we pulled it off. By the way, your girlfriend, Barb, went on a rampage in that airport garage after you left. She shot up something like forty cars and set them on fire. I'm told you could see the smoke in Santa Fe. Then she got quarantined."

"The government can afford forty cars . . . Is Barb okay?"

"She's fine. They quarantined her, but she never got it. She's fine."

THAT WAS IT for Letty and Hawkins, except for the waiting. A month after onset, they walked out of the containment area with another survivor. They were first taken into a specially prepared clean room, washed with embarrassing thoroughness with antivirals, packed into isolation suits, and then marched out through the compound's front gate, where they were hosed down with more antivirals.

Three days later, the entire compound, including the school and the church, was filled with jellied gasoline, and the parking lot sprayed with the same compound, and set afire. The church and school and everything in it, including all the medical equipment, the microwaves, the pews and crucifixes—everything—burned for three days, and was reduced to rubble. The parking lot melted, and the rubble was sprayed with the same compound—napalm—and set afire again.

The men captured in the bus at Taos Ski Valley recovered from Scott's vaccine and were indicted and charged with sixty-five counts of premeditated homicide (one of the victims on the bubble died, the other survived), and a long list of additional and essentially irrelevant charges. The U.S. Attorney for New Mexico announced that he would seek the death penalty for all three.

Underwood and his crew stayed in Taos, probing for any sign of a continuing problem, but they found nothing. Extensive blood and tissue samples from the victims, both living and dead, were sent to Fort Detrick and disappeared behind a security wall.

The victims who died were cremated on site in specially prepared kilns that reached more than 2,000 degrees Fahrenheit. The kilns were hit with napalm when the buildings were destroyed. The refractory cores survived and were later crushed and buried.

A Taos cop meeting a visiting friend at the Hampton Inn spotted Catton's Lexus in the far corner of the Hampton Inn—the same hotel that Lucas and Rae and the other marshals were staying at. None of them were parking in that part of the lot, and nobody had looked at hotel lots.

WHEN LETTY AND Hawkins walked out of the containment compound, they stripped out of the isolation suits and were met by Lucas and Weather, and by Elizabeth and Clarence Hawkins, Hawkins's parents, and by Greet, and by Rae, and by Cartwright, and unexpectedly, by the British embassy's first secretary, a friendly mustachioed fellow whose wife knew Elizabeth Hawkins's sister-in-law.

The first secretary handed Hawkins a heavy envelope with a red wax seal on it and said, "Congratulations, my boy. You are the recipient of the George Cross, the first awarded since 2017, and one of only two in the past forty-odd years. There'll be a presentation of the actual medal back in London. You are now Alec Hawkins, GC, and, I've been told, will soon enough be Sir Alec Hawkins, GBE."

Hawkins was flustered and a trifle overwhelmed; Letty asked, "Hey, what do I get?"

Rae: "You live in the wrong country to get anything."

Greet said, "Not true. We plan to take you to Smith's supermarket. Play your cards right, we'll buy you a Fudgsicle on the government tab."

"Don't even *think* about opening your purse," Cartwright said.

"That's it?"

Lucas gripped her around the shoulders and squeezed her tight under his arm: "You're alive, girlie. That's good enough. You are still walking around in this world."